# PARK AVENUE

Michael R. Zomber

First published by Dog Ear Publishing
4010 W. 86th Street, Ste H
Indianapolis, IN 46268
www.dogearpublishing.net

dog ear
PUBLISHING

ISBN: 978-160844-858-6

This book is printed on acid-free paper.

This book is a work of fiction. Places, events, and situations in this book are purely fictional and any resemblance to actual persons, living or dead, is coincidental.

Printed in the United States of America

IN THE SUMMER of 1939, Munich, the "Home of the Monks," was a lovely city. It retained a number of medieval buildings, the 15th century Old Town Hall in the Marienplatz, the 12th century St. Peter's Church, and several of the seven original 14th century town gates, Karls, Sendlinger, and the Isar, the latter named after the Isar River which flows through the center of the city. St. Michael's Church, dating from 1583, was at the time the most beautiful Renaissance church in all Germany.

The Benedictine friars built a monastery at Tergernsee in 750, and in 1157, Henry the Lion, Duke of Bavaria, granted the monks the right to hold a market where the Salzburg Road met the Isar River. The following year, the monks constructed a bridge over the Isar and fortified the permanent marketplace. The Wittlesbach family succeeded to the duchy of Bavaria in 1180, and moved the seat of their dukedom to Munich in 1255. For more than six centuries, the Wittlesbachs ruled Bavaria from Munich until Louis III abdicated in November of 1918.

Munich was a center of the arts for hundreds of years. Ludwig II was composer Richard Wagner's patron and champion. The Alte Pinakothek housed more than 500 years of Wittlesbach family treasures, an unrivaled collection of masterpieces by Albrecht Durer, Reubens, and Van Dyck, many commissioned by the Wittlesbach line of Holy Roman Emperors. Munich was so fervently Catholic that Protestants weren't granted citizenship until the 19th century.

After World War I, Munich's millennium of conservatism made it the center of German right-wing political activity. Adolf Hitler had served in the 16th Bavarian Reserve Infantry Regiment. The man who was to become the Fuhrer was an authentic war hero having won not only the Iron Cross Second Class, but the Iron Cross First Class as well. It was an extraordinary decoration for a corporal in the class conscious, rigidly hierarchical German Army. The Eisernes Kreuz 1. Klasse was normally reserved for commissioned officers.

The future Fuhrer was intimately associated with Munich, having moved there from Vienna in 1913. In November of 1923, Hitler and General Ludendorf attempted to seize power in Bavaria during what came to be known as the

Munich Putsch. Sentenced to prison for five years, Hitler served nine months in relative comfort at the Landsberg. The German Worker's Party, which he first joined in September 1919, in Munich, was founded on socialist and nationalist principles, and polled more than six million votes in the 1930 general election. After his release from the Landsberg, Hitler moved from Munich to Berchtesgaden. The month of July in 1939 was a warm one. Germany was at peace. The annexation of Czechoslovakia had taken place without a shot being fired when the Fuhrer declared the Czech nation dissolved on March 16, 1939 in a speech broadcast to the German nation from Hradcany Castle in Prague.

Enjoying the warmth, S.S. Obergruppenfuhrer Sepp Dietrich relaxed in the spacious back seat of his large Mercedes saloon car. He usually liked to drive it himself, but this morning he decided to have his scharfuhrer take the wheel so he could ride with the window open and enjoy the medieval architecture. The general knew this halcyon summer was deceptive and represented the calm before a rapidly gathering storm about to break over Europe. The Fuhrer was intent on expanding his concept of lebensraum to the East. This specifically meant Poland and challenging the Anglo Polish defense treaty. Britain and France had tolerated the Austrian Anshluss and reluctantly swallowed the much more bitter pill of Czechoslovakia. However anyone who doubted English resolve to go to war over Poland was a fool.

The ongoing violence against Jews alarmed and disgusted not only Dietrich, but many other Germans as well, had its origins in a series of increasingly harsh laws, confiscations, and persecutions that commenced a month after Hitler became Chancellor in January of 1933. The vicious anti-Semitism reached a climax in the Kristallnacht program of of November 9-10, in 1938. Thoroughly disgusted, Dietrich sent a letter to Hermann Goering, commander of the Luftwaffe, telling the Reichsmarshall he was going to resign his command of the Liebstandarte Adolf Hitler. Dietrich and Goering had been secret allies since Dietrich organized the elimination of Ernst Roehm on the Night of the Long Knives in 1934.

Goering asked him to come to Berlin and took the distraught SS general to his palatial forest estate in the Scharfheide, north of Berlin, which he christened Carinhalle after his first wife, Carin von Rosen, who had divorced her husband to marry Goering in Munich on February 3, 1922. Goering was a very popular figure in Bavaria. His gallant conduct during the Great War was recognized when he was awarded the "Pour le Merite", the "Blue Max," Germany's highest decoration. Hermann Goering knew all about Jews. Until Hermann was twenty, his mother's lover was a baron, Ritter von Epenstein, a Jew, who owned the castle of Veldenstein. The baron was also Hermann's godfather.

Seated in a chair that was more of a throne, as the rampant lions on the walnut arms were cast and chased in pure rose gold, Goering was attired in a magnificent, gold bullion embroidered sky blue, silk dressing gown. With the blue and gold Pour le Merite hanging from his ruddy and corpulent neck, the Luftwaffe commander and Reichmarshall was nevertheless an imposing figure. He was additionally a man of considerable charm and wit, the most popular of all the Nazi leaders with foreign nations as well as the German people. Dietrich was dazzled by the artistic masterpieces that hung in profusion, filling the ten-meter high walls from below eye level to the ceiling. In less than five years, the Reichmarshall's collection was very nearly equal to the one it had taken the Wittlesbach Holy Roman Emperors five centuries to accumulate. Many of the Rembrandts and Durers, as well as a number of artists officially condemned by the Nazi Party as "degenerate" works by the French artists Degas and Tolouse-LatrecToulouse-Lautrec, had come to Carinhalle as a result of the Nazi's economic spoliation of Germany's Jews.

Goering held up Dietrich's letter in his perfectly manicured fingers and Dietrich was surprised to see the Marshall marshal painted his fingernails red like a woman.

"So," said Goering in a pleasant tone, and Dietrich was struck by the fact that at forty-five, the commander of the Luftwaffe would be a strikingly handsome man if he lost fifty kilos. Goering's hair was straight, black and thick, his chin strong, and his nose noble. His eyes were light brown and radiated intelligence.

"You think the persecution of the Jews justifies your resignation, as you are an officer and a gentleman. I want you to know I share your disgust. Why do you think I allowed that vile scum of a village policeman, Himmler, to usurp my position as head of the SS? No man of honor could possibly take responsibility for the Gestapo and concentration camps like Dachau. We both know all this nonsense about Jews is just propaganda for the masses. Yes, I participated in formulating the Nurnberg Laws, that whole charade. There was altogether too much wealth concentrated in Jewish hands and now it has been redistributed and," here Goering held up his hand to forestall any possible interruption, "I'll be the first to admit I have benefited. But I am only acting as a temporary custodian of everything you see here, for I am holding it in trust for the German people. Someday, every great work of art on earth, whether it is sculpture, painting or drawing, will be here. Here you see the beginning of my dream.

"Listen Dietrich, my godfather, Baron von Epenstein, was a Jew. Do you really think I am an animal like Goebbels, Streicher, Frank, or the rest of the Fuehrer's coterie of racist trash? Not one of them would know a Rembrandt from a Reubens, a Durer from a Degas, or a Manet from a Monet. I, and I alone, have the vision and the means to create the greatest concentration of art the world has ever known. Think of it. The collections of the Louvre, the Hermitage, and the British Museum will all be here in Berlin. Now, my dear Dietrich, do you think any of this would be possible without my allegiance to the Fuhrer? Without my Nazi Party affiliations do you think I would be able to assist wealthy Jews to leave the Reich? Yes, I remember my youth. At twenty-three I was fighting British aces and shooting them down in flames. At the moment their planes bloomed red and orange from the bullets of my Maxim guns and hurtled earthward, I felt like Achilles after he vanquished Hector before the assembled Greek and Trojan hosts. You know I was chosen by the Kaiser, to succeed Baron von Richthofen after his Fokker was downed by a barrage of Australian ground fire near Amiens. I was in command of Jagdgeschwader I from that May until the war ended. Both the Baron and I won the Pour le Merite."

Goering paused to fondle the beautiful cross with his left hand and Dietrich thought that he had in fact forgotten what a heroic figure the Reichmarshall had once been. It was only too easy to dismiss him as another bombastic National Socialist when he was, in fact, anything but. As Goering pointed out, he was no Himmler, a civilian agriculture student, who had no existence or accomplishments outside of his membership in militant rightist organizations like the Reichskriegsflagg, which he deserted in 1925 to join the Nazi Party.

"I have an interesting proposal for you," said Goering with a broad and attractive smile. "The Fuehrer is much taken with soldiers who are also heroes. He loves you more than any of the generals, even Rommel." The Reichsmarshall could see the handsome general's face begin to twitch with an excess of righteous indignation, his clean-shaven visage turning red as if he were about to storm from the reception hall. Goering waited a few moments before continuing.

"Now, Dietrich, do you really think anyone believes you have anything in common with the Allgemeine SS, Muller, Kaltenbrunner, and Heydrich's band of thugs and degenerate butchers? I wouldn't waste your time or mine. No, my fiery friend, always remember you are Waffen SS, the commander of the Liebstandarte Adolf Hitler, not some Himmler lickspittle. My dear Dietrich, we both know he's nothing but political scum. You know I am your friend. The most feared police in Muller's Gestapo fawn, bow and scrape as you walk past. If anyone you know is denounced or arrested, a telephone call from you opens the locked doors of Himmler's darkest dungeon, reverses the direction of a train on its way to Buchenwald, Dachau, or Sachsenhausen." Dietrich knew that the first great influx of Jews to Sachsenhausen camp, which was three kilometers north of Oranienberg and northeast of Berlin, began after Kristallnacht when 10,000 Jews were rounded up from Berlin, Hamburg, Pomerania and Mecklenburg. He and many of his fellow Germans were only too well aware that the very first concentration camp in the Third Reich was established on March 10, 1933, on the borders of Dachau, 16 kilometers north of Munich, situated on a hill whose summit was occupied by one of the Wittlesbach castles.

"You can, of course," said Goering, "show your disdain and disgust with Himmler by leaving Germany, although considering the present situation, that is the coward's path. I remain, doing what I can for the greater good and glory of the Fatherland despite the excesses of others in high positions. And the Fuhrer listens to you."

Goering picked up Dietrich's letter once more, having laid it earlier on top of a priceless Riesener, gilt-mounted fruitwood commode made for King Louis XVI. It was, Dietrich noticed on closer inspection, not fruitwood, but mahogany enriched with mother of pearl and rich mountings of ormolu bronze displaying Reisener's characteristic rectilinear side view, and ornamentation perfectly combining exceptional richness with harmonious distribution. Dietrich regarded the chest as he thought about Goering's description service to Germany. "Could he do no less?" Then he rose from his seat and walked to the larger man. Dietrich extended his hand and Goering gave him the letter, holding it out between his left thumb and forefinger. The great hall was as still as any of the grand cathedrals in Munich in the late afternoon, when they were empty of both priests and the faithful. Dietrich took the thick, white letter paper from the soft but powerful fingers with the incongruous red painted nails and held it up by one end, standing still for a long moment, looking at

Goering, who smiled thinly and nodded his leonine head. The silence of the hall was shattered by the sound of the paper tearing as Dietrich ripped it in half. The tearing resounded, echoing through the cavernous hall as sharp and staccato as the burst of an 8 millimeter, MG-34, machine gun.

Since that fateful morning, Dietrich had not turned around any trains bound for Buchenwald from Dachau, though he had succeeded in countermanding a number of internment orders. His mere presence had the most remarkable effect on Gestapo officials who would verbally harass and physically abuse Jews on the streets. He would often walk the narrow, medieval byways near Munich's Jewish ghetto looking for plainclothes police, who would stop men and women demanding to see their papers. He liked to walk up behind them as they yelled their commands and made their crude, barbaric remarks to the terrified Jews. Dietrich would ostentatiously clear his throat and the Gestapo agents would turn to see who had the unmitigated effrontery to disturb them, and then the hate distorting their brutish faces would fade at the sight of black uniform, piped with real silver bullion braid, and the shiny black-brimmed, silver-piped black wool hat with the silver death's head at the peak. They saw all this and bowed to the overall effect of absolute power. The police would instantly salute snappily, adding a hearty "Heil Hitler," at which time the hapless Jew would be dismissed, his papers flung at him with contempt, as the Gestapo men would focus on Dietrich and politely inquire if there were anything, anything at all they could do for the Herr Obergruppenfuhrer.

The streets of Munich were crowded with passerby as well as military, police, and civilian vehicles as Dietrich's Mercedes passed over the Isar. The more he thought he knew Hermann Goering the less he understood the man. How could a man take the paintings off the wall of another man's home one day and then after robbing him advise him how to emigrate and avoid being taken to Dachau? How could Goering call himself a decent man, or even look at himself in the mirror every morning? Even as Dietrich asked himself these questions, he realized their ultimate absurdity coming from a man wearing the uniform of the SS, the most feared and loathed organization in the Fuehrer's Greater Germany. His nominal superior, Heinrich Himmler, was the chief architect of the inhuman policy towards the Jewish people of Germany and though the two branches of SS service were as distinct in their respective functions as day and night, to most Germans and even much of the SS, distinctions between Waffen and Allgemeine SS were unimportant.

## CHAPTER 2

# The Jew

SOLOMON ROTH WAS born and raised in Munich. His father, David, had served under Crown Prince Rupert of Bavaria as a lieutenant of cavalry. After enjoying initial success on the German Southern wing in Lorraine at the battle of Morhonge-Sorrebourg, the prince ordered his army to counter-attack. David was killed by fire from a Chauchaut 8 millimeter machine gun during the French counter-attack, which involved the left and center of the entire French Army. This action came to be known as the First Battle of the Marne.

David left a widow, Leah, and four children: Solomon, two older brothers, and a younger sister. David had been the manager of a small bank, and like many well-to-do German Jews, considered himself a German first and a Jew second. The Roths attended the synagogue during Pesach and the High Holy Days, and other than on those occasions, the Roth family was secular. After receiving his degree in economics, Solomon went into banking like his father, and despite the economic turmoil and hyper-inflation that followed in the wake of the war, or possibly because of it, he prospered. Solomon was a firm believer in tangible assets such as gold, silver, diamonds and property. He also bought art, mainly masterpieces by the French school, Monet, Renoir, Sisley, Gaugain, and Degas. The bright colors and every day subjects appealed to him and he hung them on the walls of his three-story, 19th century brownstone home with pride and pleasure. While all too many of his fellow townsmen were paying for coarse loaves of black-bread with million mark notes, Solomon's family quietly purchased staples and luxuries with Swiss Francs. He sent his two sons to the neighborhood Catholic school because it was within walking distance, as well as having high academic standards.

Solomon observed the ascendency of the Nazi Party with considerable misgiving, however he decided their anti-Semitism was more bark than bite, and at least they believed in the sacred nature of private property unlike the godless Communists. Like many of Munich's secular Jews, he voted for the Nazis as the lesser of two evils.

Following Hitler's appointment as Chancellor in January of 1933, there were scattered, though thoroughly alarming incidents of vandalism against Jewish properties and isolated instances of boycotts. The Nurnberg Laws of 1935 disenfranchised Jews and outlawed intermarriage between Germans and Jews. Still Solomon reasoned that for nearly three hundred years Protestants couldn't claim Munich citizenship. Besides, Jewish law strongly discouraged Jews from marrying gentiles to the extent that religious Jews would literally disown offspring of a Jewish man and a German woman.

"Better Hitler than Stalin," was the general consensus among Solomon's friends and business associates. There were those who said they'd had enough, sold out, packed up, and emigrated to the United States, Canada, or South America, Argentina was one popular destination. However there were severe restrictions on the amount of money one could take, and the Nazi authorities made the necessary emigration documents difficult to obtain. Many substantial property owners feared that even applying for exit permits would result in confiscation of their assets. After the widespread destruction of November 1938, known as Kristallnacht, Solomon awoke from his delusion to the unpleasant realization that his father's sacrifice for the Fatherland, and the pretty gold and enamel medals posthumously awarded by Kaiser Wilhelm and Prince Rupert, meant less than nothing to the Nazis. His sons came home from school in tears at having been made to stand in front of their class as teachers pointed to their noses, hair, skin, and eyes, so their classmates would learn exactly how to recognize Jews. His wife, Leah, who was so far removed from Jewish culture she attended Mass at St. Michael's Church, and had the blonde hair and blue eyes of her Catholic father, was alarmed. The Roth children were all dark, with distinctly Semitic features. Solomon spoke to the president of the bank who was sympathetic to his plight. He said Solomon could still get out with his family, providing they each left with one suitcase and took the train across into Switzerland. "But," said the man, "You will forfeit your home, your properties, and your art collection."

Solomon decided to send his family to his oldest brother. However, he would remain to liquidate his holdings and the bank president agreed to assist in transferring the proceeds to a bank in Buenos Aires. Solomon filed the paperwork with the appropriate Gestapo agency, though whenever he went to ask about the status of his request, the man in the cheap brown suit with the red, white and black Nazi Party badge, would say, "These things take time."

By February of 1939, Solomon, Leah, and the children had changed their attitude from being uneasy and anxious to being terrified. Now they could see the abyss that yawned beneath their feet. All of them knew someone who knew someone who had been plucked off the street while going about their daily lives. The SS would take them to Dachau. Some returned with horrific accounts of brutal beatings, scant rations, hard labor, and arbitrary, summary executions.

Solomon went each week to the police station, and as he looked up at the red, white and black flag, he wished for the first time that he'd left in 1935.

This time the police official snarled, "Listen, Jew. We want you to leave more than you do. Your presence blights the sacred soil of the Reich. I will bring you your papers when they come." The bespectacled bureaucrat had a pinched, dyspeptic face and stood perhaps five feet, six inches. He smiled cruelly at Roth, revealing a set of yellow, crooked teeth.

"I know where you live," he hissed menacingly.

The next day Solomon paid a call on an acquaintance. He was the former curator of paintings at the Alte Pinakothek, a Jew by the name of Friedlander. Though Friedlander had been relieved of his post, it was rumored he had influence with Reichmarshall Goering. The ex-curator told Solomon, "Yes, the Reichsmarshall and I know each other well." That evening, Roth and Friedlander met at Roth's home for supper, and after wine and food, the two men retired to Roth's study for schnapps and cigars.

One afternoon in late March Leah was on her way home from the market when she was set upon by a band of Hitler Youth who assumed she was a German living with a Jew. They beat her badly about the face, hacked off her long hair with their bayonets, all the while ignoring her loud protestations of innocence. Several neighbors turned on their heels and walked on. Blinded by blood from a laceration near the hairline, she cried out, "But I'm a Jew!"

This stopped the boys for a moment until one of them said in a vicious voice, "Even worse," and with that he drew his long, thin-bladed, Hitler Youth

Leader's dagger. The sun glinted off the flat of the lozenge-shaped blade, illuminating the etched motto, "Blut und Ehre", Blood and Iron. He pushed the point into Leah's back above her right hip. The needle sharp dagger slid in easily, piercing her right kidney, then perforating her lower intestine, allowing a flow of fecal matter to enter the abdominal cavity.

The hospital refused to admit her because she was Jewish, and she died three days later in her bed, wracked with fever, raving and in agony. The next day Solomon and the children buried her in the Jewish cemetery. Their lives had not been idyllic, even before this disaster. Leah had miscarried their first child in the second trimester of her pregnancy for reasons no doctor could determine. The best explanation from the young Viennese physician whom they consulted was, "Sometimes a woman's body just rejects the baby." The oldest son, Fritz, contracted scarlet fever and was slightly hard of hearing as a result of mastoiditis. When Fritz first began complaining of fever, sore throat, and headache when he was three, and Solomon saw the rash on his little neck, chest, armpits and groin, he thought he was going to lose his son. Then Fritz began vomiting and he was convinced Fritz wouldn't survive. The Viennese doctor recommended bed rest and a course of fluids. He assured the panic-stricken parents that as dramatic and frightening as it was, the disease was rarely fatal, however he cautioned them that the secondary and inevitable infections of the sinuses could be severe and frequently caused hearing loss. Fortunately, Fritz's impairment was relatively mild.

Solomon's other children survived the measles, mumps, chicken-pox, whooping cough, and the other assaults of childhood without incident. Leah's violent death struck him with the force of a locomotive. He first blamed himself, then Germany second, and third Hashem, the God of the Hebrews in descending order of responsibility. In the weeks that followed he must have asked himself a thousand times, "How could I have possibly have failed to understand Kristallnacht?" He cursed himself far more bitterly than Job ever did. Now, he sought out incidents of Nazi persecution, and roamed the Jewish ghetto with the smallest Leica camera he could find. He met a Jew who had a darkroom in his apartment and as Solomon surreptitiously took photographs of beatings, vandalism and murders, the other man developed his film. Concealing the camera in paper bags, pasteboard boxes and packages, Solomon became adept at taking pictures without having to look through the lens. His hands seemed to know the proper angle, independently of his eye, which judged the distance. Some of his intense self-loathing diminished, as the albums of photographs depicting Jews, maimed, harassed, crippled, and killed in the streets of Munich filled up.

At Roth's direct request, Friedlander duly informed Goering of Solomon's willingness to part with most of his art collection in exchange for safe passage to South America for his children. The Reichsmarshall was only too happy to agree, especially as Roth, himself, insisted on staying. Roth remained deaf to his children's entreaties, telling them it was his sacred duty to make a record of the evils being perpetrated by the nation that had given the world Beethoven, Bach, Brahms, Schiller, Goethe, Heine, and now in its final flowering, Adolf Hitler. Their tears flowed like the Isar, but Solomon was adamant.

There was more to his remaining than creating a photographic indictment of the country he despised even more than Hitler. Without the support of the German people, the Fuhrer would be no more than another rightist politician, marginalized by his own strident anti-Semitism. Solomon blamed the Germans for the Nazis. To him, the Nazis were no more than the execresences of a sickness that had affected all of Europe for more than a thousand years. He wanted not only to leave a meticulous record of atrocities committed against his people, Solomon also wanted to send his entire fortune abroad. He would be damned if he'd allow a single pfennig or a stick of furniture to remain once his children were safely beyond the reach of the Gestapo. His photograph albums were far too dangerous to send out with his children, but he had a German friend who, for reasons of his own, would ensure the albums were delivered safely to a large safety deposit box at the Credit Suisse Bank in Geneva.

Solomon was only too well aware that at some time in the not too distant future, the Gestapo would come for him and take him to Dachau. More than likely they would give him a beating as well; however, he was almost cheerfully reconciled to this eventuality. Since Leah died, his desire to continue living in a world which not only tolerated the Nazis but seemed to embrace them as the nations of the world did at the 1936 Olympic Games in Berlin had reached a low ebb. He was firm in his resolve to continue life alone in his brownstone home, surrounded by the now mostly bare white walls that formerly displayed his awesome collection of the French Impressionist masters. When Friedlander came to take them, Solomon was actually relieved, for in Monet's landscapes, Renoir's idyllic scenes of Argentieul, Degas' dancers, and even Gaugain's Tahitian women, Solomon saw a world that no longer existed. He lived in a nightmare world of red, white, and black swastika flags that flew from every public building and actually felt mocked by his beautiful paintings.

Immediately following the 1937 exhibition entitled Entarte Kunst, Degenerate Art, put on in Munich by Josef Goebbels and advertised as "The culture documents of the decadent works of Bolsheviks and Jews," Solomon began to acquire works by Picasso, Kandinsky, Kirchner, Nolde, Egon Schiele, and Chaim Soutine. Carefully selected from 20,000 works of modern art confiscated from German Museums on Goebbels orders, the exhibition had featured masterpieces hanging side by side with paintings by inmates of insane asylums. All of the German press was unanimous in its verdict that the paintings were indeed degenerate. This cultural stupidity was regrettably not confined to Goebbel's Volkische Beobachter, and even the more respected newspapers like Die Zeit joined the unanimous chorus of condemnation.

Leah hadn't particularly liked these new works Solomon was purchasing. She particularly objected to the Schiele portraits, which she found disturbing in their frankly erotic candor and their emphasis on emotion over decoration.

"If I must have a Sezession painting, give me a Klimt. At least they're beautiful with all their golden yellows." After Leah died, Solomon put the Klimts in the closet and hung the Schieles in his bedroom.

He hung nothing whatever downstairs, preferring to stare at the shadows left on the white walls by the missing paintings, which had hung there for so many years. The faint impressions served as a constant reminder of what he thought of as his unforgivable blindness. Thus he sought to punish himself for his failure to see what was happening to Munich, to Germany, to Europe, while he blithely went about his daily business, returning to his family and his beloved art in the evenings.

Solomon was downstairs in the drawing room, wrapping his Leica in brown kraft paper and tying it with sisal twine so it would look like an innocuous parcel. He knew the police would never suspect him as a spy, for all Jews were subject to arbitrary arrest at any time. He would venture deep into the ghetto near the Sendlinger Gate. The weather that August was fine, and would bring Germans and Jews into the streets. If any of the brown-shirted SA, much less the Gestapo, had even suspected the well-dressed prosperous looking Roth was carrying a camera, he would have been instantly arrested. If they ever developed his film after he'd taken some pictures, the consequences would be far too gruesome to contemplate. He could always call Friedlander, but even Goering could do only so much. Assisting a Jew was one thing. Helping a Jew who was also an enemy of the Third Reich was another.

## CHAPTER 3

# The Meeting

AS DIETRICH'S MERCEDES pulled to the high curb a few doors down from his destination, he saw an SS unterscharfuhrer and a small man in a three-piece brown suit beside him. The SS man was in full uniform and from twenty paces away, Dietrich could see he was sweating. The SS man was armed with the MP38 Schmeisser machine pistol, a fearsome weapon for close quarters combat and highly controllable for a fully automatic gun. Dietrich's chauffeur opened the general's door, and as Dietrich got out and walked forward, he could hear the trooper shouting in a deep voice.

"Open up in the name of the Reich! Solomon Roth, we know you're in there. We have orders to search this house!" Even in August of 1939, the SS man was unlikely to open fire with his Schmeisser. Jew or no Jew, the home was in a respectable upper-class neighborhood. The cement sidewalk was spotless and shaded by mature, specimen beech trees. The small bespectacled man was wearing a cheap civilian suit that positively stank of Gestapo. The general walked stealthily up behind the two men, who were staring at the heavy, white painted, wooden front door with the elaborate, Renaissance style, bronze door knocker and large bronze door knob.

Dietrich stood six feet one inch in his stocking feet and carried 180 pounds of sinew and muscle on his frame. He was an imposing figure without his immaculately tailored SS uniform. His general's visor cap added several inches to his stature. Dietrich rarely wore a sidearm. He had the Luger he'd carried in the First World War, as well as a Walther PP in nine millimeter short, however his uniform was all the protection he thought he needed for his Munich outings. He was not the least bit intimidated by the trooper's Schmeisser or the little Gestapo man, who no doubt had a Walther of his own.

Dietrich did have a dagger. It was a chained SS honor dagger with a black leather covered scabbard, silver oak leaves adorning the curved hilt, and pommel pieces and a superbly forged genuine Damascus steel double-edged blade inlaid with a gold inscription, reading, "In Herzlichen Kamaradenschaft, H. Himmler." Himmler's name was a facsimile of his actual signature and was presented to Dietrich by the slight, mustachioed son of a Catholic schoolmaster, who as SS Reichsfuhrer was the most feared and reviled man in the Third Reich. Dietrich had left this dagger on the back seat of the Mercedes. He loathed Himmler above all other men.

Dietrich was profoundly uneasy about his relationship with Himmler and Goering. Still, the ethical and moral compromises of his personal honor and integrity that enabled him to wear the black uniform were made less bitter by the electrifying effect the uniform had on Himmler's hirelings. Dietrich used the field command voice that served him so well in the tank corps during the Great War.

"Unterscharfuhrer, what is the meaning of this?!" The SS man and the Gestapo agent both turned on Dietrich with fury in their faces. It was all Dietrich could do not to laugh at them outright and remain impassive. His right hand twitched as he stifled an impulse to reach out and choke the man in brown. The civilian's pinched, ill-natured face put him in mind of a cockroach. For all the talk of the Aryan race being blond-haired, blue-eyed, Nordic-type ideals, in Dietrich's experience these were seen mostly in SS posters. The reality was that most Gestapo men were bespectacled, short, dark nonentities, and this one was no exception. The transformation from snarling, violent antipathy to fawning servility was the work of a second. The servile expression on the SS man's face changed to awe as his eyes locked onto the shining, silver, bullion oak leaves on Dietrich's collar. Even the Gestapo man's beady eyes opened wide and his weak chin dropped to the knot in his cheap, black satin necktie.

The SS unterscharfuhrer stood ramrod straight, thrust his right arm out in a textbook salute and said, "Heil Hitler."

Dietrich didn't bother returning the salute and said in a bored tone, "Heil Hitler."

The SS man began to excuse himself, "Herr Grupperfuhrer, this is a great honor for me."

Dietrich cut him off. "Unterscharfuhrer, this is a private home, not a public brothel. Your shouting in the street does not reflect credit on the SS. Are you drunk by any chance?"

Instead of the SS man, the Gestapo agent replied in a whining voice, which made Dietrich want to knee him in the groin, "Herr Gruppenfuhrer, this is the home of a Jew, an enemy of the Reich. The owner is suspected of smuggling his family out of Germany in order to preserve assets that were stolen by this Jew from hard working Germans. I have my orders."

"Excellent!" said Dietrich in a voice filled with hearty enthusiasm. "Please show them to me."

Dietrich smiled at the man, though he would have liked nothing better than to gouge out the man's left eye and lead him around by the optic nerve. However, he thought he'd have to be content with merely humiliating the small, poisonous bureaucrat, as the Gestapo agent had doubtless humiliated untold numbers of his fellow humans for no other reason than their having been born Jewish. The man put him more in mind of a rat than a roach.

"May I have your name, Grupperfuhrer?" he asked politely, though the request was faintly tinged with menace.

"No you may not," said Dietrich insolently. "My car is parked over there." He pointed with a well-manicured finger at the slick black Mercedes. It's carefully waxed and chamoised paint shone in the bright sunlight.

"My driver will take us to Gestapo headquarters and I will call the Reichsfuhrer in Berlin, and explain to him that not only did you refuse to obey my orders, but displayed insolence as well. Shall we go?"

The man shied away as if Dietrich had slapped his face. "I regret if I have inadvertently given offense, Herr Gruppenfuhrer. Please excuse me; I am not myself this morning. I slept badly last night. There is no need to call Berlin."

"Your orders please." The bureaucrat drew out papers from the left inside pocket of his cheap suit. Dietrich took them, read them quickly, and handed them back. "Solomon Roth is personally known to Reichsmarshall Goering, who asked me to come here on a matter of some importance. I have read your orders, however I suggest that for the foreseeable future, you leave Mr. Roth in peace. The Reichsmarshall is not someone you want to have as your enemy." Here Dietrich looked menacing. "Neither do you want to offend me. One call to the Fuhrer and you will be dangling from a noose."

The man shrugged his shoulders and spoke in what he intended to be an ingratiating tone, which only disgusted Dietrich that much more. "Your point is well taken, Herr Gruppenfuhrer. This week, next week, this month, next month, sooner or later we'll come back. We have nothing to hide. You can even tell the Jew."

Dietrich debated whether to continue abusing the policeman and decided against it, because he was most likely the sort of man who would mistreat Roth since he couldn't vent his hatred and spleen on him. The unterscharfuhrer looked at Dietrich as if to say, "I had no choice in the matter." Dietrich had sympathy for the soldier, though not so much that he was going to speak to him, which was obviously something the trooper wanted quite badly. Dietrich relented. "Unterscharfuhrer." The soldier who had been standing rigidly and unnaturally erect stiffened even more. "When you return to this home, see that it is not damaged."

"Yes, Herr Gruppenfuhrer." The soldier saluted with another crisp, "Heil Hitler," and then he and the Gestapo agent walked off down the street as the sparrows gathered in the beeches called to each other in a cheeping symphony.

Solomon Roth had been observing the men from a mullioned window on the second floor from inside his home. The window was on one of the sides of the house that projected past the front entrance in such a way as to permit a clear, unobstructed view of the entrance. Solomon knew the inevitable visit was long overdue, though like death the actual event still comes as a shock, regardless of how resigned to it one might think he is. The Gestapo man and his machine gun carrying companion, he expected. They would confiscate his home, the last piece of real property he owned, and arrest him on some entirely spurious pretext, when he and they knew his crime was being a member of a despised minority. He had no idea who was the high-ranking dignitary in the SS officer's uniform. Judging by the reaction of the two other men, he was someone of considerable importance. Roth let go of the light green velvet drape and hurried down the wide staircase with the well-worn and polished oak stairs, trailing his left hand on the rich reddish mahogany banister as was his habit.

Before Dietrich had time to straighten his hat the front door opened, and the general found himself facing a middle-aged man of average height, slim, with thick salt and pepper hair of medium length, sparkling, clear brown eyes, and a pleasant face without any obvious Semitic features. Roth was dressed in a fine, dark gray, wool suit, the product of one of Munich's premier tailors, a white silk shirt with button down collar, and an Italian tie of lustrous black silk.

"Mr. Roth?"

"Yes," said Solomon tentatively.

"May I come in?"

"Of course, how very rude of me. Please come in."

Dietrich stepped across the threshold and into the high-ceilinged entry hall. Roth was unsure of all too many things. Should he close the door or leave it open? Should he offer to take the man's hat, or would he take offense at the very idea of a Jew touching an object that bore the gleaming silver Death's Head? His Jewish hands might be seen to defile it in some way. Solomon had no fear of imprisonment. What he dreaded was the thought that the Nazis would break out his teeth with their rifle butts.

Aside from the disfigurement and humiliation, Solomon had an aversion to tooth pain. The nerves in the teeth were so close to the brain. He knew the brain itself had no pain receptors, or so the doctors said. Solomon had an impacted wisdom tooth while he was in his second year at the university and it made him seriously contemplate suicide for the first time in his life.

Dietrich was a shrewd and keen observer of men and he could see Roth's anxiety. He extended his right hand. "Herr Roth, I am General Dietrich."

Solomon thought the tall man looked vaguely familiar. He'd seen his photograph somewhere on the front page of a newspaper in connection with the death of Ernst Roehm. What he couldn't believe was the proffered hand. The gesture seemed spontaneous and genuine, though one never knew if it were a trap for the unwary, so it was best, and more importantly safest, to ask, then confirm.

"I must tell you, General, I am a Jew."

"So is Einstein, and I would gladly travel a thousand miles just to shake his hand. Don't be fooled by the uniform; I am a professional soldier, not some political thug."

With that statement, Solomon decided the man could not possibly be an ogre who would smash his teeth in for being so presumptuous as to think an SS officer would suffer the touch of a Jew. Solomon extended his own right hand, which he'd kept clasped in his left hand behind his back. The gruppenfuhrer and the Jew shook hands as warmly as if there were no immeasurable, unbridgeable gulf between them, legislated by the Nurnberg Laws and a hundred other Nazi policies put in place to prevent just such interpersonal relations.

Dietrich took off his hat.

"Would you be so good as to take my hat? As a boy, I was taught to remove it on entering someone's home." Solomon took it rather gingerly as if it were very hot, or very dangerous, and hung it on one peg of the elaborately carved, walnut coat tree in the hall.

Roth led Dietrich into the drawing room and motioned for the general to take a seat in one of the large, inlaid, fruitwood armchairs, with needlepoint embroidered seats depicting pastoral scenes in red and white thread. The chairs were comfortable much to Dietrich's surprise, as they didn't look very soft. As he looked around, Dietrich could see the after-images on the walls left by the paintings that had hung there for many years, leaving only the outline of the frame and in some cases the stretcher bars, as well as the heavy brass, picture nails, now dark with the patina of age. At one time there were dozens, hung one on top of the other, as the ceiling was fully four meters high and the outlines began at eye level or slightly below.

"I'm sorry," said Solomon, meaning what he said. "I am so nervous I have forgotten my manners. May I get you something to drink?"

"My dear Mr. Roth," said Dietrich with even greater sincerity, "please relax. I am not here to harm you in any way. As you can see, I'm unarmed. Not every Nazi is a demented anti-Semite. Some of us are simply fighting the advance of world Communism."

"I'd like to think that were the case. I had even convinced myself it was true until my wife was murdered in the streets of Munich in broad daylight on her way home from the market by a band of Hitler Youth."

Solomon's voice strangled in his throat. He couldn't speak another syllable; the lump was hard and unyielding, and tears literally shot from his eyes. Dietrich made a gesture of sympathy with his hands, and through his tears Solomon could see empathy reflected in Dietrich's handsome face.

"I have been revolted by this mindless hatred for the people who gave the world Spinoza, Einstein, and Freud, not to mention Jesus."

"General Dietrich," said Solomon after the constriction in his throat relaxed sufficiently to enable him to speak, "you did not come here to listen to my personal tragedy."

"No," said Dietrich. "However that doesn't preclude me from condoling with you, or prevent me from decrying the madness of the German people as they are led knowingly and even willingly into the sort of bloody barbarism they were only too infamous for in the time of the Caesars."

Just as Dietrich finished speaking the telephone rang. "Yes," he said, "this is Herr Roth speaking. Yes, I can do that. This afternoon will be fine. I expect to be in all day after lunch. Good bye."

Solomon hung the cylindrical receiver back on its steel hook and set down the telephone.

"Good news, I hope," said Dietrich. Solomon smiled a very crooked smile.

"General, if you'll pardon me for saying so, you seem to be a decent man. As you may see from their ghosts on my walls, I am a lover of art, mostly paintings. I owned all the great Impressionist and Post-Impressionist masters. It is thanks to my passion that my children are safely beyond the reach of the Fuehrer."

"I know. The Reichsmarshall has told me of your beautiful collection."

"Then you know it is now all in Karinhalle?"

"You are too modest, Herr Roth. Your connoisseurship ranges far beyond the bounds of the French masters."

Solomon was taken aback. Clearly Dietrich was on close terms with Goering. Either that or he was on good terms with Friedlander, and the ex-curator never mentioned Dietrich, so it had to be that he was close to the Reichsmarshall. Friedlander had just called to tell him that Goering had reconsidered Solomon's offer to sell or rather give, the Noldes, Kandinskys, Schieles, and Chaim Soutines to Friedlander in exchange for exit permits.

"Goering," said Friedlander, "will even want a few examples of the others, not only the Klimts. He doesn't think they are degenerate, but simply deformed, ugly and unpleasant to look at. Still, he recognizes their significance, and wishes to acquire them for the sake of the future art scholars who will come to Karinhalle as Christians to St. Peters, or Jews to Jerusalem. He is not a vile boor like Goebbels; with Goering it is purely a question of taste. He doesn't like them personally."

Dietrich looked at the space over the large, dark, mahogany, slant front bookcase. There was one and only one painting still hanging in the room. It hung to the left of the lattice work, leaded glass doors that protected the gilt stamped, full calfskin bindings of Schiller's and Goethe's collected works. The general's heart quickened at the sight of the elaborately carved, gilt wood frame. He didn't dare look directly at the painting, for it was a dream almost too good to be true.

He'd never thought of actually owning one. They were uncommon to begin with, though they were virtually unsalable in the artist's lifetime, and for several years after his tragic death. By 1939, they were iconic and prohibitively expensive, for there was something in them that evoked a potent, visceral response from the public.

During the course of a brief discussion with Goering, the Reichsmarshall mentioned he was acquiring the Roth Collection of 19th century French masters and Dietrich inquired if there were any paintings by Van Gogh. Goering said there was one but, "Since it is a self-portrait by the Dutch madman, I won't have it in my home. Perhaps if it were a landscape, but never one of those staring portraits. Anyone can see the dementia in the eyes. I told Friedlander that if he dared bring such a contaminated painting to Karinhalle, I would send him to Sachsenhausen no matter how great an expert he is."

Dietrich's voice sounded unnaturally calm as he said to Roth, "I see you still have one painting left."

Roth smiled, "Yes, one lonely orphan remains. It is a self-portrait, executed in mid June of 1888, shortly before Van Gogh learned that Gaugain, who was ill himself, utterly depressed and deeply in debt, agreed to meet him in Arles. Van Gogh was in the process of gradually shedding all he had learned from the Impressionists while he was in Paris."

Solomon paused as he tried to recall exactly what Vincent had said at the time. "Ah, yes. 'Instead of trying to depict exactly what is before my eyes, I am using color more arbitrarily to express myself more forcefully.' I bought it directly from the daughter of Pere Tanguy."

Dietrich thought it was an opportune time to look at the painting, so he rose and walked over to it, standing away about three meters. It was painted from the left. The bushy red moustache and beard in red and rust were thickly rendered with astonishing deftness of hand. The prominent left ear was a blend of flesh-toned paint superimposed with white. The prominent forehead with the "widow's peak" was a dazzling white, while the hair itself was rust with hints of white, brown, and beige, worn thrust back. The nose was large and impressive with a clearly defined left nostril. The eyes were dark with black pupils, white sclera, and rimmed by eyebrows as red as the moustache and beard. The ridges under the eyebrows were pronounced. Vincent had painted himself wearing a white, collared shirt, a barely visible blue cravat, and a soft coat with a wide collar and lapels, painted in fantastic strokes of red, brown, black and green. The overall effect was so striking as to create a hallucination of the artist actually being alive inside the portrait. Dietrich could well understand why Goering would shun the piece, for the eyes followed the viewer with such power that even he had a sensation of vertigo, and the Reichsmarshall being the consummate narcissist would see himself reflected in the painting with all of his own excesses, addictions, and mental pathologies. Dietrich thought it quite simply the finest work of art he'd ever seen in his life.

"You like the portrait?" said Solomon. "You may have it. Everything else has been inventoried by the Reichsmarshall's agent. It's not going to Argentina with the Schieles and Noldes, and I can't very well take it to Dachau with me, much as I might like to. It would be a comfort."

Dietrich was so utterly absorbed in the painting he was having difficulty concentrating on Roth's words. He shook his head twice and turned to face the Jew. "It doesn't have to be that way, Herr Roth. There is a plane leaving Munich for Zurich at 5:00. I have all the necessary papers."

"Good," said Solomon. "In that case, my old friend Chaim Mendelsohn can go in my place. He will be overjoyed. I, on the other hand, am not ready to leave quite yet."

Dietrich said heatedly, "Herr Roth, think of your children. The Gestapo was here when I arrived. By staying you are essentially committing suicide."

"We can't be sure of that. General, I have never been a religious Jew, however now I believe my secular ways may have been a grave error, and I don't mean that as a pun. Since my wife was murdered, I have blamed myself, Hashem whom you call God, Germany, and the Fuehrer. I refuse to think her death was some random tragic event, for then her death is meaningless and if Leah's death means nothing, then Hashem cannot exist. If there is no God, then the Nihilists, Anarchists, Existentialists and yes the Communists, are all correct. Then the universe is ambivalent if not inimical, and life is a terrible, tragicomic, meaningless farce, and we might as well all be hedonists until we die surfeited from excesses of food, drink and sex. No, I must reject that philosophy. We are all here for a reason although due to our human limitations and mortal myopia, we cannot see it. If you will give the papers to me, I will give them to Mendelsohn, and that will be a mitzvot for me, what we Jews call a meritorious, good action. I have my own personal business with Hashem that requires me to stay here. If I must go to Dachau, Hashem is surely as much there as here in Munich. Our dialog will continue regardless, and that is the only important thing in my life right now. My children are safe with their uncle. I have very much enjoyed our conversation. Please take the painting."

Dietrich looked at Solomon and could see none of Van Gogh's madness in the Jew's eyes, only an unfathomable, boundless sadness, whether for his wife, his people, or what was about to take place in Europe, he had no idea. Dietrich sincerely believed Hitler could do no wrong and that all mistakes in German political policy were due to the Fuehrer being mislead by ignorant racists like Goebbels and military incompetents like Keitel.

Dietrich had come to see Roth, prepared to pay for the painting as best he could. He reached into the right pocket of his wool uniform trousers and took out a folding purse of morocco leather, opened it and shook out thirty, bright, British gold sovereigns leaving himself only two coins. He handed twenty-eight to Roth, who looked at them as if they were fairy gold.

"Those are the good, old, British gold sovereigns from before 1914," said Dietrich.

He reached in the left inside pocket of his coat and drew out a small, blue leather box with a snap. Roth had put the sovereigns in two neat stacks on the red, marble-topped, French Second Empire table nearest to his armchair. Roth took the leather box from Dietrich and unsnapped it, opened it, and to his amazement, inside was a fairly large, mine-cut diamond in a rose gold setting.

"The ring came from my mother and belonged to her mother. I was going to give it to my wife, however I doubt I will meet my bride before I am killed in the war we know is only months away."

Two very large tears formed in Solomon's eyes, one in each, and he tried without success to blink them back. "The gold, I will accept," he said, holding the box with the ring out to Dietrich. "I can't take your mother's ring."

"The ring and the gold are the only assets I have."

"So," said Roth with a thin smile, "you are not an opportunist like Marshall Goering? Unlike so many other Germans in authority you have not enriched yourself by despoiling the Jews?"

"No," said Dietrich. "And if you feel I am despoiling you of your painting, then we will shake hands once more and I will bid you a good day."

"Listen, General," said Roth. "Under normal circumstances I would sell the house we're sitting in long before I would part with that painting. It's worth far more to me than my home. One can always buy another house. Van Gogh self-portraits are perhaps the most personal works of art ever to have come from the hand of man. Each one represents a substantial portion of a human soul, and not just any soul, but one who saw so deeply and accurately into the essence of existence and the meaning of life that he couldn't live with what he'd seen and what he knew. In the current Herionymous Bosch nightmare I find myself in, I am happy to see at least one of my earthly treasures go to a man who will cherish and protect it as I have. When I received that call a few minutes ago, I was pleased to know my beloved Klimts won't be destroyed by Goebbels and his barbarians who can't bear to look at the truth unless it is stripped of all passion, utterly banal, antiseptic and appealing to the eye of an amateur."

"Then we have an agreement Herr Roth?"

"If you include Mendelsohn, you will make me happier than I have been in many weeks."

"You have my word as an officer that Herr Mendelsohn will be on the Zurich flight this evening. The exit papers are endorsed by the Reichsmarshall himself, and bear his signature and personal stamp."

"Then let us shake hands on it, General Dietrich." They looked into each other's eyes and the Nazi SS general and the Jew shook hands warmly and firmly.

## CHAPTER 4

# Munich, 1945

FROM MARCH 23RD to 24th, Field Marshall Montgomery's twenty-five divisions, together with General George Patton's 3rd Army, swept forward across Germany meeting little resistance from either the German Army or the civilian Volksturm. The dominant desire prevailing among the German military was to have British and American forces occupy as much of the fatherland as possible before the Soviets overcame General Guderian's outnumbered troops that were holding the line at the Oder River. The Fuhrer shot himself on April 30th and Hitler's replacement, Grand Admiral Karl Doenitz, pursued a policy of capitulation. The unconditional surrender of Germany was signed on April 29th while the Fuehrer was still alive. The surrender became effective on the second of May. Several more surrender documents were signed; one at Marshall Montgomery's headquarters on May 4th, and still another at General Dwight Eisenhower's headquarters at Reims. On May 8th at midnight, the war in Europe was officially over.

In the late spring of 1945, Munich was a very different city than it was in 1939. St. Peter's Church was reduced to a pile of 12th century stones and fragments. The American and British bombing of historical, cultural, civilian architectural masterpieces was deliberate and all too accurate. As terrible as the German occupation had been on subject peoples, the Nazi toll on historical structures paled when compared to the relentless savagery of the Allies, a destruction of cultural monuments unparalleled in human history. If the Germans had leveled the Kremlin, the Hermitage, the Louvre, the Pyramids, Notre Dame, the Colliseum, St. Peters, the Houses of Parliament, Westminster Abbey, Buckingham Palace, Windsor Castle, and the British Museum, the devastation would have only begun to resemble the damage inflicted on the architectural treasures of Germany.

Munich was not an industrial city, nevertheless, Allied bombers destroyed between forty and fifty percent of its buildings. In addition to St. Peters, the oldest of the Wittlesbach residences was heavily damaged. The 16th century Residenz was obliterated, as was the magnificent 18th century Rococco Cuvilles Theater at the Residenz. The National Theater, the Alte Pinakothek, the Neue Pinakothek, and the Glyptothek, all these world renowned museums, libraries and cathedrals, lay in ruins, their countless thousands of irreplaceable works of art and literature burnt, blasted to fragments, or looted by citizens to be traded for food and tobacco with American and British forces.

Despite the horrific destruction, late May came as it always did, and blossoms bloomed in flowerbeds and even in between the rubble. The trees, those that survived the relentless bombing, leafed out wearing their bright emerald-green crowns, and the birds sang their sweet songs happy that the long winter and the continual concussions of detonating TNT were over.

It was late morning when Sergeant Henry "Hank" Dryden, who had only recently celebrated his eighteenth birthday, walked up to the Munich brownstone once the residence of the Roth family. He was tall and spare of build, still retaining much of the boy in his body, while his face was clearly older and more experienced than his years. He had enlisted on his seventeenth birthday, with his parent's permission, and was sent to France in 1944 as a private in Patton's 3rd Army. Hank earned his sergeant's stripes in December of 1944 during the relief of Bastogne. He didn't know how or why he'd been assigned to a military police detail, enforcing weapons confiscation in Munich, though he did know the Army had its own way of doing things and it was always best to salute officers and follow orders.

As a sergeant, he was issued a Thompson sub-machine gun rather than the standard M-1 Garand rifle. The Thompson was heavy, but much more compact than the long M-1. Hank had seen quite enough of war for the rest of his life and wanted badly to return to the beaches of Southern California. He'd expected to be sent to the Pacific; however once again, the Army had its own way of doing things. The Germans were invariably cooperative with the Allied weapons drive and were only too happy to turn in Lugers, Walthers, Schmeissers, and all manner of military and civilian weapons, as if they wanted nothing to do with instruments of death after the hell they'd just been through.

This particular brownstone, on the pleasant street lined with beech trees, one of the few to emerge from the allied bombing relatively unscathed, was rumored to have been the residence of the commander of the 6th Panzer

Army. SS General Sepp Dietrich had been fighting in the North near Antwerp when he was ordered to the East to reinforce Guderian's beleaguered forces. At the persistent urging of Solomon Roth, Dietrich had used Roth's home as his Munich office since before the war. Dietrich's presence prevented it from being confiscated after Solomon was taken to Dachau. Dietrich used it on the infrequent occasions he took leave of absence from his field command and except for the filing cabinets in the study where Dietrich kept regimental and personal records the house remained much the same as it was in 1939.

The front door was locked, and Hank slammed the heavy bronze doorknocker until he was convinced there was no one inside. He was reluctant to break in and add his personal contribution to the wreckage and carnage all around him. There was that, and he had no real tool for battering except for his Thompson. He wasn't willing to risk damaging the fragile wooden buttstock. He would just have to wait and come back later with Private Larson, who was a veritable wizard with a lock pick. No lock, however heavy or complicated, remained immune to his super-sensitive fingers. Just as he'd almost made up his mind to walk away, he decided instead to have a smoke, sit on the limestone stoop, and enjoy the balmy spring air. He fished a Lucky Strike out of the front pocket of his light brown fatigue shirt and lit it with the Zippo lighter he'd carried for the past six months. His mother, who's had no problem with his enlistment, would no doubt take a far less charitable attitude to his smoking. Hank had taken it up principally to mask the stench of the latrines, though the soothing effects of tobacco soon seduced him, until now he was smoking more than a pack each day. He vowed he'd quit the day he set his feet on California soil. Having leaned his Thompson against the door, he was enjoying his cigarette when he heard the distinctive sound of a door opening. Although there was a twenty-round stick magazine in his sub-machine gun, it wasn't charged, and that meant there was no round in the chamber and the bolt was closed. Hank didn't feel threatened and he made no move toward the gun.

A small, tow-headed, freckle-faced boy of no more than seven, dressed in a clean white shirt and very light beige trousers, walked up to him from the house on the immediate left, and stood staring at him with wide, cornflower blue eyes. Hank had a piece of chocolate wrapped in silver paper in the same pocket where he kept his Luckies. He kept the cigarette between his lips, took out the chocolate, and offered it to the boy, who smiled radiantly as he took it. The boy unwrapped it with a fairly clean hand, then he broke off a piece from the block, put it in his mouth, carefully rewrapped the remainder, and stowed it in his left trouser's pocket. Dryden thought the lad displayed a laudable restraint, and despite the beatific smile, there was an underlying seriousness and solemnity not just about this boy, but about many of the children he'd seen in the streets of Munich. It was as if they all suffered from a deeply seated fear that the bombings were not over after all. Their innocent childhoods had been most cruelly betrayed not only by their parents, but more than that, by all the big people of the world. Hank wanted badly to tell this boy that it was safe to smile, that the bombers weren't coming back, that hopefully they were gone forever. Regrettably, his German didn't extend much past "danke shoen, bitte sehr, guten morgen, fraulein, du bist sehr schoen, gibt mir ein glas bier bitte, and other similar useful words and phrases.

*What is the German word for airplane?* he thought. *Flugzeug? Forget it.* He tried something, "Ist der shokolad gut?"

The boy's face registered surprise, then an expression of utter delight took its place, and now Hank could see a boy, like he was ten years ago back in Del Mar, California, not a miniature adult, who spent his days and nights wondering whether a bomb was going to destroy his home and him along with it. With this one simple question the little German looked like he was relishing being alive on a lovely day in late May, who couldn't wait to go to the river, or wherever young Munich boys went on such magical days. Certainly there wasn't any Pacific Ocean where Hank had spent the hours of his boyhood that weren't taken up with school.

"Sehr gut, danke," said the boy, who then remembered why he'd come to see the tall American G1 with the machine gun in the first place. The boy had enjoyed the chocolate, and he was going to take most of it home and share it with his two younger sisters. For the past two years, his mother had cleaned the house belonging to the SS general next door to earn money while her husband was away as a Wehrmacht engineer in Denmark.

She had a key to the brownstone and when she saw the American sergeant, she'd sent Karl over with it so there'd be no need for forcible entry. While Dietrich had been fighting in the North, she'd received her payment promptly each month, however she hadn't received any money for the past eight weeks. Still, she dutifully dusted, mopped, and washed windows every week just in case the general returned. She'd heard rumors that the Americans and the British were arresting members of the SS, even heard of summary executions. The once proud and haughty wearers of the dreaded black uniform were desperate to wear Wehrmacht green, a color they used to despise, as if they couldn't distance themselves far enough from the SS. Himmler had killed himself only a few days before, and this news actually made her happy. She worried that the Americans, and worse the Russians, wouldn't bother taking the time to distinguish between the criminals of the Allgemeine SS and the brave Waffen SS, like Oberstgruppenfuhrer Dietrich, who were warriors.

Karl reached in his pocket and felt the long, brass key. He brought it out with his right hand.

"Hier ist die schlussel fur den tur."

"Danke schoen."

"Bitte sehr," said Karl cheerfully and walked back to his house.

Henry inserted the oversize brass key in the lock. Once safely inside, he closed the door behind him and began his search. There still wasn't any electrical power in much of Munich, and probably wouldn't be for many weeks, so his first task was to open the heavy, green velvet curtains throughout the house and let in as much of the May, Munich sunshine as he could. Hank was agreeably surprised at the distinct absence of dust. Usually there was a thick layer of concrete and stone dust that somehow sifted through cracks in the windows and doors of the homes that weren't occupied during the incessant bombings, and clearly this one hadn't had an occupant in some time. After searching homes for the past week, Hank considered himself something of an expert on whether or not a given home was occupied.

Hank knew that this was reputed to have been the personal quarters of an SS general, a rather famous tank commander, who had been last reported to be fighting the Russians near the Hungarian border. The home didn't look at all like what Hank had pictured an influential general's home should look like. There were picture hooks and nails on every wall, and from the outlines in the white paint, there must have been walls full of paintings as there were in museums.

As he looked under beds and sofas,

Hank saw none of the usual "dust bunnies" as his mother called them. He figured that the mother, sister, or some relative or friend of the boy who gave him the key, must be keeping the house clean. All the closets on the second and third floors were empty and almost antiseptic, as if the house were newly constructed and awaiting a new tenant, rather than being, he thought, at least a century old. The fruitwood coffers at the foot of the stripped beds, which by rights should have held bed linens, were empty and spotless as well. Only the ground floor showed signs of human habitation. The general had worked in the spacious study, which had a number of heavy oak filing cabinets. They were all unlocked, and Hank went through them, and discovered some interesting and attractive looking what appeared to be books with large, gold-embossed Nazi eagles and swastikas on them, and an elaborately engraved and gold-inlaid automatic pistol. He knew he could obtain permission from his captain to retain one or two of the guns he confiscated as war souvenirs. Hank wasn't really interested in firearms as a boy, and he had no interest in hunting like some of his friends. Hank was passionate about body surfing and sometimes surf fishing. There was good hunting to be had in the dry hills that rose to the North on the borders of the vast Irvine Ranch, though given a choice between the mountains and the Pacific Ocean Hank would always choose the ocean. Unlike all the other old First World War Lugers, old revolvers, Walthers, and old rifles and shotguns he'd turned in to his captain, this pistol looked valuable. Hank knew his captain was sending home war relics by the trunk load, but until now, he'd never seen anything he wanted. After six months of military service, his one overwhelming desire was to go home to Del Mar, get a job with the local electric power company, and marry his high school sweetheart, not necessarily in that order.

Hank was still enough of a boy to put on the wide, polished, brown leather belt with the gold-washed belt buckle, that curiously was cast with oak leaves, but not the ubiquitous, almost obligatory swastika. The belt was loose around his waist. His captain didn't call him California Slim without reason. The study had only one tall, rectangular, leaded glass window, and the light in the room was dim. There was only one painting on the wall directly across from the heavy mahogany Biedermeier desk. Dietrich had deliberately taken it from its position beside the bookcase and rehung it so that he could look up and stare at it as it stared at him. Hank hadn't paid any attention to it when he first entered the study. He was intent on confiscating any firearms. He tried to be diligent in his searching, knowing that the lives of his comrades might be saved by his finding illegal weapons, and he had specific orders to carefully inspect this particular dwelling. Wearing the general's pistol, Hank sat in the comfortable, Second Empire mahogany desk chair and looked at the picture, imaging he was the general relaxing after a dangerous month in the field, thinking how Adolf Hitler had betrayed the Army by making command decisions based on his own personal delusions, rather than listening to his fighting generals like Guderian and Rommel. Hank contemplated the painting and he thought it was uncanny how the eyes of the man whose head was painted facing slightly to the left seemed to be riveted on his. Hank rose from the chair and walked to the picture to examine it more closely. It was too large to fit in a dufflebag, and though he knew American officers, as well as enlisted men, that had helped themselves to elaborately carved, ivory tankards, silver cups, even pieces that came from the rubble of the museums, the people of Munich called them Pinakotheks. What he was thinking about doing was far closer to looting than legitimate confiscation. Unlike swords, pistols, or daggers, a painting could hardly be considered a legal war trophy.

Hank was about to leave the room when he decided he wanted the painting and the Nazi books as well. He always carried a Barlow pocketknife, which he kept as sharp as a razor. Hank took the painting down off the wall and laid it face down on the desk. He had never done anything even remotely like this in his life, and his hands were shaking as he bent the nails holding the wooden stretcher bar to the frame and removed it. Then he very carefully cut the canvas from the stretcher bar around the nails holding it to the wood, intent on preserving as much of the painting as he possibly could. He then rolled it very loosely into a tube so as not to damage the very thick paint, and tied it with a piece of ribbon he'd found in one of the file drawers. Hank broke the gold-carved wood frame into four pieces and did the same with the stretcher. His heart was racing as fast as if he'd run a mile on the beach. He exited the house with pieces of gilded wood and walked down the street to a bomb crater and threw them into the rubble filled hole. Then he returned to the brownstone and began taking his souvenirs, trying to figure out a dignified method of carrying them all out of the house without looking like he was looting it. As he was making the second and final trip to his jeep as Karl, the neighbor boy was attempting to climb onto the low hanging branch of a nearby beech tree. He saw Hank, brightened, and climbed down. Hank was somewhat burdened down with the heavy leather books, the rolled up painting, and his Thompson sub-machine gun, so he carefully set the folders and the painting down on the stoop, and reached into his pocket for the key. He threw it underhand to Karl, who caught it in his right hand. Karl clicked his heels together and brought his right hand to his brow in a passable imitation of an American military salute, then the boy turned and walked up the steps to his home. Hank picked up his treasures and walked down the tree-lined street wondering about what he'd just done. Then he thought about all the horrors he'd witnessed in the past few months. Unlike hundreds of thousands of others, more like millions, he was going home soon with his spirit and his body intact. Whatever he'd done just now really didn't mean anything in the grand scheme of things. The sun felt warm on his back and in a few months, the good Lord willing, he'd be warmed by the California sun and get himself a proper golden suntan.

## CHAPTER 5

# The Patriarch

HANK DRYDEN LIVED in the same modest home he'd lived in for nearly fifty years. At age 80, he considered himself fortunate to be living in his own home and not one of the dozens of so-called assisted-living communities, which was essentially a nice euphemism for the now despised term, nursing home. In 2007, there weren't too many WWII veterans left. He'd read somewhere that a thousand or more were dying each week, or was it a day, no that seemed like far too many, not that the number was all that important. It was the idea all the vets were dying and not the specific number that frightened him. He's outlived his wife and his only son, who died in Vietnam, another useless war of choice. Hank had vehemently opposed the war in Vietnam, as he'd opposed the war in Korea, although he'd kept his opinions about Korea to himself during the early 1950's because he valued his job.

Vietnam was an entirely different story, and Hank came out strongly against it, even leading a local group of WWII veterans that also believed it was immoral and illegal. "It isn't as if Ho Chi Minh's sampan fleet is going to sail into Long Beach Harbor and attack Los Angeles. They don't have any long-range bombers or nuclear weapons. Ho's been fighting the French for decades and he'll fight us for as long as it takes to drive us out of his country. Ho isn't Adolf Hitler. I enlisted at seventeen and I'm proud of my service. I wouldn't fight in Vietnam if they made me a general. It's only fools who say my country right or wrong. The war's wrong and that's all there is to it."

Dressed in his WWII sergeant's uniform with its service ribbons and silver star Hank marched proudly in almost every demonstration held in San Diego and Los Angeles. He was interviewed on the local television news twice.

His only son Luke dropped out of the University of California at San Diego to enlist in the army. The scene in the Dryden home was tense when he announced his decision in the summer of 1968.

"Have you lost your mind?" said Hank incredulously. Hank had hoped Luke would go on to USC or UCLA medical school. Luke was maintaining a 4.0 grade point average and showing an aptitude for chemistry and biology, not to mention he had only just gotten married. Hank's hands were shaking and his voice was shrill. Luke knew his father would be upset, but he never dreamt he'd be so utterly distraught. Hank's tan face was brick red and if he hadn't been so thin, Luke might have worried he'd have a hemorrhagic stroke.

"Dad," Luke said with sincerity in his voice that drew some of the stinging bitterness that filled Hank's heart, "it isn't that I believe the war is right or just. I agree with you that it's wrong in every way. The Gulf of Tonkin incident was a charade staged to convince Congress to go along with the military-industrial complex. That's not the point. What I see happening is that economically disadvantaged, young black, Mexican, and undereducated white men, those who can't afford to go to college and get a 2S deferment, are being drafted and sent to die as cannon fodder. I think I can go as a medic and save lives, not take life. It will be good training for my medical career."

Luke's handsome face shone with fervor and passion. "Valerie is firmly behind my decision. I thought of all people you would understand. You enlisted at seventeen. At least I'm of age. All I ask is that you give me the same credit, Grandpa and Grandma gave you."

"I didn't have a new wife either," said Hank. There was a certain justice in Luke's words, though Hank was never able to understand how Valerie could possibly support Luke's wanting to go off to Vietnam after only a few months of wedded bliss. Hank finally relented.

Luke was killed during the Tet offensive near the city of Hue. Luke was treating the wounded when their position was overrun by NLF soldiers. Though suffering from mortal wounds himself, Luke saved the lives of four soldiers before succumbing.

In 1999, eight years ago, Hank and his grandson, John, flew to Washington D.C. Hank had been there before to visit the monuments and memorials, the Capitol, the White House, and the Smithsonian Institution, but not since 1982 when the two black granite walls designed by Maya Ying Lin were dedicated as the Vietnam Veterans Memorial. The monument was as controversial as the Vietnam War. Breathtaking in its elegant simplicity, the polished granite bears the names of the more than 58,000 American servicemen and women missing or killed in action during the war. To mollify critics who couldn't understand or relate to the understated eloquence of a war memorial without statues, a bronze group of three soldiers was added in 1984, and to render it politically correct a bronze of three servicewomen was added in 1993.

Hank and his grandson left their room at the Willard Hotel and walked in the early October sunlight to the somber, black stone memorial on the Mall. They spent more than an hour searching the names. John began at the deepest part of the right angle where the wall is the highest and Hank started at the point of the Memorial aimed at the gleaming, white obelisk of the Washington Monument. Hank located Luke's name just below eye level as he stood on the black-granite projecting ramp that runs the length of the hypotenuse. Hank stood there dry-eyed, though John could tell he was deeply moved, as his fingers traced the intaglio letters spelling out Lucas M. Dryden. The two of them stood together for a long while, and John took his grandfather's hand in his, then Hank squeezed it until it was painful.

"I've seen enough," said Hank. "I've seen enough of Washington, too. You know it never really occurred to me until this minute, but amid all its carefully constructed grandeur, it's a city of death. Memorials everywhere, Arlington Cemetery, Ford's Theater and all the resplendent cherry blossoms in spring can't disguise the fact that Washington looks like an immense national version of Forest Lawn in Glendale."

John said nothing. He hadn't even been born when Luke died. He grew up with a series of male father figures, some of whom made a pretense of paternal feelings, and others who made it apparent by their attitude that they thought he was an impediment to the full and free enjoyment of his mother's company. It was Hank Dryden who was both father and grandfather to John when he was a baby, a child, and a young man. Hank took John into his home during the summer months. Thanksgiving as well as Christmas celebrations were always held in the light gray, wooden frame house in Del Mar. Hank was there for John's graduation from Del Mar High, and stood proudly beside John's mother on the USC campus when John graduated from college. Hank paid for a substantial part of John's tuition at Loyola Law School, but missed the graduation due to his wife's illness and Hank's extreme dislike of driving on Interstate 5 and 405 to reach the Westside of Los Angeles.

"It's barely a hundred miles and for some reason I've never understood it always takes almost three hours to get from Del Mar to LA. The traffic is just crazy. Cars cut you off without so much as a single blink of their flasher, and then they stop dead for no earthly reason." Hank's litany of complaints about Southern California drivers, traffic, and Cal Trans, which he saw as the anti-Christ, was always the same. "Why, those brain dead morons at Cal Trans always have to block off a lane of the 5 on a Saturday at 10:00 a.m. for guard rail repair, is totally beyond me," he would rant. "They have to pay the workers time and a half, or even golden time, and they know traffic will be heavier then than at any other time during the week. They deliberately inconvenience the maximum number of people and cause the greatest amount of pollution. It's insane."

John actually asked a Cal Trans official about the seemingly bizarre correlation between the high-volume Saturday traffic and incredibly inconvenient lane closures. John told him of five, ten, or ever twenty-mile back-ups, bumper to bumper traffic, flooding surface streets with irate drivers who speed through urban neighborhoods desperate to escape the maddening bottlenecks. The official confirmed Hank's suspicions. "We plan things so that the taxpayers get to see their tax dollars at work."

"So that's why we drivers probably pay a billion dollars a year in extra fuel, unnecessary wear and tear on our vehicles, lost time, and pump more ozone into the atmosphere and filth into our lungs, so we can see the men and women in their orange jackets at work?" John added. "And this seems sane to you?"

The man looked at John and said, "Please don't quote me on this."

"Don't worry, nobody would ever believe it anyway."

At the age of 80, Hank still drove himself, though rarely more than two miles to the market or to the beach. He never ventured onto the 5 Freeway or to San Diego, much less to Southgate, which was where John Dryden had his law office. It was situated on the somewhat seedy main street, Tweedy Boulevard, in a dilapidated brown brick and stucco building that dated from the Great Depression. John was a public interest lawyer who represented the disadvantaged minorities, which were more than adequately present in the community. John also served a few corporate clients, which helped defray the very modest rent on the building, whose reception area had a view of the dingy gray parking meters on Tweedy. Through the white metal Venetian blinds, one could see across the street to one of the parking lots, which served the sprawling St. Francis Hospital.

At least once every two months, John would drive his vintage 1967 Pontiac GTO, east on the 105 Freeway to where it dead ended into the 605 and take the 605 South to the 405 San Diego Freeway and keep heading south until the 405 became the 5, and continue till he reached Del Mar. He could have taken the 105 West to the 405 South, or taken the 605 to the 91 East to the 5 and avoided the 405 altogether. John didn't like the traffic on the 5 through Santa Ana, which was forced into fewer lanes once you passed the 57, 55 junctions, and on Saturday there was invariably a back-up with people heading south from LA and the hundred bedroom communities around the Big City, any one of which would be thought of as a large city in Montana, Idaho, or Wyoming. John assumed they were all going to the beaches of San Diego, Sea World, the Wild Animal Park, or the "World Famous San Diego Zoo." Either that or they were fleeing LA, Pasadena, Burbank, Glendale, Pomona, La Habra, the San Fernando Valley, or even Southgate. Once John was past Newport, Irvine, and the massive development of Mission Viejo, the temperature always dropped a few degrees and the air was perceptibly cleaner. Traffic generally thinned out as he drove by the huge Marine base at Camp Pendleton, and didn't thicken until the long incline where the 5 and the 805 branch off near Los Penasquitos Canyon. John knew he was getting close to Del Mar when the 5 passed over the Batiquitos Lagoon. He took the Del Mar Race Track exit west to Route 1, then turned left along the Pacific until he came to Del Mar itself. The town still retained some of the charm it once possessed in abundance before the millionaires built their mansions into the hills overlooking the ocean. Property values had increased by thousands of percent, even on modest 1500 square foot, two-bedroom bungalows like his grandfather's. San Diego was now the second largest city in California, dwarfing San Francisco. It held the distinction of being the seventh largest city in the country.

Hank anticipated John's weekly visits, whether his grandson arrived in the dull red Toyota Celica or the bright red antique Pontiac. Indeed they were the high point of his week, though on other days he would walk on the beach for hours, except in inclement weather, during which he would read the *San Diego Union* or the *New York Times*. In the past few years he had become an aficionado of Sudoku, the Japanese number puzzles. Though Hank was never really keen on crosswords, something about Sudoku intrigued him. When Sudoku failed to entice there was always the Internet. He kept up with other veterans of Patton's 3rd Army throughout the United States, Europe, and

Mexico. They would swap stories about their war experiences, children, and grandchildren. Hank thought the Internet was the greatest advance in communication in all human history far surpassing the telephone, radio, and even television. He could email a hundred people at once, or post an account of his being in a Munich hofbrau during Oktoberfest in 1945, and share it with all the people who visited the 3rd Army's website and had any interest in it. Email was far more versatile than the telephone, and the best part was that you could interact with it at your convenience. Hank and John frequently exchanged emails and instant messages throughout the day, and the luxury of being able to write and reply at his leisure, after walking, or marketing was in Hank's estimation a quantum leap better than the phone. Hank liked the phone well enough, but it demanded one's immediate attention. He carried a cell phone strictly as a precaution in the event he was stricken with chest pains, although his cardiologist told him all the walking in the sand was keeping his blood pressure at a more than acceptable level.

"In fact," the doctor said with a smile after Hank's last routine checkup, "I would say that 130 over 70 is good for a twenty-year-old and positively remarkable for a man your age. Your resting pulse is a nice steady 72 beats per minute and your weight is well matched to your height. I wish all my patients exercised regularly. I firmly believe exercise slows the onset of Alzheimer's, certain types of cancer, osteoporosis, diabetes, and probably every other chronic malady to a greater or lesser extent. Mr. Dryden, you have taken good care of your body and I see no reason why you won't live to see 100."

Hank looked at Dr. Sprague. "So those two beers I drink on the weekend when my grandson comes to see me won't kill me after all?"

"No," said the doctor. "Whatever you're doing is working brilliantly as far as your heart is concerned. If I were you, and I aspire to be like you when and if I'm your age, I wouldn't change my routine."

Hank used to smoke even after he left the army until one day in 1975, when his wife, Emily, put her foot down and insisted if he were going to continue to smoke in light of all the gruesome medical evidence, then he'd have to do it outside the house.

"I'm tired of my clothes smelling like smoke. Why, if I smell my arm, the skin stinks of cigarette smoke. More importantly, Henry Dryden, I love you and I'm not ashamed to say I need you, so I'm going to do everything I can to keep you around and that means not tolerating your smoking. You can smoke outside while you taper off if you need to. I know it's a bear to up and quit cold turkey."

Hank continued to smoke outside in the small backyard. Then on New Year's Day, 1976, he tapped his last Lucky on his left thumbnail to tamp down the tobacco, lit it with his WII vintage Zippo lighter, smoked it down until it was so short it nearly burnt his fingers, flicked it onto a patch of sand, and ground it under the heel of his tan loafers. He threw the rest of the pack in the trash and proudly announced to Emily that he'd given up smoking.

Emily was so overjoyed that later that night she treated him to a lengthy, sensuous massage, and ten minutes of the best sex he could remember. Later the same night, they made love again and lay in each other's arms as they'd done when they were twenty. Unknown to either of them at the time, Emily had a mole under her hair, which became melanoma without her realizing it. By the time she did and the symptoms were overt, the cancer had already metastasized to her brain. The end was horrifyingly swift, though Emily suffered surprisingly little pain. All her discomfort was due almost entirely to the projectile vomiting and continuous nausea from the radiation and the chemotherapy. Hank and John, together with John's mother and her new second husband, Eddie, buried her in the small non-denominational cemetery overlooking the Pacific beside Luke. That was nearly twenty years ago and Hank still visited their graves at least once each month to leave fresh flowers and make sure the simple, polished granite memorials were clean of the film left by the infrequent rains and the occasional bird droppings.

Hank looked at the time signature on the bottom left of his shiny aluminum Dell laptop. It read 10:53 and he'd been expecting to hear the throaty insistent growl of the old Pontiac's 389 cubic inch V-8 engine and its "tri-power" manifold sporting three Holly two-barrel carburators. The old 'muscle car" was still quite close to being the same car it was in 1967. Hank and Luke had gone to the Pontiac dealer in Oceanside and special ordered it in a candy-apple red. With a Hurst 4-speed shifter and nearly 335 horsepower, the car was fast and looked it, with a sinuous curve to its profile. Luke had barely put enough miles on it to break it in before he enlisted. Luke's widow, pregnant with John, had no use for such a hot-rod, and was overjoyed when Hank offered to buy it from her for full price. Hank drained the oil and put the car up on blocks in his garage until he presented it to John on his graduation from high school. Valerie was not at all happy about the gift, telling Hank the very last thing her son needed was a racing car with no airbags or even a shoulder belt. In her opinion, it was too loud and much too fast. John rarely drove it at all, which mollified his mother. He did, however, wax it frequently and thoroughly whenever he had the time.

Hank and Emily had embraced Valerie as if she were their own daughter from the first time Luke brought her home. Valerie was a lovely girl with long, naturally wavy, blonde hair, the color of dark honey in a jar, a delicately molded, upturned nose, prominent cheekbones and a golden tan. She reminded Emily a little of Grace Kelly, while Hank thought she looked more like a blonde Elizabeth Taylor. Regardless, Luke was smitten with the junior psychology student he'd met on campus in his freshman year. Within six months of their meeting, they were married in the small chapel of the Unitarian-Universalist church, which was the only one in Del Mar, and whose minister and congregation vehemently and vociferously opposed the war in Vietnam, and therefore was the only church acceptable to Hank. His attitude towards all the other so-called houses of God was one of either indifference or outright antagonism.

"Jesus said to love your neighbor, not kill your neighbor. The Vietnamese aren't even close to being our neighbors, so I suppose it's all right with Christians to drop napalm bombs on woman and children minding their own business in grass-roofed huts."

Curiously, Valerie didn't "freak out," was the expression Luke used at the time to describe strong differences of opinion. Her calm acceptance seemed out of character to Hank. John must have been conceived during the week of leave the army gave to Luke after he completed basic training. Either that or Valerie had a relationship with another man shortly after Luke shipped out for Vietnam. Hank wouldn't have been shocked, though he said nothing of his suspicions to his wife. As John grew up, Hank's concerns about his parentage faded as he saw not only Luke's physical traits, but certain extremely subtle and idiosyncratic behaviors, like the way in which John ever so slightly narrowed his eyes when he was thinking hard, as if to see through a problem to its solution. Though no psychologist, Hank was familiar with the psychological mechanism of projection and considered that he might be attributing his son's behaviors to his grandson, superimposing memories of Luke onto John. He analyzed it acutely from every aspect, and rejected the notion that John was not Luke's son. He'd read enough of the nature versus nurture debate to know he was more a proponent of nature.

Hank was no virgin when he returned from the war. The tall, spare sergeant had discovered the delights of girls only once prior to his shipping out. It wasn't Emily, but Janice, another girl from Del Mar High, who made up in enthusiasm for what she lacked in expertise. Hank found the maidens of

Munich very free with their favors, and indulged in them whenever the opportunity arose, which it did with gratifying frequency. Far from shunning him as an occupier, the Germans seemed to look on him as a liberator, and of course his ration of chocolate and generous allowance of highly-prized Lucky Strikes, served to add further luster to his status.

Therefore when Hank thought Valerie's baby-blue eyes were possibly of the roving variety, his assessment was firmly based on firsthand knowledge. He knew Luke would not have seen this, and he never said a word to Luke, because Luke wouldn't have believed him. If Hank had spoken, it would have driven a real wedge between them, and set the tone for a long, bitter, and even permanent estrangement. In every other respect, Hank thought Valerie was a delightful girl. She was pretty, well mannered, and interested in psychology, science, art, finance, anything but politics, although she had Hank's attitude towards the war. She thought Luke's rationale for enlisting was, "The noblest thing I ever heard of. He is such a good man. There's no one like him except for Dr. King." She would sit in his lap in Hank's living room and deep kiss him without any shame on the blue upholstered, Danish modern couch. Valerie's spontaneous outbursts of lavish physical attention amused Hank, though they had a tendency to make Emily uncomfortable. Hank thought her infatuation with Luke, which continued unabated in the months that followed the wedding and showed no signs of cooling, less disturbing than his wife did, perhaps because of his experience with women when he was overseas.

Valerie was very affectionate and demonstrative and only hoped Luke wouldn't find her sweet caresses cloying at some time in the future. Her parents were well to do, and lived outside of San Francisco in San Rafael. Valerie was one of four children. Her two brothers were married with children of their own. The Girards came to the wedding with Valerie's younger sister, who served as the maid of honor. Mr. and Mrs. Girard left the day after the ceremony, leaving Hank and Emily with a vague impression of unostentatious wealth mixed with arid polite urbanity. They were reserved, not quite to the point of standoffishness, though seeing Valerie hugging and kissing her stiffened mother, Hank couldn't help but wonder if the daughter were a changeling.

As he looked at the clock on his computer reading, 11:12, John was officially late, not that his being delayed was unprecedented given the horrific Saturday traffic on Interstate 5. These days even what used to be sleepy Route 1 could be bumper to bumper during a summer weekend once you turned left going south from Del Mar Boulevard onto the Coast Highway. Hank remembered the days, not too far in the past, when Del Mar was a relatively uncrowned village by the Pacific like Carlsbad, Encinitas, and La Jolla. Now they were all so-called bedroom communities of San Diego attracting hundreds of newcomers every month, or so it seemed to Hank judging by the increased traffic in the streets and people in the markets.

John was the ideal grandson, although when Hank really thought about it, he was more of a son than a grandchild. They were that close, and he owed it to Valerie, who'd pretty much left John with him and Emily for much of John's childhood. Valerie didn't abandon John, and if she hadn't been completely convinced that John needed a father figure in his life, no power on earth short of death could have made her give him up. The arrangement suited the Drydens well, and Hank's position as an executive with the electric company allowed him to spend evenings and weekends with John. Hank's job was well defined and not the sort he had to take home with him.

John grew up liking women and he'd been engaged twice, and in Hank's estimation either Laurie or Sharon would have made him a good wife. The difficulty was almost entirely John's. All of his father's and his mother's traits both the desirable ones and the less than ideal ones, seemed to be distilled in him. John had decided he wanted to become a lawyer since he began junior high school and he pursued his dream with all the fire and passion of his mother. John inherited Luke's selflessness and nobility of spirit. This ensured that he would use his legal career to tirelessly defend the rights of the less fortunate. Consequently, John lived for his work, leaving little room for romance and perhaps even less for the responsibilities and commitment of marriage.

"What do you think you're looking for in a wife?" asked Hank one afternoon following John's break-up with Sharon, a successful real estate broker. "I think you want a woman who is as devoted to her career as you are to yours, so you each have someone to come home to, eat dinner with, talk with, and have sex with. Correct me if I'm wrong."

John smiled and said, "That sounds good to me."

Hank frowned, "It does, does it? That's what I thought. You don't want a wife. You want a roommate you can screw when you're in the mood. Better yet, a dog. A dog is always happy to see you regardless of when you get back from the office, eat with you, and sleep with you. He or she will sit or lie next to you quietly while you work. Give him an affectionate pat here, a scratch on the ear or belly there, a walk twice a day to do his business, and he's happy. A wife isn't like that, no matter what she tells you she'll be happy with. Marriage is always serious and it's sometimes plain hard work."

"But you and Grandmom don't have to work at it."

"Don't you believe it for a second. There are still times after more than forty years when I have to have a little of what used to be known as pillow talk, and I know she thinks I need correction or connection during any given week, too." Hard as it was for him to accept and believe, his little Johnny Dryden was forty something, Hank couldn't remember precisely, although he could have if he tried.

He had a hard enough time believing sixty-two years had passed since VE Day. "Hell," he thought, "there's no one these days who has the slightest idea what VE Day means, much less VJ Day. All they know is the World Trade Towers and the miniature Vietnam in Iraq. Another war of choice."

Hank would gripe to John, who avoided the whole subject whenever he could. Hank couldn't fathom the American people's supine acceptance of the immoral and supremely wasteful war. Not only were there no demonstrations on college campuses against it, but except for Cindy Sheehan no one seemed to give a damn. Hank cared, but he was too old to drive to Crawford, Texas and join Cindy, so he donated money to Antiwar.com, the Randolph Bourne Institute, Code Pink, Doctors Without Borders, and read the news every morning on the Antiwar.com website.

Hank's heart may have been that of a fifty-year-old, however his prostate was every bit of eighty, and so were his kidneys. He had to wait on his urination, and despite his drinking more cranberry juice without vodka than he thought any man should have to imbibe, he had kidney stones, which caused him such excruciating agony that while in the middle of an attack, he questioned whether life was really worth living under such conditions.

Hank detested all the deterioration that came with old age, the papery skin, the sagging flesh on his upper arms, the wrinkles, bifocals, liver spots, thinning hair on one's head where it was wanted, and the luxuriant growth of hair where it wasn't, like in his ears. Still and all, as he waited for John on this pleasantly warm June day, he was relatively pain free and that was a good thing. There was no onshore flow of night and morning low clouds, called "June Gloom" by Southern California meteorologists from Ventura to San Diego. He'd already walked three miles on the beach shortly after sunrise. The Pacific swell was gentle this morning, two to three feet, and an ebb tide made the waves lap rather than crash onto the sand.

Hank always walked in the band of wet sand closest to the salt foam as it disappeared only inches from his blue-veined feet. The swell was generally predictable and tractable. Occasionally there'd be a rogue wave in one of the sets that would fool him and soak his legs with frigid water, which was fine in summer when he wore his khaki shorts. A rogue wave was a bother in winter when he was wearing rolled-up corduroys. Hank was disgusted with his thin legs, their prominent blue veins, and the total absence of the luxuriant dark hair that used to cover them. In high school, those bare legs were covered right down to the sides of his ankles with thin, wiry brown hair. Hank began noticing the hair vanishing as he entered his forties, and now his legs from his knees to his feet were as hairless and smooth as an egg. Strangely, the hair on his forearms was still abundant. This reminded him of T. S. Elliot's poem, "The Love Song of J. Alfred Prufrock", in which Prufrock is growing old and notices his arms and legs are thin.

He was just finishing an article about another suicide bombing near the so-called Green Zone when he heard the distinctive sound of a high performance V-8 engine pushing exhaust through a set of expensive finely-tuned headers, and a custom dual exhaust.

John always tapped the accelerator slightly, sending the tachometer needle to three thousand before shutting off the engine. He told Hank he did this to prime the three big-bore Holly carburetors that fed the high-octane gasoline into the high-compression cylinder heads. If John didn't open up the GTO, the old car actually got fairly good mileage on the freeway. Around town in stop and go traffic, the mileage was abysmal, ten or twelve miles to the gallon, sometimes less.

John lived in a modest home in Westchester, close to the LA Airport. The jet noise had a significant impact on the seller's asking price and made it eminently affordable. John bought it shortly after his graduation from Loyola Law School with Hank co-signing the note. John had paid it off in fifteen years and now owned it free and clear. On long trips he usually drove his older Toyota Camry, however once a month, or sometimes every two months, when the weather was fine, he would drive the Pontiac down to Del Mar. Though he was anything but flamboyant by nature, John liked to see the smiles the sight of the old car brought to younger people and older ones as well, as if it made them happy to see such a vehicle in something other than a museum. His classic car insurance policy cost him about a quarter of what he paid for the Camry and the GTO was worth about eight times as much. The State of

California gave him a substantial discount on his registration fees and classic car license plates despite the fact the vehicle polluted the air ten or twenty times as much as cars with emission controls and catalytic converter mufflers. This made John feel guilty; however when he saw the flashes of joy on people's faces as he passed by and the thumbs up they would invariably give him, he thought it was worth the few extra pounds of carbon monoxide and ozone.

John was dressed in his usual weekend clothes, black denim Levis, a powder blue, short-sleeve Lacoste shirt, and an old, well worn, extremely comfortable pair of Gucci loafers, which he planned on replacing on his next trip to Rodeo Drive in Beverly Hills. He was twenty minutes late thanks to a Cal-Trans sweeper truck running down the left lane of the 405 from the intersection of the 22 Freeway East almost to the Fairview exit in Costa Mesa. The beach traffic on Route 1 was heavy, as it usually was on a summer Saturday morning. As he parked in the driveway, John thought he'd better tell Hank that he'd overslept. Otherwise Hank would go off into a tirade about the evils of Cal-Trans, which wasn't good for the old man's blood pressure.

The screen door was closed but unlocked, and the front door was wide open. Even with its incredible increase in population, Del Mar remained relatively immune to violent crime, other than the usual domestic assaults between husbands and wives, girlfriends and boyfriends. John walked through the living room with its pine framed oil paintings of the Pacific painted by John's grandmother and the large, dark walnut framed portrait of his father standing on the beach in Del Mar, painted from life, facing away from the waves toward the artist. Valerie had painted this for Hank and Emily two months after the wedding, while they were living in an apartment near Oceanside. For a strictly amateur effort, it was surprisingly good. Valerie had captured Luke's nobility of spirit in the line of his jaw and the look in his eyes. In fact, John's mother had succeeded well enough that it was this particular image that came to John's mind whenever he thought of Luke. John couldn't really say he didn't know Luke, because Hank, and even Valerie before she married Eddie, spoke of him often, not only in passing anecdotes, but also with rich detail. Emily rarely ever mentioned her son. For her, bereavement never ended. It continued on in some level deep within her and inaccessible, even to Hank, until the day she died twenty years later.

John walked through to the separate dining room, which Hank used as a combination dining room and office. Between the rustic, thick, pine-topped dining table and four chairs, and the green, leather-topped mahogany partner's desk, which Hank purchased at a yard sale from an old retiring attorney, there was little room for someone to stand. The attorney shed real tears as he parted with the desk for he was moving from Del Mar into an assisted living situation due to his wife's Alzheimer's, and his own crippling arthritis. Hank looked up from his Dell and the Antiwar.com homepage.

"I was beginning to think you'd forgotten me," Hank said, very much tongue in cheek, since they both knew he'd come to Del Mar on Saturday mornings nearly fifty times a year without fail for more than ten years. Not that John ever thought of it as onerous or obligatory. Hank might have worked for nearly forty-five years in a comparatively dull job, however he'd risen to the vice presidential level and he had excellent health benefits. His pension ensured a monthly income in the mid four figures, and with his shares of stock and his paid off home, Hank Dryden was a multi-millionaire though you'd never know it to look at him. He supported various liberal causes and was better informed about current events than John. Hank was a voracious reader of non-fiction and contemporary literature from Thomas Pyncheon to John Barth to John Irving, with the odd Stephen King novel thrown into the mix for the sheer enjoyment of King's imagination and his well-drawn, idiosyncratic worlds. Hank owned a large and diverse collection of films on DVD, and he and John would frequently watch one of them or alternatively a rental from Netflix on the large Sharp LCD screen that hung on the wall facing the plush, comfortable, dark green sofa that replaced the blue Danish Modern where Luke and Valerie had once made out.

## CHAPTER 6

# The Advocate

"SORRY," SAID JOHN. "I overslept."

"You work too hard. And I'm not just saying that; you've got bags under your eyes."

His eighty years hadn't had too much of an effect on Hank's vision. He needed bi-focals to read or use his computer, and his driver's license required him to wear corrective lenses. The dark circles under John's eyes were rather noticeable. "You're right," said John. "I have been working overtime. There are just so few lawyers who give a shit about justice. It's all about money."

"The people who care don't have law degrees and, as far as I'm concerned, the whole country, is overly concerned with money. That's what this whole damned Iraq War is all about. Halliburton moved its whole operation to Dubai, safely beyond the reach of Congressional oversight. Now they can use congressional subpoenas to wipe their butts and send them back. What'd they get away with? Twenty billion, fifty billion, maybe more than a hundred billion! Enough for Cheney to buy his way out of anything! That's assuming anyone has the balls to take him on, which no one has for the past seven years. The war's already cost nearly a trillion dollars, all told, and at least half of that has been siphoned off, diverted, stolen is the correct term. It's by far the largest theft in history and it's all made legal by invoking executive privilege or national security."

Hank's papery skinned face was flushed with anger. "No one cares," said Hank. "Half the country is trying to survive a step ahead of foreclosure or bankruptcy, while a Goldman Sachs broker whines he's only making seventy million a year and deserves more. I know you're fighting the good fight and I love you for it. It's only that I can see the toll it's taking on you, and I think you should slow down, take a vacation, live a little. The world won't go to hell in the next few weeks because John Dryden takes some time off."

John really was tired, and he wasn't about to allow himself the luxury of condemning a civil and criminal legal system, which had nothing whatsoever to do with justice. The system was heavily stacked in favor of whoever had the money to hire the best legal talent. The merits of any given case were an afterthought. All the ethical district or city attorneys usually succumbed to the freedom and remuneration of private practice. Other prosecutors sought political careers. Defendants, regardless of innocence or guilt, usually took a plea, because if they were convicted, the judge would slam them that much harder for daring to go to trial and in judges' minds trials threatened the entire criminal justice system. Trials were tough for several reasons. The government made it a policy to excuse any juror who might have any sympathy with a defendant. Unless the city attorney wore a t-shirt with the defendant's picture on it and the word guilty over the picture, the judge would allow hearsay, innuendo, and a host of other facts that had nothing to do with the case, as admissible, while at the same time refusing to allow the defense to admit anything favorable on the record. Lastly, and most importantly, in the minds of half the jurors, any defendant must be guilty of something by virtue of having been accused of a crime in the first place, because persons with criminal records aren't permitted to serve on juries. John had often argued the utter insanity of this.

"Who better to serve on a jury than someone who has paid his debt to society and is now leading a responsible, law-abiding life?" John had in fact been up late talking with a young Hispanic man who was accused in a drive-by shooting on Whittier Boulevard. No one was killed, and John was convinced that neither Julio, who was riding in the back of the jacked-up van, nor the driver, intended to shoot anyone. They were just drunk, high, out for a good time, and fired the Jennings .380 to make some noise and punctuate their general feeling of for once being on top of the world. The whole rosy picture of being out on a warm Southern California night on Whittier Boulevard changed abruptly when a unit of the Los Angeles Sheriff's Department anti-gang detail pulled the van over and within a few minutes had them all spread-eagled on the filthy concrete sidewalk. Julio was slightly roughed up and the deputy handcuffed him too tightly. Taking all things taken into consideration, aside from a few derogatory remarks about Hispanics and gangs in general, Julio's journey to County Jail wasn't all that bad.

John received Julio's case directly from the boy's mother, Adelina, who worked as an orderly at St. Francis, and not through the public defender's office. Adelina was a single working mother, as were all too many mothers in Southgate, and had walked across Tweedy to his office primarily because John had two signs in his window. One read: "John Dryden, Attorney at Law," and the other, "John Dryden, Abogado, Yo Hablo Espanol." Operating as the State of California invariably did, under the internationally outlawed and universally condemned practice of collective guilt and punishment, the law theoretically made Julio criminally liable for various charges for simply being a passive passenger in the van. The fact that the Jennings pistol had been stolen from Tucker Loan and Jewelry several years before was not helpful. Equally damaging were the marijuana and oxycontin the Whittier Police discovered between the red shag carpeting in the back over the wheel well. Between the stolen automatic and the drugs, if the assistant district attorney really wanted to be a prick about it he could turn it over to the feds and all four boys were looking at serious prison time for their joy ride gone bad. As it was, Frank Ogden, the assistant district attorney handling the case, really only wanted the shooter, who was more than likely going to be a guest of the federal government for a mandatory minimum of five years on the gun charge unless he had some convincing information to trade, such as his source for the oxycontin and whoever sold him the Jennings.

Adelina was worried sick. Julio was a pleasant boy, about 5'10", 140 pounds, with long dark, wavy black hair, warm brown eyes, and an attractive smile. He sported a couple of small tattoos, though so far he'd resisted joining a gang. He'd dropped out of high school in the eleventh grade to work for his uncle, who had a successful landscaping business consisting mainly of clearing manzanita, sage, and other brush from hillsides in Brentwood, Bel Air, and the Pacific Palisades. Andy Aguilar had begun with a 1975 Ford stake-bed truck, two friends, and a crew of illegals he'd pick up at Pico Boulevard and Sawtelle Avenue, near the Home Depot in West LA. The work was hard and they battled poison ivy, poison oak, scorpions, tarantulas, black widow spiders, rats, and rattlesnakes to clear brush so that the rich gringos' homes would comply with the LA Fire Department's brush clearance regulations.

The Los Angeles homeowner who neglected to properly clear his or her hillside anywhere in the Santa Monica Mountains was likely to have it done for him by the county at four times Andy's rate. Andy offered a reliable alternative to the county and expanded his services into large tree work then bought a well-used but serviceable Caterpillar D-3 bulldozer, a Kubota backhoe, and sat for and passed the exam for his state contractor's license. He no longer stopped for laborers at Pico and Sawtelle except in dire emergencies. Julio was working hard and trying to get his backhoe operator's license when one joyride in the wrong vehicle threatened to send him from a poor though decent apartment in Southgate to LA County Jail or even Chino Prison. John had called Frank to explain Julio's essential decency, and the stocky, ex-high school middle linebacker from Agoura wasn't entirely unsympathetic.

"I'm in a good mood because the driver's being cooperative. Five years in a federal prison is a most amazing tonic for the memory, better than any ginkgo biloba. Kids who no habla English suddenly become fluent. Anyway, this Julio seems like a nice kid who got in with the wrong crowd, the usual story. How about a third-degree misdemeanor for malicious mischief, one year summary probation, and a two thousand dollar fine?"

"Frank, this kid's from Southgate, not Beverly Hills. Two grand is a lot of money."

"Good," said Frank. "That'll make him think twice before getting in a van full of gang bangers. Call me Monday, and John."

"Yes Frank."

Frank wagged his index finger warningly. "Don't make me go to trial on this one. You know I got a soft heart until trial day. Once the trial starts I lose my sense of generosity. Julio will go down like rock lobster and you know it."

John sighed, "I'll try to sell it like it is. That's one expensive night on the town."

"It's cheap at twice the price. If that piece of shit Jennings had killed somebody, your boy would be looking at murder one. Or Angel might have decided to shoot him on principle because he's not a gang member. Tell him to consider this a wake-up call courtesy of his guardian angel, his loving God, and the District Attorney's office."

"I know," said John with a sigh. "You're right, and Frank."

"Yes?"

"Thanks. I mean that."

"Don't mention it."

John spent more than an hour at Adelina's apartment trying to make her accept the proffer.

"But my son didn't do anything wrong. We have to pay you then pay another two thousand dollars? It will take me ten months to put that much away if I'm lucky." By midnight, John was losing his patience, perspective and sense of humor. He had to get up by seven to go to Del Mar and as wound up as he was, he knew he wouldn't get to sleep until 2:30, and that meant a maximum of four and a half hours of rest. John had a prescription for Lunesta, however he disliked pills in general and only used them the night before a trial, when he'd lie wide awake as every possible scenario of defense and prosecution played itself out on the screen of his mind, robbing him of even the lightest sleep.

"Look Adelina," he said as Julio hung his head, "I don't make the rules. I just play by them." Adelina wasn't even forty, a head shorter than her son, with a good deal of Mayan Indian heritage that showed itself in her prominent cheekbones and very dark skin. She was a hard worker and did what she could to make a home for Julio and his three much younger sisters and brother. She was enraged that the County wanted to take so much of her money, at Julio for putting her in the position of having to pay, and John as well, for when all the veneer was stripped away, he was part of the gringo establishment, the people that looked down on Hispanics regardless of whether Antonio Villarigosa was mayor.

"They're doing this because Julio is a Chicano."

"No," said John, his exasperation beginning to break through as he raised his voice.

"They're doing this because Julio was riding in a van being driven by a boy firing a stolen gun up in the air. You know children have been killed by stray bullets, and marijuana and oxycontin were found in the van."

"Julio does not use this oxycontin. If he smokes some marijuana, so what? President Clinton smoked marijuana and President Bush snorted cocaine. Everyone is such a hypocrite."

"I agree with you, but Clinton and Bush aren't being charged here."

"If Julio goes to trial we can win. He's innocent."

"Possibly, but if he loses he goes to County, then to Chino, or worse. Look at your son, Adelina. He's what they call a pretty boy. He'll be forced to join a gang, maybe La e-Me to survive and even then he'll be assaulted."

"Not if you win."

"Mama," said Julio, "please. Listen to Mr. Dryden. I'll pay you back, I promise."

Adelina finally grudgingly agreed to pay the two thousand after John told her he'd have to charge her that much or more to prepare for trial. Since neither she nor Julio was indigent under the law, they didn't qualify for a public defender. John made it clear he wasn't going to take the case pro-bono because he knew Adelina had the money and there were far too many worthy people in desperate need of a lawyer who didn't.

## CHAPTER 7

# The Walther Pistol

"ENOUGH SHOP TALK," said John. "How are you doing?"

Hank was feeling pretty well apart from some sciatica and numbness in his left leg and some dull aching in his right knee, which some idiot orthopedist suggested he undergo surgery to replace. This had prompted Hank to laugh in his face as he walked past the astonished doctor and out of the office. He also had a slight pain in his kidneys, but it was nothing out of the ordinary.

"It's amazing," he told John after the encounter with the enthusiastic surgeon. "The minute they know you have full coverage private insurance, doctors want to repair or replace every part of you that isn't working perfectly. When I was seventy, my dentist wanted me to wear braces to correct my overbite. Now this moron of an orthopedist wants to replace my knee. The only way I'll go to the hospital is for an emergency."

John had a rather jaundiced view of hospitals as well, and he knew what Hank said about doctors and insurance was sad but true. Poor people especially the very young who would derive the greatest benefit from surgery often went without while the well to do had hundreds of thousands of unnecessary procedures. Even the *New England Journal of Medicine* published an exhaustive study demonstrating that a full fifty percent of all back surgeries in the United States were not medically warranted, and were either useless or harmful to the patient. If half of all plane flights resulted in a crash, no one would fly anywhere, yet 70,000 Americans a year flocked to the operating room for back surgery at the same odds. Not that John was under any illusion about the equally shameful nature of his chosen profession. Except as sarcasm, the very word justice had no place in the American legal system. The adversarial process was no more than a beauty contest to see whether the defense or the prosecution could tell the more convincing lies, or worse, which lawyer had more charisma. Evidence, facts, and the search for truth were all irrelevant to a finding of guilt or innocence in both civil and criminal cases.

Hank thought he was feeling as well as any eighty-year-old that morning and most likely one hell of a lot better than most of his peers. "When are you going to get married and give me a great-grandchild? I'm running out of time."

"Grandpa, you know most of my work is pro-bono."

"So, donate half your time and make money the other half. You saw Erin Brockovich."

"We saw it together."

"What was that lawyer's name?"

"Masry, Frank Masry."

"Yeah that's it, Masry. You could do what he did."

"A chance like that is like winning the lottery."

"People win the lottery every week. The thing is you have to play to win."

"You sound like you're working for the lottery. We've been through this before. I didn't go to law school to get rich."

"I know. You stand for truth, justice, and the American way just like Superman."

"And what's so very terrible about that?"

"Aside from the fact that it's never been more than a fantastic dream since July 4th, 1776, and it's still nothing more than a pleasant fantasy, it's fine. I just want a great-grandchild before I check out of this life's hotel."

"You gotta one-track mind this morning."

"So give me a lethal injection. It's almost noon. Are you ready for a beer?" John really didn't want one on an empty stomach. It would probably give him a mild buzz and make him sleepy. At the same time it was a tradition, an integral component of their Saturday ritual.

"Sure, I'd love one." Hank stood up and went to the kitchen. John walked to the computer and stared at the Antiwar.com homepage with its casualty count of Americans and Iraqis. The number of dead and maimed Iraqis was truly dizzying, however life in America continued as if nothing were happening. The latest news of multi-million dollar athletes or Hollywood starlets behaving badly was far more important to most Americans than the faraway conflict, and the news media couldn't get enough of little Paris Hilton and her brief stay in the Lynwood jail. Americans were no different than the Romans during the time of Caligula. As long as the Romans had bread and circuses, who cared about the legions in Germania or Briton? Americans were on a wholly different plane of depravity than their Roman ancestors. Thanks to the media and the Internet, the American circus was on 24/7, seven days a week, non-stop all year, and food was cheap. John heard the hiss of escaping carbonation as Hank popped the caps on two Bohemia beers, brewed in Monterrey, Mexico. The beer was amber in color, rich and hoppy. Undoubtedly some masterful German brewmeister must have emigrated there long ago. Hank refused to drink anything else other than cranberry juice and water.

John turned his attention away from the computer screen, thinking if he read the body count and the articles on the website every day he would either be too depressed to work, or too angry to continue living in America, and he wondered why Hank voluntarily subjected himself to it on a daily basis.

Hank returned with two, squat brown bottles, which were so cold John could see them sweating. They clinked their bottles together before they drank. John had to admit that the beer tasted good and substantial with a clean aftertaste. Hank kept swallowing until his bottle was nearly empty. There was something about breathing the salty air that blew off the waves, even when they were only two feet high that dried him out. Of all the beers Hank had tried, Bohemia most reminded him of the brews he'd drunk as a boy soldier in Munich, even more than imported Lowenbrau. Hank set his bottle down on a thin, square, cork coaster.

"I've got some plans for this afternoon. Either we can go and see the new Harry Potter movie, which I haven't seen, or we can go for a long walk on the beach and look at the girls."

John knew Hank was quite the fan of the J.K. Rowling series, and he'd waited to see the film until the loyal legions of young people had already seen it, so the theater wouldn't be too crowded. The girls on the beach were there every sunny Saturday, so John thought that the new Potter might be fun for a couple of hours. John had nothing against the books, though he'd only read the first one, The Sorcerer's Stone, but thanks to Hank he'd seen all the films.

"I wouldn't mind seeing the movie, then if it isn't too late we could go for a walk."

"Good," said Hank.

All of a sudden Hank got a rather serious look on his face, so much so that for a moment John was worried Hank was going to tell him he had some fatal disease and only had two months to live. John's heart raced and his bowels sank. One thing that always amazed and amused him were the men's rooms at the courthouse just before court opened. The thunderous farting, squizzling, and squirting emanating from lawyers' and clients' stress-deranged bowels was unbelievable. Hank's abrupt change of expression triggered a flight or fight response from John's autonomic nervous system.

John spoke in a tentative tone, "Grandpa, are you feeling all right?" Hank was in fact feeling pretty good, as the alcohol from the beer was having a mild anesthetic effect on his arthritis and various aches and pains.

For the past month Hank had been reading articles about art objects being repatriated to their countries of origin, with a very specific purpose in mind. He read the story of the Getty Museum being forced to return Italian antiquities and the Metropolitan Museum having to give back one of their greatest prizes, a Greek calyx krater, or wine-mixing bowl, painted with scenes from the Trojan War by Euphronius, perhaps the greatest of all ancient Greek painters and potters. The bowl was allegedly taken from an Etruscan tomb prior to its being purchased in the 1960's in good faith from an antiquities dealer for one million dollars. Now, forty years later, it was going back to Italy as a result of the UNESCO treaty. More unsettling to Hank were the stories of works of art, usually paintings owned by Jews before the war, that were confiscated by the Nazis and now being repatriated by their present owners, or even taken by the authorities without compensation. A number of works on public display at the Kunsthistoriches Museum in Vienna since the 1930's were taken off display and returned to the Rothschild family, who immediately sold them at Christie's auction house on King Street in London. The stratospheric prices of paintings like the Klimt purchased by the cosmetics heir, Ronald Lauder, for 135 million dollars were staggering.

"John," said Hank gravely, "I'm going to show you something, and tell you some things that might disturb you. Just so you know, I never meant any harm. But I see in the papers, that when it comes to certain things, how much time has passed doesn't make a whole lot of difference."

Having said that, Hank left the room and John was even more mystified. All sorts of the wildest imaginings came to his mind, from an ancient murder or some other long concealed, heinous crime, to a shocking revelation about Luke or Valerie. Not just Hank, but every living man, woman, and child, had unplumbed depths to them that remained a terra incognita to even their closest relations and confidantes. John was aware that Hank was considerably more complex than his rather banal position with the power company would have indicated. Whenever John had asked him why he didn't pursue a more intellectually stimulating career, Hank would always smile and say that the very concrete and circumscribed nature of his work allowed him a greatly increased freedom of thought and action, and, "Besides, I'm a mediocre artist. I missed out on rock and roll. Honestly, for a man without college degree I think I chose my profession wisely." While John was furiously racking his brain, Hank returned.

"Come with me into the dining room. Bring your beer."

On the dining room table was a very old, gold colored shoebox. The Scotch tape on the frayed corners had the yellowed look of brittle vulnerability that only comes from being stored in a cool dark place for years. The lid of the box was dark brown. John supposed it was the color of the leather shoes it once held. There was another object of flat cardboard about two feet by three feet taped together with more of the ancient tape that held the shoebox together. The shoebox lid wasn't fastened, and Hank lifted it off and took out a small, smooth, brown leather holster. John knew it had to be a pistol and he wondered why Hank had never shown it to him before, not that John was much interested in guns. Knowing Hank, it probably had a good story to go with it. Hank smiled as he opened the strap holding the flap closed, flipped up the flap with his right hand, and drew out a small automatic pistol. John had watched the first three James Bond movies with Hank, so he knew it was a Walther PPK though Hank's was like nothing Ian Fleming had ever seen. It shone in the sunlight like pure gold and the wrap-around grip was either white plastic or ivory.

Hank handed it to John butt first. The little pistol was heavy and it was deeply chiseled or engraved all over with perfectly rendered oak leaves, and there was a gold inlaid inscription in German. As he looked more closely, he decided the grips were ivory and not plastic because of the grain. Perfectly inlaid into the grip was an eagle of high carat gold, holding a swastika in its talons. The steel of the pistol was heavily gilded or gold plated. John tried to puzzle out the gold inlaid signature at the end of the inscription. John thought that the engraver was a remarkably talented artist, for the letters and the oak leaves were exquisitely detailed and well designed as if they were by the same hand and not an afterthought. John made out the first line, "Zu Gruppenfuhrer Dietrich." The second line was, "In herzlichen Kameradenschaft," and then a facsimile signature was inlaid.

"Is the signature who I think it is?"

Hank lifted his bushy white, old man's eyebrows. "Yes it is. He was one of history's greatest criminals and there's no argument about it. The Reichsfuhrer SS, Heinrich Himmler," John thought he should feel a revulsion at touching anything to do with an unequivocally evil man, the chief architect of the Final Solution. John had read somewhere at some time that Himmler was wearing an army private's uniform when he tried to sneak through Allied lines on May 23, 1945 in Luneburg. He was recognized and arrested. Himmler bit on a vial of cyanide concealed in a tooth and died in twelve minutes despite frantic efforts by British officers to keep him alive by administering emetics. One thing John was certain of, and that was someone would pay a lot of money to own it, for it was in its own way a work of art, though a Nazi one, and it had historical value as a relic of what many regarded as the single most vile chapter of the 20th century.

"The inscription reads, 'To General Dietrich, in heartfelt comradeship, H. Himmler," said Hank.

"For some unknown reason, Himmler rarely used his first name, and come to think of it, Hitler always signed his name, A. Hitler; must be a German thing. Anyway, as you know I enlisted when I was 17, and instead of being shipped to the Pacific, the army sent me to Europe just in time for the Battle of the Bulge. That part of France was as cold as hell and the weather was brutal. An iron gray sky, day after day, week after week, such a heavy cloud cover that the bombers had to turn back to their bases with full loads. The Germans still had their Panzer units, the 5th corps under Hasso von Manteuffel and the 6th under Sepp Dietrich. These were Waffen SS, the elite fighting units, well trained and equipped, and they beat the hell out of General Omar Bradley and Field Marshal Montgomery for almost three weeks until the weather cleared and the Allied air forces could bomb and strafe the Germans at will. Patton's army went north to relieve Bastogne, which we did the day after Christmas. By May, I was stationed in Munich, a seventeen-year-old sergeant looking for illegal weapons. My CO told me to search this three-story brownstone. Amazingly it wasn't bomb damaged like almost every building in the city. There were still big beech trees standing. I was carrying my Thompson and was about to get my wizard locksmith from the motor pool to let me in. After the Germans surrendered, we didn't just break down doors unless we were looking for fugitives. The next-door neighbor boy had a key. Seems the boy's mother looked after the place while the general was away, though once I got in the place was deserted. I mean there were no blankets, sheets, pillows, towels, no indication that anyone was living there. Even the closets were cleaned out. There was furniture, a lot of it quite fancy, but even if I'd wanted some of it as a souvenir, there was no way to ship it home. Unless you were an officer, any of what we all called souvenirs, which was anything that didn't have a living owner attached to it, had to fit in a GI duffle bag or footlocker. Officers could send home anything they liked and they did, from furniture to automobiles and motorcycles.

The only room in the house that I know the general used was the study, which had a number of fine, oak filing cabinets. I found the pistol, holster, and belt in a file drawer with some Nazi books. I was worried my CO, a captain, would take it from me when he saw it. I know he sent a footlocker full of old WWI Lugers home, long-barreled ones with wooden stocks, and a couple of MP-40 submachine guns. As a matter of fact, Captain Osborne did want the pistol the minute he saw it and offered me a nice Luger and fifty dollars. Something told me that it was valuable not that fifty dollars wasn't a hell of a lot of money in Munich during those days, especially to a German, but even to a GI it was a lot. Osborne was disappointed I didn't want to sell and he could have ordered me to give it up. Instead he was a real gentleman about it and even gave me a capture paper and stamped it, after he wrote down the serial number and description."

John set the Walther down gently on the table and took the folded, creased white sheet of paper with Sergeant Henry Dryden typed on it. It was an official authorization for him, "To retain a Walther pistol, caliber 7.65 millimeter, serial number 346,278." As far as John was concerned the pistol was legally Hank's, and he said as much.

"I know it's mine," snorted Hank. "I'd like you to sell it for me. You take half the money."

"I couldn't take your money, you know that."

"Fine," said Hank with a wicked grin. "Then I'll give your half to your mother."

"On second thought," said John, "I could use that money. Thanks Grandpa."

"Somehow, I thought you'd see things my way."

"So what was all the mystery about? You scared the hell out of me, like maybe you killed a civilian during the war, something like that."

"We killed more than a million German civilians during the war. I don't think I gave one so much as a black eye, no it's nothing like that."

Hank took a paring knife from the large maple block that held his set of Henkel's cutlery and ever so carefully cut the fragile old tape on three sides of the two ancient pieces of cardboard, and opened it like a huge folder revealing a piece of old linen canvas.

"Damn it," said Hank. "Wrong side," and he closed the folder, turned it upside down and opened it a second time. All the color drained out of John's face. He said in a shaky voice, "It's a copy, right?" He repeated himself, "Right?"

"I don't know," said Hank. "Your grandmother thought it was. I'm not so sure."

"Whoever did it was one hell of a painter. You've had it checked out, right?"

"No, I haven't. I'll tell you I was more nervous about taking this than I was when all the German army was trying to kill me at Bastogne. I nearly crapped my pants when I cut it off the stretcher. I never showed it to anyone but Emily. Luke knew about the pistol, but not this. I've had it in the back of the closet for more than 60 years. I might have stolen candy from the store when I was a kid, not might have I did, got caught, spanked good and hard, and never thought about stealing anything ever again. Dietrich's house was once full of paintings; even the ceiling moldings had hooks so you could have picture wires hanging down. The pictures had hung there so long you could see their silhouettes on the empty white walls where the paint wasn't faded, because the paintings had protected the paint from the light. Out of the hundreds of paintings, the place must have been a private museum, this was the only one left, except for that drawing of a bug, you know the one that's in my bathroom. That was in one of the file drawers. It's nothing much except it used to scare you when you were little."

John remembered the tiny drawing, etching, whatever it was, of an enormous beetle with overdeveloped, toothed mandibles, resembling the antlers of a deer. The mandibles were nearly as long as the insect, and looked terrifying to John when he was three.

John couldn't take his eyes off the canvas that lay on Hank's dining room table, face up on a piece of old, but clean cardboard. As they did to people all over the world, from Japan to Canada, the paintings of Vincent Van Gogh appealed to him more than those of any other artist. Though John had never read Irving Stone's novel, "Lust for Life", or seen the film with Kirk Douglas, John liked Van Gogh's sunflower paintings and the "Starry Night," with its fantastic explosions of zinc white paint, like nuclei in green flowers, pin wheeling across the blue black sky. As much as he loved these images, John thought it was in the series of selfportraits that Van Gogh really exhibited his almost unique ability to reproduce an eternal truth using brush, paint and canvas. Van Gogh somehow distilled his very life and essence into his portraits, in a way that the viewer felt he knew him intimately, and understood both Vincent's fearful weaknesses and semi-divine powers. To put it succinctly, Van Gogh put on canvas everything it means to be a human being, a sentient creature poised between hell and heaven, life and death.

Hank's painting was particularly brilliant and eloquent, better in John's admittedly layman's opinion than the smaller, riveting portrait he'd once seen in the Art Institute of Chicago. As he looked spellbound at the picture, John recalled something Van Gogh had written to his beloved brother Theo in 1888. "The sight of the stars always makes me dream. Just as we take the train to go to Rouen, we take death to go to a star." Hank handed John a little booklet entitled "Van Gogh, The Passionate Eye", published by Abrams. Hank thought his painting was most like the portrait painted in 1887 on page three, though he felt, and John agreed, that the painting on the table was even more powerful and fully realized. In the back of the book on page 156, there was a short chapter detailing the sale of a painting of sunflowers Vincent painted in 1889. The artist was fasting when he painted it, for he was living in Arles waiting for Theo to send him 50 francs. The painting, one of five, was not considered by experts to be a major work, rather a very good, but still second tier, Van Gogh. It sold at Christie's London at a March 1987 auction for 36,292,500 dollars, which was 228,150,000 French francs or more than four million times as much money as the artist needed to live on for the month during which he painted it.

"Do you have any idea how much this is worth if it's real?"

"I've done a little investigation on the web. I don't think there's been a Van Gogh selfportrait sold since before the Second World War. A portrait of Dr. Gachet sold for nearly 85 million, and a painting of Irises sold to an Australian, Alan Bond, for over fifty million, though he never paid for it and it's now in the Getty Museum up in Malibu. I went up there to look at it after they bought it. It's pretty enough, but I wouldn't take three of them for this one, all things being equal. A portrait speaks to me in a way that a picture of flowers can't. Then, that's just me."

"You've really never sent a picture of this off to an auction gallery?"

"No," said Hank. "When I returned stateside, I forgot all about it. Then Emily looked at it and said, 'Some art student with talent must have painted it.' See, I told her all about the house and her comment was, 'You're telling me that anyone in his right mind would have taken every other painting in the house that was full of them and left an authentic Van Gogh on the wall? It's simply not possible.' I couldn't see anything wrong with her thinking. It made sense to me. So I put it back on the shelf in my closet."

"Why didn't you have it framed and hang it up?"

"Emily really didn't care for it. She said she didn't like the way his eyes looked at her."

"So what made you show it to me today?"

"I thought it was time. See, I've been reading on the Internet about all these paintings that were forcibly taken from Jewish collectors in Europe before the war. Now the children and grandchildren are demanding they be returned, and considering the millions of dollars involved, it's hard to blame them. Of course it's interesting that during the 1950's before the Klimts and Schieles were really valuable, it didn't seem to be much of an issue. Now that there's big money in them, attorneys have taken an interest, and a lot of the heirs are selling almost the same day they get them back. As a lawyer, what do you think?"

"I don't know any more than you do. In fact, you know a lot more than I do about it."

Hank smiled, "The Internet is a wonderful thing. By far the best thing to come from the 20th century."

"I'm not sure I agree with you. I will say I recall reading somewhere that the SS was declared a criminal organization in 1946, so if this painting belonged to an SS general…" John was thinking as he was speaking, "Still, unless it was used in a crime, highly unlikely, or obtained by confiscation, quite possible, in which case as you know, it would belong to the family of the original owner. Otherwise, if it was Dietrich's, I think it would belong to his heirs. Usually in America, once stolen always stolen as long as chain of title can be proven. Germany might be different. I know that in Japan, any item purchased in good faith belongs to the purchaser. I'd say unless Dietrich took it from the previous owner by force or duress, it's legally his. The pistol is legally yours, the painting..." John's voice trailed off and Hank felt sick to his stomach. He had been afraid that the story of how he stole the painting might make his grandson think less of him. "I know one thing," said John. "If I were 17 years old, searching for guns in a bombed out city, and I went to the house of an SS general, having been shot at for weeks like you were, I would probably have taken the painting for safekeeping if for no other reason."

This didn't make Hank see his action in a better light. He hadn't taken it to keep it safe. He took it because he wanted it. Wanted it more than he'd wanted anything he'd ever seen, except for Mary Beth Hayes when he was 15. He'd never been able to satisfactorily explain even to himself just how the portrait had beckoned him, so he said no more.

John recovered enough of his equanimity to think about the Van Gogh. If it were real, and that was one enormous if because he found his grandmother's logic compelling, then the painting's re-emergence after 60 years spent in a closet in Del Mar would be nothing less than sensational, rating mention on CNN, Fox News, BBC World Service, giving Henry Dryden instant notoriety, which knowing Hank as he did, was one of the last things he wanted or needed at his age. Hank was relieved that he hadn't forfeited John's esteem, though he knew that his grandson's comment about taking it to preserve it was exactly what he would have done in Hank's place. John was like his father in that regard. He believed in the rules and tried to abide by them. Hank was surprised that John's profession hadn't made him cynical about the direction America was taking, which Hank saw as either oligarchy or plutocracy, not that there was much difference. How his grandson managed to do what he did every day and keep his illusions intact was a wonder.

"So what would you like me to do with your Van Gogh?" said John with a twinkle in his eye.

"First find out if it's genuine. Then find out if anyone's looking for it. If someone is, you're a lawyer. Make certain he's the rightful owner and give it to them. Keep me out of it whatever you do. I don't want to be hounded by the media. If there are no claimants, I want you to sell it privately and confidentially for as much money as someone is willing to pay for it."

John thought Hank was being eminently reasonable. He usually was except about the Iraq War and any mention of Vietnam. "I'll do just as you say. I'll present it as the property of an anonymous owner."

"That's good," said Hank. "I like the sound of that. You may as well take the pistol and the painting when you leave."

John shook his head. "I'll take the Walther, that's fine. The painting, well I'm not too sure I want to be riding around Southern California with 50 or 100 million dollars in the trunk of the GTO. Are you sure about not wanting a public sale? You could still remain anonymous."

"No. I've been reading about some sales of art on the net. No, I don't mean that. The sales aren't on the net. The articles on the sales are, just so we're clear. Anyway, some of the largest sales are done privately. Some of the really rich people don't want the notoriety of buying at public auction and they'll pay more so the public won't judge them. Paying a 100 or 150 million for a single painting, even if you're going to eventually donate it to a museum, is a little obscene. There are thousands of little children dying every day from drinking dirty water, diseases that can be prevented by an injection costing pennies, and starving to death for lack of a half kilogram of flour. That kind of money would fully fund Doctors Without Borders for 10 years and keep a million people from dying of HIV. I'm not a Harvard ethics professor, so I don't pretend to have the answer. You see what I mean about publicity? As far as safety, it's been safe in my closet for the past 60 years and it's just as safe in Southgate. No burglar would give it a second glance, and my house can burn as easily as your office, probably easier."

"I have a fire-proof filing cabinet in my office, an old one with real wide and deep drawers at the bottom. I think it was designed to hold blueprints as well as files."

"That sounds much better than my closet. I don't know about you, but I'm hungry. What do you say we eat lunch then catch the 2:20 Potter movie? It's been showing for weeks now, so the kids have already seen it. Shouldn't be too crowded."

"That sounds good to me. Let's put this stuff back in the closet. I'll feel better."

## CHAPTER 8

IT WAS SUNDAY when John called his secretary, Carol, on her cell phone. "Carol, I need to go to Beverly Hills tomorrow. Can you clear my schedule to say one o'clock?" Carol Ramey was a very attractive black woman in her early thirties. She stood six feet tall in spike heels and weighed a solid 135 pounds. She had a pretty face with dark skin, regular features, and a nice figure. She was unmarried. Before she came to work for John, Carol had lived in Atlanta and been a driving force at the Southern Center for Human Rights on 83 Poplar Street NW. She was a premier paralegal on death penalty cases until her mother developed cervical cancer and Carol moved back to Compton. She answered John's help wanted ad in the *LA Journal* and now, as John always said, "The firm isn't so much John Dryden, Attorney at Law as it is Dryden and Ramey, Attorneys at Law."

"I don't have you scheduled in court, unless you want to see the ADA about that Mexican's plea."

"You mean Hispanic, don't you?"

"No, I mean Mexican, and if his parents were from Honduras, I'd call him Honduran. You don't call Frenchmen Europeans, or Englishmen Europeans, so why call Mexicans Hispanics?"

"Because it's safe and politically correct like calling black people African-Americans; am I right or wrong?"

"I see your point. Anyway, go see how the rich two percent live. Those stores on Rodeo sell dresses that cost more than my mother's house. I hear everything Tiffany sells is made in China. They put ten cents worth of silver in a pretty blue box and sell it for two hundred dollars. Rodeo Drive doesn't cater to glamour as much as good old-fashioned greed and narcissism."

"Thank you, Angela Davis."

"Don't disrespect Angela."

"I'm not. It's just between you and my grandfather it's like I'm living in the sixties with the Students for a Democratic Society on one side and the Black Panthers on the other. I'll try to be back by one. You can always reach me on my cell.

Carol only called John on his cell for a really dire emergency, a question of importance, or when he'd forgotten a file, which rarely happened. On Monday morning at eight, he left the house and drove to his office on Tweedy. He parked in one of the two concrete paved spaces behind the building, and inserted his key in the brass deadbolt. Once inside, John punched the code in the lighted keypad to disarm his monitored alarm system. The code was 1968, the year he was born so he wouldn't forget it. He only had the system courtesy of the previous occupant, an insurance broker who sold car and other insurance on the installment plan at usurious interest rates, and took cash down payments, which put him into profit on every policy immediately. He'd been so successful he retired to Palm Springs. John continued to pay the monthly contract for the alarm, and it was peace of mind for Carol when she was working late, especially in December when it was dark at 5:00. It was comforting to know that a touch on one of the two panic buttons would go to the central station, which would notify Southgate Police.

The Venetian blinds on the windows that faced Tweedy were closed and between them and the large sterile banana tree that grew in the sandy soil next to the sidewalk that led off Tweedy to the front door, the office was rather dark. John found it interesting that all the fruit-bearing trees in Los Angeles were sterile. The palm trees bore no dates or coconuts and with the exception of a small grove he'd passed on the east side of Highway One north of Carpinteria, he'd never seen a single banana hanging from a tree. The only thing the palms produced were dangerous fronds that fell on passersby. Those fronds were hazardous, as were the rats that nested in the tops. His banana tree, a dusty survivor with withered greenish leaves, might have housed a rodent or two and was sterile as a stone.

The darkened office was pleasantly cool and smelled ever so faintly of leather and Carol's perfume. John couldn't recall the name of the fragrance though it was familiar. It was also subtle and he liked it all the more for being so. John walked to the blueprint cabinet, which was really what it was. He mistakenly referred to it as a filing cabinet. It had a combination lock like a safe and John used it for sensitive cases. He spun the dial to eighty-five, left twice to thirty-five, and right once to fifty, and pulled down the lever releasing the shooting bolt which unlocked the drawers. He opened the bottom drawer, which was thirty-six inches wide and as deep. Even in the dim light, Vincent's eyes were luminous and penetrating. He shot the drawer closed and opened the one above it and took out the Walther in it's holster, the capture paper, and the leather belt with its gilded aluminum buckle, and packed everything in a dark burgundy-colored, finely-stitched, top-grain cowhide briefcase made in England with solid brass fittings that Carol had bought for him two Christmases ago. It had a combination lock set to 196.

John drove his red Camry west on Tweedy until he reached Long Beach Boulevard, and made a left on Long Beach to catch the 105 Century Freeway West to the 405 San Diego Freeway North. Beverly Hills was one of those places in Los Angeles that was decidedly not freeway close. One could take the 10 Santa Monica Freeway to Robertson and go north through an endless series of mind-numbingly long stop lights until you reached Wilshire Boulevard and made a left, or continue through bumper to bumper traffic to National and try to take Motor Avenue without getting lost. Once north of Motor one passed through Cheviot Hills, the less glamorous southern stepsister of Beverly Hills, with its high and dangerous speed bumps ready to rip out the undercarriage of unsuspecting Porsches or Ferraris only to dead end at Pico and the Twentieth Century Fox Studio.

John put his radio on 89.9 KCRW and NPR's Morning Edition. The meter from the 105 to the 405 North was still on, letting three cars go at one time. There were the usual people who couldn't count to three and went after the fourth car, and the timid ones who were motionless until prompted by an angry honk. Most of the drivers, John included, were solitary. All the meters giving precedence to multi-occupant vehicles and even special HOV lanes, had done little to promote carpooling. As soon as John reached Century Boulevard, the main entrance to the LA airport, LAX, John could see a sea of brake lights stretching north, as far as Manchester and beyond, across four lanes of traffic. There was always a backup north and south on the 405 through Culver City. John debated whether to get off at Sepulveda and take it north past Fox Hills. Supelveda paralleled the 405 all the way from the airport through the Santa Monica Mountains and out into the sprawling San Fernando Valley past Roscoe Boulevard. The problem was that Sepulveda had traffic signal after traffic signal, sometimes five or six in less than a mile. So unless there was a Sig Alert, an unplanned lane closure lasting more than 15 minutes. Even gridlocked as it was, the 405 was faster than Sepulveda and the freeway was one hell of a lot safer. Los Angeles drivers were justly famed for sailing through an intersection, either straight through or turning, not just in the moments after a light turned red, but sometimes many seconds later. In Los Angeles, an amber light meant speed up to avoid the red. John made it a habit not only to look before entering an intersection, he would wait a full five seconds before thinking about venturing through.

John stayed on the 405 until he took the Santa Monica Boulevard exit and made a right going east through Century City until he came to Rodeo Drive, then turned right once more. He drove south past little Santa Monica and started looking for a parking meter. The hour meters were a dollar an hour and they recently began taking credit cards as well as quarters. There were green and white signs offering two hours of free parking in underground lots as well as above ground lots on little Santa Monica, where Collis Huntington's red car trolley lines used to run before the oil barons decided they were too economical and did nothing to promote oil consumption.

John rarely came to Beverly Hills and when he did, he liked to park at a meter. As he passed by Gucci, he thought about buying a new pair of loafers, and probably would if the errand for Hank didn't take too long. Rodeo Drive had two lanes north and two lanes south, unlike many of the streets in Beverly Hills, which were one way. There was a space on the other side of the street next to Van Clef and Arpels, which if Carol were to be believed were one of the only big name jewelers that actually made and designed their own pieces and didn't outsource manufacture to China or some third world country. Not that he gave a damn and it wasn't as if he would ever consider buying anything from them. It was just one of those things that stuck in his mind at random like the AFLAC duck or the even more obnoxious GEICO lizard.

He drove down to Wilshire and made a right, then made another right on the diagonal street that began at Wilshire to put him back on Rodeo going north. John was hoping that the parking space would still be there and as he made his left onto Rodeo, a gleaming White Cadillac Escalade was trying to pull in nose first. A silver Mercedes 500 SLK was waiting patiently behind for the woman in the SUV to give it up as a bad job. John passed them both and was rewarded by a fine vacant meter north of Brighton near the Armani emporium. John did not covet an Armani suit, though he did admire them. If he ever did happen to have an extra few thousand dollars, he thought he might order a dark blue suit, because they were more than just stylish, they wore like iron. One of his friends from Loyola had gone into corporate work with Pillsbury, Madison, and Sutro, and done very well for himself. John had lunch with him about two years ago in Century City, and admired the man's suit.

"There's nothing like an Armani," he said. "They use the very finest cloth and they never go out of style because they're classics. Sure they're expensive, but they don't wear like ordinary suits. I've had this one for three years. Their tailors really care and treat you like a celebrity. Pete Sampros was there for a fitting when I bought this one."

John parked his red Camry between a black Mercedes 600 sedan and a brand new, silver Porsche Boxster with the white, temporary registration paper still inside the windshield. He fed four state quarters into the meter, verified it had sixty minutes and opened the trunk of the Camry, which he hadn't washed in two weeks. The car looked distinctly out of place between the freshly detailed vehicles that lined both sides of the street. Carrying his briefcase, he walked the several hundred feet to the glass door of Park Avenue Galleries. Park Avenue, John learned from the web, was an old established auction firm, founded in San Francisco in the 1860's, and had been recently acquired by an even more ancient and prestigious London firm. Though hardly a threat to the pre-eminence of Christie's or Sotheby's Park Avenue, it was firmly in third place, having only recently sold an iconic painting by Jackson Pollock for more than one hundred million dollars in what is known in the trade as a private treaty sale. John thought Park Avenue might be more approachable as well. The last time he'd gone into Christie's, he'd been attracted by a beautiful color placard advertising a rare book sale, featuring a first edition of The Whale, otherwise known as Moby Dick, dedicated by the author to Nathaniel Hawthorne, Melville's particular friend. This book interested John and he'd walked in to buy a sale catalog. The receptionist who looked like a Vogue model dressed by Nieman Marcus surveyed him with suspicion, as if he should have used the tradesman's entrance in the back. He asked how much the catalog cost and her thin elegant face, she couldn't have been much older than twenty-one, expressed a scarcely veiled contempt. John wasn't used to being treated with insolence and though the girl hadn't said a single word to him, he felt as if he'd been slapped in the face. Then he heard the telephone trill its electronic ring, which enabled her to ignore him completely for the next two minutes.

The girl rang off and got up to look through a shelf of catalogs.

"I'm afraid all I have is a file copy. You can look at it if you want to. You can order a copy on line from Christies.com."

This last sentence was said with unmistakable scorn, as if to say, "I know you're not a client, nor will you ever be one. Who are you trying to fool by pretending interest in books you can't afford?"

John hadn't been so utterly humiliated in quite some time. The girls they hired to work in Beverly Hills shops seemed to know instinctively who was and who wasn't a real player, just as they knew in the big Las Vegas casinos, although in Vegas they were too polite to let you know that they knew.

"Maybe," thought John. "They all have to take a special course in 'how to be a rude bitch,' and how to tell the players from the losers, sort of a John Robert Powers' School for receptionists and sales girls who have to separate the riff-raff from the billionaires."

John said as calmly and convincingly as he could, "I was interested in the triple decker English version of The Whale, presented to Hawthorne, but since you can't even sell me a catalog, I'll walk over to Bedford and see what Sotheby's has to offer."

The girl, who really was scintillatingly beautiful in an over-dressed, waifish sort of way, smiled sweetly, showing off her diamond ear studs, which were brilliant cut stones of at least a carat. They caught the light from the cut crystal chandelier hanging from the vaulted ceiling. She deftly plucked the catalog from the shelf with her long slender fingers, with medium length, freshly French polished nails, and handed it to John with her left hand. The ring on her finger, assuming it wasn't cubic zirconium, was a very impressive marquis cut diamond that would have paid for the new Boxster John had parked in front of and left some significant change as well.

He took the catalog and opened it as if he read auction catalogs every day. The Melville volume, or rather volumes, was the last lot in the sale and had a three-page write up and photographs of Melville and Hawthorne. The estimate was Refer to Department. John didn't know what this meant other than the experts didn't really know what it was worth. He closed the hard cover catalog with an audible snap, handed it back to the girl with a smile and a thank you very much, then left as quickly as dignity permitted. He would only go back to Christie's as a last resort if Park Avenue failed him.

For the present mission, he had an obviously expensive, high quality briefcase. John opened the inch-thick glass door and was greeted with a gust of cool, air-conditioned air, and a unique smell. One of John's favorite authors used the smell to characterize Daisy Buchanan in The Great Gatsby. F. Scott Fitzgerald called it "the smell of money". The girl behind the immense gilt, ormolu, bronze-mounted Louis XVI bureau plat was more Victoria's Secret than Vogue. She was carefully filing her already perfectly manicured nails. Her eyes were a startling color, almost violet, and John wondered whether they were contacts. Her full lips shone with expensive clear gloss. The face reminded him of Charlize Theron and her peach colored blouse cost more than John's dark blue suit, which he'd purchased at Nordstroms the previous summer.

She looked at him and put aside her emery board. Her look had none of the contempt he recalled all too well from his Christie's experience. He was slightly intimidated by the luxurious reception area and the girl's obvious beauty. If she noticed his discomfiture, she was used to it, and accepted it as homage to that most transient of human qualities, physical beauty. The Park Avenue girl was less artificial than most of the Rodeo Drive receptionists, hostesses, sales girls and waitress lovelies. Her feminine charms were so abundantly in evidence that she had no need for artifice in dress, manner, or speech. She would have looked arresting in a burlap sack with filthy hair.

Sondra was a graduate of the School of Art at the Art Institute of Chicago, and had come to Los Angeles after a brief stint working the reception desk of Park Avenue's Chicago office on Michigan Avenue. She was a passable sculptor, and in addition to looking for a wealthy intelligent man with a love of art, she wanted a prestigious Robertson Avenue gallery to give her a one-woman show. Her sculptures were very small abstracts cast in bronze.

She looked at John with an appraiser's eye. He was handsome enough, tall, and Sondra had no objection to his being, in her estimation, slightly less than twice her age. He was badly in need of a manicure that was one thing. His suit was obviously off the rack that was another consideration. The briefcase indicated he had a modicum of taste, as did his well-worn Gucci loafers. What fooled her was John's wristwatch, a vintage Rolex, which Hank bought at the PX in 1946, wore once, and put away until he gave it to John when he graduated from USC. Sondra had a fluty, melodious voice with a faint trace of midwestern twang, which was only noticeable if one either listened carefully or was a student of regional accents.

"May I help you?"

"Yes," said John, with what he hoped was a winning look. "I'd like to see someone in the gun department."

Sondra's tone and body language underwent a subtle alteration, and in a cooler voice she said, "I'm very sorry, but we don't have a gun department."

"You don't auction guns?"

"Oh, you mean the arms and armor department?"

"Yes," said John, nettled. "Guns, arms, weapons, implements of destruction, whatever."

Sondra wasn't at all offended by John's attempt at sarcasm, which had absolutely no effect on her. She not only didn't take it personally, she had to bite the inside of her lip to keep from laughing at him.

"Do you have an appointment?" she asked, intentionally sweetly, and batted her long, luxurious eyelashes at him in mock flirtation. This flustered John.

"No, I don't." Sondra continued to regard him and she knew he would soon either calm down or lose his temper. For her at this point, it was a scientific experiment to see if he would do one or the other.

John lifted his briefcase and said with some asperity, "Listen here, Miss. I'm an attorney. I have something I believe is of considerable value and I'm trying to give your gallery some business." He was angry and concerned that he might have just made a fool of himself. Part of him knew little of this had to do with the girl in front of him, and more to do with the Christie's girl who had so shamed him over the book catalog.

"Well," said Sondra, "we have heirloom discovery day every third Thursday of the month, excluding holidays, from 10:00 a.m. until 2:00 p.m. You can bring your treasure back then without an appointment."

John exploded, "Does the gallery pay you extra for the attitude, or do you put it on in the morning before you come to work like perfume?" Sondra gestured to the uniformed security guard with her left hand. The guard wasn't the typical Westec/Bel Air Patrol security person. He was six foot two, perhaps two hundred pounds, and was in fact an ex-Beverly Hills police detective now honorably retired from the force.

"May I help you?" said the man in a pleasant bass voice.

"No, I was just leaving. Could you possibly direct me to Christie's?" John had meant to say Sotheby's, however he was aggravated and agitated, and Christie's just slipped out of his mouth. He knew all too well exactly where Christie's had their offices.

"Christie's?" said the man. "They're at 360 North Camden, just south of Brighton on the east side of the street." Sondra was feeling a slight pang of remorse at rattling the man dressed in what she thought looked like an off-the-rack Nordstrom's suit. If he were telling the truth about being a lawyer, which was a distinct possibility then the man might be handling an estate.

"I'll give him the benefit of the doubt," she said to herself.

"Excuse me, sir," she said, this time with a genuine smile. "Could you wait just a minute?" The slight apology in her tone was enough for John to forgive her a hundred times over. Sondra pushed a button on her phone and John could hear her end of the conversation.

"Mr. Creswell? Do you have a moment? There's a gentleman at the desk, an attorney, who has something to show you. No, he doesn't have an appointment. He's on his way to Christie's."

The department head said to Sondra, "Is number two free?"

"Yes, Mr. Creswell. Shall I hold your calls?"

"Please."

Angus literally raced down the stairs. It had been a slow week for fresh property. He opened a highly varnished mahogany door at one side of the reception area and led John down a richly paneled hallway hung with framed auction posters featuring record setting pieces, including a fantastic gold-hilted sword worn by Marshall Ney at the battle of Austerlitz. The Englishman opened a door on the left and turned on the diffuse yet bright, overhead, incandescent lighting. There was a large rectangular table of inlaid walnut in the Chippendale style, with a red leather center and gilt stamped border. The walls were decorated with more auction pieces featuring art objects and paintings, including a Tang Dynasty green and brown glazed pottery horse that sold the previous June in Los Angeles for $780,000. John laid his briefcase on the table and pushed the button releasing the brass latch. The sound of it snapping up was unnaturally loud in the silent room. John handed the Walther in its holster to Angus, who opened the flap and carefully removed the pistol and laid the holster down next to the briefcase. The first thing Angus did was press the button on the side of the frame to eject the magazine.

"The Walther PP or PPK," said Angus, "has perhaps the best hammer block safety of any small automatic pistol. It's always best to put it on when checking to see if a pistol is loaded. To me, all guns are loaded until I actually satisfy myself they're not. One day one of the Doheny heirs came in here with a Parker A-l Special 28 gauge shotgun. The old lady carried it into the gallery concealed in an old long leather zipper case from Kerr's Sport Shop on Wilshire. Would you believe that the gun had two live shells in the chambers? We sold it for $225,000 plus the buyer's premium, without the shells of course."

All the while Angus was relating this anecdote, he was scrutinizing John's Walther with obvious interest. "Well, well. A presentation piece from Heinrich Himmler to Sepp Dietrich. Mint condition. Obviously the general never wore it. He was probably ashamed to carry a gift from the little mass-murderer."

"Dietrich himself was SS. They were all murderers."

"The SS had two divisions. The Allgemeine SS were the state police much like the Russian MVD, which became the KGB. Imagine the FBI being controlled by a psychotic, racist dictator. The purpose of the SS was to control every aspect of German society."

"And Gruppenfuhrer Dietrich?"

"He was actually an Oberstgruppenfuhrer in the Waffen SS, the weapon carrying SS, the commander of the Liebstandarte Adolf Hitler, the elite of the elite. General Dietrich's division of the SS was like the 82nd Airborne Division of the American Army combined with the Secret Service. Like Hasso Von Manteuffel, Rommel, and a few others, Dietrich was first and foremost a soldier."

"Yeah," said John sardonically, "he had a case of Waldheimer's disease. That's when you forget you're a Nazi."

Angus smiled at the joke. "That's really very good. Unlike Kurt Waldheim, Dietrich was convicted of war crimes, specifically the execution of 77 to 82 American prisoners of war at Malmedy, Belgium, though his knowledge of the massacre was never proven. He was sentenced to life. The sentence was reduced to 25 years, but he only served ten. Seven thousand former soldiers attended his funeral in 1966. We at Park Avenue are very sensitive to negative publicity, and we have a very clear policy about selling Nazi memorabilia, which is to say, we don't do it."

John's face must have reflected his disappointment. He'd considered the possibility that people might take offense at such a blatantly glorified relic of the Nazis. Heinrich Himmler was regarded in the West as the most evil man of the 20th century if not of all time. Stalin, who may have been responsible for even more deaths than Himmler, still had his supporters and apologists whereas Himmler had none.

Creswell continued, "That being said, your pistol is superbly factory engraved, gilded, with ivory grips, and has great historical significance, even if many people would prefer to forget the two names engraved on the slide. Personally, I've always taken Santayana's position that those who ignore the past are doomed to repeat it."

He looked once more at the Walther. "Mr. Dryden, this is a very valuable pistol."

"How valuable?"

"Let me think. Let's say $50,000 to $70,000, a $45,000 reserve, 6% commission and I'll waive all other charges, photography, insurance, no sale fees which we call BI's."

"That sounds good to me, but I'll have to clear it with my grandfather."

"Hank Dryden?"

"What?" said John astonished. "How'd you know that?"

"His name is on the capture paper."

Angus set the handgun down on the leather with great care and reached into his trouser pocket, taking out a gold card case. "Here's my card. The deadline for the November sale in London is two weeks from today. That gives me very little time to obtain the necessary export documents from the BATF. We still sell here in Los Angeles, however the laws in California are quite restrictive, and I think this piece has international appeal. The only drawback is that it can never be re-imported due to its size. On second thought, let me put it in the January sale here. That way you and your grandfather can come to the sale in person. I believe you will be very pleased with the results."

Creswell put the magazine back in the pistol, replaced the Walther in its holster, and handed it back to John, who put it back in the briefcase with the capture paper and belt. John snapped the hinges down and pressed the tongue of the locking bar into its strike plate, then spun all three dials of the combination lock. As the two men shook hands, John said, "Thank you very much. I'll be in touch."

John waved to Sondra as he was walking out and she waved back. Angus watched him leave, turned to Sondra and said crisply, "Sondra, if Mr. Dryden calls, put him through immediately. As a matter of fact, I want you to give him my cell phone number. He has a piece I want, so none of your airs and graces." Angus smiled thinly. He was well aware that Sondra Potts was sleeping with the president of Park Avenue Gallery Los Angeles, a pillar of local society named Norman Richardson. What Richardson lacked in knowledge of art, he more than made up in his extensive connections to old LA money, which translated into consignments and buyers. He was married with three young children, though that didn't slow him down where an especially nubile receptionist was concerned. Richardson knew a number of film producers and directors on a first name basis, and Sondra wouldn't be the first Park Avenue receptionist to get a small speaking role in a feature film or television program, not that Sondra wanted to be an actress for the rest of her life. However, a minor second career wouldn't be something she'd turn down. Men like David Geffen of SKG, as in Stephen Spielberg, Jeffrey Katzenberg, and David Geffen, were serious collectors and frequent visitors to the gallery, so the reception desk was as good as place to be noticed as a table in the hottest new LA restaurant. One girl who had worked the desk was on television every day with a continuing role in a soap opera. The desk was a fine career springboard for an ambitious young woman.

## CHAPTER 9

# Southgate

SHORTLY AFTER ONE o'clock, John walked through the back door of his office. The drive back took forty minutes, considerably less time than the morning drive to Beverly Hills. He'd even had enough time to eat two steak tacos from his favorite tacarilla on Long Beach Boulevard. John was a taco aficionado, and was very particular about them, much like other men were about cigars or caviar. Francisco's were the very finest as far as he was concerned. They were nothing like the hard, greasy things filled with tasteless ground beef that passed for tacos at fast food outlets like Taco Bell, which were only rendered palatable by watery cayenne pepper sauce, though they would do in the absence of anything better. The foundation of any taco is the taco shell, or wrapping, usually a corn tortilla, as distinguished from a burrito, which uses a flour tortilla. Francisco's tortillas were made fresh by his mother, as needed, from the best corn available, ground in a large stone metate. Carmen's tortillas were incredibly flavorful, thicker than usual, with a flawless texture. She also made the salsa by hand from onions, garlic, cilantro, tomatoes, and different varieties of chili peppers, depending on whether the diner desired mild or hot. The hot salsa brought tears to the eyes of most gringos, including John, and Francisco usually made John's with a mixture of half hot and half mild salsa. The meat they used was high quality skirt steak, marinated in a blend of spices, grilled over mesquite charcoal, chopped, mixed with the salsa, and wrapped in the tortilla. Like all tacos, they were best consumed immediately after they were made, before the juice from the salsa softened the tortilla. Although John sent Carol on a Francisco run three times a week, when he had the time, which wasn't often, he preferred to eat at the taco stand, even though that meant standing up. John's concept of a perfect lunch wax was two

Francisco tacos and a bottle of Crystal Geyser water. Carol didn't share John's enthusiasm for Mexican food, preferring to bring her own tuna salad with organic sprouts on Whole Foods organic wheat bread, which she kept in the small white Sears refrigerator in her private office.

As John stood finishing his second taco, listening to the cars rumble by on Long Beach Boulevard, he marveled, not for the first time, at the distance between Southgate and Tweedy Boulevard, and Beverly Hills and Rodeo Drive. Though the two cities were no more than 13 miles from each other as the crow flies, they might as well be in different countries.

No Hollywood studio ever made a feature film featuring Southgate, Downey, Lynwood, Bell, Maywood, or a hundred other places like them. People were born, lived, worked, and died in these working-class communities, unstoried, unsung, in obscurity. No one ever drove from Beverly Hills to Southgate to shop, or gawk at lowriders, or craned their necks to see who was the focus of attention in front of St. Francis Hospital. The men and women who lived in Southgate were never photographed for *People Magazine*, and never would be unless they suffered some personal tragedy so appalling it would appeal to the limitless appetite of the media for uniquely dreadful events, in which case Southgate might produce a Lorena Bobbitt, or a Susan Smith, or a child with a birth defect so bizarre as to be adjudged newsworthy.

John thought of John Denver as he looked at a filthy RTD bus roar down the boulevard and said to himself, "It's a long way from Rodeo to Tweedy."

Carol wasn't in her office. She was sitting at the reception desk, an old massive thing of unknown design made of wood from unidentifiable trees, stained muddy in a failed imitation of walnut. It was a far cry from Sondra's desk, but Carol's had its advantages. You could eat your lunch on it and not be concerned if your sweating bottle of vitamin water left rings. You could push back your swivel chair and put your feet up on the desk. It had capacious drawers, large enough for legal files.

There was a work of art in John's reception area as well, consisting of a mural depicting the San Gabriel Mountains painted on the plaster wall, by a not very talented artist, mostly in earth tones, sometime toward the end of the Great Depression when the building was new. The mural was incredibly dingy, dark from decades of exposure to smog and cigarettes from the years when tobacco companies touted their products as promoting healthy lungs. The Virginia Slims girl and the Marlboro Man were memories of a bygone era, or error. Now the message in the fine print was cigarettes cause cancer and other diseases. John figured the drop in people smoking had more to do with the price than the health warnings, dire as they were. Smoking was one more thing separating Southgate from Beverly Hills. Sometimes it seemed to John that the majority of people he saw in the streets of Southgate still smoked cigarettes, while in Beverly Hills, smoking anything but a fine cigar was distinctly frowned upon if not grounds for social ostracism.

Carol heard John come in, took another sip of her coffee, and swiveled her chair away from her computer monitor to face him. "So, you've returned from the playground of the rich and famous, and without a new pair of loafers I see. Well, you didn't miss much except for Mrs. Adams calling to say the sheriffs were coming to evict her and what are you going to do about it?"

John's somewhat expansive mood, which lingered after he ate Francisco's tacos, evaporated.

"That rat bastard slumlord! He should be paying her to live in that fire-trap. Call Judge Glass!"

"I already did. There won't be any eviction today."

"See what I mean? I'm not essential to this law firm. I think I'll go to Del Mar, move in with Hank, get a tan, meditate, find a girlfriend."

"John Dryden, I hate to say it, but you're full of shit. After a week you'd be bored out of your mind and start handing out your cards looking for some new windmill to tilt at."

"I wouldn't take me so much for granted. I might just surprise you some day."

"So surprise me. You haven't had a date since," Carol thought for a moment, "March, and if I recall correctly that one didn't go too well."

"She was an entertainment lawyer. I think my red Camry offended her."

"You should have taken the GTO. You know LA is a car town. You are what you drive."

"I don't need to impress anyone."

"That's bullshit and you know it."

"All right, you're right. I should have picked her up in the GTO."

Carol smiled, "I usually am right, you know. Especially where women are concerned."

John sighed, "I've got a phone call to make."

Carol swiveled away and returned to her monitor and her cup of coffee.

John's office was lined with the usual, obligatory, green, black, red, and gold volumes of the lawyers' edition of United States Supreme Court Reports.

They were strictly for decoration since they were available online through Lexus-Nexis in a far more convenient and accessible form. Still, they looked very lawyerly and legal to the average client. John's desk was the little brother of the one in his reception room, and on it was an 8 by 10 framed photograph of Luke Dryden, taken in Vietnam shortly before his death. Luke was photographed unarmed, dressed in combat fatigues with his left arm around a tall, African-American master sergeant festooned with fragmentation grenades hanging off him like ornaments on a Christmas tree, holding an M-60 machine gun as lightly as if it were an M-16. The two men looked as happy as if they'd just received a month's furlough. John knew there had to be one hell of a story behind the photo but Valerie said she didn't know anything beyond that he'd sent it to her and so like most things about Luke, it remained shrouded in mystery.

When Valerie remarried, she'd given John every picture and artifact belonging to Luke Dryden in her possession, which didn't amount to very much. She gave him a few letters written to her from Vietnam that she didn't consider overly personal and burnt the more personal ones in the gas grill after she was engaged to Eddie. Luke had written a few letters to Hank, who had Luke's high school yearbook and pictures of his graduation. John often wished Luke kept a journal or diary. Luke hadn't, so John had done what he could to construct an image of his father with stories and archival material, mostly from Hank.

John sat down in his swivel chair and pressed one of the speed dial buttons. "Grandpa," he said, "I only just got back from Beverly Hills. No I didn't have an appointment. The expert was very impressed; you were right. I thought he wanted to keep it for himself. Yes, fifty to seventy-five thousand. No they don't buy things they're an auction gallery. All right, I'll ask him. Talk to you later. Yes, I'll see you on Saturday. Bye, Grandpa."

As soon as John hung up, he heard the electronic chirr of the telephone and he heard Carol say, "Law office. Yes, I'll tell him." Over the intercom Carol said, "John, Valerie's on line one."

John did not particularly want to speak to his mother. He very rarely did. "Tell her I'm on an important call."

"She says it is important."

"Oh, for Christ's sake, all right."

He waited a few moments to compose himself then punched line one hard enough to hurt his index finger and accidentally put the phone on speaker. "Yes, Mom, what is it?" He tried to keep the annoyance he felt from being apparent in his tone of voice and failed as he usually did with her.

"I was speaking to Hank this morning, inquiring after his health. He said he'd given you some things. Take me off the goddamned speaker!"

John smiled grimly to himself. He knew his mother hated to be on speaker, and he couldn't help himself when he said, "I can't. You'll be disconnected."

"Fine, then call me back!" John didn't have his mother's number on speed dial. If they spoke more than once every two weeks, it meant something unusual was going on. John resented his stepfather for largely irrational reasons and John was the first to admit to himself, Hank, and Valerie that his antipathy toward Eddie had no basis in fact. The man was such a germophobe and something of a hypochondriac. He did worship the ground Valerie walked on, however Valerie had a dangerous tendency toward snobbishness and Eddie's slavish uxoriousness tended to foster all her worst qualities. John could call her back on her cell phone, which would totally piss her off and though it was amusing to contemplate, he picked up the receiver and punched the numbers of her home phone.

"Mom?"

"Why are you always so confrontational? Frankly, I'm surprised you bothered to call me back."

"Listen to yourself, Mom. Have you ever heard of this psychological mechanism known as projection?"

"You don't have to be such a smart-ass."

"If I am it's because I was raised that way. Besides, show me an attorney who isn't one."

"I won't dignify that comment with an answer." As John was about to reply with a clever remark, something to the effect that dignity wasn't one of the requirements for being a good attorney, he heard a man shouting at the top of his lungs in the reception room.

"Mom, I gotta' go, we've got some trouble here," and he hung up the phone and stood up so fast that the chair, which was on casters, slammed into the wall with such force that the adjustment knob for the height left a concave impression in the plaster a half inch deep. He raced the thirty feet to the reception area to find a large swarthy man of Middle Eastern descent, red in the face, and screaming at Carol.

"You fucking black bitch! You called Judge Glass knowing I'd been cited, and I'm trying my best to bring all my properties into compliance. America is a free country. So why can't I be left alone to manage my own business? Because of communists like you sticking their noses into my private business!"

John said, "You better watch your mouth mister!" John had never seen the man before, though he'd been the star of a Channel 2 News expose on Los Angeles' most notorious slumlords. Ahmed Nahabedian was wearing a cream-colored suit and carried two hundred, fifty pounds on his five-foot, nine-inch frame. He had the beginnings of a double chin under his goatee and was sweating through his suit at the armpits. His hands were short, stubby, and powerful with thick, black, wiry hairs growing luxuriantly on the second and third joints of his fingers. He wore a large diamond set in a heavy yellow-gold ring on the ring finger of his right hand, and a heavy gold watch on his left wrist. He was panting and John thought he could smell onions on the fetid air coming from between the man's rubbery, wet lips. Carol, who had been taken aback by the man's furious assault, was emboldened by John's appearance. She looked at the stranger in his inky, brown eyes.

"Yeah? Who you calling a bitch you fat, ugly, greasy, camel jockey?"

Ahmed was extremely agitated when he walked into John's office because Judge Glass threatened to have him arrested for contempt of the original injunction. Being called a camel jockey, when he was in fact an Armenian, sent him over the edge. Still his upbringing made it impossible for him to vent his rage on a woman and he didn't reply to her intolerable characterization. He'd been mistakenly called an Arab so many times he was hyper-sensitive to being confused with a nationality for which he felt very little if any love. Ahmed knew he had to vent his anger on someone, either that or succumb to an aneurysm. He punched John in the nose. There was a crunching sound, then a spray of bright red blood that spattered all over the lapels of Ahmed's white jacket. John saw stars and knew he was falling or floating backwards, as Carol's scream struck his ears like the whine of a jet engine. She tried to arrest John's fall without success and John sat down heavily, biting his tongue badly in the process. Ahmed's blood lust was now sated and he was calm for the first time since his attorney called him on his car phone two hours earlier with the news that they had a court date with Judge Glass to show cause why he wasn't in contempt for failing to install fire escapes and fire doors in the building occupied by Mrs. Adams. John sat stunned on his Home Depot carpet holding a bloody handkerchief to his nose.

"Carol," he said, sounding like he was under water, "could you bring me some ice in a towel?" John's nose was stopped up so thoroughly that no air was passing through it. John looked up at Ahmed, who not only didn't look chastened, he resembled a victorious boxer who'd just knocked down his opponent and won a championship belt.

"You broke my nose," said John, more in amazement than accusation.

"It serves you right," said Ahmed. "Liberal bastards like you have ruined the greatest country in the world." Carol returned with two cubes of ice in a paper towel. John held the ice next to his left nostril. John couldn't understand why his tongue hurt almost as much as his nose. Carol overheard Ahmed's comment to John as she was walking back from her office.

"If you don't like democracy, you can go back to sand land, you dune coon."

Ahmed thought he was so far ahead at this juncture that his blood pressure didn't rise so much as a single point as a result of Carol's second erroneous assessment of his ethnic origins. Still, he wasn't the sort of man who'd let another man, or woman for that matter, have the last word.

"I'll go back to Armenia when you go back to your jungle." The atmosphere in the room was tense once again. John tried to fold his legs under him before attempting to get to his feet. As he put his left hand next to his butt to push himself up, the front door opened and a large African-American gentleman, who resembled football great Jim Brown, both in face as well as build, walked into the office. He quickly assessed the scene and said in a higher voice than one would have expected, "Is there any trouble here?" Ahmed took one look at the newcomer and decided that discretion was the better part of valor, and that he would forgo the pleasure of making any more racial slurs.

"No," said John in his stopped-up nose, underwater voice. "Mr., I mean this gentleman, was just leaving. Right?" The last word was said with as much of an edge as John could give it using his froglike voice, which wasn't very edgy.

"No hard feelings," said Ahmed. "Sometimes I get excited. It's my nature. I apologize." Carol looked at Ahmed suspiciously, and he walked past the imposing black man and out the door, which he slammed hard behind him.

Carol asked John, "Do you want me to take you across the street? I think your friend Stu might be in the ER today."

"I'll be okay. Just give me a few minutes." James Johnson, the man who had walked in, was Carol's sometime boyfriend. He had in fact played football at Cal State Long Beach, until he blew out his right knee in his junior year.

James was a computer programmer for Highes Aircraft in El Segundo. He and Carol had met at a protest vigil at the First AME Church downtown to call attention to the shooting by LA police of an unarmed fifteen-year-old black youth in South Central. James and Carol went together in one of those on again, off again relationships, and John, never one to pry, thought his presence this afternoon might be a prelude to one of the on periods. James, who'd had his nose broken more than once during scrimmages, knelt down to get a closer look at John's. If it were broken, it wasn't badly smashed, and it wasn't knocked to one side.

"I don't think it needs to be set. Still, you might want to have someone look at it."

"My tongue hurts much worse than my nose. I think I bit through it when I fell. My tailbone hurts, too."

"You want me to break that fat sheeny's nose?"

"No," said John. "I see his position. And he's Armenian not Jewish."

"That's why you're such a good defense lawyer," said Carol. "You can always see the other guy's position." Then all three of them laughed, though John's tongue really bothered him. John went into the bathroom and saw how swollen his normally modest nose actually, was then returned and asked James what he should do about it.

"I remember being hit in the nose by a hardball that took a bad hop during a Little League game. My grandfather took me home and made me put an ice bag on it. The cold hurt more than the ball. My face was frozen. You're what?" said James, "Forty something and this is the first time you've ever been punched in the nose?" He laughed again. "I'd say you've led a charmed life and were long overdue. Go to your favorite market and buy a couple bags of frozen peas. The bags will conform to your face when you lie down."

John debated whether to walk across the street to the Saint Francis emergency room and decided he didn't want to wait two or three hours among people with serious medical issues.

"I think I'll just call it a day. Carol, if anything comes up, I'll be at home."

John owned a wooden frame home in Westchester, north of Manchester Boulevard and east of Sepulveda. In almost any other part of America it would have been considered truly modest, almost a shack, and though visitors to the neighborhood took note of the jet noise from nearby LAX, it wasn't unbearable. When John first looked at the house, he commented on the jets to the realtor, who told him that the noise was saving him more than one hundred thousand dollars off the price of the home. "People are like roaches," the dapper Re-Max agent told him. "They adapt to anything," as the roar of a Japan Airlines 747SP drowned out his words.

"In less than a month," he said, "you won't even lift your head when they land. You want the same house without LAX? I've got a listing in Culver City. It's 250 less square feet and it'll cost you another $150,000."

John considered the fact that the Westchester home was slightly more than 1,200 square feet, so the loss of 250 square feet for an extra $150,000 didn't sound too inviting. He thought he could learn to live with the jets for that much money. He bought the house and in less than a month, he didn't notice the jets, even on the extremely rare days when coastal fog forced them to take off to the East rather than their normal take-off pattern, which took them away from the city and out over the Pacific. He had adapted just like the realtor said he would. The traffic to and from Southgate proved more resistant to adaptation. Unless he left his office late in the evening, in which case he'd take the 105 Century Freeway, John usually took Manchester Boulevard east to Alameda north, an 11-mile trip, door to door. There were a great many traffic signals, and this was one reason he almost never drove the GTO to work. The other was the unwanted scrutiny the car attracted as he drove through the heart of Inglewood and South Central.

John parked the Camry next to the GTO. Whoever built the houses in his neighborhood in the 1960's must have had a reverence for automobiles as each one had a useable two-car garage, which opened into a miniature laundry room. John's home was furnished in a haphazard manner with pieces he'd bought on impulse from decidedly unfashionable no name stores on distinctly downscale Pico Boulevard in West Los Angeles. There was a Mexican seafood restaurant, La Serenata de Garibaldi, an upscale branch of the original down in the barrio near first and De Soto street, which had an excellent view of the apartment where Richard Ramirez, the infamous Nightstalker, spent his days resting from his murderous nocturnal activities.

The colors, styles, and fabrics of John's sofas and chairs were not uniform or even matched. John insisted on his furniture being comfortable, functional, and inexpensive. The fulfillment of the last criterion was often in direct opposition to the first two, even on Pico Boulevard. Still he persevered, haunting the showrooms on the north side of the street, both before and after eating his spicy camerones. John ranged as far east as Westwood Boulevard and as far west as Sepulveda.

He didn't bother with the frozen peas. The worst part about the hardball was Hank insisting he hold the ice bag to his face. So he had a swollen nose and looked like a raccoon? What difference would it make? Carol was the only woman in California that he knew cared about him, and she wouldn't like him any less if he didn't ice his nose. He'd listened to an annoying talk show on KPFK Pasadena, during which a Loyola law professor, no one John knew or ever wanted to know, was commenting on whether the use of torture was justifiable. The man used a combination of sophistry and hypotheticals that were evidently palatable to the majority of the callers, and the listeners ready acceptance of torture to obtain information vital to prevent terrorist attacks made John so furious he was still seething as he walked into his tiny office with a splendid view of one wall of his neighbor's yellow, stucco home. The red message light on his digital answering machine was flashing. More importantly, his pet goldfish, Thurgood Marshall, was impatiently waiting for him to arrive. The owner of the aquarium on Sepulveda in Culver City told John it was a male. It was time for Marshall's afternoon ration of specially formulated, incredibly foul smelling, food flakes. John thought they stank like an overflowing, ripe dumpster on a hot afternoon, though to Thurgood, they must have smelled better than a mesquite broiled steak. John unscrewed the blue plastic cap on the paper canister of fish food as the large bug-eyed goldfish swam to the surface of the small aquarium and broke the water splashing in his excitement.

"So, Justice Marshall, did you have a good day? I think I'm losing it. If something doesn't happen soon, I may just have a breakdown and go corporate. They don't have fistfights with irate slumlords in their offices. Here I am talking to a fish. I want a dog. That way there'll always be somebody happy to see me when I get home. Who am I kidding? I want a woman. No offense," he said to the fish, who didn't answer as he was too busy gulping the multi-colored flakes on the surface. The trick was to feed just enough and avoid overfeeding, which would quickly make the water not only unhealthy for the fish, but smell worse than an airplane lavatory at the termination of an overseas flight. He pressed the playback button on the answering machine.

"It's Carol. I didn't want to call you on the cell. Nothing urgent. Mrs. Adams called to say 'God bless you,' so that's some recompense for your broken nose. Your mother called and some woman named Sondra. Are you dating without sharing? This Sondra sounded hot, sexy. She said you'd know the number. That's it. Oh yes, James says if your nose still hurts in the morning see a doctor, and don't forget the peas. See you tomorrow." John went into his bedroom and took off his bloodstained clothes, walked into the bathroom and turned on the shower. John had removed the diverter in the showerhead, an action the Department of Water and Power would condemn as wasteful. However as a result, the pressure was strong, and he'd installed a 100-gallon hot water heater so he could spend 10 minutes in the white tile, stall shower if he wanted to, and he usually did after work. When he finished showering, he put on Levis, a lime-green Lacoste shirt, thin black socks, and his worn Gucci loafers. He walked back into his office and called his mother.

"Hello, Mom? Yeah, there was a little excitement. No, no, nothing violent. It sounded much worse than it was. It was just a little misunderstanding. I'll call you later in the week. Bye, Mom. "

A minute after John hung up, the telephone rang. It was Hank. "Well? Did you call Creswell? Did he make you an offer?"

"Grandpa, to tell you the truth, I was just too busy this afternoon. Why the sudden rush after sixty years?"

"I can think of $50,000 reasons. How about you?

Until his grandfather put it to him just now, the thought of having $25,000 in a lump sum that wasn't already earmarked for something hadn't been a concrete reality. With that much money he could really gentrify his property with a nice stucco wall, plant a few trees, put a hot tub in the back, and have thousands left over. It wouldn't be regular income, more of a long-term capital gain so Uncle Sam wouldn't take too much of a bite, though he'd let his accountant determine how best to declare the money.

"Grandpa, you're right. Actually, it was kind of a bad afternoon. I left early. I'll call him first thing in the morning, I promise. Carol said the gallery called the office. No, I won't let the deal get away. Trust me, Angus Creswell is hooked fast."

Hank knew John was an experienced negotiator and any attorney worth a damn is well versed in the art of give and take, and John was a good lawyer. Still, it is one thing to be a master of negotiation when you're dealing with other peoples' money, and another when it was your money. Hank knew himself well enough to realize he would give in too easily, whereas John would hold out for the last dollar. Hank said, "I'll call you at your office around ten; either that or you call me."

"That sounds like a plan, Grandpa."

*That's funny,* thought John to himself. *He didn't say anything about my voice sounding weird. Neither did Valerie.*

He shrugged. Ten minutes in a scalding shower had done wonders for his nasal passages, washing out dried, clotted, agglomerations of nose hair, boogers, and blood. The right nostril was open and he could breathe freely. He thought he might just lie down and take a short nap before thinking about dinner. He woke up at 9:00 p.m. He took two frozen Francisco tacos from the freezer, microwaved them for 70 seconds, ate them with keen enjoyment, drank a cold bottle of Fiji mineral water, took off his clothes, and collapsed into his king-size pine-framed bed, with its mattress of hydrostatic foam, and its three goose-down pillows.

## CHAPTER 10

# A Mishap

ANGUS CRESWELL WAS normally a sound sleeper. He and his wife were still not only friends, they were lovers as well, despite, or perhaps because, of their three young children. Angus was well-liked and highly respected in his field, a field buoyed by the recent sale of a sword belonging to Napoleon Bonaparte, by Nicholas Noel Boutet, the master artisan of the armory at Versailles for more than $6,000,000. The sale demonstrated to the art world, which had always treated arms and armor as sort of a bastard stepchild of metalwork, that fine arms were serious art objects like Paul de Lamerie and St. Germaine silver, or a bracket clock by Thomas Tompion. True, it was a very beautiful sword, but besides being owned by the French emperor, who owned a number of dress and battle swords, the sword wasn't one he carried at Austerlitz, Marengo, Waterloo, or his coronation. Napoleon's sword simply wasn't in the same league as the one presented to the Marquis de Lafayette by the Continental Congress, which brought $150,000 at Sotheby's New York in the 1970's. Angus lay awake thinking about the Dietrich Walther and that he knew the perfect client for it. Too bad it had to go to auction.

The next morning, Angus kissed his wife and children, then drove north on Robertson Boulevard to Wilshire. Traffic was light at 8:30 and he made the trip to the gallery in less than fifteen minutes, despite having to wait through two full sequences of the traffic signal to make his left turn onto Wilshire. The Park Avenue building was unusual for Beverly Hills in that it actually had a small parking area in the back opening out onto the poured concrete alley and the usual enormous Beverly Hills trashcans. One space was reserved for Mr. Richardson's large silver Mercedes with its PARKAV 1 vanity license plates.

Employees were strongly discouraged from parking in the company lot unless they were simply running in and out. Angus parked his white, 5 series BMW in the public lot on Canon.

Someone had recently consigned a cased James Purdey percussion, single-shot, small-bore rifle in exceptionally fine, original condition. Angus really should have sent it to the London saleroom, but it was a lovely piece and would look good in his next catalog and besides, his counterpart in London had just sold a factory engraved Colt model 1849 pocket revolver that would have brought 40% more in Los Angeles. In fact an American buyer had purchased the Colt. *To Hell with London*, he thought to himself.

The fine copper powder flask by Hawksley was full of old black powder. Angus thought he could either flush it down the toilet or burn it in the parking lot, though under no circumstances should he leave it in the flask in case, God forbid, some smoker choosing to break the ban on smoking would allow a hot ash to come in contact with the powder.

"It might be fun to burn it in the parking lot." Angus took a Kleenex and emptied the contents of the flask into it and carried the powder out to the lot. There were no cars parked as yet. Mr. Richardson would arrive fashionably late as usual, at ten or eleven, so Angus set the Kleenex down. There was virtually no wind, so he lit one corner of the white tissue with a Dupont butane lighter he used for his once daily contraband Partagas Havana cigar, and stepped back about five feet. He waited a few moments and it appeared to him that the flame had gone out. Angus walked up looked down and as he did, a crease in the paper flared, igniting the powder with a strong whoosh, and a miniature mushroom cloud shot into the air and hung about fifteen feet above the parking lot. Angus had closed his eyes as the powder ignited because he was startled. The heat singed off his eyebrows and left his face with an instant serious case of sunburn. The white cloud was more impressive than he anticipated. Feeling like a little boy who'd just broken a window playing cricket where he shouldn't have, Angus quickly scurried back into the building.

He walked to the men's room and was astonished at the reflection in the mirror. Ordinarily one doesn't take particular note of a man or woman's eyebrows. However, when you're used to seeing your face with them, without them you see a stranger in the glass. The fiery puff burnt off Angus' eyelashes as well. Fortunately, he'd jerked his head back in shock or he might have lost his hair, too. He washed his face with the pink liquid soap from the white plastic dispenser using cool water, because warm water stung. Angus wrinkled his brow several times and the skin was tight like it was in March when he'd taken the family to Coronado Island for the weekend. That Saturday morning it was cool and there were a few clouds, so he paid no attention to the sun and he'd gotten sunburned so badly that his face peeled despite repeated generous applications of aloe vera. This burn was slightly less severe. He could judge the degree of damage by the sensation of cold water on his skin. Angus dried his face with a paper towel. As he opened the door to the restroom, Angus saw Sondra looking into his office. She must have heard the door and she turned, then she saw him and screamed.

"Do I look that bad?" he said with amusement in his voice. Sondra never considered Angus to be a fashion plate or *Gentleman's Quarterly* material, though she gave his dress a solid 6 on a scale of 1 to 10. His face now put her in mind her of an egg. Clearly it was missing features; then she realized his eyebrows and eyelashes were gone. Sondra repressed a giggle. Without eyebrows, Angus' face seemed very round; something it actually wasn't at all.

"No you don't," she said sweetly. "For some reason you startled me. I guess I expected to see you in your office. If you'll step out into the parking lot, there's a fire truck in the alley. Something about a smoke cloud in our parking lot."

"Fire truck? I didn't hear a siren."

"I don't know about a siren. I do know there's a Beverly Hills fire truck outside."

"Thank you. I'll see what they want."

Angus tried to explain the whole fiasco to the fire captain, who was most unsympathetic. "I just wanted to render the powder harmless. I didn't want some careless smoker to hurt himself or anyone else."

The man looked at Angus' burnt face and it was all he could do to keep from laughing at the man out loud. The call had come in that there was a large cloud of white smoke in the back of the gallery. The call was from a woman jogging in the alley using her cell phone.

"You're lucky whoever saw you didn't call in a bomb threat. You'd be explaining yourself to the FBI, the BATF, not to mention the BHPD swat team. Next time you find some gunpowder you need to dispose of, do us all a favor and use the sink or the john. Or you can call the fire department for that matter."

"Believe me, captain," said Angus fervently, "you have my most solemn promise. I've learned my lesson." The fireman walked back to his command car, shaking his head and laughing to himself.

Angus hurried back into the office. He was closing the door as the telephone rang. Sondra was on the line. "Mr. Creswell?" she spoke as if it were the first time she'd seen him all day. "Mr. Richardson would like to see you in his office at your earliest convenience about the fire in the parking lot."

*Damn it,* thought Angus to himself. *I didn't see him come in and his car wasn't out back. His wife must have brought him. She usually does when she's feeling insecure.* He spoke to Sondra, "Can he wait?"

"I don't think he can. You know he doesn't like to be kept waiting."

*Shit,* thought Angus. Then he thought: *Why you little whore, you're enjoying this.*

"One second," said Sondra as she answered another line. She was off for a brief moment then she came back on. "It's Mr. Dryden, for you."

Angus stabbed at the button as if that decisive action would blot out the dismal prospect of a dressing down at the hands of Mr. Richardson. He also was venting his frustration at not being able to poke Sondra in one of her violet eyes. Angus answered in his most ingratiating tone of voice. "Mr. Dryden, what a pleasant surprise."

"I spoke with Hank," said John. For a moment Angus blanked on the name, then he remembered at the last moment before his silence became awkward. "Ah, yes, your grandfather. And?"

"He is interested in selling it."

"Excellent. I'll feature it on our back cover in full color at no charge. I'll give it the works as the saying goes."

"No. I'm afraid you didn't understand me. He wants to sell it now."

"Mr. Dryden, we are an auction company and purchasing pieces outright is against our policy. That being understood, if you insist I might be able to arrange a private treaty sale. You would still be required to pay the six-percent seller's commission."

"That's not an issue. I'll be glad to pay the commission. My grandfather is 80 years old. His only question is how much?"

"Please give me a minute. This is all very sudden."

John assumed Angus was no fool. He probably knew the ideal buyer and would be able to turn a personal profit from a private sale he couldn't get from having his company auction it.

Angus was in fact secretly delighted. In his experience, 99 times out of 100, sellers always had some price in mind. The art of the buyer or broker lay in making the seller tip his hand and naming the unknown price. Angus tried the direct approach, which was an invitation to John to name his own figure. In all likelihood it would be a high one, however with a truly unique and highly desirable piece like the Walther, the price was pretty much whatever one chose to ask within certain limits. Aside from Der Fuehrer's own Walther, which was in a bank vault somewhere in California, Angus couldn't think of a more desirable WWII automatic pistol than Dryden's PPK.

"What figure do you think would be acceptable to your grandfather?"

John considered this. The auction estimate Angus had given was 50 to 75 thousand dollars, and added to that was a 20% buyer's premium plus 8½ percent California sales tax, so call the total premium 30%. John scribbled some numbers on a legal pad. He wanted to do better than the high estimate, and he knew Creswell wanted the pistol badly; that much was clear.

"100,000 dollars," said John firmly.

"No," said Angus automatically. "That's too much. I believe the last time Hitler's own Walther was sold it brought $350,000." John said nothing. The ball was in Angus' court, and John was willing to take a chance on losing the sale, not that he thought there was much chance of that happening. John put the pressure and the onus on Creswell, as it was now incumbent for the Englishman to make the next move.

"If you need some time to think about it, or to talk to your clients, I can call you back next week."

Angus said to himself, "I should have known he was a typical weaselly lawyer." He had no intention of ending the conversation without a firm commitment from John to sell him the pistol.

"Please understand that whoever buys the piece still must pay the 20% buyer's premium. That's inviolate, not that it concerns you."

"All right," said John. "80,000 dollars net to me and the Walther is yours." This was more than Angus anticipated. He honestly thought John would come in at $60,000, maybe $65,000 at the most. Still, it was a wonderful gun. Best of all, it was completely fresh to the market with an impeccable provenance. The capture paper authorizing Sergeant Henry Dryden to retain the "following captured enemy war equipment" made the pedigree perfect. Angus had seen dozens of fake engraved WWII presentation pieces, even faked capture papers. There was absolutely no question about Dryden's Walther being 100% authentic.

"Eighty thousand dollars cash delivered to your office," said Angus crisply.

John was surprised. "You're going to bring that much cash to Southgate?"

"First of all, you don't really know me, so why would you take my personal check. Second, the client I have in mind pays cash. Where exactly is Southgate?"

"It's between Downey and Watts."

"Wonderful, that doesn't help me."

"You're coming this evening? That's fast," said John.

"As King Canute found out to his detriment, time and tide wait for no man. The client is local. I'll call you back within the hour if there are any difficulties."

John proceeded to give Angus directions from Rodeo Drive. "I'll see you at six then," said John. "On behalf of my grandfather, I can say I really appreciate this."

"See you at six," said Angus and he hung up whistling softly a Pink Floyd tune.

Richardson was certainly going to feed him a ration of shit about the morning mushroom cloud in the lot. He would rant and rave about a grown man pulling childish pranks, how he'd never heard of such immaturity, and then it would be over. His wife would meet him at Matsuhisa on La Cienaga and they would eat lunch, some of Chef Nobu's incredibly delicious yellowtail jalapeno, and this morning's mischance would be nothing more than a source of amusement to them. Once Marcia got over the initial shock of seeing his face without eyebrows, she would more than likely giggle about it for the rest of the day. He'd have a terrific story to tell his children who, like all young people, enjoyed few things more than hearing about big people, especially parents, doing very stupid things.

## CHAPTER 11

# A Revelation

ANGUS CRESWELL HAD several clients who were as idiosyncratic as they were wealthy, and they paid their accounts in cash. Park Avenue dutifully filled out the required IRS form 8300 and deposited the currency in their bank, and that was the end as far as the authorities were concerned. Angus was not averse to doing deals outside normal auction channels, as long as Park Avenue's legitimate interests were not compromised in any way. These same clients had paid Angus in cash, only he did not fill out IRS forms, nor did he deposit the money in his bank account. Instead, he put it away in a safety deposit box, and over the past six years it had accumulated, minus withdrawals for Marcia's presents, family vacations, and the occasional new suit. Thanks to Park Avenue's very liberal expense account, he rarely had to pay for dining in Beverly Hills' better restaurants.

At 6:17 p.m., Angus parked his BMW in front of John's office. He thought the neighborhood looked quite rough like one of the less desirable sections of Birmingham, or perhaps the East End in London. He pressed his BMW key to unlock the trunk and removed his Mark Cross attaché case, closed the boot, as he called it, and locked the car with the remote control key. Angus was less than impressed by the dirty sidewalk and the dusty green leaves of John's banana tree. Angus thought Southgate was a very long way from Beverly Hills.

Angus turned the cheap brass-plated Kwik-Set doorknob, though he did note the Medeco deadbolt above it. He was startled to find the door open, and he walked in. He looked around the shabby reception area and noticed that tawdry as it was, someone made an effort to keep it clean.

"Anyone here?" he called out in his English public school accent. "Angus Creswell for Mr. John Dryden." John came walking down the hall dressed in a camel hair sport coat. Angus looked at John's nose. "What happened to you?"

John stopped and stared at the Englishman's sunburned face. "I'll tell you mine if you tell me yours."

Angus laughed, "That 's a deal."

"Any trouble finding the place?"

"No, I left at 4:30. Traffic on the 405 was a nightmare as always. The 105 Freeway was even worse. It was a seven-mile-long parking lot. I don't understand how people do it day after day, night after night. More than 90 minutes to go over 20 miles, it's crazy. I'd get here faster on horseback."

"You're right. So much for progress. The traffic is one reason I rarely get to Beverly Hills."

"So tell me about your nose."

John related his encounter with the irate slumlord, Ahmed Nahabedian, after which Angus did his best to recreate the absurd events of his morning and they both laughed loud and long at their respective misadventures. John offered Angus a bottle of Crystal Geyser mineral water and brought two from Carol's refrigerator.

"Would you mind terribly locking the front door?"

"No," said John, "I always lock it after dark, but I was expecting you." As soon as John threw the deadbolt, Angus took out two thick packets of money, one from each inside pocket of his suit, and laid them on the reception desk. There were eight small bundles, each with its own bank wrapper around it.

"80,000 dollars, as agreed. You can count it if you wish."

"No," said John, "that won't be necessary. I'll get your pistol. John walked to his office, unlocked the filing cabinet, and transferred the pistol, holster, belt, and capture document to the old shoebox and returned to the reception area. Angus took the box, lifted the lid and took out the pistol.

"Mr. Dryden," he said.

"Call me John. Mr. Dryden was my father. He's passed away."

"I'm so sorry, mine too. Last year. Heart attack; totally unexpected."

"Mine died in Vietnam before I was even born." "I'm so sorry, John," he repeated, putting down the pistol and examining the capture paper. "Did your grandfather liberate any other enemy war equipment from the Dietrich home? Medals or daggers perhaps? His Knight's cross would be worth more than

$45,000. He was one of only 27 men to be awarded the Oak Leaves, Swords, and Diamonds to the Knight's Cross of the Iron Cross. The Diamonds would be worth as much or more than the pistol, but of course Park Avenue wouldn't sell them. The paper mentions two books as well as the pistol."

"I've never seen the books and as far as I know he hasn't got any daggers or medals. Sorry."

"Nothing at all? You're certain? Sometimes things that seem worthless are actually of great value."

John stroked his chin with his left hand. Angus appeared to be trustworthy, and more importantly, he'd done exactly what he'd agreed to do, which sadly was quite unusual. John decided to trust him and take the plunge. "You don't happen to know anything about paintings?"

Angus smiled, "I'm not saying I'm Bernard Berenson, Lord Duveen, Samuel Mawson or Nathan Wildenstein, but I am not wholly ignorant either. I can tell a Manet from a Monet and a Reubens from a Rembrandt, if that's what you're asking."

"If you'll excuse me for a minute I'll be right back."

He picked up the two packets of money, which were held together by rubber bands, and walked back down the hall. John put them away in the file drawer, took the cardboard folder and went to meet Angus out front. He placed the folder flat on the desk and opened the one flap. Angus took one look and very nearly passed out. John went to steady him. Angus' face went through a whole series of colors and emotions. Shock, amazement, awe, and sheer lust or greed, John couldn't differentiate. Angus' carefully cultivated English stoicism was utterly destroyed. When he was finally able to speak, he intoned reverently, "Holy Mother of God," then he sputtered, "how did…where did…ah." John motioned to the chair in the corner.

"Have a seat and I'll tell you the whole story." Angus walked to the chair as stunned as the wedding guest in Coleridge's Rime. 'He looked like one that hath been stunned and is of sense forlorn.' His knees were weak and his legs rubbery, so he sat gratefully in the soft chair.

"And that, Mr. C., is the whole story as I know it," said John as he finished. "So the big question is do you think it's a real Van Gogh?"

"John," said Angus with more fervor and passion than he'd suspected the reserved Englishman possessed. "As God is my witness, I don't *think* it's real. I know it's real. Van Gogh was the 19th century's foremost practitioner of the impasto technique. Impasto is paint applied to a canvas or panel that stands out from the surface to reproduce the broken textured highlights, like surfaces of objects struck by sunlight. Rembrandt, Franz Hals, and Diego Velasquez used impasto with consummate skill and minute intricacy to depict fine facial lines or wrinkles, the sparkle of armor, rich textiles, or jewelry. Vincent used impasto in a much more powerful, even crude way, building up and defining the forms in his paintings with thick daubs of paint. Jackson Pollock and de Kooning applied impasto to give emphasis to the qualities of the paint itself. Now, of course, the thick application of raw pigments to raw canvas is a staple technique of modern abstract painting. The impasto as it's used here is masterful, sheer genius, obviously the work of the master and not the inspired effort of even a skillful copyist or forger. You see the crackleure in the paint? Forgers use heat lamps or exposure to direct sunlight to crack modern paint in imitation of the age cracking over many years, but there are subtle differences."

He folded the cardboard over the painting and turned it over with great care on the other side to examine the canvas itself. "See?" he said. "The canvas is old French linen that has a patination, which can only be achieved by more than a century of natural exposure to air, ozone, cigarette and cigar smoke, household cleaners, and dust. It's beautiful, just beautiful. This painting has never been cleaned or relined. It is what we in the trade like to call 'fresh,' 'untouched', a 'virgin'. Your grandfather used considerable care when he cut it off its stretcher bar and he preserved almost all the original canvas. You can see how he freed it from around the nail holes. It is wonderful, just wonderful."

John thought Angus was repeating himself rather often. He didn't really know the Englishman well enough, or he would have understood that Angus was literally beside himself with excitement, and he tended to use the same adjectives more than once in the same sentence when he was agitated or less than sober.

He looked up from the painting, which he'd righted once more by turning the cardboard folder over.

"You wouldn't by any chance have anything stronger than mineral water. It's long past the five o'clock hour, and I could use a drink. Let me put it this way. If you'd come walking out of your office with Queen Elizabeth herself, I doubt if the shock would have been much greater."

John had a bottle of Remy Martin cognac one of his clients had given him for Christmas. He hadn't bothered to take it home, and being a gift package it came complete with two miniature brandy snifters. John left Angus staring stupified at the portrait and returned with the box of cognac.

"That's capital," said Angus. With a squeak of plastic foam, John opened the box and handed the inky-green, frosted green glass bottle to Angus.

"I'll go wash the glasses," said John.

"No need," said Angus, who deftly removed the black metal foil from around the cork and opened it with an audible pop. He took a glass from John, blew off a few fragments of white plastic foam, and poured a good two ounces into it. John declined the proffered bottle saying he wasn't fond of cognac, or brandy for that matter.

"Oh, well," said Angus with a smile. "Bottoms up," and he drained his snifter. As the fiery spirit burned its way down his esophagus and into his stomach, Angus began to relax. John had been waiting patiently.

"So what's it worth?" he asked. Angus refilled his glass, only this time he sipped appreciatively, cupping it in the palm of his hand, holding the stem in between his middle and ring fingers so the warmth of his hand would release the fragrant oils in the cognac.

"John, I could give you a figure, but it would make no sense. No Van Gogh of this importance has been sold in the last 50 years. The Sunflowers in 1987, the Irises, even Lola Kamarski's Portrait of Dr. Gachet, that sold for 82.5 million dollars are superb masterpieces, but in the end are not among the finest of Van Gogh's works. This is arguably the most beautiful and fully realized Van Gogh portrait in existence, the equal of anything in the Rijksmuseum Vincent Van Gogh. This painting is literally priceless. It might be the greatest single discovery in modern art since World War II. I am convinced it would set a new world record, surpassing even Klimt's unbelievable 1907 Portrait of Mrs. Adele Bloch-Bauer, which was also confiscated by the Nazis, returned to the heirs and sold at auction to Mr. Ronald Lauder of Estee Lauder cosmetics fame for 135 million dollars.

"While most of the world's citizens continue to languish in poverty if not actual privation, there is a greater concentration of wealth in the hands of a few than at any period in all human history. Two, even three, hundred million is less than a year's income to hundreds of these mega-wealthy, and there is no telling what they might pay for the privilege of owning the most valuable 19th century painting in private hands. There are simply no reasonable comparisons. In June of 1939, the Nazi government sent 126 paintings of what they considered 'Entarte Kunst,' 'degenerate art,' to auction in Lucerne, Switzerland in order to raise foreign exchange. Among the 126 works were an iconic Matisse, which was purchased by the American newspaper magnate, Joseph

Pulitzer Jr. that now hangs in the St. Louis Art Museum, and the famous lime-green ground Van Gogh selfportrait dedicated to Paul Gaugain, painted in 1882. Sold under essentially wartime conditions, the Van Gogh still sold for the equivalent of $40,000, which was one hell of a lot of money for a painting when one considers that until Gaugain's Le Garcon au Gilet Rouge sold in London for 220,000 pounds in 1958, the previous record price for any painting at auction was less than $100,000. In fact, in 1958 the combined sales of both Sotheby's and Christie's for the entire year were less than 25 million dollars."

"That's all well and good. My question is where do I go from here?"

"That's a very good question," said Angus, taking another sip. "Sure you won't join me?"

"No thanks. For some reason cognac gives me a headache."

"Pity. Unfortunately, I don't recall the Supreme Allied Command in Europe issuing orders to confiscate post-Impressionist paintings. A Van Gogh or a Klimt is not quite the same thing as a Walther pistol, which is patently considered enemy equipment. Provenance and chain of title are all very necessary to successfully sell a major painting. There was the case of an American lieutenant, I think his name was Joe Meador, from somewhere in Texas. He was stationed in Quedlinburg, Germany and helped himself to some extraordinary medieval relics, which the Church of St. Servatius had stored in a cave at Atlenburg. There were relics said to contain the blood of Christ, hair of the Virgin Mary, and a ninth-century manuscript, the Samuel Gospels, with a cover of silver gilt encrusted with precious stones, enamel, written in gold letters, an object of unearthly beauty and inestimable value. Meador died in 1980 and his sisters and brothers, who did not share his love of the artwork, tried to sell it and returned the Gospels to the German nation, and received a three million dollar 'finder's fee'. A German official and a *New York Times* reporter thwarted their attempt to sell the rest of the lieutenant's cache of stolen treasure. Two pieces, a crucifix and a rock crystal reliquary, are still unrecovered. It wasn't until 2006, that 89-year-old Maria Altmann was able to recover her five Klimts that had been hanging in the Belvedere Gallery in Vienna since 1945."

"Yes, I understand the Van Gogh has no capture paper."

"Well," said Angus, "not to put too fine a point on it or to cast aspersions, it is essentially stolen property. Dietrich probably stole it from Roth and even if he bought it from him, your grandfather took it off Dietrich's wall."

"I thought all property taken from Axis countries during the war was considered spoils of war."

"For years after the war, that seemed to be the prevailing attitude, to punish Germany and the Nazis. The English, Americans, and especially the Soviets, looted a number of private German collections and more than a few public museums. Some of the great discoveries in arms and armor, silver, ivories, and objects of art were so-called war trophies. The Nazis stole, damaged, or destroyed more than 500,000 artworks during the war, including the famous Amber Room at the Katherine Palace in St. Petersburg. At the war's end, Stalin authorized Soviet generals to take German treasures, including the more than 9,000 gold artifacts taken from Troy by the noted 19th century archeologist, Heinrich Schliemann. The Russians still hold nearly 250,000 works of art taken from Germany and have no interest in returning any of them. Peter Paul Reubens' 1610 painting of Tarquinius and Lucretia was removed in 1945 from the Sanssouci Palace in Potsdam. It recently turned up in the possession of a Russian businessman, Vladimir Logvinenko, who offered it back to the museum, which wanted to charge him with criminal possession, so instead he gave it to the Hermitage. The most renowned museum in Russia accepted the Tarquinius, restored it and hung it in its collection with pride. Still the age-old adage, 'to the victor go the spoils,' has shifted sometimes dramatically. For hundreds of years the spoils automatically went to the victor in a conflict. Much of the Louvre's collection comes from art brought back by Napoleon's forces. The British took the Rosetta stone as part of their spoils from France. Spoils as a word comes from the Latin, spolium, literally, hide stripped from an animal. World War Two and the widespread destruction caused by both Axis and Allied bombing, dramatically changed the world's attitude toward looting a nation of its art. Now museums inside countries that are signatories to the UNESCO treaties are being forced to repatriate looted artifacts."

"I know," said John. "My grandfather was reading about the Rothschilds and the Kunsthistoriches Museum in Vienna."

"Yes, there was that lovely, chiseled, French wheel-lock pistol, some superb gold-inlaid medieval polearms, nice kit as we English say. The Rothschilds sold it all at Christie's just after it was returned. Tell me what you want to do and I'll try to assist you as long as it's ethical and legal. Not that you'd have anything to do with circumventing the law."

"No, I wouldn't," said John. "Grandfather is insistent on confidentiality. He doesn't want to be the focus of a media circus."

"I'm afraid that's just what it will be. Front page news around the world, CNN, BBC, the works."

"I know. I can just see it now, 'American sergeant's priceless secret. World's most valuable painting hidden for 60 years in the closet of his modest home in Del Mar.' It just might kill him, literally. I'll have to insist on total confidentiality and trust to your discretion in feeling out what needs to be done. Either see it's returned to its rightful owner or sell it privately with no fanfare, and if the price is less than the Klimt, remember my grandfather and I have both lived this long, and the extra millions from a public sale won't be missed by either one of us."

The thought of being the agent for the Van Gogh was positively dizzying to Angus. He wanted to have another glass of cognac to steady his nerves, but he knew he was just on the edge of being over the .08 blood alcohol limit. Angus was very respectful of California's driving under the influence laws, having spent a miserable night in a holding cell at the Los Angeles Sheriff's Department jail on North San Vicente following a private party at Spago some years before.

He'd only just come to America to see the Getty Museum and visit an old school friend who'd graduated from the UCLA Film School, and was the assistant director on several feature films. Now, if Angus were ever lit-up, he either called a cab, or had someone sober drive him home.

He wistfully set down the bottle and the glass on a rather wretched presswood, Formica-topped coffee table that served as the obligatory law office waiting area magazine display.

"Rest assured," said Angus, "I will use the utmost discretion. The last thing I need is to run afoul of the authorities. The sort of information you require is available, though sourcing it out takes finesse. The Park Avenue imprimatur will be an enormous asset in our search. It's a magic name in the art world, and can open doors and archives that are tightly sealed and locked to all but the most powerful dealers and well-respected museum curators. Remember, we have our representatives on all six habitable continents. I will call you tomorrow afternoon after I make some preliminary inquiries."

Angus stood and shook hands with John rather warmly.

"Don't forget your pistol," said John. With a last look at the Van Gogh, Angus tucked the shoebox under his arm. John unbolted the front door and Angus walked out into the deepening twilight.

There were two Hispanic youths, perhaps in their early 20's with thick wavy, black hair and tattoos on their muscular forearms. Dressed in baggy pants that were slung low on their slim hips, they were both smoking cigarettes, and the taller and more menacing of the two was sitting insouciantly on the freshly waxed, right front fender of his BMW. Angus had read stories about Mexican street gangs and immediately assumed they were either 18th Street or worse. If they'd been black, he would have known they were either Crips or Bloods. They were staring at the gringo in the nice suit with the battered shoebox under his right arm. The shorter man, who was standing, spoke first in heavily accented English.

"Hey man, what you got in the box?"

The second man said in a less pronounced accent, "Yeah mano. You got some dope in there?" Angus was close to panic. He'd lived in the United States for nearly fifteen years, and he hadn't had any experience with inner city crime or criminals. He'd never been accosted on the street except by the ubiquitous panhandlers and bums who were present even on Rodeo Drive. The street people he'd encountered were smelly and filthy, dressed in rags, with or without shopping carts filled with rubbish. They disgusted him though he didn't feel they posed a threat to his physical safety or well-being.

The short man said to his companion, "Hey vato, I think you're sitting on the man's ride."

"You think so?" The man sitting on Angus' car stubbed his cigarette out with his left hand, grinding it into the hood of the BMW. Angus forgot his fear for a moment.

"Hey, that's my car. You leave it alone." This sounded so weak and ineffectual even to his ears that as he said it, Angus flushed with shame. The man on the fender took a pack of cigarettes from under the shoulder of his t-shirt, lit one with a black plastic butane lighter, puffed it until it glowed a bright cherry red, smiled provocatively at Angus, then crushed it into the hood of the car. Angus could see tobacco embers glowing on the white enamel. He thought he might stand a chance in a fistfight. However, if either of the Mexicans had a weapon he was headed for the hospital or the morgue, and he had the Walther in the shoebox to consider. He could bluff with it, though he knew bluffing with a gun might be worse than anything else he could do. The man put another cigarette in his mouth and was about to light it when something in Angus snapped. He said, "All right. You want to know what's in the box so badly, I'll show you." He flipped open the lid and with a grin he devoutly hoped was menacing and cruel, pulled out the Walther and pointed it at the young man with the unlit cigarette, whose black eyes got as wide as they were able to. Angus said coldly, "Now, get off my car."

The man hopped off. "Listen, mano," he said, "we don't want any trouble."

"I'm pleased to hear it," said Angus, who was wishing the Walther had a magazine full of 7.65 millimeter cartridges and one in the chamber. He pointed east with the muzzle of the gun toward Long Beach Boulevard.

"Now, I'm giving you a count of three to get the fuck out of here." Angus was not someone who used vulgarity on a regular basis, so when he did use it, he really meant it. If the gun had been loaded he might well have shot both boys; he was that outraged. The two Hispanics saw the gringo transform from a cringing, pathetic victim into a snarling predator, and neither one had the slightest doubt Angus would shoot. Angus said, "One," and tightened his finger on the trigger. The two men began walking east and kept walking. Angus could barely hear them talking to each other in Spanish, though the words came too quickly for him to make them out. He put the Walther back in the shoebox and in seconds he was in the BMW with the doors locked and the box on the passenger seat. The adrenalin was draining from his bloodstream and in the aftermath of his extreme flight or fight autonomic nervous system response, he was shaking and somewhat disoriented. He wanted to go home, take off his sweated-through dress shirt, take a long, hot shower, eat dinner, and tell Marcia all about his adventurous day while sipping a glass of the 30-year-old Glenmorangie Scotch he kept for special occasions. Either the Glenmorangie, or the ancient Jacopo Poli grappa, then again there was a black bottle of 40-year-old tawny port that would go down well following such a day. "No, I'm in the mood for the hard stuff. To think all that enjoyment might have ended just now on the grimy streets of Southgate."

With that almost unspeakably horrible thought echoing in his mind, he started the BMW and pulled away from the curb.

Angus was replaying the drama in his mind and as he did, he decided he'd done everything he should have. Those boys would think twice about assaulting a white man in a business suit. He saw the traffic light change to amber as he was almost to the intersection.

*To hell with it*, he thought. *The sooner I get out of here the better*. The signal was red as he drove through, though barely so. Angus didn't see the motorcycle policeman who was traveling southbound on a side street. The

Moto-Guzzi swung behind the BMW and the officer dressed in black leathers and white helmet switched on the flashing blue lights. The stroboscopic lights were hard to miss and Angus was a driver who religiously checked his sideview mirrors every few seconds. He saw the lights and said, "Shit," then pulled quickly to the curb.

The officer swung his left leg over the bike, dismounted, leaving the lights flashing as he walked to the driver's side of the BMW.

Angus pushed the plastic switch, rolling down the electric window. "License and registration, please," said the officer as he shined a large, black Mag-Lite flashlight into Angus' face, temporarily blinding him. With red after-images glowing in his eyes, Angus fumbled his billfold out of his inside jacket pocket and his hands trembled despite himself as he handed his license to the cop. The officer looked at it, then said, "Mr. Creswell, do you know why I pulled you over?"

Angus said quickly, "I saw the light change. I thought it would stay amber longer."

"A yellow light is a warning to come to a stop, not an invitation to proceed on through without stopping. Do you have any idea how many accidents, injuries and fatalities are caused by drivers who ignore yellow lights? You went through on the red. That means someone else had a green light."

"I know, I know. I'm truly sorry about my negligence."

"Registration please."

The registration was in a clear plastic pocket on the driver's side sun visor. Angus handed it to the policeman.

"Stay in the vehicle, Mr. Cresswell." The officer walked back to his motorcycle and spoke into his radio microphone. While the cop was engaged in finding out if the car were stolen, Angus was debating whether to move the shoebox from the passenger seat to the floorboard in the back behind his seat.

*If I move it now, and he's seen it, he might get suspicious,* he thought. Still, the box looked so innocuous, Angus wasn't overly concerned.

The officer returned and said, "You haven't been drinking, have you Mr. Cresswell?" This made Angus sweat once more. He knew he was close to the limit, having had two stiff brandies.

"No officer, I haven't. I thought I'd wait until I got home."

"That's always a good idea." The officer knew Angus wasn't telling him the truth because he had an excellent sense of smell, though the man hadn't been driving erratically, wasn't slurring his words, nor did he appear intoxicated. Officer Jefferson had grown up in the projects not so very far from where he was standing and he was supporting his mother and two baby sisters, as well as a new wife and his baby son. He loved being on motors and believing he was making a significant positive difference in people's lives by keeping the streets as safe as he could. If he'd thought for a second Angus was drunk he would have used his electronic Breathalyzer, which was better than a field sobriety test any day.

"Tell you what, Mr. Creswell, I'll give you a choice. I have a nice new digital Breathalyzer which uses individual plastic covers so there's no danger of germs. All you do is blow into it. You agree to do that and I won't write you a ticket for blowing that red light."

He smiled at Angus, who couldn't help thinking the whole thing was a trap. If he registered anything on the machine, he'd be guilty of lying to the police. He knew it was a crime to lie to the FBI. Martha Stewart went to Alderson Prison for five months after being convicted for doing just that.

"I don't want a ticket," said Angus as heartily as he could. The cop went back to his motorcycle, unlocked the fiberglass saddlebag and came back with a small, rectangular plastic box having a nozzle protruding out of the top right. The officer pressed a button and the machine emitted an electronic beep. The man handed the device to Angus.

"Blow steadily into the nozzle, not too hard, until you hear the beep, then give it back to me." Angus took a deep breath and exhaled steadily as his heart began to pound in his ears. He was just about out of breath when he heard a beep and he gave it back to the officer, who pushed a black toggle switch and the big red LED numbers came up on the screen. The read-out was "0.06."

"Thank God," said Angus to himself.

"Next time," said the policeman, "don't lie. I didn't think you were over the limit, but I could smell your breath." He was ready to hand Angus his registration and license when he said, "I'm curious. What's in the old shoebox? Your father's old baseball card collection?"

"No," said Angus, "some World War II memorabilia."

"Really?" said the officer. "Can I see it?"

Officer Jefferson really was interested and Angus knew he wasn't going to be able to put him off by saying he was in too much of a hurry for show and tell. Angus thought he'd best diffuse a touchy situation, this time with the truth.

"It's an antique pistol that belonged to a famous German general, Sepp Dietrich."

John was making his way down Tweedy and looking forward to grabbing two of Francisco's steak tacos when he saw two motor officers searching a White BMW 5 Series while a man who looked like Angus Creswell stood nearby in handcuffs. John had missed the dramatic confrontation with the two Chicanos in front of his office. He pulled behind one of the squad cars and recognized two of the officers.

"Hey, Manny, what's going on?"

Manny smiled, "Mr. Beverly Hills here has a gun. Imagine, an antique .32 automatic pistol. How dumb does he think we are?"

"I know," said John. "I sold it to him. It was my grandfather's. Since when is it illegal to have an unloaded gun in your car?"

"Since always," said Sergeant Ramirez. "You carry a gun unloaded and locked in the truck. Or if you don't have a trunk, unloaded in a locked container, not in a box on the passenger seat. Listen, forget about the law. A rookie seeing a gun in a shoebox on the seat might just shoot first then ask questions. Seeing as you vouch for the gun, I'll let it go."

Manny walked over to Angus as Officer Jefferson unlocked the handcuffs. They'd been put on tightly and Angus rubbed his wrists. The sergeant brought the shoebox from the trunk of his squad car. Within a few minutes the police left leaving John and Angus, as well as a number of gawkers, behind. Angus opened the truck of the BMW and put the shoebox inside.

"I'm really sorry about all this," said John.

"Sorry?" said Angus. "You saved my life."

"My fault. I should have delivered the pistol."

"Nonsense," said Angus. "No harm done. I lost two years of my life and you don't know the half of it. In the future, what do you say we meet in Beverly Hills? I think I've seen enough of Southgate in one evening to last me the rest of my life."

"All right," said John. He held out his right hand. "No hard feelings?"

"None whatsoever. On the contrary, I'm in your debt." They shook hands warmly.

"You'll call me tomorrow about the painting?"

"You can count on it. Wild horses couldn't keep me from calling."

## CHAPTER 12

# Westchester

JOHN ARRIVED AT his home in Westchester, switched on the lights and fed his goldfish. He took a shower, dressed casually in blue jeans and a black Polo shirt, sat on his bed, picked up his Panasonic cordless phone, and punched in a number.

"Hello? Oh, Eddie, it's you. Is my mother there? No nothing important. I'll call her back later, thanks."

John had no sooner hung up, when the phone rang. He pressed the white button. "Grandpa," said John. "I was just about to call you. You wouldn't believe what I have locked up in my office. How about $80,000 in hundred dollar bills? No, I'm not kidding. The painting? I think we should only talk about it in person or better yet, I'll e-mail you." There was the click of an incoming call. "Grandpa, can I call you right back? Two minutes, I promise. Okay?" John clicked the disconnect button. "Hello, this is John."

He was surprised to hear a young woman's voice. "Mr. Dryden? This is Sondra Huggins from Park Avenue Galleries. Carol gave me your home phone number."

This came as somewhat of a shock, as Carol usually protected his privacy with ferocity and never gave out either his home or cell number. Then again, she seemed to be very interested in him having a social life, more than he was at present. He'd said something about Sondra looking like Charlize Theron, so Carol assumed he was attracted to her.

"Yes, Sondra. If I seemed a bit brusque, it's only because I usually don't give out my home phone number for obvious reasons."

"I understand completely. This is very hard for me."

John was at a loss to hear Sondra so diffident. At the gallery she was the personification of self-confidence, even arrogance. John waited. "By any chance do you handle sexual harassment cases?"

"Listen, Sondra. I do civil litigation, landlord-tenant, the odd criminal complaint, and a lot of pro-bono wrongful eviction, unlawful detainers, and things like that. It's not Ally McBeal, Law and Order, anything glamorous."

"Can you do a sexual harassment case?"

"Why not go to the top? Call Gloria Allred. I assume it's someone important."

"That's just it. I don't want any publicity. The man is wealthy and a big LA society name. I don't need the attention."

"I see," said John, which in fact he didn't. The hot glare of a news conference was a great way to dry up the infection of sexual harassment, especially when the revelation sparked a veritable media feeding frenzy. "Listen, Sondra, if you want to call me at my office at eleven tomorrow morning we can discuss it further. In the meantime, let me assure you that the best cure for a big name harasser is publicity."

"Okay, I'll think about it. And Mr. Dryden…"

"Yes."

"About our first meeting. If you thought I was being a bitch, I apologize. I didn't mean to be. I've been upset by this for days. You understand."

"Apology accepted. We all have our moments. Call me tomorrow."

Sondra knew he was trying to get off the phone and this was something intriguing and mysterious to her. Usually men went to extraordinary lengths to keep her on the phone. John was brushing her off politely to be sure, but no less firmly. Sondra thought there might be more to the Don Quixote with a law degree and a vintage timepiece than meets the eye.

"Okay, Mr. Dryden," Sondra said in her most honeyed voice, one through which the twang could be heard. "Have a good evening," The implication being to have as good an evening as he could possibly have without her company and that even the best possible evening would pale in comparison to one spent in her presence. John clicked off without a second thought and called Del Mar.

"Grandpa? Sorry, damsel in distress. No, she's not granddaughter material. Trust me on this. I know. I'm doing the best I can. You and Carol need to stop busting my balls." The annoying click of call waiting hacked once again into their conversation. "Can you hold, Grandpa? Hello, oh Mom. I'm on with Grandpa. Can I call you right back? All right, I'll call him back. Grandpa, Mom's pitching a hissy fit about something. I'll call you right back. Mom?"

"You were very rude to Eddie. I won't stand for it."

The venom in her tone took John aback. "I was not. I said, 'Oh, hello Eddie, it's you.' I asked if you were home and said I'd call back. I even said, 'Thanks.'"

"Exactly. It never occurred to you to ask him how he was doing or why he was at home during office hours. You hardly ever say two words to him. You didn't like it when I was dating. You didn't like it when I remarried. As if I were insulting Luke's sacred memory. It's been more than ten years now and Eddie's your stepfather whether you like it or not. It's time you showed him proper respect."

"Mom, it's been a long day. I gotta' go."

"Always running from confrontation just like your father."

This instantly rendered John furious, all the more so because Luke died before he even knew him.

"I'm not going to listen to this horseshit! Good-bye, Mom." He clicked off and went to the kitchen to get a cold and large bottle of Grolsch beer. He popped the wire harness, listening to the hiss of the escaping carbonation. He was thirsty and drank half the pint bottle before stopping to belch loudly. He picked up the handset from the kitchen telephone and called Hank.

"Grandpa, sorry about that. No, nothing at all as usual. She was ragging me about Eddie. Yeah, he's a piece of work. Are you feeling all right? You sound exhausted. You sure? See you Saturday."

John hung up the telephone and finished the rest of the beer. He thought briefly about having a second bottle and decided against it, knowing if he did, he'd have to get up twice or three times during the night to piss after he fell asleep. He walked into his office, sat in front of his relatively new IBM monitor and went to EarthLink to check his email account. Most of it was the usual spam touting the virtues of Viagra, Cialis, and other male potency nostrums, a weight loss program "guaranteed to make you lose 20 pounds in 20 days," and one from munichman1945@hotmail.com, which was Hank's handle. It read, "Check out the Art Loss Register at www.artloss.com. John wrote back, "Will do."

John typed Art Loss Register into his Google search and in less than five seconds he was onto their home page learning about their mission to list and track stolen works of art, as well as art whose ownership was in dispute, by maintaining the largest and most comprehensive registry of its kind in the world. The Art Loss Register had been instrumental in repatriating not only paintings taken by the Nazis during their vicious ascendency, but Peruvian textiles, Etruscan bronzes, A Mayan stone stele, or calendar, as well as objects looted from the Baghdad Museum during the so-called liberation of Iraq. As a matter of fact, over 14,000 objects were taken from the Iraqi National Museum in April of 2003 and only 5,000 had been recovered. The most prized piece of all, the 3.8 inch high Lion of Nimrud, naturalistically carved of wood and ivory by an unknown artist seven centuries before the Common Era, John saw was still listed as missing. He was interested to note a lovely Monet painting of Water Lilies that had been stolen in 1940 from Paris dealer, Paul Rosenberg. Painted in 1904, it was a particularly lush, evocative work that had been appropriated by the Nazi foreign minister, Joachim von Ribbentrop, and after the war was given to the Louvre, where it hung for 50 years. Lent to an exhibit at the Boston Museum of Fine Arts, the Monet was noticed by the Rosenberg heirs, who sought the assistance of the Art Loss Register in recovering their property.

## CHAPTER 13

# Investigations

ANGUS CRESWELL WAS never so grateful to pull into his own driveway, as he was that evening. Marcia and the three younger Creswells had eaten earlier, since the children couldn't be expected to wait until Daddy got home from Southgate. His wife had made angel hair pasta with a creditable Bolognese sauce, which was made even more rich and flavorful by reheating. The children were watching television and playing with their Gameboys. The oldest was actually writing a book report on John Steinbeck's, The Pearl. As Marcia listened to his adventures in Southgate, Angus doctored his plate of pasta with fresh-grated Romano cheese and flakes of crushed red pepper. He had opened a good bottle of Italian Barolo from the Wine House on Cotner, and poured a glass for Marcia and one for himself.

"I didn't know if I were over the legal limit or not and I was thinking, 'This is just wonderful. I'll be arrested for DUI, they'll find the pistol and charge me with carrying a concealed weapon.'" Angus used his spoon together with his fork to neatly coil the angel hair on the tines before bringing it to his mouth. The pasta was hot and tasty, still al dente despite the reheating, and he said appreciatively, "This is really good."

Marcia smiled, for she was an excellent cook and used the very best and freshest ingredients available, making her sauces from scratch, generally using recipes from James Beard or Julia Child. However, she was a talented innovator in her own right with an unerring sense of spicing that resulted in the most savory and subtle texturing of flavors and aromas. She had taken courses at the Culinary Institute of America in Napa, and was a sous chef at Valentinos in Santa Monica on Pico Boulevard for several months one summer when she was a student at Cal State Northridge. As much as she liked cooking, her brief stint at Valentinos convinced her she didn't want to do it professionally. It was a great vocation for luminaries like Wolfgang Puck or Nobu Matsuhisa, just not for her. She and Angus met at the King's Head Pub in Santa Monica, a gathering place where ex-patriate Brits and Aussies meet to drink English beer and eat pub food, shepherd's pie, bangers and mash, fish and chips and the like, throw darts, and convince themselves they're still loyal subjects of the Crown. Marcia was there with two of her girlfriends from the flats of Sherman Oaks.

Angus was attracted by Marcia's long, straight, natural auburn hair, which put him in mind of an Irish girl from Belfast whom he'd dated briefly when she was studying art history at the Courtauld Institute of Art, the Trust administered jointly by the University of London and the Samuel Courtauld Trust. Marcia was captivated by the tall, handsome Englishman and more than a dozen years later, they, unlike most other married couples they knew, were still best friends and lovers. Before sitting down to his late supper, Angus had shown the Walther to Marcia.

"I'll bet I know who's going to be the lucky buyer." Angus' most revered and reverenced private client was a fabulously wealthy commercial and residential real estate speculator, the scion of a wealthy Naugatuck, Connecticut family, who left Yale to pursue an acting career in Hollywood. He was most personable and that in addition to his name, opened doors. The reality of spending hours in make-up, and then waiting more hours to spend a few minutes on set in front of the camera with the director, which was the fate of a supporting actor, wasn't nearly as romantic as appearing in Shakespearean dramas and Tennessee William's plays at Yale had been. He could see that thousands of people were moving to LA despite the 1971 Sylmar earthquake, which nearly frightened him back to Connecticut a year after he arrived. He began acquiring ranchland northwest of the city along the 101 Ventura Highway, most of it north of a truck stop and shooting range with the improbable name of Whizins. The acreage was inexpensive. Within ten years the land had doubled in value and the flat land near the highway was being used for residential development. He had the funds to wait until 1990 when the land he'd bought for a few thousand dollars an acre was selling for six and even seven figures, and he was listed in the middle of the Forbes Four Hundred without ever revealing the true extent of his vast holdings. He bought an old Ralph's Market on Wilshire, razed it and built a 21-story office tower faced with red granite, keeping the entire 21st floor for his personal offices. He collected all types of exotic weapons, even Japanese samurai swords and armor, however he would buy virtually anything if it were visually arresting and one of a kind. The Walther came up cherries on all his criteria. It was pleasing to the eye, historically significant, unique, and it could be used as well if one had a mind to shoot it.

"I'll just bet you do," said Angus, setting down his wine glass.

"You paid how much?"

"Eighty."

"Then you need 50% profit."

"Too right. As a matter of fact, I was thinking of $125,000. That way he can chip me for five and feel good about it. He probably makes that much every minute 24/7, but for some perverted reason it makes him happy to grind his vendors for a few thousand."

"You think he'd buy the Van Gogh?"

"I know he's bought some pricey Frederick Remington and Charles Russel oils. I know because they're hanging on the walls. He bought them in the 1970's and early 1980's when you could buy the best for a million dollars. He'd buy the Van Gogh for cheap money to flip it, however I don't think that's what the Drydens want. And there's the whole provenance and title thing. Imagine him buying it and it turns out he has to give it back to some rightful owner. What a nightmare."

"That would be a nightmare. He'd probably sue you."

"No probably about it, he would sue the hell out of me, bankrupt me, make it so we'd have to move to England to get away from his lawyers. No thanks. I'm going to the office early tomorrow to make some overseas calls to see if it's on the list of the missing. That's the first step. If no one's looking for it we're still far from home free, though then I can sell it with a clear conscience. Somehow I have the impression the veteran who brought it back isn't very proud of how he acquired it, and the last thing he wants is to be interviewed by CNN. The grandson's a lawyer and normally that's a big negative, since most lawyers spend their lives either screwing someone or trying to figure out how to avoid being screwed, and they always think you're trying to screw them no matter how good a deal you're offering. However in this case, if there were to be a chain of title battle there's an attorney in the mix who will have an impossible time convincing anyone that he is ignorant of the law in regards to tangible personal property."

"How much commission are you going to charge him?" "Good question. Any gallery, Sotheby's, Christie's Bonham's, Park Avenue or Pace Wildenstein would probably pay him to sell it and make theirs off the buyer's premium. Dryden knows I'm hardly an expert in Post-Impressionist art, so I have to be careful not to overplay my hand. He has placed his trust in me, and as you know better than anyone, I will do my best to honor that trust."

This was the truth. Though not even his wife would call him a philanthropist, Angus would never betray a confidence, nor would he lie in response to a direct question. Marcia raised her glass. "Here's hoping the painting isn't hot."

"I'll drink to that."

Angus arrived at the gallery shortly before eight the next morning, and the night shift security guard greeted him and unlocked the front door in response to Angus' buzz. "You're early this morning," observed the guard.

"It's already nearly four o'clock in the afternoon, London time."

Angus unlocked the door to his office, flipped the mercury switch, hung his jacket on the hanger he kept on a hook he'd screwed to the back of his door, and sat down at his plain but serviceable walnut desk. The walls were covered with framed photographs of magnificent swords, armor, and princely firearms sold by Christie's, Sotheby's, and Park Avenue. He dialed the number of the Art Loss Register, which was formed in 1991 by a consortium of the big London auction firms, including Park Avenue, Lloyds of London, Chubb, and other major insurance companies, and art industry players. Their database consisted of more than 200,000 works of art that were either known to be stolen or had disputed ownership. The old, familiar, double burr ringtone of England always made him nostalgic.

"Good afternoon, Art Loss Register. How may I direct your call?" The voice was classically English and Angus placed the exact accent somewhere in the midlands, perhaps near Kent.

"This is Angus Creswell from Park Avenue Galleries in Los Angeles."

"I've been to Los Angeles. Are you in Beverly Hills by any chance?"

"Yes, as a matter of fact I am."

"You're at the office early."

"I wanted to call before you left for the day. I need to speak to someone about a Van Gogh that's turned up."

"Certainly, transferring you to Mr. Radcliff's secretary."

"Thank you. How's the weather there? I miss it sometimes."

"Can't say as I would. It's raining and a bit chilly."

"Well, speaking as an ex-Londoner, I have to say there are times I miss it."

There was a clicking sound in Angus' ear and a woman answered. "This is Jane Goddard."

"Ms. Goddard, this is Angus Creswell from Park Avenue Galleries, Los Angeles office. I am hoping you can assist me. A private client has a Van Gogh self-portrait that came out of Germany after the Second World War. I am assisting him with provenance and as part of my due diligence, I told him my first call would be to the Art Loss Register, so here I am. I thought I should contact you, as I am suspicious of anything coming out of Germany between 1933 and 1946."

"There is nothing in our database that matches a Van Gogh self-portrait. Personally, I was unaware there were any in private collections. Are you certain it's genuine?"

"Yes I am. It came from the residence of an SS general."

"There was one Van Gogh sold in 1939 at that Lucerne auction. Are you sure it's not a copy of that one?"

"So, as far as you're concerned, there's no cloud over the ownership?"

"None that I am aware of and our database is linked with several others, as well as listings from INTERPOL and the American FBI, so you may rest assured your painting is not listed as stolen or missing as of the past few weeks."

"Well, that's very good news indeed. My client will be relieved."

"Mr. Creswell?"

"Yes..."

"Although the odds against it being a genuine Van Gogh are, in my opinion, virtually insurmountable, assuming it is authentic, such a remarkable discovery would create an international sensation, giving rise to numerous claims, which could take an army of solicitors years to resolve."

"That's not my problem, and it belongs to a solicitor."

"Is there anything else?"

"No, and I thank you for your kindness, courtesy, and thoroughgoing professionalism."

"It's my pleasure to help a fellow countryman. As much as it thrills us to reunite works of art with their rightful owners, we're just as pleased to tell people the piece they are inquiring about is not stolen or disputed."

"Well, I thank you once again and wish you a good evening."

"And a good morning to you."

Angus hung up and heaved a sigh of relief. The first and most vital hurdle had been passed. As far as authenticity goes, the painting spoke for itself. It's inherent perfection and artistic integrity testified loudly and clearly to its being an autograph work. The fact that it was found hanging in Dietrich's office only enhanced its credibility as far as Angus was concerned. He did wonder if Dietrich had any descendents or relatives. Angus typed Sepp Dietrich into his Google search and there were many pages of entries, including a YouTube video of Dietrich's son riding on a German armored car in Fort Indiantown Gap during an event commemorating the Battle of the Bulge. The video was shot in 2006.

According to the Wikipedia, Josef Dietrich wasn't an anti-Semite. Evidently Dietrich did have living descendents, but Angus decided he wasn't going to go out of his way to help them claim a fabulously valuable work of art lost for the past 60 years and that was assuming they even knew of its existence, which he sincerely doubted. Since it wasn't stolen, or rather listed as stolen, Angus could offer it in good conscience.

Angus put on his suit jacket and walked out of his office, down the hall, and out past the reception desk. He noticed Sondra wasn't there. Instead there was a dark-haired, blue-eyed girl in her late twenties or early thirties with an exotic look about her that bespoke Eastern Europe. Angus thought he might have seen her working one of his exhibitions, though he couldn't really place her.

"Excuse me," he said. "I'm Angus Creswell."

"Yes, I know," she said with a smile. "You're the arms and armor expert."

"I've seen you somewhere before. At the exhibitions?"

Angus thought she was very pretty, not an in-your-face bombshell like Sondra, more like a brunette Scarlett Johansson. She was wearing a dark, wine red, v-neck cashmere sweater with no bra, and Angus could see she had lovely, firm breasts. Her voice was deeper than Sondra's with an attractive breathy quality. There were dark circles under her eyes that gave her somewhat of an angst-ridden appearance, as if the sturm and drang of the world weighed on her more than it did on most people. She saw Angus checking her out and said, "I'm sorry. I'm Lucille Rosen. I used to be part time. Mr. Brooks called me this morning and asked if I could take the reception desk this week."

"What happened to Sondra?"

"I don't know. I think she got promoted."

"Good for her. I'm stepping out for a coffee. I have my cell phone if anything urgent comes up. I'm expecting a call from a Mr. Dryden, just so you know. Please call me immediately if he calls."

"Yes, Mr. Creswell. I have you in my computer."

Angus left thinking Lucille was a substantial improvement on Sondra, whom he never really cared for. Part of his antipathy was that she'd given him the impression that she thought the Arms and Armor Department was beneath the dignity of the gallery. The telephone rang and Lucille answered, "Park Avenue Galleries, good morning. Sondra? No, she's in the Contemporary and Modern Painting Department. Who shall I say is calling? Mr. Dryden? You know, Mr. Creswell is looking for you. I'll put you through to Sondra."

Sondra Huggins was seated at her new desk. It wasn't some lovely piece like the Louis XVI in reception. It was strictly an office desk of press-wood with a faux mahogany top. Still, it was the desk of a member of a department, not a secretary, a position she'd craved since she'd transferred from Chicago. Her salary was only marginally larger, however now she had a company MasterCard, an expense account that was generous to a fault as well as an incalculable increase in prestige.

She answered the telephone, "Contemporary Paintings, good morning."

John thought it was Sondra, but wasn't sure. "Is this Sondra?"

"Yes, Sondra Huggins."

"It's John Dryden. You called me about a possible sexual harassment lawsuit last evening?"

"Oh, yes. I don't think that will be necessary now. I was promoted this morning."

"Well, congratulations," said John. "I'm glad it all worked out for you. Usually they just get worse. I'm happy to hear your situation isn't like that. Last night you sounded pretty upset."

"It's amazing the effect a few hours can have, isn't it?"

John said to himself, "A few hours and the not so thinly veiled threat of a sexual harassment suit."

Sondra continued, "Mr. Dryden, I feel I owe you. Please allow me take you to a nice lunch. How about sushi?" Sondra's invitation was quite unexpected. Though he had any number of interrogatories and pleadings to review and draft, he always did, John didn't recall any vital appointments, though there were often walk-ins drawn by the Yo Hablo Espanol and his local reputation for successful resolution of landlord tenant disputes. He had settled several personal injury claims for high five figures and these fees helped offset the expenses for a large number of basically pro-bono cases.

Most of his clients couldn't afford to carry even the minimum liability insurance mandated by California law. They had to maintain collision and comprehensive coverage, because if they let that lapse the finance company would send out the repo-man. Therefore, since they generally needed their vehicles to drive to their jobs, the liability insurance was the first to go. The whole sordid business of selling car insurance to the working poor was essentially legally sanctioned racketeering, as the down payment covered the agent's fee and if they failed to make the monthly payments the coverage would lapse at no loss to the agent, who received his money up front. The interest on the portion financed was usually more than 50% on an annualized basis and often as much as 80 or even 100%. The insurance racket was no more morally reprehensible than the "pay-day advance loans," which could be as much as 150% or 200% on an annualized basis, or pawnshops. The whole parasitical industry living off those less fortunate and unable to borrow from banks or have fat credit lines attached to Gold Visas or MasterCard's, disgusted John.

Somehow, John didn't see Sondra Huggins as a prospective girlfriend. He couldn't conceive of her being interested in him as anything other than a casual acquaintance, she could call upon him for free legal advice, and even then she probably knew half a dozen Century City attorneys who would happily give her all the advice she'd ever need just to be seen having lunch with her alfresco on the patio near the promenade off Century Park East. They would do it for the so-called "bragging rights" attached to being in public with such an acknowledged beauty. John could have cared less about prestige dates, although even he had to admit it would be great fun to bring Sondra to Southgate just to see the look on Carol's face when they strolled in. Not that Sondra would be caught dead in grimy old Southgate, unless he mentioned the painting in the bottom drawer of his file-safe. He wouldn't consider doing such a thing though he could picture it, no pun intended, Sondra's perfectly proportioned jaw would drop to her lovely chest and her baby blue eyes would open wide in shock. The Van Gogh would almost literally knock her stockings off if she were wearing any at the time. Her first question would be, "Is it real?"

After all, John thought: *One isn't used to seeing fifty million dollar paintings in a file drawer of a dingy walk-up office in Southgate.* In the not so very distant past, you could have bought all of Southgate for fifty million dollars, and a good part of Beverly Hills as well. Hank and Carol were right about a number of things pertaining to his lifestyle, often annoyingly so. They both agreed that he didn't get out into the social Gulfstream, and even he had to agree. "You can't win if you don't play," said Carol after he'd told her about Sondra.

"You're so out of practice," said Hank, "You wouldn't recognize a pass if she made one."

John thought the two of them were conspiring against him and the worst part was they were correct. He more than likely wouldn't recognize any pass more subtle than, "I want you to take me home and make mad passionate love to me."

"It's a bit pathetic," he said to himself. He could drive to Westchester and switch cars. As long as Sondra wasn't a rabid environmentalist, which seemed out of character, she would have to like the GTO, and in Beverly Hills it garnered more appreciative looks than the more common Bentleys or a Maseratis. Girls like Sondra were not going to care if his car produced more carbon emissions than any ten new Maseratis. He'd only recently had it detailed by one of the Mexican men that did detailing at the car wash on Long Beach Boulevard, and came to John's office once a week when the weather was good to do the GTO. Carlos loved the car and would have almost washed and waxed it for free, instead of the fifty dollars he charged John. Wherever one parks in LA, you can count on having an ultra fine layer of grit falling on your freshly washed vehicle that will scratch the paint when you cover it with a fleecy car cover to prevent a thicker layer from accumulating. He decided to take the Camry to Beverly Hills and if Sondra turned up her lovely nose at it, if she ever saw it, then that was her problem and not his.

"I'm really in the mood for a good salad. Sushi sounds more like supper to me."

"Fine with me," said Sondra. "Meet me at reception at one. I'll reserve a table on the patio."

"That sounds great. I'll see you there."

John walked into Carol's office with a big smile on his face. Constant applications of a Walgreens ice bag had appreciably reduced the swelling of his nose, and when he shaved that morning, he was relieved to see he didn't look like he'd gone several rounds with Iron Mike Tyson. There was a patch of unusual yellowish brown skin under his left eye, which wasn't so much disfiguring, as it looked as if he either walked into a door or been punched in the eye.

He announced crisply, "I'm going into Beverly Hills. Call me if Mr. Nahabedian or anyone else with a grudge comes in so I can decide whether or not I want to come back later."

"John Dryden," she said with a grin, "if I didn't know it was impossible I'd say you got yourself a date."

"Yes, as a matter of fact, I do."

"Well, hallelujah, praise the Lord. Will wonders never cease? I'll hold down the fort and if Ahmed comes back, this time I'll pepper spray him the minute he raises his voice."

John groaned, "Be careful. He'll sue us for assault."

"I won't have to pay attorney fees will I?" said Carol.

"I'm sure he has an entire law firm on retainer to keep him out of jail. The city's tried for years to nail his hide to the wall without success."

"I can understand white Europeans exploiting underprivileged minorities, that's just the free enterprise system at its best. It's hard for me to fathom a man like Nahabedian, whose people were treated by the Turks the same way the Nazis treated the Jews, exploiting Blacks and Hispanics. Where's the empathy?"

"How do you know about the Armenian genocide? You were calling him an Arab only yesterday."

"I did that just to insult him."

John pointed to his nose. "You did a real good job of antagonizing him."

"He had it coming."

"Enough already, I'm leaving."

"Whatever you do, don't tell her you got punched out. Whatever sympathy that gets you will be outweighed by the fact that she'll think you're a weenie," Carol stopped and pondered a moment. "On second thought if she asks you and I'd bet my paycheck she will, just say, "You should see the other guy. Last I saw of him he was being loaded into an ambulance.'"

"What if she's poetic and sensitive?"

"Then what's she doing in Beverly Hills on Rodeo Drive?"

"I see your point. See ya'."

"Don't leave your cell in the car. I may need you."

John pulled his Blackberry out of his breast pocket.

"Is it charged?"

"Yes, it's even charged. Thank you for asking."

"Then bye," she said and turned her attention to her monitor.

It was just before one o'clock when Sondra strode up to the reception desk. She was wearing a lovely rust-colored, off-the-shoulder dress from Nieman's that cost $2,500 and on her it actually looked worth the money. The dress was part of Mr. Richardson's penance and peace offering for allowing her to languish at the reception desk, past what Sondra considered to be her time.

Everyone who worked at Park Avenue knew the fairy tales of department girls and receptionists who had married wealthy clients. One girl even married a Gulf State prince who whisked her off to Qatar on his private 747. Sondra was certain working at the gallery was a far superior venue for an ambitious young lady than the exhausting and usually fruitless path of the standard issue Southern California actress, model, wannabe. AMW's were expected to screw their way to stardom, while art consultants were accorded the freedom to pass on undesirable sexual encounters, and Park Avenue records were one hell of a lot more reliable at predicting financial viability than an assistant producer's resume, which was likely to be heavily padded and embroidered under the best of circumstances. In Sondra's experience, film industry men were flakes by virtue of their profession. If she had ten dollars for every time some phony producer came to her with an offer of a role, Sondra didn't think she'd be rich, but she could definitely buy another Norma Kamali dress.

Lucille Rosen looked up at Sondra. Lucille thought Sondra was a very pretty girl, though a bit snobbish and even pretentious. There was office talk about Sondra and Mr. Richardson having an affair and Lucille was quite sure the rumors were true, and more than likely the cause of Sondra's unexpected elevation to the painting department, a coveted position. Still the whys and wherefores of the gallery staff weren't all that interesting to her in comparison with being in such close proximity with so many works of art. Museums had their place and, indeed, most of the world's truly magnificent works of art were in permanent museum collections. However, unless one was a curator at the Louvre, the Hermitage, or the Metropolitan, the true art aficionado never got to physically handle the great tangible expressions of man's striving to probe the nature of the divine, which was what true art was all about. A visitor to the Louvre could look at La Gioconda, the Mona Lisa, but he couldn't examine it under an ultraviolet light to see how much of it was Leonardo's, and how much was centuries of inpainting. You couldn't go to the Met and handle a superb three-color glaze T'ang dynasty horse or wear the British Crown Jewels. At Park Avenue, clients were encouraged to closely examine Renoir's, Breughel's T'ang ceramics, first editions of Audubon's Birds of North America, silver by Paul de Lamerie and Thomas St Germaine, furniture by Thomas Chippendale and Bernard Riesener. Where else could a person sit down at a desk made for Marie Antoinette and mark his lots in a color catalog? Working part time, Lucille found the atmosphere at the gallery intoxicating, a museum that changed its exhibits every week and offered unlimited opportunity to handle works of art as diverse as Egyptian ushabtis and sculptures by Damien Hurst. As she sat in her comfortable stainless steel and black leather swivel chair, Lucille felt herself an integral part of the gallery, much more so than when she'd been a part-timer working the exhibitions, though that was fascinating as well.

Sondra looked at Lucille sitting in her old chair and was surprised she'd been hired to replace her. Yes, Lucille was attractive, but she looked so ethnic. Not that Park Avenue was particularly prejudiced. To the contrary, the Asian Works of Art Department was headed by a Hong Kong Chinese man, and the European Works of Art Department's expert was a Chilean by the name of Ramirez, and Lewis in the shipping department, was an African-American.

*Still,* thought Sondra, *Lucille just looks so Jewish, like the 19th century paintings of Ruth, Rachael, Leah, and Judith with those deep, violet eyes, the intensely dark, curly hair. She never has to have a perm. It's all natural like that tawny skin of hers. She doesn't need a vacation to get a tan in the winter, and she has that indefinable look of angst on her face, as if some unconscious part of her knows the Cossacks can come for her at any time.* Sondra knew that a number of Park Avenue's clients were passive anti-Semites, and the gallery was scrupulous in avoiding the taint of what was, after all the trappings were removed and reduced to its most vulgar essentials, a sort of glorified second-hand business, not far removed from a splendid pawnbroker's shop. Both enterprises thrived on the three D's, death, debt, and divorce, but Park Avenue had Amati, Stradivarius, and other Cremona instrument makers' works in the display window, instead of used Fender and Gibson guitars, though the auction house sold these too, if they belonged to Jimi Hendrix, Elvis, or Eric Clapton.

The line separating used goods from fine art wasn't nearly so sharply defined as Park Avenue and some of its upper echelon society types might like it to be. Having an obviously Jewish receptionist wasn't at all what Sondra expected as her replacement. Sondra knew of several mega-wealthy Middle Eastern clients who would take definite umbrage at Lucille's presence, though they would cloak their outrage and disgust in an exaggerated display of courtesy and politeness.

"If I know anything about the firm, her tenure will be brief." Sondra had no personal animosity for Lucille, and she experienced not a scintilla of envy at seeing her in the infamous black leather chair, made so by Sondra's predecessor having been found in flagrante-delicto with a curator from the Pinacoteca de Bera in Milan.

The handsome curator, all the Park Avenue staff male and female agreed on that fact, had come to Los Angeles for an Old Master sale to examine a Caravaggio that some cognoscenti thought might not be an autograph work by the renowned artist. Jacquiline was smitten by the dashing Italian, who, having looked at photos, Sondra had to admit was one of the most physically attractive men she'd ever seen. Lorenzo and Jacquiline thought they were alone after the Saturday exhibition had closed at 5:00 p.m. and he was naked from the waist down, sitting in Jackie's chair with Jackie in his lap, engaged in unrestrained and somewhat loud sexual congress, when Mr. Winslow from the American Furniture Department walked in and nearly had a stroke. The poor man had been cataloging a small, block front, Goddard Townsend desk that some well-meaning, but ignorant owner had over sanded then badly refinished during the early 1920's. He was trying his best to craft the prose that would minimize the irreparable damage and still convey a truthful description of the appalling damage to all interested parties, while defending the legitimate interests of the consignor. The heavy-handed sanding had turned an easy 500,000 dollar sale into a problematical one with an estimate of 100-120 thousand dollars, with an 80,000 dollar reserve, and even now it wasn't a sure sale. Wooley loved the Newport School of American furniture for their innovative interpretations of Queen Anne and Chippendale styles and their characteristic, unique, original shell carvings, which in this example were blurred by the "moron" to use his own words, "who sanded it." The sight of the couple writhing in passionate ecstasy on the swivel chair very nearly gave the scion of a very proper New England family apoplexy.

In the wake of her peccadillo, Jacquiline was relieved of her position, no pun intended, and disappeared entirely from the LA art scene. Lorenzo bought the Caravaggio on behalf of a prominent Italian industrialist for 1.1 million dollars, far too much for a school painting, and far too little for a genuine Caravaggio. The Goddard Townsend desk sold at the $80,000 reserve to a small Massachusetts museum, which wanted an example of Rhode Island School furniture and lacked the funding to buy a pristine piece.

"Hey, Sondra," said Lucille with a pleasant smile. "Congratulations on your promotion."

"Thank you," said Sondra. "It was high time."

"Can I ask you a question?"

"Sure."

"What's this Dryden guy like? He sounds nice and Dawn said he's kind of cute."

"Late thirties, early forties. Tall, nice smile, decent though thinning hair. He seems quite sweet. Not my type."

"What's he do?"

"Public interest law; a total loser attorney."

"I know you're after bigger fish. Now me, I just want a guy who isn't a selfish, egocentric prick. If you decide to throw him back in the pool, can you let me know?" Sondra looked at her with a pitying expression that a woman as good looking as Lucille would have any interest in a lawyer from Southgate.

*I suppose there are men who like the dark-skinned, full lipped, sultry Semitic types*, thought Sondra. *Lucille's a pretty girl. Definitely not long for the reception desk.*

"Do me a favor and book a table for two on the patio at Cafe Rodeo. I'll let you know all about Mr. Dryden after lunch."

"Patio table for two at 1:15?"

"That'll work," said Sondra. "Buzz me when Mr. Dryden gets here."

John was having considerable difficulty finding a parking space in one of the open air parking lots. The other day, he'd arrived before 10:00 a.m., and since many Beverly Hills regulars were only just waking up in their homes north of big Santa Monica Boulevard before coming south to meet for business and social purposes at the city's tony restaurants, the parking was relatively easy. John took Camden north to Little Santa Monica, made a right, went east to Canon, then another right and pulled into a Beverly Hills City ground level lot just as a Cadillac Escalade, one of the ubiquitous, massive SUV's driven by Beverly Hills matrons, was pulling out. He was duly impressed that anyone could park an Escalade in such a narrow space without taking out the car next door, though his Camry had more than enough room.

He took his ticket from the lot attendant, gave the man his keys just in case, and walked as quickly as he could west on Brighton Way. A glance at his watch told him he'd be at five minutes late. By the time he arrived at the gallery and opened the door John had actually worked up a light sweat. His feet felt damp in his loafers. Lucille noticed him as soon as he walked in and liked what she saw.

"May I help you?" she asked in a husky voice.

John looked at her and guessed she was in her early thirties, with a nice figure from what he could see and there was an indefinable aura around her that suggested not just intelligence, but a degree of emotional maturity as if the slings and arrows of life had found their mark in her and she survived. There was a depth to her that he didn't see in Sondra, not that Sondra was interested in him. John looked at the fourth finger on Lucille's left hand and was mildly disappointed to see a small platinum ring mounted with an old-fashioned diamond.

"I'm here to see Sondra Huggins."

"Your name?" asked Lucille.

"Dryden, John Dryden."

"As in the poet laureate of England?"

"Yes."

"Well, you're remarkably well preserved."

For a long moment John didn't have the slightest idea of what the girl was talking about. Then it came to him she was making a joke.

"I'm sorry, parking around here is such a hassle, I'm afraid it aggravated me to the point where it interfered with my naturally abundant good humor. That was very funny about a man who died in 1700 being well preserved."

Lucille liked the fact that he knew the date of the great poet's death. She doubted if most people in Beverly Hills had ever heard of John Dryden, knew of him, or could have cared less about a man who for more than a quarter of a century was the greatest literary figure in England at perhaps the most fertile time for English poetry and literature. *At last,* thought Lucille, *Someone who isn't focused on being seen at the latest 'in' club, and thank God he's not in the entertainment business.*

Lucille had several men tell her they wanted her to play a so-called 'ethnic' role. One wanted her for a daytime soap opera and the other for an evening situational comedy, neither of which came to pass. There were real producers and directors who frequented the Park Avenue receptions, men like David Geffen and Stephen Spielberg, though they never spoke to the Park Avenue girls about anything other than paintings and sculpture. John Dryden didn't look like a "loser" to her and if he were a public interest lawyer that was an indication of good character. Lucille was far from being a religious Jew and neither were her parents.

Lucille stood and offered John her hand. He was pleased to find that she had a firm dry handshake like a man, and not the limp fish, two-fingered salutation offered by all too many LA women. Her startlingly violet eyes looked into his. He liked her husky, contralto as she said, "Lucille Rosen. Pleased to make your acquaintance." She sat back down in her chair, "I'll buzz Sondra." Lucille pushed one of the buttons on her console. "Mr. Dryden is here. Yes, I'll tell him." She looked up at John. "She'll be right out." Within a few moments, Sondra waltzed into the reception area. John had to admit she was an astonishingly good-looking woman in the Charlize Theron, Cameron Diaz blue-eyed blonde mode. John had never bought clothes on Rodeo Drive, only his Gucci loafers once every six months or so, however he did window shop and knew that Sondra's rust-colored dress cost a lot more than he made in a week. She was a super flash girl who could turn heads, even in Beverly Hills, and John was willing to credit her with a modicum of substance as well as some amazing style.

She walked right up to him and shook hands every bit as firmly as Lucille had.

"Sorry I'm late," said John looking at his watch.

"Don't mention it. This is LA after all. Anything within 15 minutes is on time."

Sondra looked at him and he glimpsed a diffidence in her face that he suspected was uncharacteristic, and he found it intriguing. As annoying as it was, for John considered it incredibly shallow and prima facie evidence of an undeveloped primitive consciousness, he was feeling a powerful sexual attraction to Sondra's Barbie Doll good looks. He thought it was degrading and demeaning, and he detested himself for having the reaction, the more so as there was nothing he could do to negate it. He fought against her animal magnetism by thinking of Ahmed Nahabedian.

She smiled at him. "Could we talk outside for a few minutes?"

"Sure."

The two walked outside and John noticed the islands of flowers separating the northbound lanes from the southbound lanes. The white, pink, and yellow petunia blossoms were very different from the filthy dirty concrete islands on Tweedy Boulevard. There were no Southgate or RTD buses roaring up and down, belching noxious plumes of unburnt diesel fuel in the faces of motorists and passersby, no heart stopping, thumping hip-hop assaulting the ears and the body, only the burble of the huge SUV's and the whine of a

Porsche, or even a Ferrari. They stood on Rodeo just outside the door. "So what's up?" said John. "I'm here at your invitation. I understand the sexual harassment suit is off."

Sondra said somewhat awkwardly, "Well, I thought I was a victim. Well, hell, I am a victim. It's just that things aren't so bad right now."

"Speaking as a man, not a lawyer, I personally think sexual harassment is pretty close to rape. There's just no excuse for it."

"John, please forgive me for calling you at your home. Using gallery clients for personal reasons isn't right. It's just I felt cornered and I don't any more. Call me a willing victim, call me a coward, call me a sell-out, whatever you want. If it's all the same to you, let's leave things status quo."

"As I said on the phone, it's fine with me. By the way, congratulations on your promotion."

Sondra spoke somewhat combatively, "I deserve the position. I have a BFA and I know as much about contemporary art as anyone in the department except for the director."

John looked at her and shrugged his shoulders. "I never said a word, and Sondra if you don't mind me saying so, you seem a little defensive." A flash of anger instantly transformed Sondra's angelic face into a frightening, thin-lipped, snarling mask. The look of hatred lasted for such a brief time that John thought he might have imagined the whole thing, and then once more her face was the ideal of the fair-haired, fair-skinned young Northern European young woman. Sondra wasn't one to tolerate anyone "pulling her covers" as the current saying went, and especially not penniless lawyers from Southgate entering or in their forties. Nonetheless, she smiled sweetly.

"I'm really sorry, can I have a rain check on lunch? I'm really swamped, this being my first day and all."

*Why you little bitch,* thought John. *I drive all the way up here and you didn't have the courtesy to call and cancel. You're pissed because I told you the truth.* He gave Sondra an artificial smile, all teeth.

"I'm the one who needs the rain check. Well, best of luck on your new job." He purposely used the word job instead of position, and Sondra knew he was being catty and that he thought she had ill used him and abused his good nature.

*Tough titty,* she thought. She smiled sweetly. "Thank you, John. I knew you'd understand."

"Be seeing you," said John, and he turned his back on her and walked down Rodeo without shaking her hand or even giving her a second glance. He was talking to himself as he walked. "What a bitch. If only she knew about the painting she'd be kissing my ass literally. Well, that'll be one cold day in Hell." John wasn't paying attention to where he was going and stepped on a large wad of bubble gum with his left foot then felt the tug as he lifted his shoe. It wasn't a big thing, but he was sufficiently pissed off to begin with so it only added to his ire, and now he was hungry as well. He thought there might have been some chemistry between him and the receptionist, however the ring on her finger put him off, and knowing how women talked about men even more than men discussed women, he figured Sondra wouldn't waste any time recounting how she'd stood him up. "Screw it," he said to himself. "I'll stop on the way and get a couple of steak tacos. Better than a stupid salad any day."

The prospect of Francisco's tacos coupled with the balmy weather brightened the day to the point of whistling part of the soundtrack to the first Lord of the Rings film. He reached the lot on Canon and he wondered why neither Lucille nor Sondra had commented on his black eye. That morning he thought it made him look like a raccoon.

Sondra walked back in the gallery and Lucille looked at her somewhat taken aback. "What happened? That was a real short lunch."

"While we were talking he got a call on his cell. Some court thing. He had to go. Just as well; I've got a ton of work to do."

"Is he married?"

Sondra snickered, "If he's married, I'll shave my head like Britney Spears."

"Where do you think he got that black eye?"

"Certainly not from a woman. Nerd probably walked into a door on his way to the bathroom."

Lucille had refrained from asking him about the shiner in the event it might have embarrassed him. Sondra hadn't commented because she wanted to truncate the conversation as much as possible, and thought by ignoring it she'd avoid a potentially lengthy and tedious anecdote.

Lucille said, "Can I have his number?"

Sondra looked at her. She felt protective. "Listen honey, he's not God's gift to women. You're way out of his league. He deserves some Valley girl from Chatsworth who'll pee her panties just to go out with a lawyer."

"I think he's kind of cute."

Sondra looked at her dubiously, then rather sadly. "I'll give you his number."

The phone rang and Lucille answered it. "Yes, sir. Right away, sir! I'll tell her immediately." Lucille looked at Sondra. "That was Mr. Richardson he'd like to see you in his office."

Sondra used her left hand to smooth her perfectly coiffed hair. "How do I look?"

"Honestly," said Lucille, and she was being honest, "you look like you're ready to go to the Golden Globes."

"Thank you, I appreciate it. I'll give you Dryden's number after lunch. Oh, yes, cancel the reservation at Rodeo."

"Will do."

As he seated himself in the Camry, John decided to call Angus Creswell. He fished Creswell's card out of his billfold and punched the numbers into his cell phone. Lucille answered, trilling, "Park Avenue Galleries, good afternoon."

"Is Angus Creswell there?"

"Who shall I say is calling please?"

"Tell him it's John Dryden."

John thought Lucille's voice was very sexy, especially on the telephone. "Weren't you just here?"

"Ah yes, I was going to lunch with Sondra Huggins, but she cancelled on me."

Lucille thought to herself, *So he didn't have to go to court after all. Sondra just stood him up on the off chance the boss would take her to lunch. What a witch. And she made him drive all the way up here from Southgate.*

Lucille admired the candor of John's statement. Not too many men would admit that another woman just dissed him like that. He didn't need to make up a story to preserve his masculine ego. This was enough to make her take a risk.

"You could have come back in and asked me. I had a nice table on the patio reserved for two at Cafe Rodeo. Don't think I'm being catty when I say that Sondra is gorgeous, true enough, but with all that pulchritude come major issues of entitlement."

"Lucille, I may just take you up on that lunch. I really have to get back to my office now. Can I call you tomorrow?"

"Tomorrow's Saturday. We're closed. No exhibitions this weekend either."

"Listen. I have to drive down to see my grandfather in Del Mar. I see him every Saturday. Would you like to drive down there with me?"

Lucille considered this. Anyone who faithfully visited an aging relative, even if it were for selfish reasons, was probably a decent person and not some mentally deranged, psychopathic weirdo who'd paw her all the way to San Diego. Lucille thought he was cute for asking.

"Call me at five. I'll see if I can. Let's try the distinguished baronet, Mr. Creswell."

"He's a baronet?"

"Says he is. Knowing the immense premium the gallery places on snobbery, it wouldn't surprise me at all. A title of nobility is perhaps the single most valuable asset to those who wish to rise in the art world, or the auction business. Talent, knowledge, honesty mean little in comparison. All three put together don't count for half as much as a Sir or Lord added to the name of an ignoramus. And the ladies, baronesses and countesses are just as bad or even worse."

"You sound bitter."

"I'm not bitter at all, just realistic. So, you'll call me later?"

"On that account, you can be sure," said John.

Lucille had Angus Creswell on the other line. "Mr. Creswell, I have John Dryden on the line." Angus' pulse quickened in anticipation of talking to John, who had the potential to make him several times a millionaire in a very short period of time.

"Mr. Creswell, tell me. What do we know?" Angus thought in all likelihood his private phone was just that, however, on the off chance someone might be listening in either by accident or design, he wasn't willing to take a chance.

"John, at the risk of sounding paranoid, I must tell you this isn't the best place to discuss things. Anyone who wants to can listen in. We need privacy."

"It's that bad?"

"No, it's just that I'd prefer to talk in private. Are you in town?"

"I'm over in a parking lot on Canon. I was just leaving when I thought I'd call you."

Angus hoped he didn't sound as anxious or as desperate as he felt at the moment. To his dismay, his palm holding the receiver was actually damp.

"I'll tell you what," said Angus. "I'll meet you at your car. That way you won't have to waste time getting out of town. I imagine the Friday traffic going south is even more of a nightmare than it is during the rest of the week."

John had blissfully forgotten all about the Friday traffic. He'd driven in LA for 25 years and had yet to figure out where all the cars were going at 2:00 p.m. No one else could either, not even CalTrans. Obviously, none of the mid-afternoon commuters had 9-5 jobs, and Friday was invariably exponentially worse than any other day, as tens of thousands of cars frantically sought to flee the city. West of the 405 San Diego Freeway it wasn't too terrible. Unfortunately to reach his office, John had to go south and east, the two worst directions.

"You know the parking lot on Canon?"

"Yes."

"I'll be the tall guy with the black eye standing in the northwest corner of the lot next to the dark red Camry."

"Give me five minutes."

"I'd tell you to take your time, except you reminded me, it's Friday."

"I'll be there momentarily."

Angus walked out of his office and with barely a nod to Lucille, was out the door and walking over to Canon as quickly as he could without breaking into a jog. Down Rodeo, Angus paid no attention to any of the shop windows, even ignoring the display at Cartier, which he usually stopped to admire. The afternoon was warm enough to make him perspire and sweat trickled down his armpits as he walked. Angus entered the parking lot and saw John standing next to an undistinguished Toyota coup. He slowed his pace to a more dignified walk.

They shook hands and Angus asked him, "What brings you north to the Hills twice on successive days?"

"Actually I came up here at Sondra Huggins' request. She said she needed some legal advice, then she changed her mind."

"I'm not one to be telling any tales out of school when I say that girl will definitely need legal advice sooner or later. She's sleeping her way up the corporate ladder."

"I wouldn't be too hard on her," said John. "A girl's gotta' do what a girl's gotta' do. Face facts, at some level we're all sell-outs, so let he who is without sin cast the first aspersion."

"You're right," said Angus. "Forget what I said. I love my wife and wouldn't dream of sleeping around, much less dipping my quill in the gallery's ink so to speak. Still, I'm not blind, or so very ancient, and I must say that Sondra's a real looker."

"I'll say she is," said John. "She's simply breathtaking."

"Regarding the Van Gogh, I spoke with the Art Loss Register and the painting's not stolen as far as they or any law enforcement entity is concerned."

The look on John's face was beatific. "That being said, we've not won the Powerball Lottery quite yet. The painting belonged to Mr. Solomon Roth of Munich, a prominent banker and collector of French Impressionists. He had an even more impressive collection of the German Expressionists. Reichsmarshall Goering expropriated most of the collection. Mr. Roth's children were allowed to leave Munich for Buenos Aires late in 1939. This was an extraordinary mark of favor, doubtless a form of compensation for the lost art. Mr. Roth was not so fortunate, traveling first to Dachau, then to Auschwitz."

"So where exactly does that leave us?"

"Well, Mr. Dryden, I see it this way. The painting is not on the list of works sold under duress during the Nazi era. That being said, a public sale of such a piece would cause a host of would be claimants to spring up out of the ground as numerous as the children of the Hydra's teeth, and just as vicious with lawyers in their wakes."

"I told you, my grandfather isn't interested in a public sale."

"Questions of provenance and ownership are nothing new in the art world. Norton Simon, the Hunt's ketchup king, and quite likely the most discerning collector of Buddhist and Hindu sculpture in the 20th century, bought a fabulous 11th century Gupta bronze statue of Shiva, the god of destruction as lord of the dance, for a million dollars in the 1970's, when a million dollars was a vast sum for any work of art. The statue had been taken from the Sivapuram Temple that was very much in use. It was as if someone decided to remove the Ark of the Covenant from the Temple in Jerusalem, assuming it still existed. The sale caused an international uproar, and consequently the Shiva is no longer in Pasadena, but purportedly in a locked warehouse in southern India."

"So, as you say, a public sale is out and not just because my grandfather opposes one."

"No," said Angus, warming to the subject of repatriation. "The whole question of art repatriation is hardly new. It is as old as the controversy surrounding the Elgin marbles. Thomas Bruce, the 7th Lord Elgin, and English ambassador to the Ottoman Empire from 1799 to 1803, was a great lover of antiquities. He received permission from the Turkish High Porte to, and I quote verbatim, 'Take away any pieces of stone with old inscriptions of figures thereon.' As all of Greece was part of the Turkish Empire, Bruce proceeded to remove the friezes, pediment sculptures, and the statues from the interior walls of the Parthenon, among other ruins. George Gordon, Lord Byron, among others, accused Lord Elgin of rapacity, vandalism, and dishonesty. There was a Parliamentary investigation and in 1816 the entire collection was purchased by King George IV for 35,000 pounds, quite a bargain. For decades the Greek government has demanded they be returned, however their entreaties have fallen on deaf ears. Today there are UNESCO treaties governing national patrimony and national heritage.

"There is frequent litigation and the involvement of police agencies like INTERPOL and the FBI. Sotheby's no longer holds antiquities sales in America, and collectors of pre-Columbian pottery and gold have had their collections confiscated and the owners arrested."

John shook his head. "I know the very last thing my 80-year-old grandfather wants or needs, is to have his life disrupted with lawsuits, much less bothered by the FBI."

Angus nodded his head in agreement. "We're agreed on that. So now that we know it isn't stolen, or reported as stolen, my question is how far do you want me to take it? Should I try to contact the Roth family and ask them if they're missing a Van Gogh? There's a video on U-Tube of Sepp Dietrich's son on a German armored car shot in 2006."

John was surprised. "You're telling me an SS general's son would have a cognizable claim?"

Angus smiled thinly. "My friend, with millions involved there are always claims. Dietrich may have acquired the painting legitimately in which event, his heirs would be the rightful owners."

"I've done a little research and in 1946, the SS was declared a criminal organization."

"That's all well and good, however the fact remains that your grandfather cut the painting out of its frame and took it out of Dietrich's house. John, I'll do whatever you want me to as long as it's legal."

John wanted to sell the painting primarily for Hank's sake. Even though the money wouldn't alter the old man's life, the money certainly had the potential to radically change his own in ways he could hardly imagine, primarily because he hadn't yet allowed the prospect to be seen as a reality.

"We definitely want to sell it. First I need to talk it over with Hank."

"Do me a favor and ask him how much he wants to sell it for."

"I'm going to see him tomorrow. We'll talk about it then. I guess you and I need to formalize your fee. What do you think is fair?"

This was a question Angus had been asking himself ever since John showed him the painting. If he asked for too much John might balk altogether and look for a proper art dealer to represent him rather than using an arms and armor expert. Yet by offering his services too cheaply, Angus could very easily leave more money on the table than he would make in ten years working for Park Avenue and finessing the odd private sale.

Angus' stomach was normally robust, strong enough to function in Third World countries without an untoward gurgle, most recently in Heyerdabad, India, where he'd gone to look at the remnants of the Nizam's 19th century armory. Yet now here in Beverly Hills it was on the verge of a full-scale rebellion. It rumbled ominously and there was a spasm in his bowels that presaged a bout of stress diarrhea.

Angus knew John was a neophyte to the auction world, though that didn't mean he hadn't visited Sothebys.com and Christies.com, not to mention Park Avenue.com. The official he'd seen in India about the Nizam's collection of weapons had a current Bonhams' catalog of arms and armor on his desk with photographs of similar pieces marked with paperclips. The Internet was a two-edged sword and the ease with which a potential consignor could shop their treasures to see which gallery offered the most favorable terms was annoying.. Angus wished the Internet would tell prospects that high estimates and reserves did not always translate into high auction prices.

Too high an estimate and/or a reserve could kill the chances of a splendid work of art selling well at auction as easily as poor condition. This was very hard to explain to amateurs who always thought high estimates meant high prices. Angus made a choice to be fearlessly honest with John, and if his candor cost him the commission, at least Dryden could never accuse him of being less than absolutely forthright.

"I'll be perfectly frank," said Angus. "A piece like yours is of such a high value that Sotheby's or Christie's would not only refuse to charge you any commission, they may well offer you a negative commission, a rebate if you will, of two or three percent of the selling price, using their buyer's premium, which is normally considered sacrosanct and untouchable, however I can't say that with certainty."

John was thinking in terms of attorney's contingency fees, which ranged from 25% at the low end of the scale to 50% or even 60% at the high end with 40% being considered average. The fee structure was why personal injury, workman's compensation, and other lawyers could afford expensive billboards, print, radio, and even television advertising. John was thinking a 10% commission on the Van Gogh would be more than fair. Then again, Angus had just said the auction house might negotiate the buyer's premium.

"You've been up front with me and I think I should be with you as well. Would 5% be fair?"

Angus had been thinking 1% would be more than fair and even one half of one percent would be acceptable, assuming he didn't have to take a leave of absence from his position at the gallery. Five percent nearly took his breath away. It would be like winning the lottery only much better, because no one would ever know he'd won. The blood sang in his ears and he smiled as he said, "That's more than fair. It's really over the top if you want to know the truth."

"Then consider it an incentive," said John. "I really have to get going. It's Friday, and I'd like to get to Southgate sometime this afternoon."

Angus was trying desperately to keep control over his nerves and his bowels. "I'd best let you go then," he said.

John shook Angus' hand, opened the door to the Toyota, got in, started the engine, then rolled down the windows. "I'll call you tomorrow." Angus handed John his personal card, which read simply, Angus Creswell, in raised black letters, giving his home telephone number, cell phone number, fax, and his e-mail at creswellarmour@aol.com or acreswell@parkavegal.com

"Call or email me as soon as you and your grandfather agree on a price. We'll go from there."

John had the Camry backed up and ready to drive off. John said, "I'll call you."

As Angus walked to Canon his rebellious belly calmed down and he was confident he'd make it to the gallery where he'd relieve himself in peace, comfort, and privacy.

## CHAPTER 14

# Del Mar

JOHN PLOWED HIS way through the traffic on Wilshire Boulevard, west through Beverly Hills, past the Los Angeles Country Club on his right and on into Westwood, through the underpass below the north and southbound lanes of the 405 San Diego Freeway and took the long curving on-ramp to the 405 South. He was listening to a call-in show on KPFK Pasadena supposedly examining the legalities of the latest wiretap legislation being debated by Congress and its effect on what John firmly believed was the non-issue of domestic terrorism. His view was consistent with Hank's, which was that a nation that was so willing to sacrifice freedom for security deserved neither one. He waited for the traffic meter light to turn green, though he could see the freeway looked like a parking lot and would be stop and go, but more stop than go until well past LAX. He gritted his teeth, changed the radio station to KUSC for some classical music, and made up his mind to take La Tijera east to Manchester and Manchester to Southgate.

A miserable 50 minutes later he was parked at Francisco's taco stand, seated in his car wolfing down two tacos, listening to NPR's All Things Considered. The food was excellent, as always, and he'd purchased two extra for his dinner. The tortillas absorbed the meat juices and tended to fall apart when reheated, though they were equally delicious and he didn't like to cook for himself. Cokie Roberts was discussing a Supreme Court decision and he tried to concentrate on it and not the Van Gogh. There had to be a catch somewhere. It was all too easy. Either Creswell was wrong and it was in fact stolen by the Nazis, or it a fake after all, or INTERPOL was looking for it. There had to be something. It was too easy.

"Then again," he thought, "I have $80,000 in cash sitting in my filing cabinet from an old pistol, so it's possible. If my mother had the slightest idea, she and that weasel Eddie would be camping on Hank's doorstep."

As he came east on Tweedy, John saw Southgate police cars parked at crazy angles in front of his building, lights flashing. There was a substantial group of gawkers and the side street, which he used to access the alley behind the building was blocked by two police motorcycles with their lights flashing. John hit the speed dial on his cell to call his office and continued eastbound. Carol answered the phone and John wasted no time, the painting and his potential windfall, forgotten for the moment. "Carol, would you please tell me what's going on?"

"I was going to call you, but I honestly haven't had the time."

As she said this, John saw an Eyewitness Channel 5 news van race past him going west followed by a Fox News GMC Yukon, and two other news minivans. Carol continued, "It happened about 20 minutes ago."

"What happened?" "Ahmed Nahabedian came in waving a big, black automatic pistol around. He was looking for you. His hair was wild and he looked like a madman. He was raving that you ruined his life and thanks to you, Judge Glass was going to put him in jail with a bunch of animals. I was scared, so I ducked behind my desk, then I heard this explosion and when I stood up, Ahmed was on the floor, lying in a pool of blood, with what looked like a large piece of his skull missing. I called 911 and half the Southgate police arrived. I would have called you, but to tell you the truth I was in kind of a state of shock until the police got here."

"Did he kill himself?"

"The police keep asking me the same thing and I don't know. I remember his tramping around and he could have tripped over the coffee table and shot himself accidentally; I just don't know."

"Well as long as you're all right, that's what I care about!" and John meant every word. His instinct was to turn around and head for Westchester thereby avoiding both the media and the authorities. He had no interest in the 15 minutes of fame, promised to everyone by Andy Warhol, coming to him that evening on television. He could easily imagine the taglines, "Lawyer drives slumlord to suicide," or in a best case scenario: "Legal entanglements prompt landlord to take his own life; tragic scene in Southgate lawyer's office." As much as the local media enjoyed doing sensational stories on Nahabedian's buildings and predatory rental practices when he was alive, the same reporters who reveled in giving the public images of rodent infested hallways, leaking water pipes, and piles of rotting refuse, would rush to reveal Nahabedian's immigrant roots, painting his story as a real American Horatio Alger type rags to riches saga.

Of course it would be nothing more than self-serving sanctimonious bullshit, but John was only too well aware that all too many Americans both based and nourished their view of the world on a steady diet of the prurient filth spewed out 24/7 by a media shamelessly pandering to the most basic and base voyeurism. There was also the fact that if there were only one life preserver left in a boat and one had to choose between giving it to a slumlord or an attorney, to a man, most Americans would toss the ring to the slumlord and saddest of all John wouldn't blame them.

"Shit, shit, shit," he muttered.

"Say what? John, where are you?"

"About five blocks east of the office."

"Well I hate to tell you this, but I think you should talk to the police."

"All right," he sighed. "I'll be there in a minute," and he snapped the phone closed.

He parked about three blocks away at a meter on Tweedy and walked toward the office. As he was walking, John was stopped by a Los Angeles Sheriff's Department deputy sheriff wearing reflecting aviator sunglasses and looked like a football lineman, and not much past twenty years old.

"Where do you think you're going?" he asked in a perturbed tone of voice, as if John were another gawker hoping for a glimpse of some ghastly sight so he could tell his friends all about it later at the local watering hole.

"I work in that building. It's my law office," said John somewhat nervously and pointing to the Yo Hablo Espanol sign.

"I'll just bet it is. Now if you'll just turn around and go back the way you came."

"No really, I'm John Dryden," and he reached inside his jacket for his billfold. The sheriff moved with astonishing celerity for such a large man. He swept John's legs out from under him and John fell heavily on his sacrum, jarring all the breath from his lungs. The sheriff bent down and snapped one handcuff around his left wrist, then brought his right wrist around and snapped the other handcuff around it. Manny, the Southgate motor officer saw the action as he emerged from the front door of John's office. He walked over to the sheriff, who was standing over John. John saw Manny and said loudly, "Manny!" The deputy looked at Manny, who was trying hard to keep a straight face.

"You know this guy?" said the deputy, a note of uncertainty creeping into his hitherto supremely confident, even arrogant tone of voice. Manny was tempted by the imp of perversity to reply in the negative, however one cross word from John to his mother would make his life a living hell.

"Yes, as a matter of fact I do." The sheriff's face fell as if he'd been given some bad news, then Manny could see him gutting it up.

"Don't tell me. He really is John Dryden and he's an attorney?" Manny just nodded. The sheriff's deputy thought it best to say nothing, unlocked the handcuffs, and helped John to his feet.

"Mr. Dryden. I'm very sorry about this. It's just when you reached into your coat suddenly like that, well you know how it looked to me." John was dusting the grit and grime of the Tweedy sidewalk from the bottom of his suit pants. He wasn't really injured, but he thought the man overreacted and believed this might be a so-called teachable moment.

"Deputy," John read the gold metal nametag with the embossed black enamel letters, "Armstrong. While I sympathize with your understandable and legitimate concerns for your personal safety, I can't help but think your action was, how shall I put it, over the top as the English say, all things considered."

*Fuck me*, thought Armstrong. *This guy's going to beef me and sue.*

Though Deputy Armstrong had only graduated from the Sheriff's Academy 18 months ago, and was working out of the Lynwood Station, he already had two civilian complaints in his jacket. If he received a third one, not only would he be verbally reprimanded by his lieutenant, he'd be lucky not to be interviewed by Internal Affairs and transferred to a more remote station like Walnut/Diamond Bar. Compounding the situation was the fact that the Southgate cop knew the man, though the brotherhood of the badge was a strong one, so he didn't think Manny would automatically side with him against the civilian. "Mr. Dryden," said Armstrong in a chastened voice, "I apologize. What else can I say other than I'm sorry."

His tone sounded sincere and John thought he'd made his point, so he held out his hand.

"No hard feelings," he said, looking the deputy in the eye as best he could into the mirrored sunglasses. Armstrong took off the shades with his left hand and shook John's hand with his right in a shake so firm it was close to a bone-crusher, though it wasn't intentionally so.

Manny escorted John past the barricades, the yellow crime scene tape and the newsmen, whose vans all had their telescoping broadcasting antennas. fully extended. The Channel 5 van's antenna was perilously close to the telephone lines. Once inside, Carol, who had been sitting on her desk sipping coffee from a white Styrofoam cup, left her perch and walked to greet him, passing the bulky body of Ahmed Nahabedian as she did so. John embraced Carol and he felt her breasts press up against his chest. Carol had grown up in Compton and seen her fair share of the aftermath left by street violence. Once the initial shock of seeing Ahmed lying dead on her office floor with a considerable portion of his left temple missing wore off, her pulse rate and her composure quickly returned to normal.

"For a moment there," she said, "I thought you might bail out on me and leave me all alone to face the wolves."

John smiled. "As I was driving down Tweedy I won't say I wasn't tempted. I mean really tempted." A Southgate police lieutenant who John didn't know at all walked up. He was a man of medium build in his late forties, though he looked older.

"Mr. Dryden, if you don't mind, I have a few questions for you."

John nodded and said, "Let's go to my office. It's in the back down the hall." The lieutenant's questions weren't difficult. John's answers didn't really help him answer the problem of whether to treat the man's death as a homicide, a self-inflicted gunshot wound, or death by misadventure. He was inclined to rule out homicide. John told him about Ahmed punching him out and the lieutenant accepted John's black eye as proof.

"People who are furiously angry are homicidal, not suicidal. He probably came here to frighten you because he was scared of going to jail, that's what my amateur psychology tells me right now. Somehow he ended up shooting himself. Your secretary said he was waving the gun around wildly. A 40 caliber Glock packs quite a punch. Sort of like a hot 357 magnum. How he managed to shoot himself in the head I don't know. I'll leave that for the medical examiner and the coroner. I might need you to give me a statement about the assault. Goes to state of mind. You might want to sneak out the back that is unless you want to be on the five o'clock news. I'll tell my people. Oh, yes. Let me give you my card. If you think of anything I might have missed, I'd appreciate it if you gave me a call."

John took the card, shook hands with the lieutenant and was left alone in his office. He looked at his watch and it was nearly five.

"Damn!" he said loudly. "I'd better call Lucille. John took Angus' card from his wallet, however it was the wrong one with all his private contacts and numbers. He punched in 411 on his desk phone and was forced to listen to the artificial intelligence information operator ask him, "What listing please?" John was in such a rush that he allowed the computer to connect him for an additional 50 cents, something he bitterly resented and never did on principle.

Lucille answered with the usual, "Park Avenue Galleries, good afternoon. How may I direct your call?" Her voice sounded much better than the electronic information operator's.

"Lucille, it's John Dryden." Lucille had been watching the fine, 19th century, American inlaid, wood banjo clock on the wall opposite her desk for the past 36 minutes. She'd been about to write John off as an undependable flake. This was a disappointment to her, as she'd made up her mind to accept his offer to ride down to Del Mar, and she'd cancelled a date with one of her girlfriends to go to the Huntington Library in San Marino. Lucille wasn't as interested in the railroad magnate's splendid collection of Gainesboroughs, Romneys, Reynolds and Lawrences or the fabulous library with its incunabula and other treasures as she was in the botanical garden, which was far and away the finest in Southern California.

"It's nearly closing time." said Lucille. John detected a slight though no less distinct undertone of perturbation in her voice. He wanted to dispel any thought she might be entertaining that he was one of those people who purposely waited before calling to confirm a date thinking to establish a power dynamic in which they imagined they had control of the relationship. John knew any number of lawyers who religiously followed this paradigm in negotiating damage awards, and he considered it to be evidence of a sick, manipulative mind.

"Lucille," he said quietly, "the man who punched me in the nose the other day came back this afternoon with a gun, and either accidentally or intentionally killed himself in my reception area."

He heard a sharp intake of breath through the earpiece of the receiver. "Oh, how horrible! "Were you there when it happened?"

"Fortunately not. I was stuck on the southbound 405. My poor secretary had to witness it."

"Oh, the poor woman. She must be in shock."

"Carol's worked for the Southern Center for Human Rights. She's seen executions. And she grew up in Compton. She's seen worse."

"It's still terrible. I'm so sorry."

John was about to say it would no doubt be on the evening news, then changed his mind, as he didn't want to seem like one of the many Angelinos that courted the camera. He'd escaped the media by using the backdoor. Carol refused to be intimidated and left out the front, repeating: "No comment," to the microphones being shoved in her face. She and John had agreed that it was necessary for one of them to run the media gauntlet and they'd used rock, paper, scissors to determine the unlucky winner best two out of three. The first contest ended with Carol's paper wrapping John's rock. In the second, John's rock blunted Carol's scissors, and the third ended with John's scissors slicing Carol's paper.

## CHAPTER 15

# Del Mar Saturday

JOHN WOKE EARLY Saturday without an alarm. He had never needed one, even in college. Either his circadian rhythm was not wholly dependent on darkness or daylight, or his hypothalamus, which scientists determined to be the master center for establishing patterns and integrating rhythmic information, had his internal biological clock almost perfectly synchronized with Pacific Daylight Time. All he ever needed to do was think of a particular time when he needed to wake up before he went to sleep and he'd awaken within 15 minutes of the exact time as indicated by the bright red LED display on his bedside clock. John didn't sleep in pajamas because he was uncomfortable with the way the sleeves would bunch up under his arms during the night. Consequently, he either slept in boxers or in the nude, depending on the season.

The sun was up and light was streaming through the east-facing window in the bathroom. He brushed his teeth with a Braun electric toothbrush using the tea tree oil toothpaste he bought from the Whole Foods Market in Marina del Rey. He showered quickly, then dressed in black Levis and a pale yellow, soft cotton shirt. He brushed his hair and looked in the mirror with an appraising eye. He wasn't entirely happy with what he saw. His hairline, while not receding too dramatically, showed definite signs of retreat compared to what it had been like in law school. As long as the process didn't accelerate over the next ten years he would reach the half-century mark still in possession of a respectable head of hair. His black eye was mellowing out nicely to a pale yellow, a shade appreciably lighter than his shirt. There were two unruly hairs in his left nostril that always regrew regardless of how many times he plucked them. They were wiry and Carol would always nag him about them. On the off chance Lucille might find them offensive, he grabbed the longer of the two hairs between his thumb and index finger and yanked. Whether his nose was more sensitive than usual because of Ahmed's punch, or because he wasn't fully awake yet, the thrill of pain as the hair was torn from its follicle brought tears to his eyes. John shook the renegade hair from his fingers and grasped the second one. This time the hair slid from his grip, and he had the pain with none of the success. He tried three more times and finally succeeded in pulling the offending hair along with several others that were well concealed within the confines of his nostril. With his eyes full of tears, John left his bathroom for the kitchen where he ground up a sufficient quantity of Fair Trade coffee beans to make two cups of strong black coffee. The fragrance of the freshly ground beans was something he looked forward to each morning.

As he listened to the whine of the Braun pulverizing the dark beans into a fine powder, John wondered if Lucille were going through any of the little contortions he was, like pulling potentially offensive nose hairs. He had enough experience with women to be aware that some would undergo far more complicated and painful rituals like plucking eyebrows, waxing leg hair, waxing pubic hair, facials, not to mention hours spent in hair salons torturing their scalp to make their hair conform to some pre-conceived notion of what it should look like taken from some fashion magazine. He didn't think Lucille was the sort who would flay and flagellate herself in a sacrifice to the fashion gods. He could easily see Sondra waxing her legs and private parts, ignoring the pain and inconvenience, knowing she was only perfecting the gifts which nature had already bestowed on her in such abundance. John had dated girls from divergent backgrounds, cultures, and socio-economic levels, and though he vehemently disagreed with men who claimed a knowledge of common female characteristics, one thing he thought he knew was that men from Jesus to Sigmund Freud, to talk show pop psychologists like Dr. Phil, really had very little understanding of women.

John knew the only reason Sondra Huggins had invited him to lunch in the first place was that she suffered mild guilt about calling him at home and pumping him for free legal advice. Still, he had to give Sondra credit, as most women who looked as good as she did wouldn't hesitate to use him or any other man, and demand he think being used by her was a rare privilege. Being used by beautiful women had a long and illustrious history even before Alexandros, better known as Paris, awarded the golden apple to Aphrodite rather than to Athena or Hera. In return, Paris received the most beautiful woman on earth: Helen of Troy.

Sipping the rich, black coffee from his Loyola University mug, he wondered if he should tell Lucille about the Van Gogh. He tacitly assumed she was Jewish, both from her olive complexion and exotic facial features, as well as her last name. He thought she could possibly be sensitive to the painting having come from an infamous SS general. Then again, she might think it was only justice that the painting was "liberated" by an American GI. He didn't want to present himself as some kind of art aficionado or enthusiast, because he really wasn't. There were works of art to which he responded viscerally, however he'd never bothered to analyze or criticize either the nature or the basis for his liking or disliking a certain artist's work or oeuvre, as the experts referred to it. John did think the boundary between decorative art and so-called fine art, between art and craft, had been erased ever since Pablo Picasso put a pair of handlebars on a bicycle seat and called it sculpture, and Marcal Duchamp signed a urinal, R. Mutt. John didn't respond to Damien Hurst labeling a shark in a tank of formaldehyde as art. He reluctantly and grudgingly accepted Jackson Pollock's drip paintings, but refused to take seriously Andy Warhol's Campbell's Soup cans, Roy Lichtenstein's cartoon paintings, or Jasper Johns' American Flags. He didn't care how many people paid tens of millions of dollars for any of them. He thought they were all suffering from a collective form of insanity. Discretion being the better part of valor, especially on a first date, he thought he'd best keep such opinions to himself, principally as they were emotional and not reasoned responses, and there was the old Roman adage, de gustibus non disputandum est, "in the matter of taste there can be no dispute."

When John arrived at the long gray two-story stucco building on the west side of Beverly Glen Boulevard south of Little Santa Monica, he saw Lucille waiting. She was standing on the sidewalk dressed in designer jeans and a rust colored, V-neck cashmere sweater. She was looking at her watch. There had been the usual five miles of dead stopped traffic on the 405 North, beginning at Manchester and only thinning out as he passed the Santa Monica Freeway interchange, so he was five minutes late. Her face brightened when she saw the red Pontiac. John pulled over to the curb and she opened her door, settled in and buckled her shoulder belt.

"I didn't know they had shoulder belts in these old cars."

John smiled, "They didn't. I had then installed for safety. When I got it, the car only had lap belts, which are better than nothing, but not a whole lot better."

"That's all they give us on the airplane."

"Yes, and I've always resented it. You don't see the flight attendants wearing stupid lap belts. Oh no, they get rear facing seats with infant car seat type, over the shoulder restraints."

"Passengers are expendable, number one, and number two, passengers wouldn't like rear facing seats with complex restraints."

"People are like roaches, they adapt. The real reason is safety costs money."

"Well," said Lucille patting her shoulder belt, "I'm happy you think your passengers are worth saving."

John passed Olympic because there was no southbound onramp to the 405 and there wasn't one off Pico either. He'd make a right on Pico and a left on Overland, and take the onramp to the 10 Freeway West to the 405 South. Lucille wasn't paying attention to John's strategy to escape from LA. She was listening to the low burble of the GTO's exhaust, the feel of the pavement through its extra heavy-duty suspension, and the interested looks on the faces of the usually blasé pedestrians as they drove by. It was a typical LA early summer morning with bright sunshine, already a balmy seventy-nine degrees, and the Orthodox Jews were walking down the sidewalk dressed in their somber, dark suits, wearing their yarmulkes on their way to Shabbat services at the temple on the north side of Pico. John glanced at them and over at Lucille, who he noticed with a thrill in his solar plexus, wasn't wearing a bra. The thin cashmere clung to her less than full breasts, which were the size of medium apples. For a moment, John thought they might be enhanced, they were so round, and he was disappointed to think that Lucille would have considered herself inadequate, then again he knew far too little about her to judge her in any way, much less over something so intensely personal and private. She couldn't help noticing John looking at her chest and though she said nothing, Lucille was pleased with his attention. During the work week she always wore a bra, however come the weekend, she usually went braless just for the sheer pleasure of not having an elastic restraining device strapped around her chest, especially when the weather was warm enough to make her sweat. She only wore a sweater because she knew the temperature at the beach would be quite a bit cooler than in town, and if there were a marine layer in Del Mar as there often was in Santa Monica or the Marina, it could actually be quite cold and damp. Since she was a junior in high school, Lucille had always felt herself blessed with her breasts. They had taken their sweet time growing and she was quite flat chested all through eighth grade, much to her dismay. Then late in her thirteenth year they began to bud quite nicely until they were large enough to fill a blouse or sweater quite adequately, though not so heavy as to require a brassiere at all times. They were unusually round, which misled more than one man into thinking she had implants, something she took as a compliment rather than an insult.

"In case you're wondering," she said, "they're one hundred percent original equipment, as received from the manufacturer." John blushed a fiery red. He could feel the flush on his neck.

"I wasn't, I mean I didn't mean to stare." He was so completely discomfited and so boyish in his chagrin that Lucille, who wouldn't have minded if he'd been staring with lewd and lascivious thoughts in mind, was charmed and disarmed.

"You've heard the expression, don't get out much," said John. "Well, I really don't get out that much. What I mean is that I haven't been in my car with a pretty girl, except for my secretary slash paralegal, for quite a while. You'll have to pardon me."

Lucille was very tempted to lift up her sweater and really give him something to stare at. The only reason she didn't was she didn't want to give him the mistaken impression that it was easy to get into her designer jeans. That, and she didn't want him to have an accident. She mastered the impulse and smiled at him, "Don't worry," she said with a lilting tone, "I'm not one of those girls that values a man simply because he goes out with a lot of other females. Fine feathers are hardly indicative of fine birds, nor are many mates, not that I have any objection to fine feathers when they're part of the whole package. After all, say what we like, we do judge books by their covers until we know the contents. It's human and animal nature, and anyone who claims that he or she doesn't is deluding themselves."

John was attracted to both Lucille's thought process as well as her candor. In LA where style nearly always trumped substance, and form ruled over content, he found Lucille's way of looking at and practicing interpersonal dynamics refreshing and novel. He had been cruising down the avenue at forty miles per hour in fourth gear at slightly over 2200 rpm, and the green and white sign for the 10 Freeway West was coming up on his left. He very rarely floored the GTO, allowing all six barrels of the three Holley carburetors to open fully. The stop and go nature of Los Angeles city driving caused unburnt carbon to build up and going full throttle resulting in a plume of black exhaust smoke, not half as thick or noxious as an RTD bus. Nevertheless, John could see how any driver behind him might find it mildly offensive. He made his left turn onto the onramp and he had a good quarter mile of clear road in front of him.

"Would you mind if I open the car up a little?"

"Not at all," said Lucille. "My father, rest his soul, thought the two very best things about America were its inexpensive, fast, luxurious cars and what he called its 'magnificent highways.' I know enough about muscle cars to tell you that yours has a 389 cubic inch engine and that's a close ratio Hurst gearshift. So as long as we're not going to be pulled over for reckless driving, have at it."

John double clutch downshifted into second and punched it, causing the Goodyear Bluestreak Speedway Special tires to chirp and Lucille was pushed into her seat by g-forces as the Pontiac accelerated from 35 to 75 in less than four seconds. John had speed shifted from second to third so the transition was unnoticeable except for the lower exhaust note of the lower gear and the snick of the Hurst shifter as the gears in the transmission meshed perfectly. The sensation was similar to, though not as powerful as, taking off in a Southwest Airlines 737. Lucille was reminded of her father's tales of his old Dodge 440 Coronet, which her mother insisted he sell shortly after she married him. He always talked about buying a Ferrari 308GT, though Rachael kept him behind the wheel of an eminently sensible and practical Volvo sedan until he died unexpectedly of a coronary at age 54. Lucille was 23 at the time.

John merged smoothly onto the 10, exhaust booming under the Overland Avenue overpass, and he could see traffic already beginning to slow in the distance where the connector from the 10 West to the 405 South choked two lanes down to one. John downshifted from fourth in anticipation of the slowdown and looked over at Lucille expecting a smile, and instead he saw her cheeks were wet with tears.

"Is there something wrong?" he asked softly. The morning broadcast of the BBC World Service was over and there was a rebroadcast of an old edition of Ira Glass's This American Life on KPFK, which wasn't one of his more inspiring chronicles, so John hit the CD button, which gave him an Emmy Lou Harris album. He decided it was too melancholy and changed it to Dvorak's Symphony number 7 in D minor. Lucille sniffed and dried her eyes with her hands, using the sides of her index fingers.

"I'm sorry," she said. "I'm very emotional about certain things. It's a character flaw I have. I could see the pleasure you were getting from your car and all I could think about was all the years my father spent behind the wheel of his Volvo, when in his heart he yearned for his Dodge Coronet with the huge V-8. I know it sounds incredibly childish, stupid, and even pathetic when you consider all the people in the world that are starving, gasping for breath from one minute to the next, or in mortal agony from trauma wounds, third-degree burns, cancer, kidney stones, whatever. Still, I know my father had to chisel off pieces of his square peg soul to fit in the round hole of social convention, and the Volvo was just one visible manifestation of his self-mutilation. So when I saw your spirit soar for those few brief seconds, I saw superimposed on that vision of sheer joy, a portrait of my father, like a bird beating his wings against the bars of a cage, a cage of his own making and choosing to be sure. Like Jacob Marley's ponderous chain in the Christmas Carol, he too forged his own bonds link by link, until the burden of carrying their accumulated weight finally broke his heart."

Traffic on the 405 was dead stopped as cars merged and attempted to exit at Venice Boulevard. Generally the Pontiac ran cool with the needle of the temperature gauge comfortable to the left in the cool blue area and this morning was no exception. John regularly changed the thermostat as well as the water pump, the hoses, and all the drive belts, and flushed and drained the radiator each year. As a consequence of his rigorous maintenance schedule, he was as confident of the old Pontiac as he was of his Toyota.

John told Lucille the GTO was his father's dream vehicle. He told her how his grandfather and Luke had gone to the Pontiac dealer in Oceanside and ordered it. Luke had taken his new bride in the new car on their honeymoon up Route 1 to Carmel, where they stayed at the Highlands Inn for a week, hiking in Big Sur, horseback riding, and driving into San Francisco, all of which John only knew anecdotally, since less than a year later Luke was killed in action during the Tet Offensive in February near Hue. This last revelation made Lucille cry in earnest and tears poured from her eyes.

"You must have been a tiny baby," she said through her sobs, as if she could see him as a fatherless little baby, and she were weeping for everything that the infant and the deceased parent would never have.

"Actually, I wasn't even born when Luke died,“ said John, who wasn't made too uncomfortable by Lucille's open display of raw emotion. He did wonder how anyone so sensitive had survived on a planet so awash in human misery and suffering, much of it self-inflicted to be sure, without being on Prozac, Zoloft, Paxil, or some other psychotropic medication. One could either take drugs or withdraw from life to a greater or lesser extent to avoid the pain. She didn't act as if she were on drugs. Even if she were they weren't affecting either her mentation or perception.

"That's just so sad," she said and wiped her face and eyes with her hands. Lucille thought it was one of the most pathetic stories she'd ever heard, using the term in its purest sense as in an experience that arouses sympathy from the Greek word for suffering, and not the more colloquial use denoting scornful pity.

They were past the South Bay Curve, nearing the exits for the 110 Pasadena Freeway North, and traffic was moving briskly at sixty-five, although there were cars in the fast lane traveling at seventy or seventy-five. John knew on any Saturday morning there were black and white California Highway Patrol police interceptor Mustangs as well as Moto Guzzis looking for speeders, especially those weaving artfully in and out of the endless lines of cars.

"Actually," said John, "growing up fatherless wasn't all that bad. My grandfather, the man we're going to see, really stepped in, and my mother arranged it so I practically lived with him and my Gran for the first eleven years of my life. He'd worked for the power company since 1947, so when he inherited me he already had twenty years seniority; he could pretty much engineer his schedule around mine. He was there for more school plays, PTA meetings, and little league games than most of the other kids' dads, and Gran was there for me when I was a baby, so though I might have missed out on having a biological father, I didn't grow up fatherless. Hank was the best father any kid could ever dream of having. I received the benefit of everything he and Gran learned raising my father."

"And now you see him every weekend."

John said proudly, "Last year I missed two Saturdays out of 52. It isn't like I feel I owe it to him. It's not like that at all. I want to see him. He's been my best friend since I can remember, my whole life. That's going on forty years."

"He sounds like an amazingly warm and generous person."

"He's a truly remarkable man and I love him with all my heart."

"You said he fought in World War Two. He must be in his eighties."

"Actually he enlisted on his seventeenth birthday in November of 1944. He pestered his mother until she gave him written permission. He won the Silver Star at the Battle of the Bulge. He was totally against the Korean War, but it was Vietnam that put him over the edge, and not just because my dad died there. Hank opposed the Diem regime as early as 1956, writing letters to President Eisenhower denouncing American support for the man who opposed the Geneva Accords elections, was stridently anti-Buddhist and ran a regime rife with corruption and nepotism. Ngo Dinh Diem made Saddam Hussein look like a model ruler.

When Kennedy started sending thousands of military advisors in 1961, Hank was writing letters and sending angry telegrams, though he was an ardent supporter of Kennedy at the time. FBI agents came to question him, and far from intimidating him, they only increased his belief that America was committing a criminal act in Vietnam. When my dad told him he was enlisting, it broke Hank's heart, however Luke was going over as a medic to save lives, so there wasn't a whole lot Hank could say."

John talked about Hank's post-Vietnam anti-war activism and his current support of Code Pink and the Randolph Bourne Institute, his disgust with what he regarded as the prevailing climate of fascism in America that most people were happy to embrace as long as their own personal oxen weren't being gored, how the so-called Founding Fathers, especially Thomas Jefferson, would have encouraged a revolt against the government as it was presently constituted. Hank detested the American peoples' supine acceptance of the war in Iraq. In his view it was an elective war if there ever were one. He despised the support for it, which he regarded not as patriotism but treason.

As they were passing by Mission Viejo, Lucille felt enough pressure in her bladder that she wasn't certain she'd be able to hold it all the way past Camp Pendleton to Del Mar. Lucille had never been to Del Mar, though she had been to San Diego several times, and once to San Ysidro, where she and some girlfriends took the bus across the border to Tijuana for the day. She was startled and appalled by all the small brown children busily hawking tiny packets of chewing gum to the gringos and gringas traveling north. Their dark dirty skin, straight black hair, and shining black eyes haunted her dreams for weeks afterward, something she'd never told her three girlfriends, who'd simply regarded the excursion as a lark to buy cheap leather goods and silver jewelry. Lucille didn't know if any of the three girls saw the Indian children as she did. To her, they were a youthful form of the ubiquitous shopping cart people that most Angelinos stepped over or around from time to time with less concern than they would have shown avoiding stepping in dog shit. Perhaps they did see them and assumed the children weren't their concern and the situation while deplorable, wasn't anything they could do something about. Not that Lucille thought she could do anything to change their having to grow up breathing diesel exhaust for hours to make a few extra pesos or American quarters. There was the occasional one or rarely a five dollar guilt offering, thrust out at the very end of white hands through a driver's or passenger's window, a window which was immediately rolled up tight afterward.

As they drove by the bright orange tiled roofs of the Spanish style buildings and the blossoms that formed the large Mission Viejo sign on the hillside to the East of the freeway, Lucille announced, "I have to pee." John eased into the far right lane and took the next off-ramp, not sure if there were a service station at the bottom or not. There was a Chevron off to the right, and he pulled in and parked next to a pump.

"You go ahead," he said. "I might as well top it up as long as we're here." John inserted his credit card in the reader and pressed the button for premium fuel. Even though the premium gas was several octane levels lower than the regular gas refined in the late 1960's, it would have to do. The only place he knew of that sold true high-octane fuel was a Union 76 station on Chatauqua in Santa Monica Canyon, and they charged a dollar more per gallon than the highest priced unleaded premium. The GTO seemed to adapt to the 93 octane unleaded Chevron premium without too much incomplete detonation or "pinging" and though the absence of lead was probably having a negative effect on his cylinder heads and engine block, his mechanic, a muscle car enthusiast, had carefully recalibrated the carburetors to drink the unleaded fuel. Lucille came back just as he was shaking the nozzle to be certain no drops of gasoline spattered on the enamel paint, although considering how much hand-rubbed carnauba wax was on the car, any spilled fuel would wash off harmlessly with a little water. John inserted the nozzle in its holder, twisted the gas cap locking it into place, and flipped the flap closed.

He opened the door for Lucille, and she squeezed gracefully between the island and the car as she got in. John walked around the front of the car and thought momentarily about checking the oil, then dismissed the idea. He was fanatical about changing the oil and filter every two thousand miles, and carefully inspected the smooth clean concrete floor of his garage for any leaks before he even started the engine.

Soon the twin, white, concrete cooling towers of the San Onofre Nuclear Power Plant were in view off to the right as the 5 Freeway neared the Pacific Ocean for the first time, since it began at the Oregon border. The towers looked exactly like two female breasts complete with protuberances on top that were the size and proportions of nipples. The morning sun was dazzling, and the snow-white sand of the beach, the creaming Pacific swell, the light and dark blues of the water, and the aqua blue of the sky were a feast for the eyes.

Lucille said playfully, "I'll bet I know one of the thoughts you've had in the past few minutes."

John figured she was referring to the twin cooling towers and said, "That's a wager I wouldn't make, because I know I'd lose."

"I read somewhere that McDonalds made the Golden Arches and the logo purposely to make people think unconsciously of their mother's breasts when they see them."

"Yes, I heard that too, though I don't think those towers are very subliminal. More like blatant."

Lucille laughed. "Yes, I think so, too. What does your grandfather think of nuclear power?"

"He's all for it as long as companies are willing to pay the costs of safe storage for the waste. Of course Hank says there's no mandate for safe storage, so he's against it as presently constituted. He's all for conservation, and that's what he was in charge of at the power company for the last ten years of his career."

"But if people use less electricity, then power company revenues will decline."

"Grandfather says energy conservation represents an inherent conflict of interest, like civil attorneys telling people to file fewer lawsuits, or divorce lawyers telling their clients to work out their differences outside the courtroom. All the lights people leave on in their houses, yards, and especially office buildings makes him crazy."

"He probably doesn't like Las Vegas."

"That's the understatement of the day. Between the misuse of Colorado River water to nurture a city that has no business being there in the first place, the profligate waste of electrical energy and the fact that the entire purpose of the place is to separate people from their money in the most obvious, tawdry manner imaginable, he loathes the city. I was trying to quote him. He can go on for hours naming statistics. Please don't mention Las Vegas under any circumstances unless you want to hear a Jeremiad."

"Are there any other subjects to avoid?"

"Please don't talk about Iraq, anything to do with terrorism, the government, politics, consumerism, economics, health care, things like that." Lucille hadn't been all that keen on meeting Hank, particularly as it was her first date with John. Meeting a close relative on the first date was to be expected in high school, however as adults, such a meeting generally took on a different tone, as it could be seen as prefatory to taking a relationship to a more serious level. Her initial interest in John was sparked by Sondra's desultory comment that he was a public interest lawyer and Dawn's opinion that he was cute. The day Sondra stood him up, she was able to agree with Dawn, and John's candor in admitting he had been stood up had added to her favorable impression. She was surprised by his invitation to drive to Del Mar and she debated with herself long and hard before making up her mind to accept. When he didn't call until almost five o'clock yesterday afternoon, she was about to tell him to go to hell until she heard his explanation. Now as her gaze drank in the beauty of the brown foothills and sand dunes, and beyond them, the blue Pacific dappled with the flashes of a thousand wave prisms reflecting the strong sunlight of the late morning, Lucille was more than glad she'd come.

"I guess art is a safe subject," she said.

"Oh, yes," laughed John. "Very safe. Literature, the arts, films, history provided it's pre-1900, no forget that, otherwise you'll hear Hank's own abridged version of Bury My Heart at Wounded Knee, or how all America's wealth has its roots in the African slave trade."

"The more you tell me about his views the more fascinating he sounds. Whatever made him so idiosyncratic? Was his father some kind of communist or socialist?"

"No, and from what I know speaking to my mom, Hank was pretty much your typical California boy growing up. The war changed him. I know the death camps changed his outlook on life in general. The fact that Roosevelt and Churchill knew all about them early in 1944 or even 1943, yet didn't even bomb the train tracks leading to Auschwitz, Treblinka, and the rest. There were countless tons of bombs available to drop on women and children in Dresden, incinerating as many innocents as at Hiroshima or Nagasaki, and yet there wasn't a single bomb dropped on the train tracks in Poland. Well, let's just say Hank spoke very little about the war until Korea when he became a closet pacifist."

"How did all that square with the good old boys at the power company?"

"I don't think they ever knew. He didn't really go public with his views until Kennedy sent those additional 10,000 'advisors' into Vietnam. Even then he didn't take his radicalism to work with him. When he made the local papers as a leader of World War Two Veterans Against the War, there were men who called him a coward and a flag burner. However, he did have his Silver Star, which he returned to the Secretary of the Army with a scathing letter, and the papers printed that story, too. Remember back then the government and the media weren't as inseparable as they are today, and the fourth estate would occasionally speak truth to power. Now he maintains his own blog, a website, and sends his social security checks to anti-war causes in addition to large checks from his other income."

"Do you ever see your mom?"

"Mom's kind of a sore subject," he sighed. "I love her because she's my mom and I know she had a hard row to hoe being widowed after less than a year of marriage, left pregnant, essentially penniless, and dependent on her father-in-law, She did the best she could under the circumstances, which was to leave me with Hank when I was one, finish her degree, and begin a career as a commercial artist. Then she met this lawyer whose mission in life is to defend incompetent doctors and hospitals from having to face the consequences of their negligence, donate money to the Republican Party, and protect the status-quo with every fiber of his being."

"I take it the lawyer and Hank don't get along."

"No, Eddie thinks Hank is almost as bad as Osama Bin Laden, and Hank sees Eddie as a twenty-first century Nazi."

"What about your mom? She had to be an idealist to marry your dad."

"The hippie girl of the 1960's sold out with a vengeance. She drives one of those Cadillac Escalades and hosts Republican fundraisers."

"When was the last time you saw your mom?"

"About a month ago. If she's in town, which she generally isn't, I see her on her birthday and I see her for lunch once in a while."

"What about the holidays?"

"I generally go to my paralegal's for Christmas Eve then on Christmas morning I'll drive down to Del Mar and spend the day with Hank. Sometimes we'll drive to the La Valencia Hotel in La Jolla and eat dinner, or we'll go to the Hotel Coronado on Coronado Island in San Diego. How about you?"

"I don't really do that much for the holidays. I'm not that religious. I go to temple for a few hours on Yom Kippur and that's about it. I don't observe Chanukah and I have nothing against Christmas except it's little more than an excuse to spend money thoughtlessly. I like the decorations that Beverly Hills hangs over Wilshire and all the colored lights. They're cheerful." John would have liked to ask Lucille about her mother, but he figured if she wanted to talk about anything having to do with her parents she'd do it, and if she didn't it was because she didn't want to for some reason.

John took the exit for the Del Mar Racetrack heading west, and the two-lane road ended at California Route 1, the Pacific Coast Highway. John made a left at the junction and a short time later he parked in the driveway of Hank's home. Hank heard the low rumble of the GTO's exhaust and walked to the bathroom where he dry swallowed two Percocet tablets. He'd spent the morning hoping the pain from his kidney stones would lessen from the quart of cranberry juice he'd drunk. When he heard John's car he said to hell with homeopathic remedies and took the narcotics. His stones weren't responding to ultrasound and he wasn't having surgery. Hank had a relatively high pain threshold and for him to take two codeine pills was unusual. Since he seldom took them, Hank could depend on the drug to be effective when he needed it, and he figured that within fifteen minutes, he'd be relatively pain free. He very much looked forward to John coming on Saturday and he knew the six-hour round trip took some effort, so he wanted to be with his grandson and not have his attention focused the entire time on the sharp, stabbing pains in his lower back. He had hardly slept at all the previous night, partly due to the pain in his kidneys, partly because sleep at his age was somewhat elusive under the best of circumstances. And as much as he hated to admit it even to himself, he was excited at the prospect of selling his Van Gogh. For sixty years, give or take a couple, he had kept it a secret from everyone except Emily, who'd dismissed it as the work of some talented art student. It had rested quietly, hidden with Dietrich's Walther and the books as he referred to them, in his closet. Now was the time to do something, before he passed on to whatever, if anything, lay beyond this life, and Hank could see no reason why there wasn't something besides the conscious world. In fact, he thought the Hindus and the Buddhists were correct in seeing existence as a wheel, rather than some linear progression with a finite definable beginning and end. He had yet, despite his eighty years, to figure out the purpose of life, except to think of it as a process of trying to perfect one's spirit so as to eventually, whether in the present incarnation or a million incarnations, merge with the original energy that created all worlds and all universes. This energy was the Unknown and Unknowable that man was forced to reduce to an anthropomorphic form he called God or Theos.

In the time it took Hank to walk from the bathroom to the bedroom to fetch his old Bass penny loafers, the pain had already receded by a degree. He knew there was no way the codeine could possibly affect him so quickly, so it must be his mind anticipating the relief and making it a reality. Hank generally left the screen door unlocked and the white, painted wooden door open when weather permitted, which in Del Mar was most of the year. Aside from the four to six weeks in late spring or early summer when the marine layer didn't dissipate until early afternoon, and the brief rainy season that usually ensued in February, the weather in Southern California, and particularly San Diego, was in Hank's opinion and millions of others as well, pretty close to ideal. The temperature was never so cold that a man needed to wear more than a sport jacket or sweater or so warm that one was driven indoors by excessive heat.

John opened the screen door for Lucille and he followed her in.

"Your grandfather just leaves his door open?"

"Del Mar is a long way from Los Angeles. Aside from the occasional burglary and the usual domestic disputes, there's very little violent crime here."

Lucille and John made it to the very modest living room when Hank called out.

"Is that a woman's voice I hear?" and he walked quickly into the room. At eighty, Hank Dryden was still nearly six feet tall, standing in his loafers, and Lucille could see where John got his stature. Hank's skin had the characteristic fragile, parchment quality of advanced age, and although his face had its share of wrinkles, they were mostly from exposure to the sun. Hank had John's intense blue eyes, and more than half the hairline he had as a young man. His hair was still thick and an attractive gray rather than white. Hank disliked having visible nose and ear hair. He spent time in front of a mirror each week, tweezers in hand, eliminating them both. The skin hanging under his lower jaw, like the skin hanging from his upper arms, was a sad though unavoidable consequence of old age, and nothing short of cosmetic surgery, or stretching the skin taut by putting on weight was going to improve the situation, and Hank considered the cure in either case to be more disgusting than the condition. He was wearing a pair of well-worn, light brown corduroy pants and a beige golf shirt. Lucille thought he looked very much like she'd pictured him being from John's stories and his description. Lucille thought he looked quite vibrant considering his age, and handsome in his own way. If John only aged half as gracefully, he'd be a fortunate old man.

Hank was shocked to see Lucille. She was dark and exotic looking, beautiful in the way Elizabeth Taylor had been in A Place in the Sun and Giant, and not at all like the Barbie doll types that John seemed to be attracted to. He said in a hearty, welcoming voice, "John, it's good to see your face, boy." He turned to Lucille and smiled, revealing a remarkably well-preserved set of teeth, carious to be sure, but fairly white and quite complete.

"And this lovely lady is…"

"Lucille," she said, putting out her right hand, which Hank took in his large warm paw and pressed lightly.

"I'm pleased to meet you, Hank Dryden."

"It's my pleasure. I've heard so many things about you, I feel as if I already know you."

"He's probably been telling you all about his wildly eccentric grandfather, what subjects to avoid talking about for fear I'll go off and get up on my soapbox like the English cranks at Speaker's Corner in Hyde Park. Am I right or wrong?"

Lucille couldn't help herself and started giggling. "You know your grandson, Mr. Dryden."

"Hank," he said with a twinkle in his eye. "Since I see you're a lady of discernment, you can call me Henry if you like, or even Harry, but none of this Mr. Dryden nonsense."

John was taken slightly aback. Hank rarely allowed anyone to call him Henry much less Harry, not that Hank had anything against the name Henry, it just wasn't what people called him.

Lucille smiled at Hank. "Henry it is then. I love the name Henry."

"Grandpa," said John, "you don't even let me call you Henry."

"I want Lucille to feel privileged."

"Well, I do," said Lucille. "And I want you to know it's appreciated."

Lucille really was appreciative. Generally, she was an acute judge of human character when there was sufficient distance to prevent passion from coloring vision. Of all the adults she'd encountered in the past three months, none could compare to Henry or John. Lucille had a positive visceral response to both men, and the usual unease she experienced from being in a stranger's home vanished within moments, something that was foreign in her experience.

"It's been a long time since I saw my grandson with a pretty girl, or any girl for that matter." As much as John prized his grandfather's habitual candor, this angered him. Even though John never considered himself a player as far as women were concerned, neither was he the shy, retiring, wallflower type, and as much as Lucille didn't seem like the sort of girl who'd be attracted to a playboy, she was a good-looking female who undoubtedly had any number of suitors.

"Don't say that. You're embarrassing me, Grandpa."

"Please don't be on my account. I told you I don't find a man more attractive or desirable simply because he's being pursued by other women. As a matter of fact the less he puts himself out there the better, as long as he isn't deliberately playing hard to get. I like to flirt, but flirting's not game playing, and most men are too obtuse to distinguish between them. One is an art, the other artifice, as in artificial. As in posturing for its own sake."

John thought about what Lucille just said, as Hank chuckled. "Lucille," said Hank, "a man could learn enough being around you to be really dangerous to the ladies. You don't pull your punches. It's all straight from the heart."

Lucille liked it when a man understood that she generally meant what she said and didn't particularly care for what people called "small talk," principally because it usually took the form of gossip. "You have no idea," said Lucille.

"You'd be surprised at some of my ideas," replied Hank. "Please sit down. You must be thirsty after that drive. John usually likes a cold beer, but I have water, coffee, and cranberry juice."

"I'll share a beer with someone, but I'm not up to drinking a whole one this early."

Hank rose from his chair, went to the kitchen, opened three bottles, and brought them back. He handed one to Lucille and another to John. "Lucille, drink as much or as little as you like and if you want a glass I'll get you one. We don't stand on ceremony here. I want you to know that. If there's anything you want, just ask for it."

Lucille took a sip of the beer and she liked the taste. She studied the brown and gold label, which featured an Aztec warrior in a feather headdress. The Percocet had all but eliminated Hank's back pain. The alcohol in the beer potentiated the pills' analgesic effect. "This beer actually tastes good," said Lucille. "Most beer has a bitter aftertaste. This one leaves a clean taste."

"I'm glad you like it. So, Lucille, what kind of work do you do?"

"I work the reception desk at Park Avenue Galleries. As a matter of fact, I just started. Before, I worked for them part time whenever they had an exhibition."

"So you know Mr. Creswell?"

"I do indeed."

"And what do you think of him?"

"Once you get past the stuffy British baronet routine, he's okay. He seems to be well respected in his field. He doesn't hit on the girls; I know that."

Hank got up and excused himself to go to his bedroom, where he opened the bottom drawer of his old oak dresser. Underneath long disused sweaters that he couldn't quite bring himself to donate to Good Will, primarily because they were birthday presents from his wife and had sentimental value, were two leather document cases that resembled large books. The red Morocco case was substantially thinner and less impressive than the larger white leather one, which was massive and elaborate, almost like a folio volume. One had a large eagle with outstretched wings and held a swastika in its talons, stamped into the leather in what appeared to be pure, bright, yellow gold. The larger case was very elaborate with a huge raised eagle with folded wings in what appeared to be silver gilt. He tucked them under his arm and walked back into the living room, where he laid them down on the low, reproduction Sheraton, walnut coffee table. He'd never really liked the table, however Emily had thought it was the last word in elegance and style, so he tolerated it. Lucille took one look at the red leather folder lying on top of the thicker white one, curled her upper lip and said with disdain, "Uggh. Nazi stuff." John hadn't seen them before and was wondering what other treasures Hank had liberated while he was in Munich. Lucille picked up the red folder and opened it. Inside the case was a beautifully printed, thick, white piece of paper held in the corners by triangles of silk. The paper looked like vellum or parchment.

"Can you read German, Lucille?" asked Hank hopefully.

"I can read a little. My grandmother was a German speaker and a Holocaust survivor. She was in Dachau for two years and somehow she was never sent to Auschwitz or another one of the extermination camps. She was fluent in English, so perhaps they made some use of her. She would never talk about it. I took a year of German in high school when I should have been learning Spanish."

"What does it say?" asked John.

Lucille was having some difficulty with the elaborate Gothic-style lettering. "It says something like this: 'In the name of the German people and the fatherland Gruppenfuhrer Josef Dietrich is awarded the Knight's Cross to the Iron Cross, 5th July 1940, by Hitler. It has Hitler's signature in the lower right hand corner written in black ink.'"

Hank was concerned. "I hope I haven't given offense by asking you to read such a thing. If I have, I did so unwittingly and I apologize."

Lucille laughed loudly and long. "Bother me? I should say not. I only regret that Hitler and Dietrich can't know that a Jew is handling their sacred documents. I can only hope their souls are suffering added torment as I read each word. We don't sell Nazi memorabilia at the gallery and I know it's prohibited on E-bay, too. Personally, I think it's ridiculous. You give something power by suppressing it. Angus tells me that several of the major dealers and two of the biggest collectors of Nazi relics are Jewish, and I see that as the greatest justice. What could be more poetic than having Jews buying and selling Nazi artifacts, not as objects with ideological power, but as commodities."

"That's a relief," said Hank. "After I put them down, I remembered what if you were Jewish? I would have been the most thoughtless, callous, person you ever met."

Lucille carefully laid down the Knight's Cross Document folder and picked up the elaborate white case. The actual award document was far more detailed and decorated looking like a page from a medieval illuminated manuscript, printed in glossy black and outlined in gold leaf. "This one," she said, "awards the oak leaves to the Knight's Cross of the Iron Cross to Obergruppenfuhrer Josef Dietrich 31st December 1941. That's Eichenlaub zum Ritterkreuz des Eisernen Kreuzes. The oak leaves must have been a much bigger deal than the Knight's Cross considering the quality of the folder and the printing."

John's face lit up. "Mr. Angus Creswell is going to flip over these. He asked me if you had anything else. You said all you had was the pistol."

"John," Hank said with a smile, "at the time you asked me all I was thinking about were military items like guns, swords, daggers, not books. I always thought these were some kind of books."

Lucille set the heavy folder down. She'd peed in San Clemente, however the few sips of beer had stimulated her bladder and she had the urge to go again, not insistent though her gynecologist told her she shouldn't hold it unless she really had to. Lucille liked Hank very much and if John were half the man his grandfather was she thought she might be able to have a relationship with him, though it was early days yet. *He might as well know up front*, she thought, *that I have something of a weak bladder.*

"Excuse me, Mr. Dryden. No, I mean Henry." As she said this John involuntarily jumped. Hank didn't permit Valerie to call him Henry. Only Hank's wife had ever successfully claimed that privilege and now Hank had given it to Lucille minutes after meeting her. This was truly astonishing. If John's mother ever found out about it, there'd be hell to pay. Lucille said brightly, "I need to use your bathroom. Beer goes right through me."

"Down the hall, second door on your right." Lucille got up and walked out.

Hank's bathroom was a pleasant surprise in that it was antiseptically clean, painted in an eggshell blue with matching deep pile carpets, towels and hand towels on the wooden towel bars, blue Kleenex tissues on the carpeted stand tank, and a soft plastic toilet seat. She decided that Hank must have an exceptionally competent maid, because in her experience, men living alone generally did not pay such close attention to their bathrooms. Even the mirrored face of the medicine cabinet was immaculate and free of fingerprints and toothbrush spatters. She unbuttoned her jeans, pulled them down, and sat, thinking that old Henry Dryden was a man of sensibility.

John took a moment to examine the white folder and document. Hank couldn't wait any longer. "What did Creswell say about the painting?"

"He says he can sell it. There'll have to be a final authentication by the buyer. What he really wants from us is a firm price."

"I'll leave that to you. You did such a good job with the pistol."

"The pistol was something understandable and quantifiable. Ten or even twenty thousand one way or the other, serious money to be sure, but nothing like we're talking about with the painting. Ten million is more than I'll make in my whole life. I tried to get Angus to name a figure, but each time I thought I had him, he'd throw it back on me."

"He's a pro. That's his job."

"I think we should just decide on a price and stick to it."

"What if Creswell tacks on an additional figure besides his commission?"

"I thought of that, then I said to myself if he sells it and we get ours, what do we really care?"

"So what do you think? You've been talking to him."

"I was thinking about sixty."

"Tell him seventy-five and that's firm. Otherwise, I'll donate it to Doctors Without Borders."

"I thought you didn't want any publicity. That's what this private sale is all about."

Lucille's attention was arrested by the glass-covered colored reproduction of a magnificent stag beetle by Albrecht Durer, dated 1517. It was an extremely odd image to hang in a bathroom. She finished buttoning her jeans, looking at the print as she did. The engraving exhibited some brown spots from foxing and other staining, but the colors were brilliant and there was no publisher's name in fine print at the bottom of the image. She wanted to take it off the wall for a closer look, though that was the height of bad manners. There was a luminous quality to the work that intrigued her.

*No*, she thought. *It couldn't possibly be a drawing. Durer was famous during his lifetime and his works have been held in high esteem through the centuries. No it's impossible.*

She left the bathroom and as she walked into the living room, John and Hank were both looking at her curiously. "Did I take a long time?" she said, amusement evident in her tone. "I'm sorry I didn't mean to. One doesn't expect to see a Durer print of a stag beetle on a bathroom wall, unless you're in Windsor Castle as a guest of the Queen and probably not even then."

"That big bug?"

"You could call it that. It's one of my favorite Durer images."

"Who's Durer?" asked Hank.

"I'm sorry. Albrecht Durer is the greatest German artist of the Renaissance. In addition to his magnificent oil paintings, he was a master draftsman, etcher, engraver, and printer."

"And here I always thought the AD above the date stood for Anno Domini."

"No," said Lucille. "Although I can see why you'd think that. It's his monogram; A over D are his initials."

"And here I thought it was some old picture of a bug. My wife thought it was funny, so she hung it over the toilet in the guest bathroom."

"The frame looks old. It's certainly19th century, maybe older. Wherever did you get it?"

"Are you all right, Grandpa?" Hank shook himself all over like a wet dog drying himself. He sniffed and wiped his face with a white Kleenex he pulled from his hip pocket.

"I'm fine. You'll both have to forgive me. It's just that I didn't sleep that well last night. To answer your question, Lucille, I found the bug in a filing cabinet, together with the award documents."

"Really?"

Hank smiled indulgently. "John, why don't you take Lucille for a walk and show her the real reason Del Mar's such a special place?"

"What about you?"

"I've already put in my three miles today and my knees are reminding me, and won't let me forget. You two go along. I'll fix something for lunch."

"I'll stay and help you," said Lucille.

"You're very sweet, but I really want you to enjoy our beach. It's a perfect day for it and I want to surprise you when you get back."

The beach was only a few short blocks from the house and there was a traffic light and pedestrian crosswalk to facilitate access. Even on Saturday in summer the beach wasn't crowded with sunbathers and their boom boxes. The waves were coming in the usual sets of three on the Pacific swell about three feet high before breaking into a dazzling creamy foam, much to the delight of some young body surfers and a pair of pre-teen, sun browned, bleached blonde-haired boys on boogie boards.

John and Lucille walked hand in hand on the fine sand as close to the water as they dared without wetting their shoes. They came to some dark rocks where John took off his loafers and socks. Lucille removed her sandals. Having placed their footwear high out of harm's way, they rolled up their jeans past their knees and continued their walk on the edge of the surf in the yielding sand.

Hank had shopped on Friday and bought organic lettuce, cucumbers, tomatoes, and onions for salad. The extra virgin olive oil and balsamic vinegar he had in his kitchen. He didn't like the roast beef, it was too well done for his liking, and the cooked shrimp were usually too salty for some reason and worse than that they weren't completely deveined, and in his opinion shit was shit and just because it was in a shrimp instead of a large mammal it was still excrement. Hank had settled for one of the roasted free-range chickens, and then added a loaf of crusty French bread to his basket.

After John and Lucille left, he tossed the salad, unwrapped the chicken, and arranged three place settings on his small, mahogany, Duncan Phyfe reproduction, dining room table. He liked what he saw of Lucille. She was obviously intelligent, sensitive, and to his eyes, physically attractive. Lucille had a way about her that reminded him of the anti-war, hippie girls he'd met during the late 60's and early 70's. She seemed to share their passion without their stridency.

The one great regret in his life was that it seemed more and more likely he would die without seeing John happily married, much less have a great grandchild. Hank and Emily had tried unsuccessfully to have another child after she had Luke. For the next four years Emily practically wore him out three nights a week trying. Not that Hank minded.

John had come close to marrying twice. These were actual formal engagements that for whatever reason never ended in nuptials. John broke off the first one after coming home early one afternoon, unannounced, to find his lovely blonde, Barbie doll fiancé dressed in Frederick's of Hollywood's most revealing black lingerie, on her knees, having sex on an old boyfriend whom she'd supposedly sworn off for a number of very good reasons. Hank was concerned for John's masculine ego at the time, but John told him about the episode in such lurid and graphic detail, and added so many humorous touches that Hank was relieved of any anxiety on that account. Hank never cared much for Anita in the first place. She owned a small dance and exercise studio in the less fashionable part of Santa Monica near Venice.

He did like Janet, a personal injury attorney, who worked for a large Los Angeles law firm and was their principal pro-bono lawyer. At first, it seemed like a match made in heaven, and John excitedly reported to Hank that she was the one, and yes they were going to be married in November. That was in August. Then came one of the rare weekends when John told Hank he wasn't coming down to Del Mar because he and Janet were going up to San Francisco on a mini-vacation.

When John called Friday evening to tell Hank he wasn't in fact going to be married, that he and Janet had a fight and he'd broken off the engagement as well, Hank was bitterly disappointed. It turned out that Janet had a drinking problem, and John had made it a condition that she would seek counseling for it before they married and Janet had enthusiastically agreed. They'd flown up to San Francisco early Friday morning, checked into a suite at the Huntington Hotel, then gone to Berkeley for lunch at Chez Panisse. Over John's objections, Janet insisted that they drive up to Napa to visit the wineries. By late afternoon, Janet was drunk and demanding to go to several more wineries. John was tempted to leave her at the Duckhorn tasting room in Rutherford, however he persevered and drove her back to San Francisco, dropped her off cursing at the intersection of Mason and California and managed to catch a 7:30 flight back to Los Angeles. Janet returned the following day and checked into the Betty Ford Clinic for a month. Following her release she and John had an on again, off again relationship for a year. Then Janet married one of the senior partners at her firm, twenty years older than she was, who had decided to trade in his wife of thirty years for a younger model. John didn't judge her and even sent her an expensive sterling silver teapot from Geary's as a wedding present.

Hank didn't think John had ever dated a Jewish girl, although he knew John had had a brief and torrid affair with a Korean waitress. He couldn't help wishing John would marry Lucille, and given a choice between selling the Van Gogh and seeing John married there was never a question that the latter was more important to him. Still he couldn't help speculating on the effect millions of dollars would have on his favorite non-profit anti-war organizations. They would really be able to get the message out and wake up the American people to what was going on in Iraq, the hundreds of thousands of Iraqi casualties while American technology limited American losses to a few thousand expendable volunteers from the underclass.

Some of the millions would pay for full page informational advertisements in *USA Today, Time, People, Newsweek*, put anti-war congressman in office, in fact, quite literally change the course of history, which Hank thought was in desperate need of a significant course correction. The money wouldn't dramatically change his life and he didn't think it would change John's that much either.

His former daughter-in-law and her husband would be physically ill if they even had the slightest idea that Hank had been concealing a vast fortune for sixty years, though they'd never find out from Hank and John would literally swallow his tongue long before he said anything to either one of them. John really didn't know if it would even be a good idea to talk to Lucille about the Van Gogh. He was fairly certain she was not the sort of girl who'd like him more if she knew he was soon to be a very wealthy man. Hank had his own qualms, which had more to do with a reluctance to discuss financial matters in front of guests, so he thought he'd leave any mention of the painting to John.

John and Lucille were bent over some rocks looking at an anemone in a miniature tidal pool. John gently put his finger in the middle of the animal and the light, almost lime-green, petal-like tentacles gently closed around it as John drew his finger out. Lucille looked at John.

"You're teasing the creature, making it think your finger is a fish." This statement made John's heart warm towards her even more. If she were this sensitive and concerned about the feelings of a sea anemone, it augured well for the man who entrusted his feelings to her care. Tidal pools had always held a fascination for John and he told her all about anemones.

"Some anemones paralyze their prey such as small fish and other marine animals. Most anemones are either male or female, discharging their eggs and sperm into the water. The female draws the sperm into her gastrovascular cavity. Some species reproduce asexually by longitudinal fission, and in other species the pedal disk by which they attach themselves to the rocks actually breaks into fragments which grow into new anemones."

Lucille skipped nimbly backward as a rogue wave higher than the swells, which had been washing their ankles, soaked John's jeans to the crotch. "Hey," said John. "Thanks a lot for warning me. What's wrong with 'John, look out, there's a big wave coming!'"

Lucille was howling with laughter and her throaty laugh thrilled him. "I'm sorry," she said through the laughter. "It was just one of those situations like when you're at the market, and you can just see that someone's grocery bag is about to burst or lose its handles, or when you're a kid and you see some other kid about to dump his books all over, you know what I mean? It's not like you were in any danger."

"No," said John.

"I just hope you won't be offended when I take my pants off and put them in Hank's washer. I don't like sitting around in soggy jeans and then there's the sand."

"Oh," grinned Lucille. "I doubt very much if you have anything I haven't seen."

"What do you mean? I wear boxer shorts."

Lucille looked at him dubiously.

"It seems your boxers are as compromised as your jeans."

"I'm beginning to think you're not warning me was a well-laid plot to see me naked."

"You'll excuse me for saying so, but I have a hard time believing I need to resort to subterfuge to get you to undress."

"No, I suppose you're right about that as well. What do you say we leave off teasing the anemones and go back to the house?"

"That sounds good to me. All this sun and salt air has given me an appetite. Don't know about you, but I'm hungry." Lucille had eaten breakfast, which consisted of a carefully measured bowl of granola, low-fat milk, a two-egg-white frittata with basil and a sprinkling of mozzarella cheese, and two cups of inky black, French roast coffee with no milk, cream, or sweetener. She was a borderline hypo-glycemic, and preferred to eat frequent small meals rather than several large ones. Hank was pretty trim and fit for his age, so she assumed that he paid some attention to what he ate, either that or he had a miraculous metabolism. "Does your grandfather cook?"

They were walking hand in hand back to the rock where they'd doffed their shoes.

"Actually he makes a decent lasagna, good coq-au-vin, penne puttanesca, and a fair beef Stroganoff, when he has a mind to be in the kitchen. Most of the time he grills chicken or fish and tosses a salad. You're not a Vegan are you?"

"No," she said with a smile. "Though I can't say I'd wouldn't like to be because I can't help thinking it's a higher consciousness way of living. Maybe I'll be vegan in my next life. For the most part I'm a lacto-ovo, fish-eating vegetarian, who will consume the odd fowl and very rarely a steak. That being said I pass on red meat, mostly out of disgust with the way cattle are raised and slaughtered, rather than a belief they are highly conscious creatures."

They sat down on the rock and John cleaned his feet as best he could with his hands, and donned his loafers without his socks. Lucille bent over to slip the back strap of her left sandal over her heel and John caught a good glimpse of her chest through the v-neck sweater. They were round, tawny colored, with dark and prominent nipples. He quickly looked away at a sandpiper running along the strand on its pipe cleaner thin legs, always one step ahead of the furthest reach of the waves. He thought to himself, *If I keep this up she's going to think I'm some kind of total loser with a tit fixation. Though I must say hers are as nice as any I've seen in person.*

Lucille had noticed him looking then looking away, and she thought it as charming and disarming as she had earlier in the car. She had known enough men who looked at her as a piece of ass and even that sort of ultra-crude and crass admiration didn't offend her, though it did turn her off instead of being a turn on.

John, Lucille, and Hank sat down to lunch. John was dressed in a pair of Hank's ancient, rust brown, wide whale corduroys, which were slightly short on him. His clothes were in the washer. Lucille helped herself to a second plate of salad, which consisted of a mixture of romaine, mesclun, and herbs, dressed with ideal proportions of olive oil and balsamic vinegar, so the acerbic quality of the balsamic complimented the spicy flavors of the organic greens. Hank had sliced some tomatoes and fresh buffalo mozzarella, garnished with fresh basil leaves, and this too appealed to Lucille. John applied himself to the cold roasted chicken with a will and Lucille accepted two very thin slices.

"What a perfect lunch," said Lucille and she finished her last bite of tomato. This pleased Hank no end. "I thought you two might build up an appetite rambling on the beach."

"We did. And your grandson told me all about the sex life of sea anemones."

"Did he really? That must have been fascinating."

"Actually it was interesting. I never knew there were male and female anemones and the male produces sperm which fertilizes the egg."

"The real question," said Hank with a gleam in his pale, blue eyes, "is whether or not the female can turn him down if she's not in the mood."

"One thing's for sure," said John. "It's not like she can walk away."

"No," Lucille said. "That's true. But I'll bet she can just close up if she wants to."

"I never knew that people and sea anemones had so much in common, or that my grandson was such a marine biologist."

John was enjoying himself and he could see that Hank and Lucille were getting along famously, which was important to him. Hank had tolerated Anita out of politeness and liked Janet, more for her college cheerleader good looks than her abilities as a conversationalist regarding matters of interest. John hadn't asked Lucille to come with him out of any need or even desire to win Hank's approval. He liked her from the brief encounter they'd had at the gallery, and their telephone conversation after the disturbing events of the previous afternoon. John had slept poorly, for him, waking up three times during the night, and once at 2:15, he didn't fall back to sleep for nearly an hour. He didn't think he was even indirectly responsible for Ahmed's suicide, if that's what it was, and the police seemed to agree with him. Still his unlawful detainer action certainly brought Ahmed's name to Judge Glass's attention.

The television coverage was treating the death as a tragedy in the working class community of Southgate, complete with a teary-eyed interview with his young son and daughter, his wife being too hysterical for the camera. The children, both in their late teens, the daughter enrolled in pre-med at USC, and the son at UCLA, were both very credible. Forgotten was the evil slumlord and remembered was the kind, hard-working father, who was the embodiment of the American dream. Clearly Shakespeare was wrong when he wrote in Julius Caesar what the good men did in life was interred with their bones.

*In Ahmed's case the evil was interred,* thought John as he watched the news that night.

Doreen Nahabedian blamed her father's death on a legal system that sought to scapegoat those, who at great personal and financial sacrifice provided the only affordable housing in Los Angeles. Hike, the son, angrily indicted the tenants themselves saying, "If there is trash, let them pick it up. This is an apartment building, not assisted living. If they'd spend half as much time taking care of their units as they spend complaining, when they use sinks as toilets, destroy walls, plumbing, electrical fixtures, and fire escapes, there wouldn't be any problems in the first place. If they choose to live like wild beasts, then how was my father supposed to maintain his properties? They expect him to clean up after them. He never piled up filthy mattresses, box springs, broke water pipes and tore out plaster. He chained the doors to keep junkies and crackheads from shooting up and sleeping in the hallways. My father was a good man. He was murdered by a system that apologizes for people who are unwilling to assume any sort of responsibility themselves. He lived the American dream and died for it."

John watched both the Nahabedian children on Channel 5 Eyewitness News at 10. Carol was on it as well, looking like an African-American television star, a Halle Berry type, repeating a brisk, "No comment! No comment," to reporters' questions. She had called him after the segment concluded to hear his critique, and he told her she looked great, and he liked her on-screen presence.

"Maybe you have a future in television," he said much to her amusement.

"Now I know you John Dryden, as well or better than you know yourself in many ways. Now you have to promise me that if you take this on as part of the burden of guilt you carry around with you that you'll let me know so I can tell you it's got no more to do with you than if you rented someone a car and they got drunk and crashed into a tree. Yes it's too bad Ahmed's dead and it's sad it had to be at your office, but shit happens. You're not God and you can't accept responsibility. Man has free will, and Ahmed brought that pistol to Southgate of his own free will. The devil didn't make him do it, God didn't, and sure as hell you didn't. He waved his Glock around and shot himself. End of story. And if you believe in karma, then it was meant to be."

"On second thought, maybe you should consider a second career as a psychiatric social worker."

"I'm happy being your paralegal and though my heart goes out to Ahmed's family, the world is a better place without Ahmed coming down to Southgate and terrorizing me."

"I feel you. Isn't that how they say it in the hood?"

"You got it, counselor. I'll see you Monday; give my best to Hank.

"I will. And Carol?"

"Yes."

"Thanks for taking care of the media."

"Hell, no need to thank me for that. It was fun." In spite of all Carol's well meant and acute observations, John couldn't help feel somewhat responsible and he had a nightmare in which Ahmed rose from the carpet, his skull missing enough bone to expose the brain just above his bloody right eye, and walk toward John with an accusatory expression on his ghastly, ghoulish face, pointing a pudgy forefinger and speaking in a sonorous sepulchral voice, "You made me do it. Even so, I love you because you must love your enemies because they are the instruments of your destiny." It was from this dream that John awoke in a sweat at 2:15 a.m. He knew he'd read or heard the quote Ahmed used, but couldn't recall where or who'd said it.

Since picking up Lucille, he hadn't once thought about Ahmed and his untimely demise, until now, and John immediately shunted it aside, and turned his thoughts to the Knight's Cross documents and how much he was going to enjoy telling Angus all about them. Although he was very tempted to tell Lucille about the Van Gogh, what he really wanted to do was take her by his office and casually show it to her to see what she thought of it. In the meantime, he'd content himself with Angus' reaction to the documents.

---

Angus and his son had just returned from a soccer game at Rancho Park. They had stopped at a Thai restaurant on Pico for lunch, as Robert liked the satay chicken there as much as other children liked McDonalds' hamburgers. Angus enjoyed eating lunch with him away from his two sisters, considering it to be quality father and son bonding time. Marcia encouraged these boys' Saturday lunches out and they were a sort of Creswell family ritual during the spring and autumn soccer seasons. Robert's team had lost the game though Robert, a forward, had played well and Angus told him that his playing well was more important than the final score. The opposing team had two fourth graders, while Robert's team consisted of third graders and one precocious second grader, so the outcome was no great surprise. Still, Robert was a little depressed about losing, and Angus allowed him to have his feelings and didn't try to negate them. Angus was buoyant himself. He had just made nearly a whole year's salary on the Dietrich Walther pistol and was poised on the threshold of making several million dollars on Dryden's Van Gogh. He was not counting the money as yet, for there was still the possibility, however remote, that it might be an antique copy, though with the Roth provenance that was highly unlikely. Legally speaking, if Dietrich had obtained it legitimately during the Nazi era, it belonged to his heirs. If the general had obtained it by force or coercion, then it made no sense whatsoever that the Roth heirs wouldn't have registered a claim with the Art Loss Register. The Roths had sold some important Expressionist paintings at Christie's in the late 1990's setting several records at the time for Soutine, Schiele, Nolde, and Kokoschka.

The Roth children would certainly be aware if their family were missing a Van Gogh, as if any painting by the master could be anything but important. This was more than a Van Gogh. It was a self portrait of such luminous power that Angus thought it ranked with the greatest portraits ever put on panel or canvas, on a par with Albrecht Durer's "Self-portrait in a Furred Coat," in the Alte Pinakothek in Munich, or the very best of Rembrandt's astonishingly transcendent images of himself. Angus had carefully considered the possibility of a circumstance in which the Roths could conceivably have forgotten about the painting and discarded it as far too absurd. John and Hank Dryden's insistence on absolute confidentiality and secrecy almost but not entirely relieved him of any ethical considerations regarding his duties and obligations as an employee of Park Avenue Galleries, which in the ordinary course of business should have had their private treaty department handle the sale of the Van Gogh. Angus had, in fact, mentioned this to John, who told him he was satisfied to do business with him, and neither he nor his grandfather wanted the gallery to be involved in the sale if at all possible. Angus' conundrum was how to locate a private buyer without alerting the entire art world.

Angus knew a Frenchman, Phillipe Lebrun, who had been the director of Sotheby's Latin American Painting Department before retiring to Buenos Aires to be a private dealer. In all likelihood, Phillipe knew the Roth family and Angus wondered if this might not present a problem. Also, a man who deals primarily in Rivera, Botero, Zuniga, Siqueiros, and Orozcos would not necessarily know a client for a major Van Gogh. There were a number of immensely wealthy people in South America, including the woman who'd paid a world record price for a J.W.M. Turner, so there were serious buyers for European art as well as Latin American works.

Angus had faith in Phillipe's discretion. That wasn't the issue. Angus was waiting for a firm figure, then it was a relatively simple process of sending good digital images and arranging a personal inspection. There was a question of whether Phillipe would be comfortable authenticating the piece. The buyer might not be comfortable with anything less than the imprimatur of the Rijke-museum Vincent Van Gogh, though the Roth collection history should be sufficient. That and assuming the fact that there was no little known forger of Van Goghs with the talent of a Hans van Meegeren or an Elmir de Hory.

Angus was kissing Marcia on the lips when his cell phone trilled Mozart's piano concerto in C major. Marcia pulled away. "Angus, why is it whenever I call you you never have your cell phone with you? All of a sudden you're carrying it in your pocket? What's going on?"

"The man who sold me the Walther has some other items and he's visiting his grandfather as we speak."

"Is it about the Van Gogh?"

"I'll tell you in a minute." Angus pushed the answer button. "Hello. Why yes, Mr. Dryden. No, no, it's perfectly all right to call my cell. That's why I gave you my card. No, no, you're not interrupting anything. I'm just now returning from my son's soccer game, as you call it here. No, as a matter of fact he lost. Yes, he was a little disappointed, though he and his mates played well and that's the important thing."

John could hear the tension in Angus' voice underlying his habitual cheery British breeziness.

*Well,* thought John, *I've got something that will rock him.*

"I'm down here in Del Mar and my grandfather just showed me two large leather document cases. They look like books, especially the more massive white one. They have large eagles stamped in gold on the covers and a swastika. Inside are documents awarding the Knight's Cross and the Oak Leaves to the Knight's Cross to Dietrich."

"The white book as you call it is very large, larger than an encyclopedia volume and very impressive?"

"That describes it to a tee, about half again as large as the red one, almost as large as an atlas."

"How is the condition of the leather? Any scuffs or tears?"

"No, they look like what you call mint condition."

"And the documents themselves?"

"They're like new. No fingerprints or any of those brown stains you get with old paper."

"And the paper itself, it feels thick? Not like cardboard, more like..."

"Like parchment or vellum. When I was a kid, I remember my grandfather giving me a copy of the Declaration of Independence. It was printed on thick, cream-colored paper. It feels almost silky."

"That's exactly right," said Angus. "How much does your grandfather want for them?"

"How much are they worth?"

Angus thought quickly. Considering the Van Gogh it would be wise to tell him the absolute truth down to the dollar.

"An average Knight's cross document and folder typically sells for between eight and ten thousand dollars. Of course given Dietrich's notoriety and the fact he was an SS Gruppenfuhrer, I could see his bringing thirty thousand dollars."

"And the oak leaves?"

"There are four Knight's Cross awards. The Knight's cross by itself is the lowest. In ascending order of importance there are the oak leaves, then the oak leaves and swords, and then the ultimate, which is oak leaves, swords, and diamonds. An oak leaves document and case belonging to the famous SS general Hasso van Manteuffel sold at auction some twenty years ago for thirty-five thousand dollars, which I considered a bargain at the time, though to be sure I was still at university and could no more afford such a thing than I could buy a Gulfstream V jet aircraft today."

"I assume prices have risen in the past twenty years."

"Prices on Nazi memorabilia haven't gone up as much as one would think. For one thing, there is still a stigma attached, quite understandably, and for another there are a whole lot of superb forgeries coming from former Eastern Bloc countries, not that we have that problem here, but it had adversely affected the whole market for Third Reich material."

"So, what's your best guess on the oak leaves?"

"I'd say sixty thousand dollars. Your best buyer would be the man who bought the Walther."

"I figured that. How does fifty thousand for the pair sound?"

Angus thought it was a very fair price and the purchaser of the pistol would most certainly be keenly interested in the awards. They would make an ensemble and complement each other. "Are you certain there're no daggers or medals?"

"No, I'm positive. Well, I suppose that makes sense. The general would have worn the medals and possibly the daggers as well. They're more than likely lost somewhere in Russia. Too bad."

"What about the documents?"

"Oh, I'm sorry. I'll have them. Do you want me to pick them up?"

"No, I'll bring them up to Southgate, then I'll come to Beverly Hills."

"That's most kind of you. I've seen quite enough of Southgate for one lifetime."

John laughed. "I suppose you have at that. You could come to my house in Westchester. It's off Manchester near LAX."

"Whatever is more convenient for you, though I prefer if you didn't bring them into the gallery. The executive staff is very sensitive about Nazi things, and large items with big gold swastikas would upset them. Third Reich artifacts don't fit in with the whole painting, furniture, and jewelry crowd, some of whom are children and grandchildren of Holocaust survivors. Best not to offend."

"I can see their point."

"Thank you, I appreciate it. Now about the painting."

"We'll talk about it when you pick up the documents. Unless you have something else planned, how about corning to Westchester tomorrow around three?"

"The address?" "One three seven nine one Las Palmas Avenue."

"I'll MapQuest it and see you at three."

"You can call me if there's any problem."

"There won't be, and John."

"Yes Angus."

"Thank you, and I mean that."

## CHAPTER 16

# *Lucille*

JOHN AND LUCILLE left Del Mar shortly after 3:30 so Hank could take his afternoon nap, which was an almost inviolate routine. Occasionally John would stay overnight, and when he did, he would retire to his grandfather's computer room to work on cases during the hours of four and six, or he would go for a long walk on the beach. With all the events of the past week, John had done very little legal work, and though he wasn't so very far behind that any of his clients would suffer, he did have briefs that needed to be filed Monday, so John intended to use Sunday morning and afternoon to prepare them. Lucille knew very well that Del Mar was a day trip before accepting the invitation. As they were driving east on Del Mar Boulevard to catch Interstate 5 North, with the Knight's Cross documents safely in the trunk, Lucille said, "Your grandfather is a very special person. He loves you just like you were his son."

"He's the only father I've ever known and I've never felt lesser than or deprived because of it, thanks to Hank. Although, of course, I would have loved to know my real father."

"I got the distinct impression that as happy as he was to have us there, he wasn't unhappy when we left."

"No, Grandpa has his routine and he sticks to it. His blogging and anti-war activities are pretty much a full time job."

"He looks great."

"Yeah. I only hope I look that good in forty years. You'd never know it, but he suffers terribly from kidney stones. Sometimes the attacks are so bad he has to be hospitalized. Aside from that I think he's quite healthy."

"He's sure still engaged in the world around him. Lots of older people kind of withdraw into themselves."

John smiled broadly. "No one would ever say that of Henry Dryden."

"I take it Angus was pleased with the Nazi stuff."

"Oh, yes. He sounded like a little kid at Christmas. One that gets the present he wanted the most."

"Beneath that stiff upper lip, public school facade, he is a little kid. He nearly blew himself up in the executive parking lot the other day."

"Yeah, he told me all about it."

"He's very lucky the boss didn't fire him, give him the sack as the Brits say."

As they were passing by the massive Marine base at Camp Pendleton, John said, "You know if it weren't for the Marines, all those beautiful hills would be covered with subdivision houses and townhomes like Mission Viejo. Look at what the Irvine Corporation did with all that lovely rolling ranch land in Laguna Niguel."

"People have to live somewhere. But I know what you mean. We must be grateful to the federal government for unintentionally preserving a few miles of Southern California coastline from urban sprawl."

John finally made up his mind that he wanted Lucille's input on the Van Gogh. She had formal schooling, a BFA in art history, and she worked for the gallery. Now that he'd spent the day with her, much of it alone in the car talking, he trusted her not to mention it to anyone. Equally important, he knew the painting wouldn't have any effect on their relationship. It would either blossom or wither, quite independently of his association with either the Van Gogh or the millions it represented.

The Saturday afternoon traffic northbound on the 5 wasn't that heavy and as he approached the great divide where the 405 begins and the 5 continues, John and the other drivers had to make their choice, and if they wanted the 405 North through Newport they had to cross a number of traffic lanes to the right. For vehicles in the far left lane of the 5, this meant crossing as many as seven lanes of traffic to make the transition to the four lanes that swept off to the right and over the 5 at 70 miles per hour. The GTO's 335 horsepower engine made changing lanes easy, a brief sensation of speed and a sinuous up down movement of the wood and aluminum Nardi steering wheel was all it required to change lanes at speed. If he were going to Lucille's apartment on Beverly Glen, which was on the far eastern border of Westwood, taking the

405 would be the logical choice despite the guaranteed several miles of stop and go traffic past LAX through Culver City. He wanted to show her the painting, so he stayed on the 5.

"Aren't you going to take the 405," asked Lucille, who rarely drove her Honda Accord on the Santa Ana Freeway, and hadn't been so far south in years.

"I'd like to stop by my office if it's all right with you?"

"You're the driver. I'm fine with it. It's strange, I don't think I've ever been to Southgate, and here I've lived in Los Angeles my whole life except for college."

"Well, there are no museums or cultural attractions, though the Watts Towers are nearby."

"I'm ashamed to admit it, but I've never seen the Watts Towers."

"Most people in LA haven't. Did you know that Watts used to be called Mud Town, until it was renamed after C.H. Watts, a Pasadena real estate dealer, who had a ranch there?"

"No, and I'll bet the people who live there don't know that either."

"I won't take that wager."

They were driving past El Toro. "You know, when I was a little kid, I remember all this land being covered with orange groves. Now most of the groves are further east in Riverside County out by the 215, and out towards Hemet where property isn't so valuable."

"Sometimes I think of the land buried under millions of tons of asphalt and concrete, and I feel suffocated. Not only suffocated, but I feel sad it has to be that way. Look at the Los Angeles River, forced to flow through concrete pipes and channels like a sewer just so it can't flood anyone's land. It all seems so unnatural."

John sighed. "I know what you mean and that's one of the things I like about going to Del Mar. The ocean is as wild and free as it was thousands of years ago. You recall what Joni Mitchell wrote, 'They paved paradise and put up a parking lot.'"

Lucille looked at him with a blank expression. "Sorry, I don't know that one. The sea, yes. The creatures are becoming rare or extinct, and we use the ocean as a combination trash dump and cesspool."

"It costs money to treat sewage, and money and time to recycle trash. People won't even consider taking an hour out of their day to work with their refuse. If you even suggested it they'd think you lost your mind, but if you tell them about some totally meaningless hour-long television program, they'll thank you for the information and watch it. Of course what they do with trash is a million times more relevant to their lives and the lives of their children than any television show. The problem is that they don't have to deal with their garbage personally and trash isn't entertaining."

"So are you a serious recycler?"

"Not really, and I know this car is putting more hydrocarbons into the atmosphere than any ten cars with catalytic converters, so I guess I'm a hypocrite."

"We all are, except for some lost tribes in the Amazon rainforest and some indigenous cultures in Papua, New Guinea. We're all guilty to a greater or lesser extent of crimes against the earth."

"That's true. It doesn't make me feel any better, though I'm not going to do anything radical like selling this car, or leaving it up on blocks in the garage."

"Nor should you. It's more than metal and glass. It's a legacy from your father, from a time before we really understood that we were choking and irreparably damaging the earth."

"As strange as it might sound, when I drive Dad's car I feel a connection with him I don't feel at any other time. Almost like I'm channeling some energy he left here for me. Even though he never knew me, he did know my mom was pregnant. They didn't have ultrasounds back then, so he didn't know if it were a boy or a girl. He only knew he was going to be a father."

Lucille was very close to tears thinking about Luke Dryden, who was little more than a boy himself, in a strange land thousands of miles away, long before cell phones, reading a letter telling him the woman he loved was pregnant, and being unable to hold her or even call her to tell her he loved her, and how happy he was. This image engendered a wave of empathy so powerful it threatened to make her break down completely in a torrent of sobbing and at the same time, she was thrilled with John's sensitivity and willingness to share his feelings. She mastered her sadness by choosing to think of the man sitting next to her and not the lonely boy in Vietnam who had died long before she was born.

The GTO was in the second lane, purring past Anaheim and Disneyland off to the left. Traffic was relatively light for an early Saturday evening, and if they could make it up to the 91 Artesia Freeway West, John thought he'd take that rather than continuing north on the 5 to the 605, because there was all too often several miles of backup beyond the 91. He'd take the 91 West to the 605 North, then take the 105 West to Long Beach Boulevard. If there were no accidents, that should work well.

"What do you think happens when we die?" asked Lucille. This was a question John did think about from time to time, and it had been on his mind in connection with Hank, and then actually seeing Ahmed's dead body lying on his office floor the previous day really brought such thoughts to the forefront of his conscious internal dialogue.

"Considering death is something every person must experience sooner or later, there is an almost unbelievable lack of scientific data on the subject. Scientists can't even agree on what death is, whether it's a process or a state that can be defined by irreversible apnea, such that death can be defined as brain stem death."

"That's interesting though it's not really what I'm asking."

"The way I see the eschatological aspect is that everything is energy, living, dead, animal, vegetable, mineral, light, it's all energy. We are energy, so it makes sense that some of the energy would persist after the life force is extinguished by death. Either that or life is utterly meaningless, a terrible sort of cosmic prank that of all life forms only men, dolphins, and primates have the cognitive ability to know what a cruel hoax it all is before they perish."

"I agree with you. It's all too strange. One minute Ecclesiastes says, 'the day of death is better than the day of birth,' and that men and beasts suffer the same fate, 'as one dies, so dies the other. They all have the same breath, and man has no advantage over the beasts.' Then he completely changes his mind saying, life is all that matters. 'A living dog is better than a dead lion.' Make up your mind, Preacher. Does life have any meaning or is it all vanity and a 'chasing after wind?'"

"Well, you know what Shakespeare said in Julius Caesar: 'Of all the things I yet have seen, it seems to me most strange that men should fear. Seeing that death, a necessary end, will come when it will come.' Then of course the Bard from Stratford on Avon has Macbeth say: 'What is man? A poor player that struts and frets his hour upon the stage and then is heard no more. Life is a take told by an idiot, full of sound and fury signifying nothing.'"

"That sounds really depressing."

"It's better than the Hindu and Buddhists who have no special rites for dead infants because they think the child must have been a monster in its previous life to have incurred such terrible karma. Infant mortality is put down to the child's own evil and requires 84 lakhs of rebirth to expiate each lakh being 100,000 rebirths."

"As difficult as that might be for a European to swallow, it's very similar to the whole doctrine of original sin, which I think is a crock and I'm Jewish. The Buddhist belief answers the question Ivan Karamazov poses to his younger brother Aleksi when Ivan refuses to acknowledge the existence of a benevolent God who allows innocent children to suffer unspeakable torments. If in fact the children are paying for their evil deeds from a previous incarnation, then one can give that answer to Ivan. It's hard to accept, even though it makes more sense than any other explanation."

"I have to agree with Ivan. As for dying, in Europe and America, it's a by-product of technology. Medical doctors pay almost no attention to the sick, Instead they reify the illness. They see death, not as inevitable but more as something alien and totally negative, the ultimate failure of all their therapeutic efforts as if death is a personal insult to them."

Aside from a mile of slow traffic on the 91 before the lanes of the on-ramp to the 605, John made good time and soon they took the Long Beach Boulevard exit off the 105 and headed north to Tweedy. They talked about Kubler-Ross' popular works on death and dying and they both agreed that the experiences she recorded were peculiarly American, and that her so-called six stages of death beginning with denial and ending with acceptance were hardly universal and that a Buddhist or Hindu would find them as bizarre and absurd as Kubler-Ross would find 84 lakhs being required of the soul of an infant who dies in childbirth.

"Then my question for you," said Lucille as John made the turn onto Tweedy, "is if there is a soul as the Western religions call it, or the atman of the Hindus actually exists, are they no more than concepts that permit humans to describe the indescribable unknown? For more than 2000 years, Hindus have taken Buddhists to task by asking if they believe there is no immortal soul, so how can rebirth take place? Essentially, the Buddhists deny there is anything to be reborn.

"So what is their answer to the Hindus?"

"Some seek to explain existences in rebirth by invoking the continuity of ever changing identity like fire, which is unchanged in appearance and is different in every moment."

"But fire changes its appearance constantly."

"I agree with you. It's only a way of explaining a seemingly irreconcilable paradox, as if every mystery must be reduced to a level where man can understand it or it's invalid."

"Whether men can comprehend it or not, valid or invalid, we're all going to die."

"And then we'll either know, or we won't know. It's all a mystery, one that won't be solved by anyone until it's too late to return and tell about it."

"So, you don't believe in all those returned from the dead stories about going through a passage toward a marvelous light?"

"No, though I do think that's quite possible. Look at it this way. You take it as an article of faith, every time you close your eyes to sleep, that you will wake up alive when you open your eyes in the morning. However, no one knows this for a fact, and you could easily never wake. You believe we are going to your office, and so do I, though we can't be positive we'll get there. An earthquake, a speeding car, a pedestrian, any number of things could happen to change the tapestry of phenomenal existence. Odds are they won't. What I mean is, how can we insist on certainty in philosophy or religion, when the only certainty is that nothing is certain."

John smiled, "Except for death."

"If death is a physical end to the existence of certain forms of protoplasm in the natural world, I agree, but just as everything is energy, energy can be neither created or destroyed. You're running this car with the decayed remnants of plants that died two or three hundred million years ago. Their stored energy powers nearly everything in every industrial society on earth. If there is anything like a soul that continues on, then death ceases to be an end, and is only the beginning of another process or journey. Death loses its finality and becomes a stage like a cocoon or chrysalis lasting for an unknown duration while a metamorphosis takes place."

"So what do you believe?"

"I believe that what we so blithely call life is extraordinarily complex and takes place not just in the phenomenal world of human senses. There are infinite levels and dimensions, universes within universes. I mean why do we have such absurdly large brains when we use only a tiny part, maybe five percent? It's not like any of us uses five percent of our heart or our lungs, so why our brains? That 95% isn't vestigial like the appendix, a relic left over from some earlier time of hominid existence, although there again is speculation that maybe ancient men had what we would refer to today as paranormal powers to read other men's thoughts, and perhaps pick up signals from earth's magnetic poles the way birds and other animals do. How do horses and dogs find their way home over hundreds of completely unknown miles? Animals have capacities humans can only dream of, and not only the physical senses like smell, sight, and hearing. It's the extrasensory abilities they have, as in a dog making its way back home to Nebraska after being driven to Missouri. The story might make the local news, but does anyone think how the dog did it? I mean the dog didn't use MapQuest or get directions at the Shell station. The swallows don't return to Mission San Juan Capistrano every year on March 19th using a calendar and the 5 Freeway as a navigational guide."

Tweedy was not very crowded with cars, and the passersby on the grimy sidewalks who ignored the occasional flash of mica from the surface took notice of the GTO with a turning of heads and smiles as John made his way to the office in third gear. Tweedy was not a favored cruising street like Whittier Boulevard or Van Nuys Boulevard in the Valley, though with the windows rolled down John could hear the heart-stopping thump of super-amplified hip-hop coming from lowered and raised Chevy trucks, and other radically altered vehicles. The evening was relatively warm and it wasn't yet full dark. This was assuming that full dark ever existed in the LA basin, which produced enough ambient light to be seen for fifty miles from vantage points in the Angeles National Forest near Valencia and as far north as Lebec on a really clear night. John parked in back and they exited the GTO. John unlocked the solid core, wooden back door and punched in the alarm code in the pad inside, which lit up at the first press, and beeped each time John hit a key until Lucille heard it give out a prolonged beep.

"It's off. I would have had to call the alarm company if we came in after nine, and if we stay after nine I'll have to call them to verify my identity, but between seven am and nine pm any day of the week, all I have to do is disarm it when I arrive and reset it when I leave."

"Even on Saturday and Sunday?"

"Seven days a week. I usually come in on Sunday and stop in for an hour or two on Saturday on my way back from Del Mar."

"Can't you work at home?"

"I can and I do. It's just that there are more distractions at home."

"Like what? You said you weren't going with anyone."

"No, I'm not. But there're books, movies, and television."

"Somehow you didn't strike me as the television type."

"I don't know about that. Between Bravo, A&E, Discovery, The History Channel, American Movie Classics, not to mention HBO, CINEMAX, and Showtime, I could spend all day watching if I'm not careful."

"I'm not much on TV. It's too vicarious, too passive. I'd rather rollerblade between Venice and Santa Monica by the ocean or go for a hike off Mandeville Canyon or the Palisades, anything that's not sedentary. I do enough sitting at the gallery."

"I know what you mean, though television can offer you a sense of wonder. How else would the average person know that all heavy elements present on our planet were produced from hydrogen inside stars by the incredibly high temperatures and densities present in their centers. Most of the atoms and molecules on earth and in our bodies owe their existence to processes within the stars."

"It's amazing when you think of it."

"Honestly, as stunningly remarkable as it is, it hurts my head to think of it. Since I only use five percent of my brain, my mind has difficulty grasping the concept that I'm stardust. Like Joni Mitchell wrote, 'We are stardust, we are golden,' he hesitated for a moment.

"What's wrong?"

"I'm sure Joni Mitchell wrote those lines, but I remember them from Crosby, Stills, and Nash singing about Woodstock."

"You mean, 'I came upon a child of God, he was walking on down the road, and I asked him where are you going, and this he told me. Said I'm going down to Yasgur's farm, think I'll join in a rock and roll band, going to camp out on the land and set my soul free.' That one?"

"Yeah, the next line is the one about we are stardust. How do you know? You weren't even born yet."

"No, but I know people who were there and I watched the movie. You weren't exactly there either, unless your mom took you as a baby."

"If she'd been living anywhere within a thousand miles she would have taken me diapers, bottle, and all. At the time, Mom was something of a hippie girl."

John flipped on the light switch and he and Lucille walked down the short, narrow hallway to his office. He turned the switch to the overhead light fixture, which was a chandelier of sorts made of brass and white plastic bulb holders that he and Carol had chosen from the selection at the Home Depot on Jefferson west of Culver City. The frosted, candle-shaped bulbs, and some walnut-stained pine bookcases, gave the room a vague sort of library/study atmosphere, an ambience enhanced by finely framed 18th century legal documents, written with quill pens in India ink on parchment and vellum affixed with large, impressive embossed, red wax seals. These were interspersed with a set of six genuine Currier and Ives color lithographs of steamboats. He had a vanity wall behind his desk featuring his college diploma, his law degree from Loyola, and his license to practice law in the state of California.

"I want you to sit down at my desk and close your eyes." Lucille was admiring his prints, which were 19th century examples and in good condition for the most part.

"Are you sure you didn't invite me to your office to look at your etchings?"

John laughed. "No, I have something even more exiting in mind."

"Now remember this is a first date, and Woodstock was decades ago."

"I'll keep that thought. Now if you'll just sit down and close your eyes."

Lucille didn't think he was going to do anything freaky like strip off his clothes and wiggle his dong at her, or put on some bizarre mask or dress up in drag. Still, a girl couldn't be too sure of a man she'd known for years, much less one she'd been with for less than nine hours. She sat down on his swivel chair covered with what her father used to refer to as hide of the nauga and closed her eyes hoping John wasn't going to do anything to damage her positive impression of him. She felt affection for him, and she hated the thought that he might be weird in some disgusting way.

John spun the dial on the combination lock to the blueprint cabinet and opened the shooting bolt. Lucille was tempted to open her eyes as she heard the snick of the bolt and the smooth sound of a perfectly balanced metal drawer sliding on ball bearings.

Lucille felt the soft rush of air on her face as John opened the cardboard folder. John couldn't help the response of his involuntary nervous system as he opened the folder. There was a sensation in his solar plexus almost like the one he had when he stood in a fast descending elevator. He had always liked art, however he never experienced the visceral response to any painting at the LA County Museum or the Norton Simon that the Van Gogh evoked. It was powerful enough to border on actual discomfort and the fact that a small piece of canvas was probably worth more money than the huge St. Francis Hospital across the street was amazing.

"All right, you can open your eyes." Lucille hadn't known what to expect. First she looked up at John, then she saw he was looking down at his desk and her focus shifted and locked on the painting. John could see the tan of Lucille's face blanch as her eyes opened wide in astonishment.

"Oh my God!" she said with a sharp indrawing of breath. Lucille was very happy she was sitting down, because she was sweating and cold. The Van Gogh self-portrait at the Art Institute of Chicago was her favorite painting in the whole museum. Penetrating and potent as that image is, in fact the first time she saw it in the corner of the gallery she had such a strong attack of vertigo that she sat down on the polished maple floor to avoid fainting. An elderly, uniformed security guard had helped her to her feet and expressed concern. Lucille told him she was fine and that she needed some fresh air. She walked outside the museum and sat down on the granite steps near the huge, greenish bronze lion on the right side of the entrance. The lion was not anatomically correct, a bowdlerization she always thought was offensive to the whole purpose of art, which was to portray the truth as the artist saw it. The cold air off Lake Michigan in October quickly cleared her head and she went back inside to face the portrait once more.

She returned to the painting because she needed to understand how Van Gogh had created a rendering of the human eye that so plumbed the depths of the viewer's soul and simultaneously permitted the observer to experience a portion of the overwhelmingly passionate intensity that animated the artist's own soul. The reddish orange of his beard glowed as if Vincent's face were aflame, and the light bluish-green background, far from being surreal or unreal, lent a greater reality to the work, as if empty space were actually thick with color, the way some people claimed they could see colors in the auras around people. Lucille thought Van Gogh wasn't mad at all: he was only a super-sensitive person who not only could see other people's auras, but his own as well. There was no other plausible explanation for the unearthly effect of his painting. The Dutchman could see auras around physical objects as well as sentient beings. This accounted for his extraordinary night skies, his incredible interiors, and his unique appeal to all people regardless of culture. Of all Western painters who ever took up a brush or palate knife, Van Gogh seemed to be the most accessible. Young or old, Occidental or Oriental, it made no difference.

At the same time he was an unbelievably complex artist who sought to paint what he saw as the truth with a single-minded dedication unmatched by almost any other artist. Lucille knew that the popular notion of Vincent being an untutored genius, who had a ten-year period of incredible productivity immediately preceding his suicide attempt using a revolver, was both a misconception and a myth. A drawing of a stone bridge dated 11 January 1862 when Vincent was nine years old is of such exemplary quality that it could easily pass as having been drawn by Rembrandt and for many years art experts questioned its authenticity and authorship. At age 11, Vincent gave his father Theodorus a drawing of a barn with a steeply pitched roof that once again looks as if it were a Rembrandt. When Vincent was fifteen, having finished his studies, on the strength of his Uncle Cent's recommendation,Vincent was hired by the renowned art dealers, Goupil and Co., as a seller of prints and engravings. Vincent worked for Goupil's offices in The Hague, London, and Paris until he tendered his resignation in April of 1876. Vincent's mastery of art appreciation gained by his years with Goupils is easily seen in a letter to his brother, Theo, written in March of 1878 in which he describes the Borinage Valley. "Generally there is a kind of haze hanging over it all, or fantastic chiaroscuro effect formed by the shadows of the clouds reminding one of the pictures by Rembrandt, or Michel, or Ruisdale." Vincent saw people as figures in well-known works of art, describing a mine foreman as: "When I met him for the first time, I thought of the etching by (Jean-Louis Ernest) Meissonier that we know so well."

The accepted truism that Vincent never sold a work of art he'd created was false as well. He sold a small drawing to Tersteeg at Goupils for 10 florins in 1882, and a series of 12 pen and ink drawings of The Hague for 30 florins in March of 1882. In November of 1882, an art dealer who saw Vincent's lithograph, Sorrow, asked for a set of prints to be made especially for him. Van Gogh may have been a tormented artist, but he was anything but unappreciated. Paul Gaugain, Pere Tanguy, and the art critic Gilbert Aurier, all recognized him as having an unprecedented genius and talent for painting. Aurier was so impressed, he published a story about Van Gogh entitled, "The Isolated Ones, Vincent Van Gogh," six months before Vincent's tragic suicide in July of the same year.

Dryden's portrait was even more powerful than the Art Institute's. Lucille sat stunned, even forgetting to breathe. Then John saw her rather full lower lip quiver and her violet eyes fill with tears that shone in the overhead light. They welled up and rolled down her cheeks. Then she covered her face with both hands and burst into a paroxysm of sobbing so deep it seemed as if her heart were broken.

John never expected anything like this reaction and he was dumbfounded. He stood there by his desk looking at the seemingly inconsolable girl, as all sorts of thoughts raced through his mind from guilt at setting her up for the whole sequence of events, to a desire to keep the painting, for he was by no means immune to its attraction. Possession of such an icon, a totem so imbued with the distillation of a man's reaching out to the Divine, the source of all significant representational art, absolute truth, was not something to simply be sold off. He would never again own anything remotely as ineffable or as beautiful. Perhaps no one on earth owned anything as precious. Hank probably wouldn't object to keeping it in the Dryden family except that the money generated by its sale would benefit all mankind by funding efforts to end the wars in Darfur, Iraq, Myanmar, Columbia, Afghanistan and a hundred other places in the world including Gaza. The painting really belonged in a public collection. It was a unique record of the collective consciousness of humanity, frozen forever at a single highly concentrated moment in time. The impenetrable veil that separates ultimate truth from man, whose greatest aspiration is to be at one with that truth, had been torn asunder by Van Gogh for a few sublime, transcendent hours. The divine knowledge burned in Vincent's brain and may have driven him mad, however he had known the truth long enough to paint it on canvas, rather than seeing it lost to use the words of Blade Runner's Roy Baty, "like tears in the rain." Vincent's painting could only be considered a daring and holy act, like Prometheus stealing fire from the gods. Lucille knew the painting wasn't a completely pure expression of truth, or it wouldn't exist in the physical world. It did have such a very high percentage of truth captured within it that experiencing it was revelatory yet terrifying. This was the quality that enabled people to see something in the painting, to be touched in some aspect of their soul, whether or not they knew impasto from pesto sauce, Post-Impressionism from a postmortem, or a painter's canvas from a canvas duffle bag.

Lucille stopped crying and as she looked up at John with her tears shining on her face, John thought he'd never seen a woman so beautiful. Her very soul had been rendered transparent, washed clean by Vincent's vision. Even Southgate, grimy and unappealing as it usually was, could look clean and fresh following a rainstorm, when the sun was freshly revealed by a break in the clouds, and Lucille was an attractive woman under normal circumstances. As a result of that look, John instantly passed from liking Lucille a great deal to loving her.

He recognized it as his very own Jay Gatsby moment, when he, "listened for a moment to that tuning fork that had been struck upon a star," and his own eyes filled with tears. For Lucille, the violent squall of emotions had passed over, leaving her calm and serene. There were questions in its wake, however they were not so much metaphysical as practical.

"It is real," she asked, "isn't it?"

"I don't know. You're the one with the BFA in art history. You're far more of an art expert than I am." Lucille looked closely at the canvas, studying its physical characteristics. The impasto was classic Van Gogh as was the way the artist used thick paint to build up and define the form of the nose and chin. The crackleure appeared natural, and the painting had the patina that usually comes from exposure to indirect sunlight, tobacco smoke, household cleaning agents, dust, and automobile exhaust over a period of many years. The slight yellowing of the old, lead-based oil paint indicated the painting hadn't been cleaned with solvents since it was painted.

"Unless Van Gogh had one of his artist friends copy one of his self-portraits at the time, I'd say it's authentic. I'm sorry I broke down like that. I hope I didn't frighten you."

"No, but I was feeling guilty for springing it on you like that. I wanted to surprise you not make you miserable."

"Art critics who are notorious for trafficking in counterfeit emotion, by that I mean they attribute qualities to works of art that in and of themselves have no essential truth, like to talk about the shock of recognition. Well, you sure shocked the you know what out of me."

"I apologize."

"Please don't. The whole purpose of great art is to rock the psyche and establish a different dialogue between the viewer and the world, whether that world is the physical world around him or the world within him. How else but by literally knocking you out of your usual orbit can you hope to see the truth the artist is trying to show you. If you see a painting and think, 'Oh, that's pretty,' and experience it with your eyes alone while your heart remains detached the whole time, then that painting is a mere decoration and nothing more."

"How about Duchamp's and Picasso's so-called 'ready-mades?'"

"By using common urinals and signing them R. Mutt or by taking a bicycle seat and a pair of handlebars and creating a bull, they were making a statement and trying desperately to divert the flow of people's understanding of art from it's old and well worn channels and send it flowing in new, hitherto unknown directions, and they succeeded."

"I think I understand what you're trying to say, that there's artistic truth in ordinary objects, even urinals. It's all a matter of perspective. I still think the two of them must have laughed themselves silly reading the critics' comments."

"Duchamp created his first 'ready-made' in 1913, entitled 'Bicycle Wheel,' which was the wheel from a bicycle mounted on the seat of a stool. The Dada Movement, Dada being French for hobbyhorse, was essentially anti-aesthetic, a protest of bourgeois values and despair over the First World War. Duchamp used techniques of creation relying on chance and accident. Duchamp wholeheartedly embraced the movement and became its leading exponent and champion. He asserted that the 'intellectual expression' of the artist was of much greater significance than the object created."

"I still think a shark preserved in a tank of formaldehyde is just that. If I want one, I'll make my own. Same with a picture of the Virgin Mary in a bucket of piss."

"I know what you mean. I'm not one of Damien Hurst's big fans, then again he has so many he doesn't need me either. That's enough about his rotting shark that needs to be replaced and the nature of art. How did this painting find its way to your office in Southgate?"

John told her the story Hank had told him, word for word, as closely as he could recall it. Then he brought her up to date with the pistol transaction with Angus, and Angus being his agent. Lucille was incredulous.

"You're going to let Angus Creswell handle the sale?"

Lucille's tone made John anxious.

"What? You don't think he's capable?"

"No, it's more that it's out of his league. He may be a player in the arms and armor field but this is worth exponentially more than any object that was ever sold in his field."

"Well, if you think he's not competent, I'll tell him the deal's off, though I did give him my word and shook hands on it."

"Then I guess you're stuck with him. He's a pro, so he'll have enough sense not to burn it no matter what."

John was close to panic. "What do you mean burn it? Of course he won't burn it."

Lucille was highly amused. "Slow down a minute, buckaroo. In the art world, a piece like this that hasn't been offered for sale in generations is said to be 'fresh to the market.' I know it makes it sound like a head of lettuce or a box of strawberries but it's art dealer talk. If the piece is offered around to the usual suspects and no one buys it, either because it's priced too high or there are doubts as to originality or history, then it's no longer considered 'fresh' but shopworn, what we call burnt. If you put it up for auction and somehow it failed to sell, whether because of condition, too high a reserve or estimate, there are many factors, the painting would be burnt as well and failing an after-sale private treaty, the best thing to do would be to take it off the market for a minimum of five years to 'season' it. With a painting of this importance, I think you're going to have a severe provenance problem. Surely someone in the Dietrich family will claim it. Not that I care about whether the family of an SS general gets a dime out of it or not. As far as your other major claimant, the Roth family, I can't imagine assuming they have a claim of any sort, why they never went to the Art Loss Register, unless by the time the Register was founded, they'd given up all hope of ever seeing it again."

"Angus double and triple checked with the Register, INTERPOL, and even the FBI, and no one is looking for it as far as they know."

"That's all to the good, then again after nearly sixty-three years who knows." "How do you forget a Van Gogh?"

"Good question, especially seeing that there were more books and theses written about him from 1890 to 1942 than about any other artist, including Rembrandt and Michelangelo. Still, anything can happen."

"My grandfather has insisted on a very private sale. He doesn't want to be the focus of a media circus."

"Now, even though I only met him today, I can say in all honesty I love him, and I don't blame him at all. With the Roths out of the picture, the question is less a legal one than an ethical issue. Like I said, taking it from an SS general isn't theft, it's a mitzvot, a blessing. Despite what the Dadaists and the Existentialists say about the universe being governed by happenstance and chance, I believe as I told you earlier, that everything happens for a reason. Christian's say the Lord marks the sparrow's fall. The Jews say Hashem knows the outcome of a matter at its inception. What I mean is that it's no accident your grandfather took that painting and it's not by chance that he's kept it a secret all these years."

"So, then Angus is meant to sell the painting."

"The universal pattern is a work in progress and because of free will things can change within the bounds of certain parameters. Of course we mortals don't know what those boundaries or parameters are."

"It's all dizzying when I think of it. Only yesterday I was looking at a dead body in the front of this office and now a little over twenty-four hours later, here I am looking at a Van Gogh with a beautiful woman."

"I can't help asking. How much are you going to ask for it?"

"Hank wants 75 million."

Lucille wrinkled up her forehead, raising her thick, dark eyebrows.

"That seems like half of its real value, maybe even less than that. Someone is going to get the biggest bargain in the art world since I don't know when."

"You really think so?"

"I do. All of this is assuming you surmount the provenance problem and authenticity hurdles."

"But you and Angus both say it's real."

"What we say means nothing, less than nothing, when push comes to shove. Most big money artists have their own particular expert or museum authority whose opinion on authenticity is accepted by museums, auction galleries, dealers, and collectors. In the case of Renoir, it's Daniel Wildenstein, for Rembrandt, it's the Rembrandt Project, and for Van Gogh, it's the Rijksmuseum Vincent Van Gogh in Holland. If this painting were to be sold at public auction as an autograph work by Van Gogh the gallery, Sotheby's, Christie's, Bonham's, or Park Avenue would want and need the blessing of the museum."

"Even when it's obvious to you and Angus that it's real?"

"You have to remember that we know the provenance is from Roth and that your grandfather personally cut it out of the frame in the spring of 1945. We're believers partly because we know its history. Whoever buys it won't know these things except by heresay."

"Well, either it will sell or it won't. And if it doesn't, I guess either Hank or I will just keep it and enjoy it."

"You'll have to keep it in a fire-proof vault."

"My blueprint file is fire-proof and remember it sat in Hank's closet all those years."

"That was before he knew what he had. Forget about its intrinsic value as a stunning work of art. Would you keep 75 million dollars in your filing cabinet? Of course you wouldn't. Who would, other than some wildly eccentric billionaire or a drug kingpin? You have a responsibility as the custodian of an irreplaceable work of art."

"Listen, I couldn't afford the insurance."

"Not too many people can. That's why sometimes collectors leave precious pieces in a vault rather than on the wall or in a drawer."

"I think it's a shame to leave beautiful things in a vault where no one can appreciate them."

"I agree. Then again, most museums are like icebergs with the vast majority of their works of art in storage, in so-called 'study collections,' and they never see the light of day."

"Then they should sell the stuff and use the money to open up more exhibition space."

"That's a story for another time. John, I need to use your bathroom and then we can get something to eat."

Lucille really wanted to go to a sushi restaurant on Beverly Glen up past Mulholland Drive located in a small upscale shopping area, however the food was pricey and she didn't want to take advantage of John. Then she remembered he'd just sold some Nazi pistol to Angus for more money than she made in the last two years.

"Do you eat sushi?" John liked sushi. He'd been thinking of a Francisco's taco for the past two hours, but Lucille wasn't much of a carnivore, and thanks to Hank, he had more disposable income than he'd ever had in his life, so he could easily afford to take her anywhere she liked without a second thought.

"I do like sushi. Not all kinds though. I can't eat uni, or the raw egg things. I like the magoro, toro, hamachi, anago, things like that."

"Me, too. I know a great little place off Beverly Glen tucked away in a sort of high-end strip mall."

"That sounds great. It's Saturday night. You think we can get a table?"

"It'll be packed, but I eat there at once a week and the hostess knows me. She'll get us a table. We might have to wait fifteen minutes. It's a nice place and they have benches outside."

"Let's go. Let me put Vincent back in his cabinet and you can use the bathroom. It's down the hall on the left."

# CHAPTER 17

# The Tarot

WESTBOUND TRAFFIC ON the 105 was clipping along at 70 and it wasn't until they were north of LAX that the 405 became a sea of red tail lights and dead stopped vehicles, which thinned out as usual once they passed the 10 Santa Monica Freeway.

"Take the Sunset exit," said Lucille. "That way we avoid Wilshire and Westwood."

They didn't have to wait long for a table, as most of the patrons preferred sitting at the sushi bar, which was fine with John. They each ordered a flask of hot sake and then shared a large Kirin Ichiban beer. When the young, pretty, and distinctly non-Japanese waitress asked John if he wanted another flask of sake, he declined and deferred to Lucille, who also passed. When the waitress smiled and walked off, John said, "It's not that I wouldn't like another flask, it's that one more would probably put me over the limit, and I don't think driving while impaired is a good thing to do. Strictly speaking, even the little I have drunk makes me a less safe driver than if I had only tea with my dinner. Call me old fashioned, lame, a square as Hank would say, but if I'm going to drink, I generally don't drive."

"I don't think you're lame. I think you're kind and considerate. I can't understand, knowing that tens of thousands of people die and hundreds of thousands are injured every year in accidents involving drunk drivers, why there isn't a law that all vehicles must have a breath test interlock that prevents drunk driving."

"You'd be penalizing drivers who don't drink."

"I've never hijacked an airplane, yet I'm penalized every time I have to go through security at LAX, and drunk drivers kill and maim one hell of a lot more people in two months than all the terrorist attacks in the United States since the Oklahoma City bombing."

"I see your point, believe me. I have to listen to Hank and read his emails about how ridiculous this whole phony terrorist menace really is. It's just an excuse, according to him, to suspend the Constitution and Bill of Rights, and institute warrantless wiretaps and searches. As Hank says the easiest way to control a nation is to 'tell them they are being attacked, and denounce the pacifists for lack of patriotism and exposing their country to danger; it works the same in any country.' Do you know who made this observation?"

"No, who?"

"Hermann Goering."

Lucille made a disgusted face. "I'm still glad you don't drive when you've had one too many. You're a good man, John Dryden. It was well past nine when they snaked their way down Beverly Glen Canyon. Traffic was relatively light, especially after John made the right on Sunset and then he immediately turned left back onto Beverly Glen, because Beverly Glen intersected Sunset in such a way that it was actually discontinuous for a few hundred yards. John had the radio on 91.5 KUSC, and the Academy of St. Martin in the Fields, conducted by Sir Neville Mariner was performing Chopin's Fantasie in F minor as he neared Lucille's apartment building.

"See if you can find a parking space," said Lucille. John was silently grateful that she'd solved a problem he had been wrestling with since they passed Wilshire. He was physically tired. He'd driven nearly seven hours, walked on the beach for miles, and thanks to Ahmed Nahabedian, he hadn't slept well the night before. Though he had spent the day with Lucille and he thought they'd really gotten to know each other, it was still a first date, and in the 21st century, unless the girl was exceptionally active sexually, a man had no right to expect anything beyond a quick hug and a kiss on the cheek with a promise to call, and that was if the woman liked him. John thought there was both physical and romantic chemistry between them, however that didn't mean Lucille was going to invite him into her home. Lucille had dropped some subtle hints that in spite of her provocative, bra-less look, she wasn't by any means prolix with her favors. She'd made reference to the crass stupidity of men who assumed if a girl didn't wear a bra, she was more likely to want to have sex, that she was advertising her wares so to speak.

"I hate that sort of sexism, don't you?" At the time, John agreed with her that all such men were swine, although if he told the truth in his heart, he thought there might be a grain of validity to the male chauvinist view.

The part of him that naturally sought peace and quiet made him hope that Lucille would give him a quick hug, perhaps a kiss on the lips instead of the cheek at the passenger side of the GTO. He would tell her he would call, and they would both know he meant it. Another part of him wanted her to invite him in for a nightcap. They would continue their discussions about art and metaphysics. He would sit next to her on the couch and with a little finesse, more serious deep kissing would take place. He would touch her and she would stop him saying she wasn't really ready yet, though she really did like him. They'd get up from the couch, Lucille would say it was getting late, and he would agree. Then they'd embrace at the front door. He'd feel her pressing against his chest as they kissed with tongues gently exploring and she would know he was aroused from the erection in his jeans. Lucille would open the door, he would kiss her once more, and then within a minute he'd be inside the GTO having told her he'd see her this week. She'd have said yes, that sounds wonderful, knowing she meant every word and they'd see each other one night during the week. When Lucille asked him to find a place to park, he instantly discarded the first scenario, and began thinking with pleasurable anticipation of the second one.

Lucille's apartment was a walk-up on the second floor. There was no security except for a deadbolt and a Judas hole in the solid-core wood door. The lighting outside was good. Once inside, John saw the apartment was a spacious one bedroom with a kitchen, living room, bathroom, and even a powder room. Lucille had painted the walls a cream color and there were contemporary, mostly non-representational paintings in both oil and acrylic on the walls. Several were very large. John liked some for the bright colors, though there were others like the one that consisting of shades of black in varying intensities he neither understood the meaning of nor the artist's intention.

They were seated on a comfortable, dark green couch, upholstered in a cloth that was much like velvet or velour. Lucille had opened a bottle of Argentine Malbec and poured each of them half a glass in thin red wine goblets. John and Lucille raised their goblets simultaneously, clinking them softly. Lucille said, "Here's to a lovely day. I enjoyed every minute of it."

John smiled warmly, "And to the beautiful lady that made it happen." With that, she snuggled close to John, then put her glass down on the low, highly-varnished pine table and squeezed his left hand with her warm right one. She got up and changed the station on her Bose stereo, which was one of the better non-component systems on the market, and passed by several classic rock stations before settling on KPFK Pasadena and "Evening Becomes Eclectic." The show was featuring some hip-hop reggae, which John thought was interesting, so when Lucille looked at him questioningly, he nodded and she left it on. She opened a tall rectangular cardboard box, took out a very long wooden match, struck it on top of the box, and walked around the room lighting candles in their glass holders. When the room was aglow with their soft light, she turned the rheostat and lowered the intensity of the rice paper lamps that hung from the ceiling. Satisfied with the level and mood of the light, she used the match to light two sandalwood joss sticks that protruded erect from their flat rosewood holders.

Lucille walked back to the couch and stood in front of John.

"Let's go into the bedroom." John thought this was strange, since she'd just arranged a romantic mood in the living room. He looked up at her.

"No. On second thought there's something else I want to do first. Now it's your turn to close your eyes and don't you dare peek. I didn't." John dutifully closed his eyes, thinking that Lucille was going to undress. KPFK gave way to the sensuous sounds of some unidentifiable New Age CD that reminded him of the music that was playing while he had a massage at the sumptuous Nob Hill Spa in the Huntington Hotel during the otherwise disastrous weekend with Janet.

He'd gone there without telling her before leaving for the airport. It was the best 45 minutes and one hundred and twenty dollars he'd spent on that abortive trip. He'd seen the spa as they were checking in, since he'd left their bags with the bell captain. He was able to retrieve his luggage without alerting his drunken girlfriend when he dropped her off at the corner. He parked the car in the garage and the bellman brought his overnight bag. It was slightly before 5:00 p.m. and he should have driven straight to the airport, but he asked the girl at the spa desk if there were any massages available and miraculously someone had just cancelled their five o'clock appointment, so he decided to go for it. How he managed to catch the 7:30 flight and return the car to Hertz, he couldn't even recall. That fifty minutes worked all the tension out of his neck muscles, and on the flight back he was as relaxed as if he hadn't just broken up with the woman he intended to marry.

Lucille's incense tickled his olfactories and he thought of the massage and that he'd made a resolution to have one once a week when he returned to LA, and of course never followed up on his decision. He heard Lucille padding around the apartment, then a riffling sound as if she were shuffling cards.

"All right. You can open your eyes." John blinked and he was looking at Lucille, who was holding a deck of oversize cards, and she'd cleared the copies of *Art News* and *Artforum* as well as their glasses from the pine coffee table in front of the couch.

"I want to make love to you," she said in her raspy, and to John, oh so sexy voice. "But before I do, I'd like to do a Tarot spread. I already know what you're thinking. 'Just when I think I really like this girl, she turns out to be some New Age wacko who believes in Area 57, the Roswell conspiracy, UFO's, and putting copper rings on my car's exhaust pipe to increase my gas mileage. Either that or else, 'This chick's lost in the sixties, incense, candles, the next thing's she's going to bring out a hookah and a gram of hashish.'"

Actually, John did have an automatic negative reaction to the Tarot as he did to all magical ways of manipulating human behavior, though he recognized the extraordinary effectiveness of magical thinking in advertising, the reliance on so-called "secret" ingredients and "secret" processes to market everything from acne creams to the magical eleven herbs and spices in Kentucky Fried Chicken. He deplored the hucksterism of TV evangelists, selling everything from ''holy water' to 'holy' scriptures', all for exorbitant prices to people desperate for something tangible to believe in. The Tarot was inextricably linked with divination and fortune telling. To most people the cards had a distinctly Satanic feel about them like drawing pentagrams.

"I want you to suspend any preconceived feelings you may have toward the Tarot. They come from the devil, death, and hanged man cards of the Major Arcana. People might as well say Albrecht Durer was Satanic because of his famous copperplate engraving of Knight, Death, and the Devil or his Four Witches. No one knocks or fears Shakespeare because he has witches; the Weird Sisters control men's fates in Macbeth. They even have a cauldron and speak of eye of newt. But all most people think of when they see the Tarot is the black arts. It's ridiculous. As much as I hate to say it, I think most of the negativity people have towards the Tarot cards comes from the fact that they are intimately associated with Gypsies. To most of the people in Europe in the 16th and 17th centuries, both Gypsies and Jews were seen as being in league with Satan. Even in the 20th century, Hitler sent 400,000 Gypsies to the extermination camps as well as six million Jews, this despite the common knowledge that all Gypsies are Aryan by definition.

The historical record shows that Tarot cards are first known in the very Christian countries of France and Italy in the 14th century. The Christian nature of the Tarot is shown conclusively by the Death card being number thirteen and that the Hanged Man, Jesus, is number XII. It wasn't until the 18th century that European writers began associating the Tarot with mysticism, divination, ritual magic, and alchemy. There are 22 cards of the Major Arcana and 56 of the Minor Arcana. My mother taught me that the Tarot is no different from any technique to plumb the unconscious. The cards are a mechanism to see into the person's soul by interpreting his reactions and listening to what he sees in them, much like psychoanalysis. The purpose of the Tarot is to allow a person to access himself by providing structured, interpretable ambiguity. The cards are very much in the tradition of Karl Jung's archetypes in that they are symbols of the collective unconsciousness of the entire human species throughout its history.

Now that you know the Tarot isn't a devilish device and I guarantee you I don't have any horns hidden under my hair or a tail coiled in my jeans, let's go into the real business of the Tarot, that is if I haven't lost you along the way."

"No, now that you've explained it in a psychoanalytic context, it's very interesting."

"Just promise me you'll keep an open mind."

The truth was John did find it interesting, now that Lucille told him the way in which the cards worked, that the meanings were purposely ambiguous, and not so specific that his actions would be poured into a mold and labeled.

"I promise."

"Good. The meaning of any individual card can be modified, depending if it's upside down, or rightside up, its position in the spread, and in the context of its adjacent cards. Generally speaking, the cards of the Major Arcana, the face cards if you want to think in terms of a normal deck of playing cards, refer to spiritual matters and significant trends in the life of the questioner. The Minor Arcana, the number cards, are divided into coins, which refer to material comfort, swords, representing conflict, cups pertaining to love as in loving cup, and wands, which deal with ambitions and business matters. It's important to keep in mind that just because you're dealt the Death Card, it doesn't mean you or someone you love is in imminent danger of death, any more than the Hanged Man means you're going to the gallows. The Tarot is far more complicated than that. It is concerned with archetypes, not specifics. Like any type of spirituality and psychology, its value is not intrinsic but extrinsic. A person who has no faith in psychiatry is wasting his money on analysis."

John couldn't help himself. "But someone who's bi-polar is bi-polar whether he has any belief in his therapist or not."

"Very true, and this holds for the Tarot as well. Unfortunately there are many amateurs, some well meaning, others more perverse, who use the Tarot as a sort of parlor game like a Ouija board or crystal ball. No one can precisely predict the future, because it hasn't happened yet. Still one can make predictions based on a person's past behavior with some reasonable expectation of a future result. By no means am I a master like my mother, still I think she taught me well." Something about the Tarot was tickling John's mind like a tiny feather in the back of his throat, then all of a sudden he had the reference.

"Doesn't T.S. Eliot talk about the Tarot in the Wasteland?"

Lucille grinned knowing she was on very firm intellectual ground. "You mean, 'Madame Sosostris, famous clairvoyant, Had a bad cold, nevertheless, is known to be the wisest woman in Europe, with a wicked pack of cards. Here said she, is your card, the drowned Phoenician Sailor, those are pearls that were his eyes, Look!'"

She paused, "I can go on if you like. It's interesting that you bring up the Wasteland. I don't know how far you got into the poem, but Eliot based a great deal of it on Jessie Weston's book, From Ritual to Romance. Eliot wrote that, 'Not only the title, but the plan and a good deal of the symbolism of the poem was suggested by the book'. It was Weston who traced the symbols used on the Tarot cards to the symbolism of fertility cults, the Fisher King, the god of vegetation whose death is mourned with the dying of the year, and returns triumphantly to life in the spring. She makes the case, which I happen to doubt, that the Tarot was used in ancient Egypt to predict the rising of the Nile. I'm getting off track here talking about the Wasteland. You're not doing this to postpone your reading by any chance are you?"

"No, not at all. It's just that I don't often get an opportunity to talk about poetry with someone who knows what they're talking about."

"Oh, I have a feeling you'll be doing a lot of literary criticism in the coming months if you play your cards right, and I intended to use that pun."

"I'll hold you to that. I want to know all about the Latin and Greek preface to the Wasteland. One more thing. Who wrote that poem about the pearls that were his eyes?"

Lucille was delighted. "You mean, 'Full fathom five thy father lies, Those are pearls that were his eyes, Of his bones are corals made?'"

"That's right. Who wrote it?"

"I'll give you a clue. It is a song that young Prince Ferdinand hears as he wanders disconsolately about the island believing his father has drowned."

Now it was John's turn to be triumphant. "I remember. It's Ariel's song from the Tempest."

"Good for you. There's more to you than the law, John Dryden. Then again, I expected nothing less from a man with your illustrious name. Now, let's proceed. "

There was intensity in Lucille's expression that was intimidating and for a time earlier during her monologue, John thought she might be hypnotizing him. Looking around him he felt he needed to break out of what was very close to an alternate reality created by the candles, incense, and Lucille's presence. His mindset was similar to one he recalled from college, when his first roommate turned him on to marijuana. Marijuana had a disorienting and disconcertingly disconnecting effect on John and the roommate told him he'd get used to it and learn to love it.

"Think of it as skiing or rollerblading with your mind. You have to consciously allow yourself to relinquish control and then re-balance. Once you do it's easy. You're free to glide effortlessly, like flying. I'm sure baby birds go through the same experiences when they learn to fly. At first there must be uncertainty, even terror in falling, and then the inexpressible joy and the most incredible sensation of freedom and release."

"I feel like the bird that didn't flap his wings quite right, and fluttered down to the ground where a cat will come and eat me."

John tried smoking a few more times, and he got to the stage where he could see how someone might like the effect, however he decided that getting high on mind-altering, illegal substances wasn't for him.

Now, in Lucille's apartment, as sweat trickled down his underarms, and his stomach was queasy, and not from the delicious sushi, and his head felt light, John wondered if he weren't experiencing a mild panic attack. He was aware that in all likelihood Nahabedian's violent death in his office had an impact on some deep, unconscious level in his psyche and additionally, he was out of his element in an unknown environment. He knew his anxiety had absolutely no basis in reality. Lucille wasn't going to harm him, far from it. She was the most charming girl he'd met in years. He detested these rare panic attacks, which ambushed him out of the blue, always at the most inopportune moments, never at his home, his office, or at Hank's. John hadn't had an attack for more than a year, and the last one was when he was with a girl named

Leslie. They'd gone to a movie at the Third Street Promenade in Santa Monica and were eating at a nearby Italian restaurant. The attack was so severe he began hyperventilating and nearly fainted off his cast iron chair. Then he drank a second full glass of Chianti and within ten minutes, he'd stopped sweating and enjoyed the remainder of their date. Leslie remained blissfully unaware that he'd undergone something similar to a near-death experience.

"John, are you all right?" asked Lucille with real concern. "You look pale and you're sweating."

Of course Lucille would have to notice. She was exquisitely aware and sensitive.

"Do you need to go outside for some fresh air?"

"No," said John. "It's not that. It's just sometimes I get these sort of mild panic attacks. They're not really debilitating, more of a nuisance than anything."

Lucille put down the Tarot pack, sat down next to him, then put her arm around him and looked into his eyes.

"Maybe this is all going too fast for you. The last thing I want to do is overwhelm you and I have enough self-knowledge to be aware I have a tendency to do that. It's only that our time here is so very brief; it's almost a crime to waste any of it waiting. Not that I'm one of the "just do it" people; I'm anything but. However when it's right, I think I know it, and I go for it."

Confessing his weakness made him feel much better. He could never have been comfortable explaining his sudden, generalized anxiety episodes to Leslie. Lucille's nearness was reassuring, rather than stifling or suffocating. His pulse, which seemed like it were racing only moments ago and thready and erratic as well, slowed to its normal, steady, predictable rhythm.

"Ahh," he said, "that's nice. Once the attack passes it never recurs on the same day or even in the same week. It's got nothing to do with you. I've had them in court in front of judges I eat lunch with. I can't predict them or I'd get a prescription for something, Then again, I'm not much of a pill taker."

Lucille was certain John's attacks could be managed by learning breathing techniques. Lucille had learned them from an Indian philosopher and guru she'd met at the Self Realization Fellowship Temple in the Pacific Palisades, off Sunset Boulevard, near the Pacific Coast Highway. Pranayama had a therapeutic effect on a number of disorders, and anxiety was particularly susceptible to a deliberate reduction in respiration. One of Lucille's girlfriends had literally controlled her colitis through pranayama, to the praise and astonishment of her gastroenterologist, who began recommending it as an adjunct form of therapy in addition to pharmaceuticals. There was so much she wanted to share with John that would open him up to the wonders of the phenomenal world and he, in his turn, could share his love and dedication to the cause of the dispossessed, an unusual and precious quality in a society that values property above humanity, and grants legal rights to corporations, trusts, and legal fictions as if they were flesh and bone. Lucille considered this state of affairs proof positive that the American legal system was utterly preverse.

"I think I'd like another glass of wine. And then I'd like you to do my Tarot spread."

"Are you sure?"

Lucille really didn't want John to think he was being pressured in any way.

"This isn't your male ego talking here, making up for admitting to being vulnerable?"

John laughed. "Lucille, you can't imagine what a relief it is to be with someone I don't have to pretend around."

"Oh, I wouldn't be too sure about that. My imagination is a law unto itself. I can promise you I don't pretend. I might flirt and play games, even role play and dress up in a different incarnation entirely; however I'll let you know in advance so we can both be in the same play."

She got up, filled his glass, and brought it to him. Then she picked up the Tarot deck and shuffled it as expertly as any Las Vegas blackjack dealer.

"In the eighteenth century, the French nobleman, Court de Gebelin correlated the 22 cards of the Major Arcana, also known as trumps, with the 22 letters of the Hebrew alphabet, thus linking Tarot with the kabbalah, which as you know is esoteric Jewish mysticism. The Sefer Yetzira, the Book of Creation, is the earliest extant text on cosmology and magic. It appeared about 1500 years ago, and explained creation as a process involving the ten sefirot, the so-called divine numbers, and the 22 letters of the alphabet."

"So that's how the Tarot cards became linked with the Jews as well as the Gypsies."

"Exactly. However, they are much more than a tool for telling fortunes. By definition, the future is unknown, because it hasn't taken place as yet. One can see a pattern by looking at the present and the past, then make a prediction based on what has taken place, however nothing in the tapestry of existence is sure until the knot is tied in place by time. As the poet Omar Khayyam put is so beautifully and eloquently in his quatrain from the Rubiyat, "The moving finger writes and having writ moves on, nor all your piety nor all your wit can lure it back to cancel half a line, nor all your tears wash out a single word of it."

"That's a depressing thought."

"Yes and no. Anyway, enough of Persian poetry. Back to the Tarot. In their purest form the Tarot are a means to exalt individual consciousness. A system of symbols to free the mind, no hallucinogens required."

"That's a good thing, because psychotropic drugs and I don't really get along very well, but that's a story for another day as well."

Lucille had nothing against mind-altering drugs as long as they were from nature and not some laboratory, however they were no more than a means to an end, not an end in themselves, and with the passing of each year she had less and less use for them.

"I'm going to do a horseshoe spread. Later when you're more familiar with the path, and more aware and open to the whole process, I'll do something more elaborate, like the Tree of Life or the Celtic cross."

John was feeling comfortable and relaxed as he sipped his wine, enjoying the soft golden light cast by the numerous candles, the delicate fragrance of sandalwood, and contemplating Lucille, who was concentrating hard on the cards as she laid them down on the table in the shape of a horseshoe.

"Now, remember that absolutely nothing of what I say or what the cards reveal is set in stone. The pattern of existence encompasses only present and past. Tarot cards cannot in and of themselves yield concrete judgments and anyone who says they can is misusing them in a potentially dangerous, destructive way. Like Jungian analysis, the Tarot is only a path. Now, bearing all that in mind, the card to your right is indicative of your present status."

Lucille deliberately turned the card over.

"The seven of cups. I know I said earlier that cups were associated with love. Even so, the context is not certain. The card really means you have a choice to make that requires serious consideration."

John said nothing, though he thought making considerate choices was a wise thing to do under any circumstances. Lucille thought she knew exactly what he was thinking; that making considered choices was rather obvious, however she knew the cards would become less predictable very soon.

"The next card signifies current expectations."

Lucille turned up the Ace of Wands.

"An ace is sometimes assigned a high value as it is with modern playing cards, however in the Tarot the ace represents the lowest value card, though once again, a low number value does not equate with insignificance in the scheme of things, just as in certain situations a pawn may be of equal or greater importance than a knight or bishop, sometimes even the queen in chess. Though wands are often thought to concern business or career matters, in this particular context, the ace indicates you have a strong creative energy within you. The center card of the horseshoe represents the unexpected."

John was interested though, as with the deliberate decision revelation with the cups card, Lucille hadn't really said anything startling or revelatory. She turned over the next card and it was the Page of Swords. She was trying hard to keep her face neutral and impassive, still John could see she was far less than thrilled with this card.

"Lucille, you look less than happy. What's up?"

"Either there's something in trust for the future or there's someone you should beware of. Don't be alarmed yet; it's the final two cards that represent the future. The first is the immediate future and the second reaches out into the long term."

Lucille took a long, steady breath, exhaled, and turned over the Nine of Swords." John took one look at it and he was frightened. The card was positively terrifying in appearance.

"You can't possibly tell me this one is good news." The colors on the card were vibrant and appealing, though the scenes depicted were anything but. John went on, "Swords, and a woman who looks like she's lost everything she ever held dear in life. Either that or she is about to be tortured and executed. It's a portrait of ultimate despair. No wonder people are scared of Tarot readings. I'll stick to astrology; it's more equivocal."

"Now, you promised to keep an open mind. That being said, I'll be the first to admit that it's not the most auspicious appearing card in the deck. Though you'll admit after I revealed the first card you were saying to yourself, 'It's just the usual fortune telling routine. Anyone knows you should be deliberate in your choices.' No seer ever tells someone there will be great misfortune in his or her future, though it's as inevitable as death. Now, you're unhappy because of a card, which on the surface looks anything but auspicious. However, if you regard the card closely, you'll see the swords are not actually piercing, or even touching the woman's body. Your immediate future will present you with some significant difficulty; possibly a series of difficulties, however it or they will be no more than the darkness before the dawn." Between Lucille's sonorous, husky voice, and the incense perfumed, candlelit room, John was sitting spellbound and filled with a keen excitement for the final card to be shown. With a suitably dramatic gesture, Lucille used the index finger of her right hand. She inserted her fingernail under the edge, and flipped it end for end. John was ecstatic. The card portrayed a man in regal dress, obviously a king, the King of Cups.

"Well, well," said Lucille, the satisfaction evident in her voice. "The King of Cups. How very interesting. Cups in the Tarot deck correspond to hearts in the playing card deck, and therefore they are often associated with love. The deeper meaning, though, is more obscure. I would say in your case the card is most appropriate and auspicious seeing as you're a public interest lawyer. Taking into account its position in the spread, it represents either a call to self-introspection, or it's a reflection of a deep and abiding love of humanity. Remember, it's the final card of the horseshoe, so it sees toward the long-term future."

"So it doesn't mean that sometime in the distant future, I'll be the king of hearts?"

"No, Don Juan, I'm afraid not."

"Is it a good journey as far as horseshoe spread Tarot readings go?"

"By no means the best I've ever seen, but very far from the worst, believe me."

Lucille gathered up the cards, shuffled them three times and replaced them in their paper container, folded the flap closed, and placed them on a mahogany bookshelf that had a selection of hard-bound books with gilt stamped titles. She turned to him and smiled innocently. She'd only given him one level of meaning for several reasons. One was that she knew John was skeptical of the cards, associating them with Ouija boards, so-called black magic, as if they were tools of the Devil, when in fact they were far more closely associated with Christ and Christianity. Also it was one thing to know intellectually that all the elements in your body were created once in the depths of a star, and another to accept this incredible scientific fact as something so transcendent as to make the most ordinary person on earth, a wonderful phenomenon surpassing all human understanding, a reason to celebrate the sacredness of life, greater and more powerful than any contained in all the sacred writings since the beginning of recorded history. John was still mesmerized by the Tarot reading, yet at the same time he really wanted to connect with Lucille and give her something in return for the lovely gift she'd given him.

"I read somewhere," he said, "that a philosopher is a poet of the mind, but a poet is a philosopher of the heart. Lucille, you are poetry in action." Lucille's eyes widened and she warmed John with her smile.

"I like that. I like that very much. Now give me a minute to do a few things."

A few minutes later, Lucille called John into the bedroom. His heart was racing, though it wasn't due to a panic attack. All of his physical weariness vanished and in its place was excitement. He hadn't had sex with a woman in months, although he pleasured himself in the shower from time to time just to ensure his system was still viable and he wasn't suffering from the dread ED, erectile dysfunction. As he entered the bedroom John could see that at least half of the floor was taken up by a surprisingly luxurious, walnut four-poster bed topped with a dazzling white cotton canopy. Wooden sconces placed strategically on the walls held crystal candlesticks, which lit the room as if it were an altar in a cathedral. Small brass censers smoked gently giving off a heady aromatic fragrance that smelled like frankincense. A haunting and dimly familiar piece of New Age music was playing low and sweetly on a small CD player. Lucille was standing to one side of the bed dressed in a sheer chiffon negligee that emphasized her breasts and large nipples.

"Take off your clothes," she purred. John quickly stripped off his shirt and unbuckled his Gucci belt, dropping his jeans, then used the left heel of his shoe to remove his right loafer, repeated the process with his right stocking heel, then kicked his jeans under the bed. He moved to take her in his arms, but she adroitly sidestepped his advance.

"I want you to know that I don't sleep around. I don't do one-night stands. If that's what you're in to, you'll do us both a favor by putting your clothes back on and leaving right now. There'll be no hard feelings, I promise. Now, don't get the idea that I suddenly want to marry you and bear your children either, or that I want to live with you or have you move in with me. Oh, and one more thing. I'm on the pill so you needn't worry about me getting pregnant. I don't have any sexually transmitted diseases, and if you do, please have the decency to tell me and I'll either get you a condom or we'll pass on intercourse altogether and just fool around. You don't look like the STD type, then again these days you can't be too careful. I apologize if my spiel turns you off. Think of it this way, there's nothing romantic about herpes or venereal warts, much less HIV."

"I can't say I've ever heard it put quite so directly. I will say I admire your candor."

"Good. Then take off those silly looking boxer shorts and come to bed."

With that, Lucille hopped up onto the huge bed, which had a super-abundance of fluffy feather pillows in satin pillowcases. John wasted no time ripping off his socks and boxers, and within a very short time he was pressed against Lucille and kissing her passionately. Lucille's mouth was soft and warm, tasting of wine and peppermint, a combination he found delicious. Their tongues were dancing with each other and he let Lucille lead, showing him the pressure and direction she wanted him to use and follow. Lucille had been kissing boys since junior high school and considered the passionate kisses they were exchanging to be a very intimate and serious act of passion, something not to be entered into lightly or carelessly. She knew men who considered kissing to be no more intimate than shaking hands or hugging. Lucille responded to their advances with a quick buss on the cheek or the lips, keeping the velvety, moist interior of her mouth safely locked away from their crude addresses.

When she was in her early twenties, she would occasionally even let them have intercourse with her, although she did that only with men who really turned her on and this after she made certain they weren't some type of freak. After one of her girlfriends had gotten knocked around by a perfectly normal looking, Century City entertainment lawyer she'd met at Huston's bar, while she and Lucille were waiting for a table after watching a film, Lucille, who'd always been what she believed to be discerning and cautious about dating, became even more so. She'd taken a chance with John, partly because she liked his looks, and then when she found out he was a public interest attorney, a "loser" as Sondra so succinctly put it, she reasoned he must have more than a modicum of decency in his nature. Not that his ostensible concern for his fellow man necessarily precluded his being a bizarre creep who might give her a black eye if she turned him down for sex on a first date, or a second, or a fourth. No one ever knew everything about themselves, much less about other people. Lucille had personally experienced more than one Jekyll and Hyde type and the triggering mechanism was almost invariably alcohol. Use of any drug other than marijuana or hashish was an automatic disqualification for her having anything to do with a man, although long past use of even cocaine didn't bother her. She had used cocaine casually for about a year in her early twenties, however she'd seen its effect on several girls who became regular users. Their lives rapidly deteriorated into little more than a constant search for more of the drug, and the men who provided it to them were invariably disgusting. She was taking a chance with John, driving all the way to Del Mar and back, but the day had exceeded her expectations on every level.

As they continued to kiss, she was pleased at his willingness to follow her lead and not insisting on asserting his masculinity by forcing his tongue down her throat and gagging her, or crushing her soft lips against his teeth as one performance artist she'd dated had insisted on doing. Lucille had seen him at a gallery on Main Street in Venice, and after the show, she'd agreed to a date. The man was both talented and attractive. They had dinner at Chinois on Main, which was sublime, and he'd persuaded her to go to his apartment on Fourth Street near Montana in Santa Monica to look at a David Hockney watercolor. The watercolor was a good one, however as she was enjoying looking at it, the man embraced her without her inviting him to and smashed his mouth down on hers hard enough to split her lower lip with his front teeth. He apologized profusely, telling her he thought she was so sexy that he couldn't help it if his libido overcame him. She insisted he call a taxi to take her back to Main Street and she swore to herself as they waited for the cab, while watching a re-run of an interview with Meg Ryan in the Actor's Studio on Bravo, that in the future she would never let any man talk her into going to his place in his car. "Rule Number One," she'd said to herself. "Always take your own car no matter what. If you've had one too many drinks, then take a cab home."

John was so turned on he could hardly think. Lucille's skin was smooth as glass and warm against his genitals. The difference in their heights was enough so the tops of her thighs were rubbing up on him and he knew that if they continued to kiss and rub, he was going to have his orgasm all over the two of them. John normally didn't have any sex problems, however that was when he was in an ongoing relationship. It had been a long time and Lucille's body was more than just appealing, it was as lush and inviting as it could be without being thought slightly plump, which John didn't mind either, provided the woman was tall enough to carry the weight. Lucille's mouth was at once exotic, yet in a way familiar. Better still, it was a place he longed to be. John wanted to slowly drift through the lovely sense memories the kissing was unlocking, like the time he kissed beautiful Caroline Off during the Junior Prom at Del Mar High. In the midst of his reverie, he could feel a tingling sensation in the nerves on the underside of his penis that meant he was very close to orgasm. This had happened to him several times over the years, and there had been women who were actually offended, including a very pretty paralegal named Cindy, whom he'd been trying to bed for several months. She was very sweet about it at the time, then she told him the next day she was seeing someone else. This juxtaposition might have been just a coincidence, though John didn't think so. The incident bothered him enough to make an appointment with a urologist in Hawthorne who had the almost unbelievable name of Julien Wiener pronounced like the hot dog. Doctor Wiener asked him if he'd had any trouble maintaining a second erection and John told him no, he didn't.

"And the second time, do you ejaculate immediately as well?"

"No, as a matter of fact I can pretty much control my orgasm with my thoughts the second time around."

Dr. Wiener regarded him through a pair of wire-rimmed bifocals that magnified his watery blue eyes. "Then I'd say you are a most fortunate young man."

"Isn't there something you could prescribe for me, some cream to desensitize my penis? It's embarrassing. It makes me feel like some teenager who can't control himself, spraying all over the poor girl."

"Listen here, Mr. Dryden," he said in a thin reedy voice. "Everyday, I see men who would willingly trade their left arms just to have one erection. Not only should you not be embarrassed, the lady should be flattered. If she isn't, she's not worth a second date, believe me on this."

"Actually, they're usually disgusted. I can tell by the looks of pity on their faces. Like I said, it makes me feel like a teenager."

"And that's a bad thing? Seriously, I think any woman who has a man ejaculate all over her just before having intercourse should take this as homage to her sexiness. If you failed to become aroused, now I could see that engendering a sense of rejection in a woman. I think your sex partners are perhaps rather immature, fixated at an infantile level, either that or they're narcissists."

John walked out of Dr. Wiener's office somewhat relieved, though far from convinced. He actually seriously contemplated ordering a Staying Power cream he'd seen advertised in an issue of *Penthouse* he'd idly flipped through at a convenience store near the office. The episode with Cindy unnerved him to the extent that he considered discussing it with Carol to get her take on it. There wasn't much he couldn't talk to her about. They were that close, and he knew that religious as she was, she wasn't any shrinking violet. They'd decided by mutual agreement when she first began working for him that under no circumstances, regardless of the temptation, would they ever allow their relationship to go beyond friendship between a female and a male colleague. If one or the other found himself or herself wanting more than that, then that would be the cue for Carol to move on. For years now, Carol had been his closest friend and confidant. As a matter of course, she approved or disapproved of his girlfriends. She had not the slightest compunction about voicing her opinion, and he did much the same about her boyfriends. Carol had even asked him about the date with Cindy, however he didn't go into what he considered the disgraceful details. Carol was curious because John had seemed so keen on her, but she was content to bide her time until he wanted to tell her everything. She knew he'd gone to the urologist because she'd booked the appointment. She assumed he was seeing the doctor as he was nearing forty and a checkup of the plumbing was purely preventative in nature. Though he was far from being a hypochondriac, John had no reticence about voicing physical complaints and visited a chiropractor once every four months or so to treat a persistent stiffness in his upper back.

On his way to his office, he was thinking about the Staying Power cream, and if it numbed the penis wouldn't it numb the vagina, and God forbid if the woman wanted to perform oral sex, what then? By the time he got to the office and poured a cup of Carol's excellent coffee, he started telling her all about his abortive night with the hitherto much desired Cindy, and his subsequent half-hearted attempts to address the problem. Carol was sympathetic, although she didn't condemn Cindy as Wiener had.

"You have to see it from her point of view. How would you like it if Cindy gushed all over your leg and had her moaning orgasm before you were even erect?"

"I would love it. Absolutely love it. My dream girl would do that."

"That would kind of take the pressure off you having to hold back until the lady was satisfied."

"You got that right."

"Still, I wouldn't be too hard on Cindy."

"No pun intended I'm sure."

"No, though now that I think of it, it was a pretty good one. Listen to me. There's girls that'll think it's lame and girls that'll think it's a compliment like the doc said. And like you said, using some cream might be a cure that's worse than the disease. Best find a girl who likes it wet. Either that or there's always those thick latex rubbers."

Yeah, I thought of that, only putting one on long before sex seems kind of presumptuous, don't you think?"

"Well, if you're at the point where your prick is exposed, then I think you are safe in assuming that you're having some kind of sex."

"That's just it. You said some kind. These days with all the STD's, who can blame any girl for stopping at a hand job or oral sex?"

Carol considered this, sipping appreciatively at her collectible coffee mug from Clinton's second inaugural with the presidential seal in raised gilt. "You're right about that. There're a lot of people walking around carrying the gifts that keep on giving long after they're gone and not just HIV and herpes."

"Maybe abstinence is the best policy."

"Well, you should know all about abstinence."

"Carol, that's cruel."

"Sorry, I couldn't resist."

"And coming from my best friend." "As Mark Twain said, 'It takes two people to hurt you to the heart. Your enemy to slander you and your best friend to tell you about it.'"

John had laughed at the time. Now, however, that time was far away. John really liked Lucille. More than that, he thought he could very easily fall in love with her and that she might well feel the same way about him. The proverbial adage, "You never get a second chance to make a first impression," was even more valid in dating than it was in business.

"What to do," he said to himself, and the situation was desperate. Three or four more up down rubs against Lucille and he would climax. John had three choices. He could tell her, say nothing and let nature take her course, or he could interrupt their embracing and say he needed to go to the bathroom.

Lucille was in a state of bliss. Even though John had eaten sushi and drank red wine, his breath wasn't fetid, and his mouth and tongue tasted clean. She was acutely sensitive to halitosis, and wouldn't kiss men who didn't take scrupulous care of their teeth and gums. She had dropped more than one boyfriend because of his breath. John's body was easy for her to like. He had just enough chest hair to look and feel masculine, though not so much that it was atavistic. Hairy backs were a turn off to her. He wasn't a muscular hunk with six pack, rippling abdominals, and he could afford to lose ten pounds, however as he was over six feet tall the excess avoirdupois wasn't off-putting. He seemed to be the sort of man who was interested in more than just his pleasure and this was a favorable sign.

Lucille loved her body and did her best to care for it as though it were an exquisite instrument. In the future, she would teach John the precise fingering techniques and ways of holding her that would best please her. As far as Lucille was concerned when it came to discussing sexual matters, far too many women and men expected their partners to read minds, or respond to cues so subtle as to be worse than useless, as if the repositioning, or any verbal communication of a desire, would vitiate all the romance from a passionate moment. It was as though communication would kill the act of love as effectively as a pitcher full of ice water.

Lucille knew from the wooden hardness of John's dick, and the tightening of his testicles, which she could feel on her thigh, that he was very aroused. She disengaged her left hand and encircled the head of his dick with her thumb and forefinger. He was circumcised, and she was glad he was, not that she would categorically reject a man for having an intact organ. She preferred circumcised men just as she preferred men who weren't excessively hairy.

As Lucille's warm fingers touched him, John knew his options were dwindling. He experienced a brief, though in its own way endlessly sublime moment of suspension, where his mind blanked out into a brilliant white light. There was an exquisite tingle in his groin as if his very soul were being kissed lasciviously and he erupted in an orgasm as powerful as those he used to have as a teenager.

"Damn," he said. "I'm sorry." Lucille was astonished at John's production, which she cupped in her hand.

"There there," she said in a low soft voice. "Nothing to be sorry for. I'm happy I turned you on so much. It makes me feel good. There's no rush, no pressure. We have all night, and believe me when I tell you, your climax is a beautiful thing."

Lucille got up from the bed, carefully keeping her hand cupped, walked to the bathroom, ran warm water over her hand, dried it with a fleecy towel, and bounced back onto the bed on top of John and kissed him long and passionately.

## CHAPTER 18

# Shattered Glass

THE NEXT MORNING was Sunday. Lucille made egg-white omelets with reduced fat Jarlsberg cheese and organic chives. She made Ezekiel bread toast with Horizon organic butter, and her signature strong French roast coffee. John was wearing one of her fluffy, soft terry-cloth robes and they were eating at the clear pine table in the small dining area that was an extension of the kitchen. There was a fairly large window that faced east, out toward Beverly Glen so the morning sunlight streamed in through the blue curtains. A beam of light struck Lucille's face and John could see the fine down on her cheeks, and thought she was lovely without any make-up. He knew if a woman looked this good in the morning just after waking up, then she would only look better as the day progressed. Many an evening beauty looked frowsy in the morning light, and the good-time party girls were especially prone to appearing rough in the a.m.

Alcohol, drugs, and late nights were not kind to anyone's skin and dissipation had a way on manifesting itself in extremely fine red veins on the nostrils, wrinkles at the corners of the eyes, and puffiness in the skin around the lower parts of the orbits. The warm California sun was celebrated in Dennis and Brian Wilson's deathless lyrics, "The west-coast has the sunshine and the girls all get so tan." John didn't remember all of the next line. It sounded sublime when the Beach Boys sang it though now, whether it was due to global warming or holes in the ozone layer, women with an affinity for the California sun over twenty of thirty years suffered not only increased incidences of melanomas, but puckered, leathery skin on the neck and chest that put John in mind of iguanas. A golden brown tan might look alluring, however the cost of such beauty might not be mere disfigurement but death. Lucille had lovely natural olive skin, very long luxuriant eyelashes, and thick dark eyebrows that were very close to a unibrow. The omelette was light, fluffy, and delicious, and John was effusive in his praise.

"Just don't get used to it," she said with a puckish expression on her face. "I usually have a slice of dry toast, an apple, and a cup of coffee." Lucille's left breast was partially exposed by a fold in her own robe and she made no effort to conceal it, consciously giving John license to enjoy it. "I think I hear your cell phone," she said. John looked at the kitchen clock, which read 7:58.

"I can't imagine anybody calling so early on Saturday morning." His stomach sank. He couldn't think of anything it could be other than some sort of bad news, more than likely Hank having to go to the hospital. He walked quickly into the bedroom, though by the time he found the phone, it had already stopped ringing. He'd left it on her dresser and he picked it up, pressing the missed call button and punched Send. It was Carol's home number and Carol answered immediately.

"Carol, what's up?"

"Pacific Alarm just called. Southgate police called them. The girl said something about a broken window. I'm dressed and I was going to head over and check it out if I couldn't reach you. Otherwise, I was going to attend early services at my church."

"You go to church; I'll drive to the office. There's no traffic at this hour."

"Call me on my cell after 10:30 and let me know what happened."

"I'll do it."

"Bye John."

"Bye Carol and thanks."

Lucille walked into the bedroom. "What was that?"

"Carol, my secretary and paralegal. Actually she's more like a partner in the firm. The police called about some broken windows at the office."

"It's probably some fallout from what happened Friday."

It had only occurred to him as he spoke to Lucille that the two windows might be connected to Ahmed's suicide. He had been thinking in terms of some kids joy-riding down Tweedy with a pellet rifle. Then again, he'd had the office for more than ten years and never had a broken window or a break-in. The sterile banana tree obscured a good part of the large front window, which consisted of two, thick glass panes. Except for relatively small windows just above head height along one side, the building was basically windowless stucco.

John took off his robe and began dressing in a hurry. Lucille was disappointed. She had been hoping to talk John into a morning walk on the beach south of Big Rock in Malibu, then maybe a light brunch at the Ivy at the Shore in Santa Monica. As she was lamenting this turn of events, her entire mind changed instantly. She'd forgotten all about the Van Gogh. However enchanting and romantic a morning ramble in Malibu might be, a half an hour alone in John's office with the painting would be a privilege reserved exclusively for her and a few fortunate curators either after hours, or on days when their museum was closed to the public. No one with her capacity for appreciation had spent time with this particular piece since the 1930's. The previous night, after she recovered from the initial shock, she'd taken in as much of the painting as she could without being completely swept away by it.

"I'd like to go with you. First, I'm not ready to let you go quite yet, and second, I want to spend some time alone with Vincent. That is, as long as you won't be jealous." John was thinking about how long it usually took girls to get ready in the morning. If Lucille were reluctant to part he was even more so. Lucille doffed her robe, donned blue jeans, a maroon tank top, sandals, brushed her teeth, washed her face, and was ready to go at the same time he was.

At just after eight in the morning on Sunday traffic on the Los Angeles freeways was as thin as it is at 3:00 a.m., and sometimes even thinner. They made it to John's office in less than thirty minutes by taking the 110 Pasadena Freeway to Manchester. This was a route he'd never dare take on any other morning. He parked right in front of the building at a meter. He got out, walked to the banana tree and he could see both panes were shattered, and when he peered into the dark office he saw what looked like two bricks or stones lying on the reception room floor in shards of glass.

He and Lucille entered through the back, after John turned off the alarm, though he knew Pacific Alarm had already disarmed the system since their tape was broken.

"Shit," he said as he picked up one of the two red bricks lying on the office floor, hefted it and then dropped it onto the magazine table.

Lucille's eyes looked shocked. John said, "This has to be part of that man's suicide."

"I saw his son and daughter on television."

"They blame me for everything. I think I'd better call the police."

"I don't think you should."

"Why not? Whoever did this should be taught a lesson. Someone could have been seriously injured."

Lucille walked with care and grace, avoiding the fearsome slivers of glass. The force of the impact had driven daggers of glass under Carol's desk and out into the hall. She took John's hand and pressed it.

"Look at me, sweet man. Losing a father is really painful, as we both know from personal experience. Whoever did this is suffering a lot of pain and feeling a whole lot of hostility towards you. Do you really think the police are going to pull usable fingerprints off bricks? They might question the young Nahabedians, though I doubt they'll do even that much. No one was hurt, nothing important stolen, just a mess of broken glass. Call one of the board-up services and tomorrow you can contact your insurance carrier. You do have insurance, don't you?"

At first John wanted to protest, then he realized the police weren't going to treat this crime as if it were a terrorist attack. All it really amounted to was a few hundred dollars of vandalism. The police weren't about to go to Beverly Hills and arrest either of the Nahabedians who had appeared on Eyewitness News at 5 and again at 10 as suspects.

"You're right. I just hope it isn't going to escalate into some kind of Armenian vendetta."

"Do you have a dust pan somewhere?"

"I don't really know. That's one of Carol's departments. You're not going to sweep up glass wearing sandals."

"I'll tell you what. You call the board-up people. Ask them if they'll sweep up all the glass. If they do, great! There will still be minute pieces of glass they won't see. I'll be very careful, I promise. Remember, I'm not a masochist. I generally try to avoid pain. I'll be very careful." An hour later they were sitting in John's office waiting on the board-up people. John was working on a brief and Lucille was rapturously contemplating the Van Gogh to her heart's content. The office telephone rang and John let the answering machine pick up. They listened to the message,

"You have reached the law offices of John Dryden. The office is now closed. Please leave a message. If this is a legal emergency please call the following number." John heard an English accent saying, "John, it's Angus Creswell calling. It's Sunday," John pushed the speaker button.

"I'm here, Angus."

"I tried you on your cell, but it went to voicemail on the first ring."

John fished his cell phone out of the pocket in his jeans. Angus was right. It had so little battery it would go straight to voicemail. "I was hoping to catch you, so I tried your office. I figured you were like me and probably worked on your day off."

"More often than not, though rarely this early on Sunday. I wouldn't be here, except someone threw a brick through my window."

An icy shaft shot through Angus' bowels.

"Nothing stolen I hope."

"No, just glass everywhere. So are you coming to Westchester?"

"Actually that's why I'm calling you. Do you have a digital camera?"

"Not here."

"I have an interested party and they want a series of high quality digital images before proceeding further. That and a price."

Lucille shifted her attention from the painting to the conversation, which wasn't difficult, as John had deliberately left the phone on speaker. "I told my grandfather what you said and he took that into consideration. Remember, he's spent hour after hour on the web studying auction results, as well as verified private sales including some Jackson Pollock that reportedly sold for more than 100 million. He thinks his Van Gogh is worth more than the 135 million dollar Klimt."

*Here it comes:* thought Angus. *I knew it was too good to be true. The old man will want more than the Klimt, and the deal will be dead on arrival.*

This was one reason why he hadn't been out with Marcie looking for a new home. Even if Dryden's price were in the realm of reason, which it wasn't going to be, the sale would have to be fast as well as discreet. The world of art had one thing in common with the world of clandestine intelligence, the saying that three can keep a secret if two are dead. Phillipe was completely trustworthy as far as he knew however no dealer had full control over a buyer. A buyer with the resources and sophistication to spend a hundred million dollars on a single work of art would certainly demand ironclad provenance and authenticity. That meant revealing the painting as coming from the collection of Solomon Roth. The Roth provenance was every bit as good as one from Baron von Hirsh, Peggy Guggenheim, Dr. Albert Barnes, or Rockefeller. Without a certificate from the Rijksmuseum Vincent Van Gogh, the only real surety for a buyer was the Roth pedigree. Angus had a firm conviction that anyone with a good eye and a modicum of experience with late 19th century oil paintings could tell from the crackleur, impasto, patina, and canvas that the piece was either a Van Gogh or a fantastic period copy. Though Van Gogh had no recorded contemporary imitators, Angus knew that wouldn't be enough for the client. Christie's insisted on a freshly issued certificate from Daniel Wildenstein on every Renoir they sold, no matter if the piece came from a well-known collection and was listed and photographed in the Wildenstein Institute's own catalog raisonne.

All the auction galleries acted out of an abundance of caution, each one having been mired in litigation at some time as a result of differences of opinion among experts concerning a given work's authenticity. Old masters, in particular, were so problematic that Sotheby's, Christie's, Bonham's, and Park Avenue refused to guarantee the authorship of any work of art executed prior to 1870, "As it is subject to scholarly opinion which may change." There was a bewildering though legally meaningless scale of authenticity for pre-1870 paintings, drawings, and sculpture ranging from the highest degree of certainty such as Rembrandt, then descending to Attributed to Rembrandt, Circle of Rembrandt, and School of Rembrandt, all of which meant nothing in light of the disclaimer in bold print absolving the gallery of all legal responsibility for authorship. Unless the work in question were a deliberate forgery i.e. a work executed at a later date with intent to deceive, the ancient Roman rule of caveat emptor, buyer beware, applied to almost all works of art sold ay auction.

The problems of fake drawings and guaches so bedeviled the works of Amadeo Modigliani that the expert, Christian Parisot, had been sued for refusing to 'vet' certain works on paper and include them in his catalog raisonne. Parisot reacted by refusing to authenticate any works on paper that weren't recorded in the Ceroni catalog of the artist's works.

Angus knew John and Hank Dryden were both blissfully unaware of these vicissitudes in the art market, and even if he tried to educate them about these issues, they might very well misinterpret it as his attempt to diminish the painting and lower the price. He probably shouldn't have been so positive about it or so enthusiastic. It was just that the painting was so stunning that his habitual British reserve evaporated before Van Gogh's genius. Angus wasn't going to berate himself for having a positive response to a masterpiece. If the day ever came when something truly extraordinary didn't shake him out of his daily orbit, when he saw the most sublime expressions of man as another commodity like so much gold bullion, stocks, or anything mass produced, even a vintage Ferrari, he'd retire and teach English literature at the private secondary school his children attended.

John was on the verge of arbitrarily lowering the price. He and Lucille had talked about the difficulties posed by the sale of an iconic Post-Impressionist painting without a current certificate from the recognized authority on the artist. She told him that even paintings listed and described, as well as photographed in a catalog raisonne, still had to be personally examined by the designated expert prior to sale. Although digital images were good enough for provisional acceptance the final imprimatur had to wait for the maestro's naked eye to physically examine the work. Consequently John's price would have to be attractive, and in all likelihood whoever purchased it would sooner or later make arrangements to have it brought to Holland for exhaustive comparison with other Van Gogh's and scientific analysis of pigments, canvas, and varnish. She reminded him that most valuable canvases were either on stretchers or laid down on board. This one was carefully cut off its stretcher, making it convenient to transport. "However that is exactly what art thieves do when they take paintings from museums and private homes."

The Van Gogh looked exactly like it had been "liberated" from the Nazis. He asked her about restretching the canvas and finding a frame and she said that she knew a conservator who had worked for the Getty Museum, though it would be best to have any restoration done in Holland.

Thanks to Lucille, John knew far more than Angus gave him credit for. He now knew many of the details, difficulties, and possible pitfalls associated with a successful sale, though he hadn't been able to talk price with Hank. He and Lucille had solved the complex ethical issues involved, such as whether John had an obligation to inform the Roth family. Lucille thought that given the Roths prominence in the art world, and their intimate familiarity with the auction process that, "If they were missing a Van Gogh as a result of Nazi persecution, pressure, or spoliation, the Art Loss Register, INTERPOL, and the whole world would know all about it. The Roths have already successfully reclaimed any number of paintings from Goering's Karinhalle, as well as substantial monetary reparations from the German government after the war."

As for the possibility that Gruppenfuhrer Dietrich might have acquired it legally without duress, Lucille thought that even supposing he had, "His heirs, if any, can go straight to Hell as far as I'm concerned." John tried to tell her that the sins of the father shouldn't be laid at the doorstep of his children or relatives.

"I'd agree with you in any other case, but not as far as Nazis are concerned. I don't care if Roth gave it to him as a gift. Dietrich was SS. I mean look at the gun you just sold. Who gave it to him? You think Himmler gave expensive presents to people he didn't like?"

"In my opinion, anything belonging to a member of the SS should be forfeit by virtue of the fact the SS was a criminal organization. The fruits of a criminal enterprise are subject to confiscation. Aren't they?"

"You're the lawyer."

"Yes I am. What you're saying is that if a member of the Mafia buys a Renoir, his children shouldn't be able to inherit it when he dies."

"That's exactly what I think."

"All right. Let's take it one step further. Suppose a young policeman goes into the Mafioso's home, takes the Renoir off the wall, and keeps it for sixty years. No one ever complains about the missing painting, if in fact anyone knows about it. What then?"

"It's not the same thing. A war is fundamentally different from a police action. Theoretically the police can't bomb your home, shoot you on sight, kill your children, your pets, your neighbors, or send you to a death camp. Your grandfather was a liberator not a Nazi. He very likely saved the Van Gogh from destruction."

"I'd like to think that was the case."

"Think of your grandfather. He'll put the money to good use. It will save lives."

"There is this concept called due diligence. I'm not sure Angus' call to the Art Loss Register constitutes making a reasonable effort."

"John, listen to me for the last time. If the painting were considered stolen or taken from Mr. Roth under duress or any questionable circumstances, it would be on the Art Loss Register along with the paintings stolen from the Isabella Stewart Gardner Museum in Boston, which by the way is an incredibly beautiful place. Like the Frick Museum in New York, it was a home, and the art is arranged exactly as it was at the time of her death in 1924."

"So you don't see an ethical need for me to seek out the Roths? You made your feelings toward the Dietrich heirs quite clear."

Lucille shook her head.

"In all honesty, I don't see why you need the Roth's permission to sell. They know all the in's and out's, and if they don't they have attorneys who do. Still, they're only human and if it's sold publicly they'll more than likely put in a claim on general principle, even if Dietrich had a bill of sale. Multi-million dollar paintings tend to attract litigation just like airline disasters. The more I think about it, using Angus as a sales agent rather than the more obvious choice of a major dealer like Wildenstein might actually be a good strategy. If upper management knew about it they'd be furious and that's for sure, though I doubt there's anything in his contract specifically prohibiting Angus from repping it, assuming he even has a contract. Auction gallery experts may be stars in their respective fields, however they don't have elaborate contracts like sports figures and actors. Park Avenue is always hiring people away from the other auction firms. Most of the really talented experts eventually go into private dealing like Mary Ann Martin. She almost singlehandedly created the market for Latin American paintings when she worked at Sotheby's. Gerald Hill did much the same for Russian works of art, long before there were any oligarchs in Russia collecting them."

All this input weighed on John's response to Angus.

"What would you say to fifty million?" Angus was so relieved he felt lightheaded. Whatever warts the painting had would be cured by such an attractive price. Even a protracted court fight with a phalanx of litigators in United States and German courts would be palatable at fifty million. Japan had virtually no mechanism for repatriation of stolen art, and even England required only a few years of possession in good faith to establish title. As long as the buyer bought in innocence and good faith, the owner of a stolen painting, especially one missing for 60 years, had little recourse. However, if the painting ever returned to the United States for exhibition it could be seized like the Monet from the Louvre, and the Dutch might present issues when and if it was sent to the Rijksmuseum for vetting. He had called the Art Loss Register, so he was covered.

"And my commission?" John looked at Lucille, who shrugged her shoulders.

"We'll leave it at five percent."

"That's extremely generous. All I need are some good digital images and I think we should have a buyer by week's end. Of course everything will be predicated on a physical inspection by either the buyer, his representative or both."

John looked at Lucille, who nodded her head affirmatively. "That sounds good to me."

"I have a professional grade, Canon digital camera. It takes great pictures, however it's not the camera or even the lens that's really important, but the lighting. If memory serves, the lighting at your office is not ideal. Would it be too much for you to bring it to Westchester? No, on second thought forget I even suggested it. Best not to move it around, especially unstretched, you could lose paint, and God forbid you have a car accident. If you have the documents with you, I'd like to come to Southgate."

John had in fact, left the documents in his living room. He had taken the Camry to the office and left the GTO in the garage. "I don't have them here. I left them at home knowing we were meeting at two." Angus wanted the documents badly. They were more tangible and immediate than the commission on the painting, even though the profit was miniscule in comparison. Besides, Nazi award documents fell within his area of expertise, and he didn't need anyone to support his opinion of their value or authenticity. He had the perfect client, and essentially they were sold before he even paid for them. Though the sale of the Van Gogh would be a life-changing event, the last thing he'd allow himself to be was desperate.

"I think photographing the painting is more important. We can deal with the documents later at your convenience."

"All right then. I'll wait for you. If you leave right now, you'll miss the heavy traffic through the Slauson Freeway Marina exit, otherwise, after about 10, the 405 South's a nightmare on Sunday."

"I'm leaving in ten minutes."

John checked his watch. "You should still be okay."

"I hope so. I'll see you soon."

"Good bye, Angus." John punched the speaker button and he could see Lucille was once again absorbed in the painting.

"Those board-up people should have been here by now."

"It's Sunday morning. The boys probably had a big Saturday night."

John grinned. "Well, I sure did."

She smiled back, "So did I." Then she wrinkled her brow.

"What's wrong?"

"I hope Mr. Creswell doesn't think it's strange that we're here together."

"Why should he?"

"No reason, except he might be uncomfortable having me know he's doing deals on the side, though it's common knowledge such things go on. Considering the meager salaries paid to gallery experts a certain amount of private dealing is expected, but nothing on a grand scale much less selling a Van Gogh. The ten percent buyer's premium alone would pay Park Avenue's operating budget for months."

"Well, I'm not going to take you home. First of all, I don't want to. Second, I have to wait for the board-up folks."

Lucille stood up and put her arms around John's neck. "I just don't want to make things awkward for you."

"Lucille, you made me see the sale from the buyer's point of view, and thanks to your perspective, I saw Hank's figure as unreasonable. If it were up to me I'd put it up for public auction and if claimants come out of the woodwork, so be it. That's why we have lawyers and judges. I like discretion as much as anyone, but I have to tell you I'm not keen on secrecy and subterfuge. I've had my fill of it being an attorney and it goes against my nature. I wish Hank weren't so dead set on a private sale. Once he makes up his mind about something, he will change it, but only if you make one hell of a good case why he should."

"When you're his age, you'll probably be the same way. Age has its prerogatives."

"So what do you want to do about Angus?"

"If there's a Starbucks nearby, I could go for a coffee and read the Sunday *New York Times*, or if there's a Kinko's I can spend hours there."

"Southgate isn't really Starbucks country. Three-dollar cups of coffee aren't in vogue here. There might be one, but not in easy walking distance. There's a Kinko's on Alameda. Honestly, I'd really rather you stay. You know more about Van Gogh than Angus."

Lucille laughed. "That might have been true a week ago. According to his secretary, actually he shares one with the Ethnographic Department, he's a quick study and he's not afraid to spend hours doing fairly exhaustive research. The materials available on the web can make you an authority in very short order. All you need is a retentive memory and the ability to think symbolically. In seconds, you can access superb digital images of almost every Van Gogh in public collections throughout the world. You can enhance and enlarge the pictures on your monitor, download and print. It's astonishing what you can do once you know how to find the data. Ordinary people can do high quality research on artists in hours, work that it used to take genuine experts months. In pre-Internet days one had to rely on extensive air travel, and contacts at major museums, just to see the works, but no longer."

As he listened to Lucille, John thought he could put in Knight's Cross document into a Google search, and probably come up with the most recent sale prices, since all auction galleries from Christie's to little specialty auctions in towns he'd never heard of made their catalogs and listings available on-line. Then again he knew from experience, once you were on-line, one path leads to another, and the hours melt away like the sand in an hourglass. Besides, he was willing to bet money that Angus had given him a fair price to ensure he'd be retained as the sales agent for the Van Gogh. "I still want you to stay."

Lucille wasn't really all that concerned about Angus except in so far as he might feel some constraint being seen dealing privately on an unheard of scale. She knew she was in the clear herself, as Park Avenue had no policy stated or implied about employees dating clients. If anything such liaisons were tacitly encouraged, though not so overtly that anyone would even think the gallery had anything to do with it. The very last thing management wanted was to give the impression that girls were hired for their physical charms, though this was an important factor in hiring. Angus would be more than surprised; he would probably be panicked. Well that really wasn't her look out.

"I'm equally happy to stay or go. I think Mr. Creswell might really freak out if he sees me."

"Well, he'll get over it. I can't worry about his feelings."

"The thought of all that money really doesn't mean that much to you does it?"

"I look at it this way. At this point, it's all still a possibility, not reality. When and if I see a deposit slip or a bank wire, then I'll believe it, and I'll deal with it at that time. Until it actually happens it's no more than a pleasant fantasy. I lived all these years without wealth and I can continue for the foreseeable future not having it. I'd like to see Hank get the money because he can leave a legacy that will benefit future generations and that will make him happy."

"You're about to get half of 47 million dollars."

"Forty seven and a half million dollars," said John with a broad smile.

They heard a man's voice calling loudly. "Mr. Dryden?"

"Yes."

"AAA Board-Up."

"I'll be right out." AAA Board-Up had a special GMC truck with glass as well as plywood on either side of the bed in special racks. The driver was a fairly well spoken white man in his mid-forties. He wore a freshly pressed, white cotton uniform with AAA embroidered in bright, red letters over his shirt pocket. His assistant was a young Hispanic man with a lovely smile and the svelte build of a soccer player. Between them they had all the glass swept up and plywood bolted over the window frames in less than 30 minutes. George, the older man, asked John if he wanted them to replace the glass, which he said he could do Monday for three hundred dollars complete. "Is that a good price? I've never had to replace the glass before."

"You can call around and get estimates, and call me later."

"No. Let's just go ahead and do it. I trust you."

John didn't own the building, though he did have insurance, and the board-up and cleanup cost him slightly more than two hundred dollars with the tax. Part of the high cost was due to it being an emergency and the fact it was a Sunday. George apologized for the price and told John broken windows on Tweedy weren't that common, though on Long Beach Boulevard there were windows shot out every few weeks. John thought he'd let Carol decide whether it was worth filing a claim, since if he remembered correctly his policy had a fairly high deductible. The rent was more than reasonable, less than a dollar a foot and one of the reasons was that the landlord, who lived in Palm Springs, didn't want to be bothered with minor maintenance, and expected John to keep the building painted and in good repair, in return for a monthly rent that paid the property taxes and not much else.

George and Vince had just left the premises when Lucille started laughing. "What's so funny?"

"It just occurred to me. Sondra made some snide remark in reference to you're being a public interest lawyer. If she knew you owned a Van Gogh, she would have fastened onto you like a leech. Oh, the things she would have done for you and to you, I don't even want to imagine. This painting would have launched her career like a Saturn 5 rocket and she's ambitious enough to have ridden it to the top. I have to give credit where it's due and Sondra's smart enough not only to recognize it, but to do it up right."

John was wondering. "What about you? You have a BFA in Art History."

"Yes," said Lucille. "I do, but I'm more the academic type. Wealth and notoriety aren't my raison d'être. If I ever become famous, it won't be by my design, or my willingness to pay any price for it like Sondra. Not that I'm knocking the girl by any means. On the contrary, I admire her tenacity and willingness to sacrifice in order to succeed. It's just not me."

"What I'm saying is that if you want to sell the painting instead of Angus, or if you want to work with him, maybe you can split the commission 50/50."

Lucille tried to be honest with herself and she had to admit the idea of making a million dollars on the painting was intriguing, however she knew

John had already given Angus his word. More importantly, aside from the obvious potential buyers like Steve Wynn, the Getty Museum, Baron Thyssen, and Francois Pinault, the owner of Christie's, she neither knew nor had special access to private clients. Of course she could talk to Sondra's boss, but Angus was a department head and he could do it more easily than she, so it wasn't as if she were going to make a significant independent contribution to the sale process. She was John's lover for all of one night and she had a BFA. That and three dollars plus tax would buy a grande coffee at Starbucks.

"John, you don't have to do anything. Sure I wouldn't mind making all that money. Who wouldn't? I'm no Jainist monk, and I'm not that altruistic or otherworldly. I'd love a nice little house in Playa del Rey or Benedict Canyon, but I'm not going to horn in on your Van Gogh, especially after you've already made an arrangement with Angus. If I had a private client for the painting, that would be one thing. Then I'd have something to contribute and we could at least talk to Angus about recasting your agreement to reflect my inclusion."

John hadn't given a second's thought to this being a test of Lucille's character. He'd made the suggestion purely as a result of the extensive advice she'd given him on the sale, both in the car the previous evening and at the restaurant, as well as his feeling a powerful upwelling of good will toward her at the moment. Then he thought about what she'd just done and it struck him as extraordinary.

"You know, you may have just turned down an easy million dollars."

"You mean an easy one million, two hundred, fifty thousand dollars don't you?"

---

Except for a minor bottleneck where the 10 Freeway West narrows from two to one lane as Angus made the transition to the 405 San Diego Freeway South, and slow traffic from Venice Boulevard to the 90 Marina Freeway, traffic wasn't too dreadful, and the 105 East was wide open to Long Beach Boulevard. Angus parked at a meter in front of John's boarded-up building, and was startled to see the front door wide open, though Tweedy was very quiet on Sunday morning. He'd brought his Canon digital camera and a 36-inch square of white poster board made of extremely light plastic foam sandwiched between brilliant white-coated cardboard, that he used extensively for taking pictures at home of arms and armor. The foam was exactly two inches too large to fit in the trunk of the BMW, so he carried it in the back behind the driver's seat. Angus was casually dressed in light beige Levis, a lime green cotton Polo shirt, and buttery soft dark blue Ferragamo loafers. He picked up the camera and the board, and set the board on the hood of the freshly waxed car. He closed the doors, pressed the key to lock them and set the alarm, picked up the board and walked inside.

"Hello John," he called out as he entered the reception area.

"Back here, Angus. Close the door and come on back." Angus closed the door and turned the deadbolt, then walked back to John's office. He saw a woman with her back to him looking at the Van Gogh, which was lying on the low, dark walnut, stained coffee table. He didn't recognize Lucille from behind, and when she turned, he hardly recognized her dressed in a tank top. Angus had seen her working the weekend exhibitions for the past year and he knew she'd taken Sondra's job at the reception desk. She had assisted at one or two arms and armor views, and even asked him some questions about the European swords, which seemed to interest her. One sword in particular seemed to intrigue her. It was a solid gold hilted, 19th century English small sword with two colored enamel plaques, made by a prominent gold and silversmith, and was presented by the City of London, to First Lieutenant Thomas Hall, during the Napoleonic Wars for "His exceptional heroism and gallantry in leading the successful assault on the Dutch at Demerara."

The estimate on the sword was 100 to 125 thousand dollars and sold above the high at the auction. Lucille had always appeared to be an intelligent young woman and he didn't perceive her presence in John's office as a potential threat to his making the sale, or as a possible problem in terms of office gossip that might filter up to senior executive staff. If he'd encountered Sondra or one of the girls from the Impressionist and Modern painting department, now that would have shriveled his testicles.

John walked to Angus and held out his hand. "Angus, it's good to see you again. See, Southgate's not quite so bad on Sunday morning."

Angus shook the proffered hand warmly. "No, it seems blessedly peaceful, except for your windows. What happened?" Without going too deeply into the details, John sketched out what he knew of the bricking.

"Hopefully there won't be any further fallout."

"I sure hope not," said John. "Of course you know Lucille Rosen."

"I have that pleasure," said Angus and Lucille offered him her hand, which he took warmly. Lucille had expected Angus to have a somewhat different reaction, and she carefully conned his face as surreptitiously as she could, searching for signs of displeasure or hostility, and finding none, gave him a very genuine smile, for she was no longer an employee being deferential to higher level staff. For the day they were equals.

"Let me go back to your reception area. I left a bit of pasteboard I like to use as a background." The three of them spent the better part of an hour behind the building with Angus standing up on a chair, and John and Lucille positioning and repositioning the painting, and an old wooden yardstick from Home Depot, until Angus was satisfied. The Van Gogh was carefully returned to its resting place in the blueprint safe, and Angus connected the camera to the PC in John's office so they could view them.

"You don't have Adobe Photo Shop by any chance?" asked Angus.

"No, I don't, but Carol might. She has all sorts of software on her machine including, Movie Magic and Final Cut Pro, stuff for editing digital films. I keep on kidding her about being a screenwriter. She once wrote a treatment about a death penalty case. I don't think she got beyond the preliminary stages."

"I'll guarantee she's got Photo Shop," said Lucille.

"If it's not on her machine, I'll edit the pics at home," said Angus. "I just thought since this was a cooperative effort you'd like to see them."

They adjourned to Carol's office. Angus hit the spacer bar and the monitor lit up. The screensaver was a photograph of the Mississippi State Prison at Parchman. "Password," said Angus to John.

"Legalchick33."

"That's it. We're in business," said Angus looking at the icons at the bottom of the monitor. As much as he loved pre-industrial arms and armor, Angus truly enjoyed working with the computer, although he recognized that the Internet was a mixed blessing in many ways. Knowledge and expertise that took him years of painstaking reading, traveling, research in museum basements, was available to the general public at the click of a mouse. Prices realized at public auctions with catalog pictures and descriptions could be had for free without paying hundreds of dollars for print catalogs. Very often there were series of images on the web that were far better than anything in the catalog.

The virtual world and instantaneous communication had made his life easier. The negative was that anyone with a computer and a little savvy could price his sword, gun, or antique by comparing them to similar items sold at auction. A man in Siberia could accurately price his great grandfather's kindjal dagger, Faberge saltcellar, Novgorod School icon, or Order of Saint Alexander Nevski. This had made negotiating estimates and reserves far more contentious than in the past, when a prospective seller would have had to go through the tedious process of ordering and reading paper catalogs assuming he wanted to spend the time and the money, or even knew where to obtain them. Now all a prospective seller had to do was type in 17th century Italian morion into a Google search and every morion offered for sale in the past five years in an auction would be listed on one of the search pages. The Blue Book of Gun Values was on line as well, which meant that a woman in Cochabamba, Bolivia with a rare Luger carbine would know the price in 90% condition as well as he would with his well-stocked library in Beverly Hills. Clients invariably tended to overrate the condition of their pieces. Whether this was the product of ignorance or because they were personally invested in Dad's sword, made no difference, the effect was the same. Also, although the Internet had no problem with national borders, antiques in general, and antique weapons in particular, often couldn't leave their country of origin without a bewildering amount of bureaucratic interference and red tape that could take a year and perhaps longer to negotiate. Any piece incorporating ivory, tortoiseshell, whalebone, red coral or Brazilian rosewood was subject to CITES regulations, which made export and import difficult if not impossible. The international Convention in Trade in Endangered Species was a nightmare road to navigate even for experts. It was all very well and good to know the sale price of something in a London, New York, or Los Angeles saleroom, however if you couldn't export it legally, then the New York price was meaningless. More than once, Angus had politely told a seller who'd insisted on a value they'd determined by researching the piece on the Internet as a reserve to "sell it to the Internet," after they refused to accept his suggested estimate and reserve.

The glorious part of the Internet was that he could download and send his digital images of Dryden's Van Gogh to Phillipe in Buenos Aires within a matter of seconds. In the past, he'd have had to take the pictures with a 35 millimeter camera, wait for them to be developed, and if they didn't come out right, reshoot, then have the second roll developed, and send them by Federal Express, which would take a minimum of two days, then wait until Phillipe called him.

Angus figured he might as well expedite the whole process and send them from Carol's computer. This would give John Phillipe's email address, unless Angus used his own email account, however he wasn't bothered. Phillipe wasn't the type to cut out the middleman, and even if he were, Dryden seemed like a straight-up bloke to him. There was never any sense in overly-orchestrating any given transaction, even one involving a Van Gogh. He'd witnessed the masterful players at Sotheby's over-sell the Van Gogh Irises to the Australian financier, Alan Bond, only to have the record-breaking sale explode in their faces when Bond couldn't pay for it.

Angus used the Adobe program to saturate the color and duplicate the actual hues of the painting as closely as possible, then neatly cropped the images, typed a short email to Phillipe, attached the photo flies, and pressed send.

"The Internet," said Angus. "It's truly a marvel, but like so many things that are revolutionary, a two-edged sword. Instant access to every major museum, auction gallery, and library, has given the public information that used to take years of effort to acquire. No more costly overseas trips to see objects, no spending days in churches, museums and reading in dusty library stacks. It's all free and easy to anyone with the click of a mouse. Fortunately, one still needs to sort, sift through, and analyze the raw data, so we experts have a place. It's just no longer nearly as important as it was in times gone by, when catalogs were hard to obtain and costly. I foresee the day coming soon, just as computer graphics are so incredibly sophisticated that cadavers will no longer be vital to medical students for purposes of dissection, when art dealers will be able to examine museum pieces in three dimensional virtual reality just as if they were handling the piece in person."

"Speaking of handling things in person," said John, "what about the documents?"

"I actually have the money with me. Well not with me, it's in my briefcase."

"I don't know whether you can answer this or not, but am I under any obligation to report cash transactions to the IRS other than as ordinary income or a capital gain?"

Angus looked slightly uncomfortable. "Actually, under IRS regulations you must file a Form 8300 if you take in ten thousand dollars or more in cash. They define cash as currency, cashier's checks, art, antiques, real estate, anything worth more than ten thousand dollars, probably even a live horse. There are exceptions based mostly on foreign residences, however there is a big exception, which states a transaction is exempt from reporting if it is not in the course of the person's trade or business. You're a lawyer, not a dealer in Third Reich memorabilia. Your and Hank's only obligation is to report it as income or a capital gain, but that's between you and your accountant. As far as having to file a Form 8300 within 24 hours of receiving more than 10K, as far as I know you're under no obligation. The buyer of the Walther gave me cash, so that's how I paid you. If you'd rather take a personal check, I'll be happy to oblige."

"No, no," said John. "I'm happy with cash money. You're not a militaria dealer either."

"No, thankfully I'm not."

"I hope your client isn't going to pay cash for the painting."

Angus laughed aloud. "No, not hardly. Figure a million dollars weighs approximately ten pounds, that would be a quarter ton of paper. Payment will undoubtedly be by wire transfer. Make no mistake, given the worldwide paranoia about terrorism, a wire like that coming from abroad will receive some high level scrutiny, however since it's inbound to the States, I don't think you'll receive a telephone call, much less a personal visit from a representative of your government as a result."

"My bank won't believe it."

"Probably not. We'll cross the bridge of wiring instructions when we come to it."

"How long do you think it will take?"

"I wouldn't want to be held to a schedule. Let's see, it's Sunday. With luck, I should be able to tell you when the representative for the buyer is coming to inspect the piece as early as this afternoon."

"So we're still on for two at my place?"

"Two sounds good to me."

"Do you need directions?"

"No, I put the address into MapQuest right after I spoke with you."

## CHAPTER 19

# *Phillipe*

PHILIPPE MACLET WAS actually a distant relation of the artist, Elysee Maclet, a follower of Impressionism, who achieved a minor reputation in his lifetime. Maclet's still-lifes of fish and oysters, as well as his landscapes, appealed to Americans who hung them in the dining rooms and drawing rooms of their Manhattan apartments. Phillipe couldn't draw or paint. He did have a gift for speaking foreign languages and after he completed secondary school, his parents sent him to the University of Paris, but not the Ecole des Beaux-Arts. While a student, Philippe took a part-time position as a porter at the Hotel Drouot, France's pre-eminent auction house. Philippe's fluency in English and Spanish, as well as his obsession with Latin American art, brought him to the attention of upper management. Following his graduation an offer of permanent employment was accepted with enthusiasm. When Christie's and Sotheby's broke the Hotel Drouot monopoly on the French auction business, the chairman of Christie's Europe hired him away, first to London, and then to New York for eleven highly successful years. On a trip to Buenos Aires to ensure the consignment of a truly superb, late oil painting by Henri Matisse, he fell in love with the city and Argentina. The wealthy collectors of South America welcomed him with open arms and checkbooks. They were only too happy to have a renowned expert living among them. After less than two years, Phillipe had a circle of old monied families and new telecommunications billionaires that relied on his expertise in buying and selling European paintings as well as South American works of art. His interest in Botero, Zuniga, Riviera, and Sequiros made up in energy what it lacked in expertise.

When Angus first emailed him about the Van Gogh. Phillipe was not at all excited. Van Gogh's notoriety, greater than that of any painter in the history of art, had attracted the unscrupulous of the art world since before the First World War. High quality copies and superb deliberate forgeries were commonplace. The Roth provenance was an immense factor in its favor, but he knew one of the grandsons of Solomon Roth, who was President of the Roth Foundation, a pillar of the Buenos Aires philanthropic community, and he couldn't imaging Carlos Roth leaving such a painting off the Art Loss Register. If it were genuine, and that was one huge if, the odds against it being authentic were on the order of a thousand to one, even considering the plausible acquisition history. If it were an autograph work, it would rank as perhaps the greatest art discovery of the past 100 years. Solomon Roth had never published an inventory of his collection, nor had he lent to public exhibitions, except on very rare occasions. He preferred his masterpieces to remain anonymous once they entered his home. He collected only paintings with impeccable provenance and documentation. He would make rare exceptions to this rule as well, since his own connoisseurship was of the first magnitude. For a banker without formal training, Roth had an excellent 'eye', as it's known in the trade, and a Roth Collection pedigree was a virtual guarantee that a painting was one of the better examples of a given painter's oeuvre.

Phillipe was in Caracas staying at the guesthouse of one of his clients, who wanted him to arrange a cleaning for a Monet painting of the Houses of Parliament he'd purchased some years ago at a Sotheby's London, Impressionist and Modern sale. Philippe knew the work in question intimately, and it was true that the varnish had yellowed slightly. One could see it in the color plate from the catalog, however Philippe didn't care for the way some restorers left a painting so shiny that it reflected light as if the varnish and the paint were still wet and far worse, they all too often skinned the high points off the impasto.

The Monet held a prominent place in Mr. Rodriguez's office and a decade of thick Havana cigar smoke had definitely dulled the subtle pinks, blues, and greens, of the diaphanous, misty, incredible evocative, almost other worldly rendering of the famous structure. Phillipe agreed it would benefit from a very gentle cleaning. There was no one in Caracas Phillipe trusted to do the work without over cleaning it. He knew a man in Buenos Aires with the deftness and sure sense of just how far to take it. Sergio was a brilliant restorer who took an inordinately long time, often weeks, though when he ministered to a canvas or panel, it was with love and understanding and respect for the artist's original intention. Sergio mixed his own solvents, wore a set of magnifying lenses when he worked, and used the very finest mink and sable brushes, cleaning a square centimeter at a time. His inpainting, when it was required, was so skillful and the pigments he used so closely duplicated the original, that unless someone knew where to look, and exactly what they were looking for with a strong black light, the repairs were nearly undetectable. Cleaning the Monet would be child's play, however moving multi-million dollar works of art from one South American country to another presented problems. There were customs issues, questions from the insurers, and Senior Rodriguez really wanted Sergio to come to Caracas. Phillipe was reluctant to agree to this primarily because he was concerned that the billionaire would hire him on a full time basis. So he told the man that it would be impossible to clean the Monet outside Sergio's studio where the solvents, lighting, and brushes were all in their proper places. Rodriguez didn't want to put the painting on his Gulfstream and fly it to Argentina, though this was looking more and more like the only viable option. Lloyds of London was less than thrilled about having a 35 million dollar Monet sitting in a restorer's studio for a month without so much as a fire safe, much less an alarmed temperature controlled vault.

Phillipe was almost ready to give in and have Sergio come to Venezuela solvents and brushes in hand, though there was no way Varig or Aerolineas Argentinas would knowingly allow him on a plane with flammable liquids, either in his luggage or on his person. Driving was put out of the question because of the distance, not to mention there was a certain element of risk in driving the Pan American highway through the Andes.

Philippe ensconced in the luxuriously furnished guest house, seated in front of his laptop, which rested on a genuine but not particularly good example of a walnut Sheraton style desk, composing an email to Sergio to see if he were willing to leave his wife and three children for three weeks in Caracas, when Angus' email made its presence known. It was a Sunday afternoon and Mr. Rodriguez was visiting his estancia in the country -for the day. Philippe had been invited, but begged off saying he wanted to do some research on the forthcoming New York sales at Sotheby's and Christie's. Philippe was leaving Venezuela late Monday morning.

Philippe read the e-mail and used Acrobat Reader to open up the attachments. As the first image materialized centimeter by centimeter from the top of the screen, he was literally awestricken. As much as he liked Lola Karmarski's Portrait of Dr. Gachet, it paled in comparison with the image on his computer. Phillipe seldom thought in terms of his personally owning the art he sold or bought, but this was something he could envision selling everything he owned in order to possess. As Angus' pictures filled his screen, one after the other, Philippe experienced something like a hot flash, seated as he was in a good mahogany copy of a Jacobean armchair with a thick embroidered cushion.

The fifty million dollar price was more than just reasonable. It was a tremendous bargain. He was sufficiently impressed with the quality of the images to have no doubt as to the Van Gogh's authenticity. Aside from the obvious vitality of the painting, something copyists, regardless of talent, had trouble capturing, there were the technical details, the unmistakable Van Gogh impasto, the poisonous chemicals that made the zinc white and other colors were no longer manufactured, and although modern computer technology could duplicate any color, the texture, once dried, wasn't so susceptible to recreation. Crackeleure could be faked, however an aging process artificially brought about by heat was not quite the same effect as the finely variegated cracks of a hundred years of natural aging characteristic of 19th century oil paints. There was a possibility that an unknown artist of incredible talent, working sometime in the early 20th century, might have decided for whatever reason to paint a Van Gogh self-portrait without actually copying an existing work. In that incredibly unlikely event, the anonymous artist would still have had to devote intense study to Van Gogh's palate, as well as extant paintings, and this would have had the effect, though extremely subtle, of inevitably infecting the Roth portrait with the fatal stiffness of a copy.

There were anomalies about the piece, which were mildly disturbing though they were purely mechanical in nature. The surface was untouched and uncleaned which was to the good, however there were cracks, not just crackleure, resulting from decades of being off its stretcher and not properly laid down. Extreme care would have to be taken in transport to ensure the canvas would lie flat in one position at all times. As much as he hated to say it, a relining was necessary so it could be restretched and framed. Angus had cropped the images well, and Philippe could sell it using them, however he would no more present the actual painting to a private buyer in its present state than an agent from William Morris would present his biggest film star to the press unwashed, poorly dressed, no make-up, hair awry, with a terrible skin rash on her face.

A ten thousand dollar carved, ghessoed, gilt wood, antique frame, and a gilded bronze name plate with embossed black enamel letters reading "Van Gogh 1886", and a month of Sergio's tender loving care with his sable brushes and solvents, relined and restretched, would render Vincent ready to meet his new owner. The blessing of the Rijksmuseum Vincent Van Gogh would be the final touch. With that, Philippe believed he was looking at the most valuable work of art in private hands, surpassing Ronald Lauder's Klimt. A Klimt, however luminous and splendid, wasn't a Van Gogh. In very little time, perhaps three months, restoration, framing, and certification would yield an almost certain profit of 100 million dollars and very probably more. The deal was basically a fait accompli except for chain of title issues. The people who could afford eight or nine figures for a work of art were generally purchasing something their vast wealth alone could not, which was the indefinable quality referred to colloquially as 'class,' and equally as important, recognition from the general public that they possessed 'class.' Philanthropists from Andrew Carnegie to Warren Buffet and William Gates insisted that their names be liberally plastered all over museums, hospitals, universities, and foundations during their lifetimes. They needed the bronze plaques, names carved in stone, concrete monuments to their generosity that reminded the public as they passed by or entered of the sacrifices made by the wealthy, and their selfless commitment to the uplifting of society. Philippe often wondered how well a museum would fare if its policy required all bequests of money or art, or construction, to be made anonymously in the name of common humanity. As much as he benefited from it, Philippe had a deep and abiding disdain for the current mania among the rich to veneer their abysmal ignorance of art and culture by purchasing works of art to donate them to public collections so that a bronze plaque would be screwed to the wall attesting to their artistic credentials and civic mindedness. There were here and there among the Forbes 400 types, a few true art aficionados like Norton Simon, the Hunt's Ketchup king, purchaser of the ill-starred, stolen Shiva, and the charming Rembrandt portrait of Rembrandt's son, Titus. These men relied heavily on their own connoisseurship to make purchases. Others used people like Philippe to purchase works of art the same way they hired lawyers, accountants, and stockbrokers to handle their affairs in those fields.

Philippe wasn't old enough to recall the scandal over the Shiva though he was well aware of the forced repatriation by the Metropolitan Museum of the Euphronius calyx krater, which was a major embarrassment to the director,

Thomas Hoving. Given the underlying motivation of most wealthy art collectors, which was the burnishing of their public persona, to establish their high cultural bonafides with fellow plutocrats, or some combination of the two, any association with a stolen work, or even more disgraceful, a painting taken from a prominent Jewish collector who was first sent to Dachau and then died in the gas chambers of Auschwitz, was something to be avoided at all costs. If the Van Gogh had been on the Art Loss Register list, he would have had nothing to do with it other than saying, "I'm not interested and don't ever contact me again or I'll inform INTERPOL."

Angus' painting wasn't 'hot' in that sense and Philippe couldn't account for it not being on the list. He had to proceed on the assumption that it wasn't stolen or even disputed property. There were dealers he knew who would place works of art with dubious histories. There were men of considerable means in Columbia, Bolivia, and Peru whose income was derived from American and European demand for the refined crystal alkaloid of the coca plant, Erythroxylum coca, in the form of a hydrochloric salt. Like their counterparts in legal businesses, they too sought to acquire art and burnish their images, and acquire prestige and bragging rights by owning famous pieces of art, though they had few scruples with provenance. Philippe had been approached on more than one occasion by men from Cali, Columbia and Medalin, seeking to invest large quantities of American dollars in works of art, even offering to purchase stolen masterpieces, at a substantial discount of course. Philippe carefully and courteously refused all such offers, pleading the scarcity of quality works outside the auction room, which had strict reporting rules concerning payment in currency, and his complete and utter ignorance of anything to do with stolen paintings and sculpture.

Angus had written that the seller of the Van Gogh was an attorney. Philippe saw this as a significant plus in the equation. Angus also said the vendor would provide a properly endorsed bill of sale, however he wasn't certain of a guarantee of clear title. In the event that legal disputes did arise, Philippe wanted to make sure the burden of litigation would shift to the seller. Construction of a risk-reward paradigm was clearly dictated. The risk component was 50 million dollars plus his customary ten percent commission. His 10% would include framing, Sergio's time and Philippe's expertise, together with his personal warranty of authenticity. Philippe's warranty, while certainly worthwhile, was no certificate from the Rijksmuseum, though it would have to suffice for the time being. The reward was a potential profit of between 100 and

150 million dollars if and when the painting was resold. This profit was predicated on the blessing of the museum, and an absence of legal challenges from the Roth family and the heirs of SS Gruppenfuhrer Dietrich. The worst case scenario he could foresee was some pain in the ass American federal judge would award the painting to the Roths. A European, or more particularly, a German court would probably award the painting to Dietrich's son, the one videotaped riding in the Nazi armored car. A painting worth nine figures would attract claimants with the very remotest and tenuous connections to either family, as surely as bloody offal dumped in the ocean would bring sharks.

Sooner or later the painting had to be sent to Amsterdam, and there amid the news headlines in print and television, Internet blogs, and chat rooms, suits would be filed and the piece seized by the authorities until ownership could be adjudicated. His buyer would request a ruling from the International Court of Justice at The Hague. In the event of an adverse ruling, the vendor would have spent the 50 million, further legal action would be meaningless and the purchase price irrecoverable. Since he could prove he acted in good faith from the outset, a position bolstered by the legitimate bill of sale, Philippe would not be required by either Argentine or international law to refund his commission. His client might have hard words for him or never speak to him again. Still having exercised his due diligence the five million dollars would be his. If there were no question of title, Philippe wouldn't hesitate to ask 125 million dollars, regardless of Angus' asking price, then again if the painting were free of all impediments, Angus wouldn't have it for sale in the first place.

"To think this unique sequence of events came to pass as a result of an American GI and a stupid Nazi automatic pistol," said Philippe to himself.

The logical buyer was the Japanese who bought Dr. Gachet and Philippe knew the financier from his days at Christie's, but he would require a certificate from the Rijksmuseum. He could offer it to Rodriguez, but the telecommunications czar's first question would be, "Where is the certificate?" and when Philippe told him there isn't one, the next question would be, "Why not?"

Philippe typed up an e-mail accurately outlining the risks and the rewards, the fifty million dollar asking price, his commission, a confidentiality agreement, attached the very worst of Angus, photographs, and e-mailed the whole package to another Japanese collector with a 48-hour deadline for a response. He sent a separate e-mail to Angus telling him he should have an answer for him by Tuesday at the latest.

## CHAPTER 20

# *Sunday Afternoon*

JOHN DROPPED LUCILLE off at her apartment after they agreed he would come over at 6:30 for another sushi dinner at the upper-class strip mall off Beverly Glen. He drove to Westchester, microwaved two frozen Francisco's tacos, and ate them at the kitchen counter, drinking a bottle of cold Fiji water, which he'd recently taken a liking to. At five minutes to two, Angus pulled his BMW into John's driveway.

The Knight's Cross documents and folders were everything Angus was hoping for with the exception of the oak leaves document. Someone, probably Dietrich, himself, had carefully folded it at some time, perhaps to show it to someone without having to carry the bulky and heavy white leather folder. The crease was noticeable, and though it wasn't as bad as a hole drilled through an otherwise valuable coin, there were purist collectors who wouldn't buy it as a result, and others who would insist on discounting the price rather drastically. The document in the red folder was very nearly pristine with a pen-signed Hitler signature rather than the stamped signature found on most awards from later in the war. At fifty thousand, taking into account the folded document, they were nonetheless a bargain. Although if he didn't have the ideal client to whom he'd sold Dietrich's Walther pistol, the oak leaves might have been a hard sell.

"These are lovely," he said to John. "Except for one thing. You see this fold?" John had in fact seen it and dismissed it as not worthy of mention. All the gold leaf and the exquisite hand lettered printing on the document were perfectly legible and the paper itself spotless, devoid of greasy fingerprints or the brown dots of foxing that old paper is generally subject to.

"I didn't really pay it that much attention. I figured the general must have folded it and put it in his pocket to show it to someone, then put it back in its case." John could see Angus wasn't entirely happy about the documents. His attitude lacked the enthusiasm he'd showed about the Walther.

"If you think it's a big problem, you don't have to take them."

"No, they're great. It's kind of like finding a beautiful 1974 Jaguar v-12, XKE with a crease in the right front fender. Only unlike a vintage motorcar, a paper once folded can't be returned to its pre-folded state. You just have to live with it." Having offered Angus an out if he wanted to take it, John wasn't going to spend any more time on the documents. Angus opened up his brief-case and handed John five bundles of hundred dollar bills, each with its bank wrapper still intact.

"Thank you very much," said John, as he put the money on the living room table next to the documents for the time being. "Any word on the painting?"

"Yes. The man I contacted said he should have an answer by Tuesday if not sooner."

"And did he say anything about the chances for selling it?"

"Let me be honest with you. Your grandfather's insistence on confidentiality is making everything more difficult, primarily because we can't send it to the Rijksmuseum Vincent Van Gogh for their imprimatur, which is universally accepted worldwide. Asking a client to spend 50 million on even a trusted expert's say so is asking a lot."

John hadn't told Hank he'd lowered the price by 25 million and his not having done so had nothing whatever to do with a fear of Hank's reaction. When Hank gave him carte blanche, the old man meant exactly that, and Hank was no Monday morning quarterback. If John sold it for 10 million, one million, or decided to keep it, Hank wouldn't criticize his decision, trusting that whatever John did, there was sound reasoning behind it.

"Angus, let me be frank with you. The Van Gogh can go into a bank vault and I'll visit it once in a while. I'll survive and so will my grandfather. Maybe that's the best thing to do under the circumstances, what with all the chain of title questions."

Angus' blood ran cold in his veins, this despite a sort of prickly heat at the back of his neck and under his arms. He'd given any number of clients the 'good news' 'bad news' treatment over the years. It was very much standard operating procedure throughout the auction business from Christie's on King

Street in London to the obscure gallery in the midwest. Experts would wax enthusiastic about property until it was consigned. Then just before the catalog was printed, if the original 'come-on' estimate were too optimistic, the softening up process would commence and flaws in the piece that were overlooked in the first flush of getting the consignor to sign the contract would be disclosed, and all sorts of potential sale difficulties raised. All auction gallery contracts, without exception, are written to offer the maximum protection to the gallery as consignee and little or none to the consignor. In the days before a major sale, any uncertainty about the viability of important items would be addressed by telephone calls and e-mails to the seller advising him or her to lower the reserve to ensure a sale and guard against unsold lots, known in the trade as BI's or bought-in lots. Some BI's were to be expected, however an inordinately high number could result in the department head being reprimanded or even fired following a sale.

Angus had no contract with John other than a gentleman's verbal agreement, and the pre-sale 'bad news' to lower the reserve and seller's expectations was not the right tack to take. Angus was so accustomed to telling consignors of the problems involved in a sale that he made the comment about the Van Gogh almost without thinking about the consequences. Part of it was that he couldn't accept the fact that the Drydens didn't seem to really care about millions of dollars. They were not wealthy, and even the richest people he knew, those listed in the Gold Book with a 10± in the wealth column next to their names, paid attention to fifty million dollars. Angus knew at several billionaires who acted as if a thousand dollars were a matter of life and death. It was a question of respect for money in general, and their money in particular.

"If I have given you the impression that the sale will be difficult, please forgive me, it won't be. Many times people come to me with a vastly inflated idea of their item's value. In your case, the reverse is true. We both know the painting's worth much more. It's your grandfather's insistence on utter confidentiality that is making things slightly more problematic, but I understand his reasons and I respect them."

"Good. For a moment there I thought you were trying to discourage me."

"John, believe me, that was the last thing on my mind."

"Remember I'm a lawyer, and we do the 'good cop, 'bad cop' routine in our sleep, especially when settling personal injury claims. Give them a rosy picture of their financial recovery, then a few weeks after the retainer agreements are signed, trot out the real numbers, which you get from the hospital's lawyers. I don't do that much PI work, but trust me I know the drill. I'm afraid I'm hypersensitive to anyone trying it on me. I apologize for thinking you were doing it."

"And I'm sorry for falling into the usual expert pattern with a client. You've been nothing but candid and accommodating with me, and I appreciate it sincerely."

"No hard feelings?"

"None at all. And if you're serious about a vault instead of your filing cabinet, there are several firms in Beverly Hills that offer secure storage for high value artwork. They're approved by Lloyds, Chubb, and every other fine arts insurance company." Angus smiled. "Then again, I seriously doubt you'll need their services. Sometime this week, protecting the Van Gogh will be somebody else's problem."

"That'll be great."

Hank had never taken on the rather substantial burden of insuring and caring for the painting. It had resided in his closet for decades without incident, out of sight and out of mind. Only within the past week had it become a source of concern and John wondered exactly what had changed.

*I'm the same person I was,* thought John. *The painting is the same one that was in Hank's closet all these years. It's our perception of what it is and what it represents that has undergone a change.*

John had given somewhat more thought to the nature of reality as a result of owning a 50% share of the Van Gogh. *If Lucille or I say the thing is genuine, it makes no difference. Angus says someone might pay a few thousand dollars for it as a copy because it's a good painting. If Angus says it's a Van Gogh, it's still worth very little, though he has enough credibility to have someone look at computer images and ask fifty million dollars and be taken seriously. Nothing physical has been altered and yet there's been a quantum leap from let's say three thousand to fifty million.* John wanted to discuss these things with Lucille. Amazingly, John did not think the most important event of the week was the discovery of the Van Gogh or the unfortunate demise of Ahmed Nahabedian. He sincerely believed the advent of Lucille Rosen in his life was the most significant thing to happen to him in a very long time. Carol and Hank were much more than just good friends and confidantes, he loved them both dearly, however there are certain secrets of the heart that can only be properly shared with a lover, otherwise they remain locked within and appropriately so. A great artist, whether poet, actor, painter, composer, or singer could choose to share some of their sacred inner secrets with their audience, though even they reserved part of their heart for private consumption. In medieval times, men and women despairing of meeting a suitable earthly lover could choose to marry God in a monastery or convent and share their heart with the Divine, and often did so deliberately. Given a choice between the Van Gogh and Lucille's love, John would choose Lucille, though he told himself he'd rather have both. He'd inherited his father's other-worldliness as well as his mother's need to analyze and weigh consequences.

As he walked Angus to the BMW and watched Angus tuck the Knight's Cross document folders carefully into the soft folds of an old, pink, wool knitted baby blanket he'd put in the truck before he left, John was thinking of Lucille's full, soft lower lip, the spicy warmth of her mouth and how much he was looking forward to 6:30.

"Does your wife know you're using that blanket?"

"As a matter of fact she doesn't. I was rummaging through the closet this morning, looking for something soft to wrap the documents in, and I happened across it."

"I'll bet she didn't see you walk out of the house with it." Angus smiled and gently closed the trunk. The servo in the electric motor made a soft whirring sound as it inexorably pulled the trunk lid tight against the rubber seal. Angus' wife had an annoying habit of slamming the truck closed as if there were no automatic electric mechanism and try as he might, he couldn't break her of it.

"I see you can be quite the ruthless cross-examiner when you want to be and quite the detective in the Conan Doyle School of deduction as well."

"A lawyer has to be a detective. I always ask a client, 'Have you told me everything I need to know so there won't be any surprises?' And they look at me with their totally sincere expressions and I just know they're lying. The difference between a good, and by that I mean effective, not good as the antithesis of evil, lawyer and a poor lawyer is that the good advocate knows his client isn't telling the whole story and is willing to take the time to drag the truth out of him, while the poor lawyer accepts his client's story at face value because it's easier. I figure that blanket belonged to your daughter when she was a baby, and if your wife knew you were using it to cushion militaria in your truck, well let's just say she more than likely wouldn't be overjoyed."

"Are you sure you've never met my wife?" said Angus coyly.

"No, I mean yes, I'm sure."

"Have you ever been married?"

"No, though I've been engaged twice."

"Well, as perceptive as you are I'd say you'd make some woman a good husband."

John held out his hand and Angus took it. "I appreciate that, Angus, and I'll keep it in mind."

"Do you want me to update you by email or telephone?"

"All things considered, I think both, although I really like the emails because I can just forward them to Hank. That way he's part of the action."

"If you want to give me his email, I'll just copy him."

"I would expect he's made it crystal clear he doesn't want to be involved in any way directly. He's more than a little embarrassed about how he came by it and he's concerned about being vilified by the media if the story is known. Hank's nobody's fool, even at eighty. I love him to death. He was literally and figuratively my father when I was young, not that he ever let me forget for a minute that Luke Dryden was my dad. Still, you can bank on the fact he's relying on attorney-client privilege applying to every aspect of his role in the sale. He was there for me when I was a baby and all through my life, and he knows I would literally die before I'd let anyone hurt him, not that he's the vulnerable type. For a man who weeps over pictures of injured Iraqi children, he can be tough as rhinoceros hide about anything to do with the American government. He pays his taxes though he complains vociferously about the government using money for torture and murder. I'll bet he donates every dollar from the Van Gogh to UNICEF, Smile Train. They're the doctors who repair cleft palates in third world countries, and Doctors Without Borders. He'll do it for no other reason than he doesn't want to pay the government long-term capital gains tax."

"Well, I've never met your grandfather and if the subject ever comes up, which I doubt it will, as far as I'm concerned, you're the only person involved."

"That's the way Hank wants it and I'm all about making him comfortable."

Angus opened the driver's door and slid in, put the key in the ignition, started the engine, and rolled down the driver's side window. John closed the door firmly, taking care not to slam it.

"How would you like to come to my home for dinner and afterward you could teach my wife how to close the trunk without slamming it?"

"I've got a vintage GTO; I don't slam doors, hoods, or trunks."

Angus was pleasantly surprised. He turned off the ignition. He'd taken note of John's watch, though it never occurred to him for a second that John had a vintage Ferrari. The office and home, the furnishings, were altogether too modest for a man with a high six or low seven figure antique car. Still, stranger things were known to happen, like John having a fifty million dollar painting and more than a hundred thousand dollars worth of Nazi memorabilia.

"I'm not leaving until I see your car." John walked back to the house and as Angus exited the BMW, John opened the electric garage door revealing a Toyota Camry and a car covered by an expensive cloth car cover. As Angus walked up the driveway to the garage, John deftly pulled back the elastic edges of the cover and folded the soft bluish cloth up and over the trunk. This was not the type of GTO Angus has expected, though clearly it was a valuable collectible automobile. It was a Pontiac and not a Ferrari with a sleek body by Pininfarina or Bertone. The chrome bumper was so shiny, it looked to be newly plated, and the paint was waxed to a depth and luster that would have passed inspection at a Concours de Elegance like Hershey or Pebble Beach. Even though the body was by Fisher of Detroit and not Bertone of Turin, Angus could see the car was a ninety-point plus specimen. It sported a California classic license tag, so it had to be more than 25 years old.

"What a lovely car," he said. "Though to tell you the truth I was expecting something with more of an Italian accent."

"You seriously thought I had a Ferrari GTO? No, not hardly. Where would a public interest attorney get a 500 thousand dollar car?"

"That was a question I asked myself when you mentioned it, but I've learned that there are more things in heaven and earth and all that, so I believe anything's possible."

"Well, I suppose you're right. No, my Gran Turismo Omologato was built in the Motor City for my father. It's probably got more horsepower than a Ferrari of the same vintage, 1967, and I think it would hold its own in a quarter mile race. Now, in a road race I'd take the Ferrari. In a straight line, I think I'd win easily up to 110 miles per hour and after that the Ferrari would have the edge and begin to walk away."

John popped the hood, and for a car that was driven on the street, Angus was impressed with the engine, which was spotless. The three Holly two-barrel carburetors featured a free flow, chromium top air cleaner, with clear plastic gas lines, clear plastic spark plug wires, a special dual point distributor, and a highly sophisticated exhaust by Hooker, that Angus recognized as one of the attributes of a racing car.

"Would you like to hear it?"

"Yes I would, very much so." John opened the door, took a key from under the driver's seat and inserted it in the ignition. He turned the key and the engine caught on the first rotation of the starter motor, and thrummed like a powerboat. John got back out and stood next to Angus.

"Listen to this." John took the accelerator bar that was connected to the three carburetors and flicked it back about an inch, and instantly the engine responded with a roar, which subsided immediately after John released the bar.

"I'd say that's a responsive motor."

"Sorry it's not a Ferrari."

"Believe me, I'm not disappointed." John gently but firmly closed the hood, reached in through the driver's window and turned off the engine. "Would you like to take it around the block?"

Angus looked just like a little child at Christmas.

"As a matter of fact, I'd love to."

"Give me the keys to your BMW and I'll park it in the street."

"They're in the ignition."

"You know the shift is in an H pattern, first is forward. Reverse is a slap to the left and then forward. You okay with a standard shift?"

"My first car was an old Triumph TR-4. No worries on that score." John opened the door for him. "Have at it then."

## CHAPTER 21

# The Samurai

MAKIO ONISHI NOT only thought of himself as a samurai, he could actually trace his lineal descent from the daimyo of Choshu Province. Many of Japan's wealthiest men had samurai ancestors who made a successful transition from daimyo, or feudal lord much like a baron or even a duke, under the last of the Tokugawa shoguns, to owners of zaibatsu, trusts or cartels under the modern post Tokugawa emperors, Meiji, Taisho, Showa, known in the West as Hirohito. Mitsui, Mitsubishi, Yasuda, and Sumitomo emerged as the big four. The Allied occupation government attempted to dissolve the zaibatsu, however after the Japanese government signed the peace treaty of 1951, many companies began associating into kigyu shudan, or 'enterprise groups,' organized around major companies and financial institutions. Though the policy coordination of these groups was more informal and their financial interdependence more limited than with the old zaibatsu, the cooperative paradigm of these direct descendents of the zaibatsu was the primary factor in the so-called Japanese economic 'miracle.' It was no accident that that the three industrial-economic leaders were Sumitomo, Mitsui, and Mitsubishi.

Makio had seen the potential in semiconductors early on, then invested heavily in broadband technology, fiber optics, and cellular services. At age 54, his wealth was rated at 10 in the Gold Book as opposed to the Sultan of Brunei who rated a 10+++. He was more than satisfied with his position and status, as well as his physical and spiritual well being. Makio had little love or respect for Western culture and in general and American culture in particular. He despised the unabashed worship of materialism and found it barbarous. The spectacle of American corporations stealing hundreds of billions of dollars from America through wars in the Middle East that had nothing to do with 'spreading democracy', but were no more than elaborate charades to serve as camouflage for the massive theft to a idiotized public amused him. The rest of the world was aligning itself with Russia, China, and India. The 21st century would be an Asian one, just as the 20th century had been an American one, and the 19th century an English one. By the time the Americans awoke from the torpor induced by their foolish self-gratifying culture, assuming they even wanted to, they would see that despite their nuclear weapons, and impressive military, they were a second-rate nation. As long as a country had even ten nuclear weapons and the means to deliver them, the actual number was irrelevant. Any nuclear exchange, even one involving five weapons, would effectively end civilization in the countries affected and disrupt life in every other industrialized nation for decades.

Makio and most Japanese conservatives understood the mathematics, and as the still potent legacy of Hiroshima and Nagasaki was finally beginning to wear off, they could envision a day in the not so distant future when Japan would build its own nuclear arsenal. Either that or closely ally themselves with China. This would be difficult. Unlike Westerners, who thought of history in terms of months, Asians understood the concept of generational change, and the Japanese 'Rape of Nangking' in 1937, during which between 300 and 400 thousand Chinese non-combatants were murdered, was still relatively fresh in the Chinese psyche despite the Internet age.

However much Makio despised popular Western culture, he admired certain Western artists, especially Van Gogh, whom he considered the greatest of all. There was a kinship between the Dutch master and the great Japanese artists, Hokusai, Utamaro, Hiroshige, and Kuniyoshi. Makio knew Van Gogh owned a number of woodblock prints by these artists and that in 1887, Vincent was so enamored of all things Japanese he painted Japonaiserie, a homage to Kuniyoshi, now hanging in the Rijksmuseum. In a letter Vincent wrote to his brother, Theo, shortly after arriving in Arles on February 21, 1888, after a sixteen-hour journey by train, he describes the landscape: "And the landscapes in the snow, were just like the winter landscapes that the Japanese have painted." Van Gogh covered the walls of the tavern on the Boulevard de Clichy, Le Tabourin, with Japanese prints bought at the shop of Samuel Bing. Agostina Segatori, one of Edgar Degas' models who managed the restaurant, had a brief affair with Vincent. When she ended it, Van Gogh broke down the door of Le Tabourin to recover his Japanese prints.

Makio was the underbidder for the Portrait of Dr. Gachet. He passed on the Irises, feeling that fifty million was excessive. He, himself, stopped bidding at thirty million and declined to purchase the painting when Sotheby's offered it to him after Bond defaulted on the purchase.

Makio liked the Irises well enough, however in his opinion the greatest paintings of flowers were those of the Kana school artists like Kana Sarakyu, working during the Aizuchi-Momoyarna period. Of the European artists, none surpassed the Dutch Baroque artist, Jan Davidszoon de Heem's, still-lifes. Vincent's Sunflowers were another story. Makio had bid on the Sunflowers at Christie's, dropped out and lost them. He still recalled the sale on March the 30th, 1987 at 7:30 p.m. Greenwich Mean Time. The work cost more than five billion yen at the time and he regretted not buying it to this day, though he quit at two billion. Today he would have bought the picture, however he was in his early twenties at the time and was reluctant to spend such a major percentage of his liquid assets on art. At the time it was the best of five large canvases Vincent painted of sunflowers while he lived in the famous yellow house in Arles. It is now universally regarded as the finest and most important of the iconic series.

Makio understood the secret of Van Gogh's tremendous appeal. The secret was simply that at age 35, when he painted the Sunflowers in January of 1889, he had found ultimate truth through his art. This truth was something even the sublime artist Katsuhika Hokusai was still insatiably seeking as he breathed his final breath at the age of 89 on May 10, 1849. Hokusai wrote his manifesto of the artist's quest in 1834 at the age of 75.

"At the age of 73, I finally apprehended something of the true quality of birds, animals, insects, fishes, and of the vital nature of grasses and trees. Therefore at 80, I shall have made some progress, at 90 I shall have penetrated even further the deeper meaning of things, at 100 I shall have become truly marvelous, and at 110, each dot, each line shall surely possess a life of its own."

Makio knew that Vincent, at the age of 37, had achieved what Hokusai was looking forward to at 110. Each one of Van Gogh's lines "surely possessed a life of its own." Makio wasn't a rabid Sinophile. He didn't resent the fact Van Gogh was a European and not a Japanese, any more than he resented the Buddha being Indian or Confucius being Chinese. Makio empathized with Vincent, who had paid a fearful price for looking long in the light of truth until it burned his desire to live in this world to cinders.

Makio was in his penthouse apartment, which occupied the entire top floor of a fifty-story high-rise. The floor to ceiling windows offered spectacular views of Tokyo Bay, Mount Fuji when the air was clear, as well as the Ginza district. Makio's wife and children were out of the city at her parents' home near Kyoto. Makio was sipping a Grey Goose martini that his personal assistant had shaken to perfection in crushed ice made from his favorite Japanese mineral water, with a twist of peel from an organic lime, and a Kalamata olive.

Makio hadn't looked at his computer monitor all day, which wasn't unusual. He'd had an exhilarating day at the office meeting with the recently appointed Chinese minister of Economics about a semi-conductor manufacturing facility nearing completion in Chongging in Sichuan Province. The minister had given his unqualified endorsement to the project. Beijing, Shanghai, and Tienjin, Chongging were administered by the national government, which eliminated all the usual local provincial interference.

Makio seated himself at the desk in his home office. The desk was an original, designed by the renowned Bauhaus teacher, Marcel Breuer, and made of Honduran mahogany by the ISOKON firm. His chair was also a Breuer design, an invention inspired by the design of bicycle handlebars in tubular chromium known as the Wassily chair. He tapped the spacer bar on his keyboard and refreshed the page with his email account. There was an interesting email from Philippe in Buenos Aires with attachments. He opened the email and read while the attachments were downloading. His highly advanced Panasonic computer had a processor that made Intel's Pentium 3 look slow and the largest downloads were the work of a moment. He opened the first image and he reached for his martini and took a deep draught. The portrait on his monitor took him aback. The time signature on his monitor read 6:47. He knew New York was fourteen hours behind, or 4:47 the previous day. He couldn't remember if Argentina was on New York time or not, then again he thought: *What difference does it make?* Like most Japanese, Makio valued etiquette and protocol in both social and business transactions because they made it possible for people to live in close quarters and still maintain their personal space and privacy.

He instantly wanted the painting more than anything he'd ever seen in his life. The very power of the desire astonished him. He was neither acquisitive nor covetous by nature. Makio truly believed that the world was an illusion, and everything material was maya as the Buddha taught and he did not burn with the fires of lust for gain. He was a Buddhist in the deepest recesses of his being. Nevertheless, like so many of the most wonderful Japanese artists, his Buddhist beliefs did not diminish his appreciation of the evanescent, lambent beauty that existed in the world of illusion, or lessen his passion to experience the truth contained in a work of art. To know that the Van Gogh was itself an illusion and still to respond to its appeal was a paradox. Zen Buddhism not only made allowances for such irreconcilables, it used them as one of the foundations of teaching. The essence of a Zen koan, the succinct paradoxical statement or question used as a meditation discipline is designed to wear out the analytical mind and the self-involved will, forcing the mind to respond intuitively rather than intellectually. Makio repressed the immediate impulse to telephone Philippe and instead sent a terse email asking for payment instructions, and to make arrangements to have it in Buenos Aires as soon as possible. He knew Philippe was a reputable dealer who would no more represent a stolen work of art than he would steal one.

He thought, *There must be some problem with the title, some dispute, or the price would not be so low*, he thought. Then again this was not necessarily a problem for under Japanese law if he bought it in good faith and owned it for two years, the painting was his. Philippe would give him a properly endorsed bill of sale and that would be the end of the title issues. Strange, Philippe made no mention of a certificate from the Rijksmuseum Vincent Van Gogh, though this could be easily remedied. The curator and Makio were on very cordial terms, because the official knew it was Makio who had persuaded Saito San to allow Dr. Gachet to go on exhibition at the museum three months after the world record breaking auction. The painting proved quite a draw in much the same way as Rembrandt's Aristotle Contemplating the Bust of Homer had in the 1960's after the Metropolitan Museum paid 2.3 million dollars for it, a world record at the time. Makio knew of several private sales that equaled the auction price Mr. Lauder paid for the Klimt. Someone with far more money than sense had even paid in excess of 100 million dollars for a painting by Jackson Pollack. If Kilmt and Pollack were worth 100 million dollars, Dr. Gachet was worth billions and so was this self-portrait. Even with his admittedly limited knowledge and expertise, Makio was confident of the painting's authenticity. So was Philippe or he would never have offered it to him to begin with.

Still the thought of paying fifty-five million dollars for a few francs worth of oil paint and canvas, which was all it was worth without a certificate from the Rijksmuseum, was slightly disconcerting. Then again, with an up-to-date certificate or letter from the museum, which was what Sotheby's, Christie's, Bonhams, or Park Avenue would require, verifying that it was in fact the painting in question and not a copy, the price would triple or quadruple. He could solve the whole problem by emailing one of the photos to the curator in Holland, however that might alert a possible competitor to the existence of the piece and ignite a bidding war. Though Angus had laid great stress on the absolute need for confidentiality, one simply didn't place similar strictures when approaching a client with the stature requisite to buying a major Van Gogh for obvious reasons, and Philippe hadn't made references to the need for secrecy in his email to Mr. Onishi. Makio decided the most prudent course would be to wait until Philippe actually had taken possession of the painting, and then he would email the photos to the curator. He'd lost the Sunflowers in a bidding war, and he had no intention of losing the self-portrait the same way.

## CHAPTER 22

# Winning the Lottery

SUNDAY NIGHT PROVED even more enthralling for John than Saturday had been, if such a thing were possible. He hadn't taken a change of clothes over to Lucille's because he didn't want to appear presumptuous, for after all it was only their second date. Lucille even asked him if he'd brought a jacket or a tie and John told her he hadn't because he thought that would be taking too much for granted. After hearing this, Lucille smiled, wrapped her arms around his neck and kissed him passionately.

"John Dryden, where have you been all my life?"

John left Beverly Glen at 6:30 in the morning, hoping to make it to Westchester before the 405 became a parking lot. He needn't have worried, as the horrendous traffic coming in on the 101 Ventura Freeway into the 405 South from the San Fernando Valley usually dissipated once you passed Wilshire Boulevard. He had a court appearance in Southgate criminal court scheduled for 9:00 a.m., representing a young Hispanic woman in an assault case. The woman was out on a personal recognizance bond and Judge Garcia was usually sympathetic to women, however he was a stickler about attire and would make caustic comments about counsel appearing before him in anything less than a three-piece suit. As far as he was concerned, a sport coat and a tie indicated a lack of sufficient respect for the court. John chose a dark blue, single-breasted light wool suit and noticed he was missing his billfold. Not only that, he wasn't wearing his watch. As small waves of panic washed over him, he frantically searched his pockets then finding nothing, ran to his car. He looked frantically under, on, and in between the seats, all to no avail. Worse, he couldn't find his cell phone either. He tried desperately to remember Lucille's home telephone number and failed.

John was thrown completely off balance. He thought he must have left everything at Lucille's apartment, only he couldn't remember forgetting anything. He shouldn't be operating a motor vehicle without a license, although the registrations were in the glove compartments of both the GTO and the Toyota. He didn't have time to drive back to Beverly Glen, and even if he did, Lucille might well have gone into Beverly Hills for breakfast, as she'd told him there were several Italian restaurants that served delectable coffees from their elaborate machines. John was drinking his own home brew, which was freshly ground and dripped, fragrant and strong. He wasn't in the mood to make scrambled eggs, and he was out of the whole wheat bread he used to make toast. The telephone rang and he lunged for it, hoping it was Lucille.

"Hello," he said somewhat anxiously.

"John, it's Angus. I called your cell and it went straight to voicemail." Angus had read Philippe's email at 6:15, and he'd waited an hour to call John. When John didn't answer his cell, Angus was ready to panic. The deal was all but done to his way of thinking. There was a willing buyer and a willing seller, and the terms and conditions were acceptable to both parties. Now it was only a question of the actual mechanics, examination of the goods, the transfer of funds, then of the painting itself. Philippe wrote that he was coming to Los Angeles on a chartered jet, flying into either Van Nuys, Burbank, Santa Monica, or LAX. He was leaving the choice of airports up to Angus. Angus preferred Santa Monica because he disliked the Valley in general and Van Nuys Airport in particular. He had met clients at Van Nuys before and he had gotten lost traveling west on Sherman Way, besides he avoided the 405 Freeway during daylight hours whenever he could. He'd seen numerous corporate jets land at Santa Monica and he knew all he had to do was take Bundy Drive south and he'd run right past the airport, and it was much closer to Southgate than Van Nuys. LAX had general aviation, but it was congested at the best of times unless one wanted to land in the small hours of the morning. Long Beach was a good airport except it was further south than Van Nuys was north. Santa Monica was definitely the most convenient, assuming they would permit Philippe's plane to land there. Angus knew Santa Monica could take a big jet like a Gulfstream 4. Even a Gulfstream would have to re-fuel, probably in Panama City. It sounded like the trip from hell to Angus. The problem was that a jet with transcontinental range was usually too large and costly to fly just one passenger. Regular commercial airlines would present problems carrying the painting flat, even in first class, and then there were the customs issues;

Angus didn't even want to think about. He assumed Philippe had Argentine customs used to the idea of almost priceless works of art coming into the country. Then there was the question of insurance, which might be easier to obtain using a private jet.

John knew something of significance must have transpired in the hours since Angus sent the photos from his office. There was a tangible sense of electricity animating Angus' British reserve. This could only mean that he and Hank were very close to winning the lottery so to speak. The reality of all that money, which had been so amorphous and illusory as to not affect John's thinking at all, was beginning to take form. He could found a law firm with the yearly interest on the principal that would employ ten of the most talented young lawyers in Southern California. He could pay them a salary equal to that paid by Fortune 500 corporations. The disenfranchised needed civil as well as criminal representation. He would send Carol to law school, not that she didn't already know more about the type of law that interested her than the teachers. She could prep for the bar right now and probably pass it with flying colors. John was sure that all kinds of opportunities would present themselves in time.

"Are you sitting down?" asked Angus.

"Well, no," said John. "I have to be in Southgate in less than an hour and then drive to downtown Los Angeles."

"The painting is sold. The buyer's representative is on his way as we speak by chartered jet. He has agreed to the price. I have to email his office with your wiring information so the funds can be transferred simultaneously once the painting is inspected. Of course there may be a twelve-hour or even a two-day delay because instantaneous wire transfers only exist in John Grisham novels and Hollywood movies. In real life wires take time, but considering the parties involved, we shouldn't have to wait that long."

John almost said, "I'll have Carol email you my account number." Then he paused. He hadn't told Carol about the Van Gogh and she would be seriously pissed off that he'd kept her in the dark, and she'd have a perfect right to be. It wasn't at all like him to keep secrets from her. In this case it had just happened without any element of volition or intention on his part. His grandfather had been so damned insistent on confidentiality, primarily, John thought, because he was ashamed that he'd liberated the Van Gogh, and liberated was really nothing but a pleasant sounding euphemism for looted or stolen. It wasn't as if Hank had just been overwhelmed by desire for the painting and run off with it; he'd carefully and deliberately cut it off the stretcher, then disposed of the frame and the stretcher bars so as to leave no trace. He had taken it from the house of an SS general, and possibly saved it from being taken by someone other than the rightful owner, whoever that might have been. Although the transaction was taking form, it was still very far from being a done deal to John's way of thinking, though now it seemed the money would not be an issue.

*Maybe I'm just being paranoid, because I always think if something's too good to be true, it is,* thought John. The ability to perceive and foresee any conceivable danger or pitfall in any given course of action involving humans or institutions was simply part of being a good lawyer and had nothing to do with intentionally negative thinking or outlook. A lawyer who only saw the best possible outcome rather than a worst-case scenario, and blew sunshine up a client's rectum rather than giving him the awful truth of what could occur, was in John's opinion, the vilest sort of traitor. He asked Angus, "When do you think your man will arrive in LA?"

"He's coming in from Buenos Aires, so I think he'll have to stop to refuel. He should be here sometime this evening. I'm sure he'll email me from the plane as soon as he leaves Panama City."

"What do you want me to do?"

"I need the wiring instructions ASAP. I'll email you the Bill of Sale and Assignment of Title format he wants you to use."

"Wait just a minute, Angus. We already talked about this. Bill of Sale, I have no problem with. As for title, given the circumstances involved, I can't sign my name to a fraudulent document. Not even for fifty million dollars." Angus heaved a sigh. He'd anticipated this and told Philippe in his email that Dryden was an attorney and might balk at signing a standard guarantee of good title.

"I'll tell you what," said John. "I can guarantee the painting has been in the possession of the seller since 1945, has never been offered for sale, and that to the best of the seller's knowledge there are no liens, encumbrances, or claims against the property. Much past that, I'm afraid I can't and won't go. I know what he wants, which is to say it was purchased in good faith and acquired legally, and you might as well know now that isn't going to happen. If it's a deal-breaker then so be it. Nothing I can do about it. I can't convey legal title to property taken in wartime, especially after the terms of surrender officially ending the hostilities had been signed."

"I understand all that," said Angus.

"But without an assignment of title, what exactly is the buyer getting for his fifty million?"

"He's getting physical possession of a Van Gogh self-portrait and a properly drawn bill of sale showing he's buying it in good faith. Except for the United States and Canada, after keeping it for a few years he owns it. He's the legal owner in Britain, the European Union, Japan, and most countries in the world."

"I don't know that a Bill of Sale offers that much in the way of legal protection."

"Speaking as a lawyer, I can tell you it does, as it demonstrates it was purchased legally and paid for. As for a guarantee of legal title, since the seller is unsure of his own title, he can hardly offer any assurances to the buyer beyond conveying physical possession. As you've pointed out, the Getty Museum has bought Italian antiquities with no more than a Bill of Sale."

"And there's been an ongoing legal battle and the curator involved has been indicted in Italy as a result. A number of the disputed items have been repatriated."

"Angus, I have to be in court by 8:50 or I'm going to be in trouble with a judge who won't hesitate to make my life miserable. You work it out and let me know what you want me to do."

"What if it's either a title or no deal?"

John's answer didn't require a moment's thought. "Then I won't be a rich man after all."

"I'll see what I can do to maneuver around it."

"I don't have my cell phone. I seem to have mislaid it in all this excitement. I should be in the office by noon."

"I'll call you at noon."

---

Philippe was jostled violently as the Gulfstream alternately rose and dropped in the disturbed air over the Cordillera de los Andes. The cabin of the executive jet was carefully and comfortably furnished like a living room. He was watching an old Clint Eastwood film, Unforgiven, on DVD. The more he thought about it, the more he was convinced this was the strangest deal he'd ever heard of, much less been a part of. Lupe, his secretary, had called him on the Iridium satellite phone he'd bought just for this mission. Lupe thought of buying it just before he left Buenos Aires. His regular cell phone would have probably worked in the States, but she didn't want to take any chances. As far as he was concerned, everything was happening much too quickly. Philippe liked transactions to proceed in an orderly, even stately fashion, much like any other dramatic production. This was far too chaotic and too hurried to make him comfortable. Mr. Onishi had made it abundantly clear that if he thought the work was genuine to take possession of the painting immediately. Questions of title, provenance, even ownership were to be regarded as of little importance weighed against the condition of the painting and its authenticity. As long as it wasn't stolen or on the Art Loss Register's list of problematic WWII pictures, Philippe was to spare no expense in securing the Van Gogh. Philippe was humbled by the extent of the Japanese billionaire's faith in him. Makio had trusted him to the extent of having the full fifty-five million dollars wire transferred to Philippe's account in Nassau. Philippe fantasized about picking up the painting and leaving the States the same night, however he knew this would be impossible, as the crew needed to sleep a full eight hours and he had no intention of flying with drowsy pilots. The charter company had booked the two crewmen into rooms at the Sheraton Plaza La Riena on Century Boulevard at LAX, and arranged for a limousine to pick them up at the general aviation terminal on Imperial Highway at LAX. Philippe wasn't that bothered by LAX, however Angus seemed to think the federal authorities at LAX might be more intrusive than the officials at a less congested airport. Philippe thought the reverse, assuming the customs in a place like Santa Monica would be more aggravating by virtue of the fact they had comparatively little experience with private international charters, while at LAX they were commonplace.

The pilot had once flown into LAX at night and told Philippe it had been almost as uncomplicated as landing at the airport in Santiago de Chile. Admittedly his one landing had been at 11:00 p.m. and as they would be landing much earlier in the evening, the massive airport might very well be congested. Philippe decided to take a chance and land at LAX. No doubt the American Homeland Security officials would want to go over the aircraft thoroughly with sniffer dogs and inspectors to make certain no one had secreted any packages of cocaine in the wheel wells or elsewhere.

As the Gulfstream sped down the runway at Panama City and climbed steeply, banking to the West out over the Bay of Panama, Philippe could see the bright blue-green ribbon of the Canal as the plane leveled off. The jet touched down on the far south runway at LAX shortly after 7:00 p.m. Pacific

Daylight Time just behind a United Airlines 757 that was inbound from Denver. Customs clearance at the Atlantic Terminal on Imperial was much less of a headache than Philippe had expected and by eight the pilot and co-pilot were inside a Lincoln Towncar and Philippe was in Angus' BMW. Lupe had booked a villa at the Peninsula Hotel on Little Santa Monica Boulevard in Beverly Hills and as Angus made his way east on Imperial to the entrance to the 105 Century Freeway. Philippe, who had taken a long nap on the plane after Panama, was feeling quite fresh despite his more than fourteen hours en route. Much of the credit was due to the excellence of the charter amenities including fine food consisting of a delicious Argentine beef tenderloin in a mushroom red wine reduction sauce that was actually prepared so that 90 seconds in the convection microwave would enhance the flavor rather that reduce it to a chewy piece of leathery beef. The Catena Cabernet was an estate bottling that compared favorably with a fine Bordeaux, and the bread was crisp, a perfect accompaniment to the excellent cheeses.

Angus wondered just how much the Gulfstream cost and asked him. "Between the fuel, the crew, and the rent on the plane, say a close to two hundred thousand dollars."

Angus took the long, sweeping, two-lane transition ramp onto the 405 San Diego Freeway North, which was an unmoving sea of red brake lights beginning just past Century Boulevard. Within less than three minutes they had gone from seventy miles an hour to a dead stop.

"Can you believe this? It's 8:15 on a Monday night and this freeway is stop and go all the way from Century to the Santa Monica Freeway. It will take us twenty minutes to travel the next five miles."

"Is there another route?"

"I could take La Cienega north, but there are traffic lights, dozens of them, all unsynchronized. During the day it's an interesting drive through Baldwin Hills and the oil fields. You never think of Los Angeles as an oil-producing city, though it's been one for decades. Union Oil and Exxon-Mobil own most of the wells."

"That's really interesting. All you associate with Los Angeles is the film industry."

"In their first fifty years beginning in 1921, the Signal Hill fields eventually boasted 2,400 wells and pumped nearly a billion barrels of oil."

"So all along as the world was focused on the glamour of Hollywood, it was petroleum that fueled the city."

"It made the Dohenys and the Hancocks multi-millionaires back in the days when you could buy a Rolls Royce for a few thousand or a new Ford for five hundred."

"Any chance of seeing the Van Gogh tonight?"

"I've been trying to call him on his cell all day. He didn't have it on him this morning and I know he was in court until 12. I called his office this afternoon and got a recording. I don't know what's going on. I'll call his office again. He works late." Angus pressed 411 and for the extra fifty cents, allowed the electronic operator to connect him to John's office. The phone rang and went to voicemail.

"No answer."

"How far is Dryden's office from here?"

"Maybe twenty minutes."

"Good, let's take a chance on catching him. Sometimes when I work late I don't answer my office phone either."

Angus had been hoping Philippe would be more interested in having a good dinner at Crustacean, one of Beverly Hills premier Asian seafood restaurants. The hostess, who knew Angus as well as most of the Park Avenue staff from their frequent lunch reservations, was holding a prime table for two near the artificial stream at 9:30. Angus took the Manchester exit, made a left at the top of the ramp, and another left to get back onto the 405 South to catch the 105 East to Long Beach Boulevard. Angus knew he could have simply taken Manchester Boulevard, however he was wary of driving a route that would take him through Inglewood, South Central, and skirt the north sector of Watts. In his mind it made no sense to take surface streets through impoverished, black neighborhoods in his new BMW with two white faces in the front seats.

John's court appearance before Judge Garcia had gone well. The judge even complimented him on his choice of suits. Consuela Aguilar was a free woman. He'd wanted to stop by his office, but he barely had time to race to the federal building on Los Angeles Street to an immigration hearing before a federal magistrate involving a Guatemalan woman, which went his way as well. He used the pay phone in the building to call Lucille at the gallery. She had found his watch, billfold, and cell phone carefully placed on one of the wooden sconces in her bedroom. She apologized for not noticing them before he left. By the time she did see them and called his house, he'd evidently already left for court. Lucille offered to drive to downtown Los Angeles on her lunch hour, but he told her he didn't need them that urgently.

"I'll be as connected as I need to be once I get to the office, and if by some twist of fate I need the billfold, I'll send Carol to pick it up."

"Well, I have them all safely in my bag if you need them."

After he arrived at his office, John spent a good 45 minutes with Carol telling her the whole story of the Van Gogh, Sepp Dietrich, and the Walther pistol as well as the Knight's Cross documents and folders. He showed her the painting, which she admired, though she couldn't understand why it was worth so much money. Carol did understand why Hank didn't want anyone to know he'd taken the painting off the wall of someone's home, even the home of a Nazi general.

"I look at it this way," she said. "Say that Van Gogh painted a thousand paintings in his life. Some better and some worse. Let's give them an average value of ten million dollars. That means all of his works are worth ten billion dollars. Does that make sense to you? For ten billion dollars you could own a good percentage of a major corporation like Ford or General Motors. See what I mean? Say what you want about rappers like Master P, JZ, and Fifty Cent throwing their money around; there aren't none of them buying fifty million dollar paintings."

"There are those who say great art represents the very closest approach the human spirit makes to the divine force that creates the universe."

"If I feel the need for that, all I have to do is go to church on Sunday and it doesn't cost me a dollar unless I want it to go into the collection plate. Don't get me wrong. I like art. Maybe this painting is worth a million dollars because it's beautiful and powerful and the artist is famous, but past that I can't see it at all, especially when you think of it in terms of a thousand Van Gogh's."

"Van Gogh painted more than 700 oil paintings in his life and sold only one, the Red Vineyard."

Carol looked at John as a thought came to her. "Considering that Hank took the painting off the wall, how exactly are you going to transfer title legally?"

"That's the fifty million dollar question. I told Angus Creswell, the man from the gallery who bought the documents and Dietrich's pistol, that I'll give him a bill of sale."

"John Dryden, sometimes I know you better than you know yourself. Somehow I get the impression you're not really comfortable with the whole thing."

"No, I'm not. The gun was one thing. Supreme Allied Command in Europe ordered all firearms to be confiscated. Their order was legal and binding. In a theater of war, the laws of property are different, however looting is still illegal, though everyone knows it's commonplace. The Nurnberg Tribunal declared the SS a criminal organization in 1946. Property belonging to a member of a criminal organization is theoretically subject to confiscation. Hank 'acquired' the Van Gogh in late spring of 1945 before the Nurnberg ruling and he was under no orders to confiscate anything other than weapons."

"So he shouldn't really have taken those documents either. Listen, I love Hank. He's a great guy with a heart of pure gold, but you and I both know when all is said and done this painting is hot, and dear old Hank stole it. That's why he never showed it to a soul until now, sixty years after the fact. You're not happy with your position, and don't bother trying to tell me you are."

"Carol, hear me out on this. If Dietrich had taken it from Solomon Roth by force or even under duress, his children would have reported it to INTERPOL and the Art Loss Register years ago. And if it belonged to Sepp Dietrich, he was an SS general and a criminal by definition."

Lucille had told John and all but convinced him that even if Dietrich had a daughter in a convent much less a son who would proudly ride around on Nazi armored vehicles, she shouldn't profit from anything her father owned while he wore the black uniform. Assuming the painting legitimately belonged to Dietrich, Lucille was fervent in the belief that being in the SS made him forfeit all rights to any property whatever.

Carol looked at John. "You say Van Gogh only sold one oil painting in his entire life, the Red Vineyard?"

"That's right," said John. "He sold it for 400 francs to Anna Bach six months before he shot himself on July 27, 1890."

"I don't know how much 400 French francs was worth in 1890. Let's say it was close to 4 dollars for 20 francs. Eighty 1890 dollars are worth what today? Gold was twenty dollars an ounce actually it was fixed at 20.67. So call it 4 ounces of gold and I'm being generous. At a thousand dollars an ounce, that Red Vineyard is really worth slightly more than five thousand dollars today, and that's valuing the gold on the high side. You're telling me that the Red Vineyard is worth twenty thousand times its value in gold? If there's anything wrong with my math or my logic, please tell me."

John thought about Carol's logic, and it made perfect economic sense to him. Her formula was based on the price of gold and allowed for inflationary increases from twenty dollars an ounce to a thousand dollars an ounce, a factor of fifty times or five thousand percent. Using Carol's formula, Van Gogh's Red Vineyard had increased in value by nearly one million percent in a little more than a century. John thought of the Dutch who bought the isle of the Manhatto Native Americans for trinkets and cloth worth sixty Dutch guilders, at the time equivalent to about 18 ounces of pure silver. Valuing silver at ten dollars an ounce, that made New York worth 180 dollars using the Carol formula and he told her. She responded immediately, "You can't compare a theft, which is what the white man always did to the Native Americans, to a legitimate sale. Those Indians didn't have the slightest idea that they were giving up ownership of their land. They had no concept of private ownership. How could anyone own something the Great Spirit gave freely to all people to enjoy as long as they were alive?"

"Okay, I agree with you; bad example. How about Alaska? Seven million dollars at the time in 1867, and the American people thought Secretary of State William Seward was wasting the public's money calling it Seward's Folly and Seward's Icebox. Using your sixty times, 6000 percent formula, that makes Alaska worth 420 million dollars. Even at the Van Gogh multiple, Alaska's worth only two and a half trillion dollars, although that's a substantial figure."

There was Hank to consider as well, and all the positive, philanthropic uses he would make of the money. Even the soon to be sainted Mother Teresa didn't inquire too closely into the source of some of her funds. If her money came from narcotics traffickers, well then her use washed it white as snow. John threw this up to Carol as well.

"I read where Mother Teresa said she'd take money from drug lords and that she didn't care where the funds originated as long as it was put to good use," said Carol. "I'm not judging her and I'm sure her heart was in the right place, but her thinking was wrong, dead wrong. I'd say it to the whole world on Oprah that in this case, Mother Teresa was full of shit. It does matter where the money comes from and you know it as well as I do."

John broke out in a cold sweat. He knew the main reason why he hadn't told Carol wasn't because of Hank's insistence on complete confidentiality. It was because he knew she'd probably disapprove of his selling it secretly. Carol had worked on enough death penalty cases, spent time with prisoners condemned to die, and witnessed more than one execution. Carol wasn't some iconoclastic, didactic moralist by any means. She did have a highly evolved sense of right and wrong, and very rarely allowed her emotions to overrule her ethics, even when it was an issue affecting African-Americans like affirmative action or the fact that 10% of young African American men had either been in or were going to prison.

"All right, Carol. How would you suggest I handle it? Bear in mind there's a buyer on a chartered jet who's due to land in LA sometime this evening."

Carol smiled rather grimly. "Did you tell Angus that you weren't going to guarantee ownership?"

"Yes, I made that point clear. Not just clear but crystal clear, and I reiterated it several times."

"Then I'd say the buyer is aware that the painting has a, and I use the term advisedly and in a spirit of generosity, clouded title, and he's still flying in tonight?"

"Yes."

"Then I'd say he's not overly scrupulous to begin with. He knows the risks involved in making, shall we say, unsavory deals. You haven't put anything in writing?"

John tried to remember if he'd sent Angus any emails about the Van Gogh, and nervous as he was, he couldn't recall any."

"What if I sold the painting and gave the money, all fifty million dollars, to charities like Doctors Without Borders and your old law firm there in Georgia?"

"That might do a lot of good and salve your conscience. Nevertheless, you'd still be a fence. The most glorious fence anyone ever heard of, but still a fence. It would make a great Lifetime movie or Movie of the Week with your character as the Robin Hood hero."

"But you'd think I was a receiver of stolen goods?"

"Not to put too fine a point on it or judge you in any way, but yes."

"This is bad! What am I going to tell Angus? Hell, what am I going to tell Hank?"

"I don't know about you, but I need a cup of coffee."

"Coffee be damned; I need something stronger!"

"I noticed you opened the Remy the other day. You want me to bring you a shot?"

John laughed, "How about a cup of coffee and a shot of brandy?"

"I'll bring it to you. You just relax and think about things." John knew Angus Creswell wouldn't take the news well at all. Whoever was flying in would be way past pissed off. He knew it had to cost the better part of a hundred thousand dollars to fly a private jet, even a tiny one, from Argentina to LA and back, maybe two hundred thousand, and someone was going to lose all that money. Lucille would think he was a sanctimonious horse's ass. Hank would be disappointed in him. No, he'd be more than just disappointed. After living with the painful secret for sixty years, he'd be devastated. There would be no expiation of his theft. He would die knowing he was a thief, and that was more than terrible to John, it was unimaginable. Angus would lose his two million dollar commission. Carol brought the coffee in a Loyola Law School mug and as he took a sip he could taste the brandy and it tasted good.

"There's an email from someone named Lupe asking for our bank account number, the address of our bank, routing numbers, so they can wire money. What do you want me to do?"

"Don't answer it. I need time to think this through."

"What are you really afraid of? You're afraid of how Hank will take it, aren't you?"

"Yes, I am. The shock of it could easily kill him. Not immediately. He's too healthy from all that walking. It's just that he has such high hopes for the money and all the lives it would save."

Carol sipped her coffee. She'd put just enough Remy in hers to give it taste, not that she'd tell John she was tippling on the job.

"You never know. Maybe no one will come forward to claim it. Then it's yours free and clear."

"I've read enough about other pre-WWII works of art coming to the market after decades of being lost. Any public sale brings attorneys and claimants out of the woodwork, including those with totally specious claims. There are very complex jurisdictional questions involving international law and nations that can take years to resolve. Just defending Hank's claim would cost more than either of us has to spend."

"Last time I checked, you were a lawyer. You can do the defending."

"I'd have to bone up on international property law, UNESCO treaties, all the recent cases. It's a job for a big firm, not our little shop."

"Well, I don't know what to tell you. You can always put it back in Hank's closet."

"I thought about that. I would and yet when you think about it, I really can't. Angus and the buyer know about it, and the buyer has digital images on his computer. He's going to be highly pissed off and that's a masterpiece of understatement. What's to stop him from going to the media and saying the reason he didn't go through with the purchase was that he discovered the Van Gogh self-portrait, potentially one of the most, if not the most valuable paintings in the world, was stolen? Then I've got INTERPOL, the FBI, and God only knows what police agencies at my doorstep."

"That's not a very pleasant prospect, although it does have a silver lining. All the publicity would be good for business."

"What? Like Nahabedian's suicide helped make the phone ring off the hook?"

"As a matter of fact while you were in court I received a good thirty calls from prospective clients, not that we need any more pro-bono landlord tenant disputes, though five sounded interesting and potentially lucrative."

"The phone hasn't rung since I got here."

"That's because I have it set to go directly to voicemail. I knew from the look on your face when you came in that you had something on your mind. Between that and the email from Lupe asking for our bank information I knew something was up."

"Enough about the Van Gogh."

"I agree," said Carol. "Let's us talk about this Lucille girl. You haven't had anything approximating a real date in months, and suddenly you spend the night with a girl who makes you, of all people, forget your wallet, cell phone, and your precious gold watch."

As flummoxed and trapped as John felt, he couldn't help smiling as he told Carol all about Lucille, his taking her to Del Mar, her meeting Hank, the two of them being at the office yesterday, and how they naturally seemed to get along, as if he were the yang and she the yin, and together they formed a whole. He didn't go into any details describing the fantastic sex and Carol didn't inquire. He also omitted the tarot reading as he regarded that as a private matter between him and Lucille.

"She certainly sounds like a great girl. I take it from what you told me that she doesn't see the painting as stolen because the owner was in the SS. I can see her point. If I were a slave in America before the Civil War, I wouldn't think twice about robbing my master if I could get away with it. Hell, I even sympathize with Denmark Vesey, Nat Turner, and John Brown. I could see it if

Hank were Jewish and he were avenging the injustices perpetrated against his people."

"So you could say Hank was avenging humanity for the evils of the SS."

"You could have said that if Hank had donated it to a museum right after the war. He didn't. Instead he hid it in his closet in Del Mar for sixty years."

As John finished his coffee, the tumultuous events of the past several days caught up with him, and he literally had an overwhelming urge to sleep.

"Carol, would you think any the less of me if I lay down and took a nap for an hour?"

She guffawed.

"You're not used to life in the fast lane. Romantic late-night dinners in Beverly Glen Canyon, racing up to Beverly Hills, wild love making till all hours of the night, multi-million dollar deals, drinking during the day, it's no surprise that it's all too much for you."

"Yes, I'm the first to admit it. It really is too much for me, and I'm not ashamed to say it either."

"You go to your office. I'll keep the phones quiet. We can return all the calls tomorrow. None of them was life and death or involved imminent incarceration."

John was so exhausted he could hardly concentrate on what Carol was saying.

"If Lucille or Hank calls, be sure to wake me up right away."

"I'll do it."

John put the Van Gogh back in the bottom drawer of the blueprint safe and sat in the thickly upholstered armchair across from his desk, stretched out his legs and was asleep as soon as his eyes closed.

# CHAPTER 23

# Denouement

JOHN SLEPT SOUNDLY until 5:19 p.m., when he awoke with a stiff neck from sleeping in the chair, a left foot that was completely numb, and a ravenous appetite. He didn't dare stand up immediately. He waited as the renewed blood flow restored sensation in his foot. The pins and needles of the reawakened nerves and blood vessels were sharp and painful, serving as a spur to his mind. He had been dreaming of Ahmed Nahabedian, who'd come to his office dressed in a Nazi uniform, demanding that John return the Van Gogh he'd stolen from him. Nahabedian was flanked by two massively built men in cheap black suits, with the shoulders of gorillas, and pitiless, stony expressions on their faces. John dreamt that he told Ahmed, "It is all a mistake; I haven't stolen anything," then the scene changed and Nahabedian together with the two black-suited men, were leading Lucille out the door to the street and she was pleading to him, "Please, please, whatever you do don't let them take me."

Then John had Dietrich's Walther pistol in his right hand and pulled the trigger, shooting Nahabedian in the head. When John looked closely he saw a small, round black hole in Ahmed's head oozing dark blood, just above his right eye. Ahmed just smiled and said, "You know you can't kill me," and with that, Ahmed had a Luger in his hand, pointed it at John's belly and pulled the trigger. The scene changed abruptly, and John was sitting at the window of a Boeing 737 about to land at LAX and he knew it was going to crash into the tarmac. As he fought against his terror, just before the rending fiery impact, he woke up.

John carefully tested his foot on the floor by putting some, but not all, of his weight on it, and finding it would support that, stood and turned his head sharply to the left. His cervical spine made a loud cracking sound, and all the painful stiffness vanished. He walked into Carol's office.

"Well if it isn't Sleeping Beauty. Or is it Rip Van Winkle?" She looked at his puffy sleep-swollen face, disheveled hair, rumpled suit, red-rimmed eyes, and smiled.

"All right, so I fell asleep. It's not like I was out for twenty years. I mean the world can't have changed that much."

"No, but I did get three more e-mails from Lupe, each more urgent than the one before."

"You didn't answer them?"

"No, I didn't. Did you ever make up your mind about the painting?"

"I thought we did that before I fell asleep. What'd you put in my coffee? A Mickey Finn?"

"No, just three fingers of your Remy."

"Well it knocked me out like an injection of Lord knows what, sodium pentothal, Versed, morphine?"

"Lucille called. I offered to wake you and she told me to let you sleep. Said you had better husband your strength. We chatted awhile."

"What about?"

"Nothing important, just girl talk."

"I hope you didn't tell her anything that was just between us girls."

"John Dryden, you know me better than that. I wouldn't dream of embarrassing you in front of the only girl you've dated in the last X number of months. Not unless I couldn't help myself."

"You didn't. Please don't tell me you told her she was the first date I've had in a year."

Carol knew John was only half serious, and she and he were close enough that she liked to twit him about his non-existent love life, though not so viciously as to wound his feelings.

"Don't worry. We basically talked about what a great person you were, that you actually cared for your fellow man."

John was relieved.

"Anyone else call? Angus Creswell perhaps?"

"There were more calls from people who saw Ahmed and me on the nightly news."

"Hank didn't call?"

"He almost never calls during office hours. You might want to check your email."

Carol poured a cup of steaming coffee from the Pyrex carafe.

"I just made it."

John took it and sipped with satisfaction. "Thanks, I needed that. You didn't spike it did you?"

"No, I didn't. One thing I know for sure is that anyone who says you're a heavy drinker is a liar. You want me to check your emails?"

"No thanks, I'll check them myself. I don't know about you, but I'm starving."

"I suppose you want me to drive down to Imperial for two steak tacos?"

"Would you? That would be just short of heavenly."

"All right. I'll go under one condition."

"What's that?"

"You take Lucille and me to a nice Italian lunch in Beverly Hills sometime this week."

"I will, assuming she's still talking to me after I tell her I decided not to sell at the last minute."

"She won't think any less of you, trust me. Now that Englishman and whoever's flying in from Buenos Aires on a wild goose chase might have a different attitude. You want me to have my boyfriend go with you when you meet them? Or are you going to let them know by phone or email?"

"Which do you think will piss them off less?"

"Given a choice, assuming I was in the air and couldn't turn the plane around, I'd rather hear it in person from the prick who backed out at the last minute."

"That's an unkind cut, below the belt, especially since you made me rethink the whole thing."

"Don't blame me. That still, small voice inside you knew it wasn't right. If an action has to be done in secret, unless it's charity, there's something not right about it. Like I said, you know I love your grandfather, but he stole that painting the same as if he walked into the Louvre and took it off the wall."

"SS generals didn't live in the Louvre. Hank wasn't sent to the Louvre to confiscate firearms."

"Fine. You go into a person's house looking for cocaine, that doesn't give you the right to take his Renoir off the wall."

"If you're the American government it most certainly does."

"Since when are you on the side of the Supreme Court, which has eviscerated the Constitution of all its privacy protections? Fine, you go through with the sale then."

"No, you're right. It's just hard for me to accept that the man who basically raised me, whom I love and revere as a father, is a thief."

"Hank was no more than a kid at the time, fresh out of high school, seventeen years old, in a foreign country during a terrifying war. He acted on impulse. I might have done the same thing, and you, too. We weren't there, so we can't really say what we would or wouldn't have done."

"The hardest thing for me was listening to him tell about how he disposed of the frame and the stretcher. He knew exactly what he was doing or he wouldn't have covered up the theft."

Once a man sees another man's action in a completely different light, for whatever reason, his thoughts tend to swing in an arc like a pendulum to justify the new perception. Usually this means the new attitude tends to be more extreme and exaggerated than is really justified. John was no exception to the rule. Having hitherto justified Hank's actions by using the war as an excuse together with Dietrich's being SS, Hank was now off the pedestal John had placed him on for the past thirty-five years. Carol was aware of this and that there was little she could do to soften the grandfather's fall, though she would say what she thought needed to be said after she returned from Francisco's."

When she returned twenty minutes later, John was in his office, seated at his desk, left hand on his forehead, staring at his monitor. He looked up at Carol. "There's an email from Hank, but I haven't opened it. I don't know what to say to him. If I look at it from a strictly legal standpoint, he's asked me to be an accessory after the fact. The entire sale could be portrayed as a conspiracy to sell stolen goods. With the amount of money involved we would be looking at more than a few years in federal prison under the sentencing guidelines."

Carol handed John the white paper bag with the tacos. John unwrapped the foil and wax paper from the first one and wolfed it down in three bites. "Thank you, Carol," he said as he unwrapped the second one.

"John, before you send Hank off to Lompoc or Terminal Island think for a minute. Hank had no reason to think that painting was anything but a copy. He probably had never been to a museum in his life. He was a beach boy, a teenage surfer. The painting reached out and grabbed something deep inside him like it was supposed to do and he was nervous. He couldn't help himself.

After all he's done for you, loving you as his own son, now all of a sudden you see him as a common thief because he made a mistake and succumbed to temptation?"

"That's not what bothers me. What I'm having a problem with is that he insisted on confidentiality because he wants to avoid media attention. I think that is bullshit. I think he wants to avoid the whole question of how the public would judge him for taking the painting the way he did. People might excuse him because it belonged to the evil SS general, or he'd become the poster child for the wickedness of looting in wartime. The worst part is that the war was officially over before he took it."

"Over for how long? A week? A month? No, I don't think the issue is whether there were bombs falling or artillery shells raining down or not. It's more of whether the old 'to the victor go the spoils' rule holds true for Americans, who despite the overwhelming evidence to the contrary from slavery to Wounded Knee, to Waco, consider themselves better people than everyone else, and have a 'holier than thou' attitude in general."

As hungry as he was, the tacos seemed even more toothsome than usual, and the incipient headache that was the result of brandy on an empty stomach and sleeping sitting up was gone. John hadn't opened Hank's one email or the two from Angus. A part of him was very angry with both of them for placing him in an equivocal position. As a lawyer he believed he was firmly on the side of the angels, locked in combat with the devilish legal bureaucracy and the America's Prison Industrial Complex that actively sought to destroy economically disadvantaged young men and women who ran afoul of laws specifically tailored to take advantage of their distress. The mandatory sentences for possession of crack cocaine that were far longer than the time served by most murderers, immigration laws that permitted federal agents to devastate families, were but two indictments of a legal system gone utterly insane. John had allowed himself to be carried away from his principles by his desire to please his grandfather. He should have stopped the whole sordid process when Angus initially questioned his refusal to give the buyer the courtesy of an implied conveyance of title, much less a proper guarantee.

When Hank took the Van Gogh, he was a teenager toting a submachine gun for Uncle Sam in a foreign land, having fought his way through the Battle of the Bulge. Hank could always plead youth and innocence, whereas John could plead nothing of the kind. John didn't want Hank to end a good life being labeled as a thief and given the present mania for celebrity that held the entire human species in its thrall, he could just see Hank on CNN.

Carol had given him a good five minutes to allow her words to sink in then she continued. "Everything that happens in life has a purpose. I have to believe that. I know you're worried that the media will do their usual sensationalistic hatchet job on Hank, chop him into small pieces, and feed him to the sharks. That would probably be the case at the beginning. Think of it this way. We've all done things we're not exactly proud of, even I the 'heroine of the death chamber' as one Alabama paper once referred to me, have strayed off the path. If Hank goes public with this, he'll get it off his chest before he checks out of the game. It would be a salutary object lesson in this time when everything's about money, and honor, service, and integrity are seen as relative at best, and the traits of suckers at the worst. If Hank's confession and story helps one young person to see that winning the lottery isn't the be all, end all to life, then it's worth it. At last here's a man with an incredible fortune in the palm of his hand and he chooses to question the source. Who knows what will happen? Maybe he'll get to keep it after all. Maybe he'll get a multi-million dollar reward from the rightful owner. Anything that serves to foster a meaningful public discussion of right and wrong is a positive. You, John Dryden, can't sit there and tell me you were comfortable selling to some mysterious South American."

"No, I can't."

"So open Hank's email."

"If you get me a bottle of Fiji water."

"One cold Fiji water coming up. Wait until I get back to open the email. Please."

Carol left and returned a few minutes later with a bottle of John's favorite mineral water. He took it, twisted off the plastic cap, and drank half the pint without pausing for breath. His heart was pounding in his chest as he opened Hank's email. John could feel Carol's breath as she leaned over his shoulder. The email began with Hank's usual salutation to his grandson.

*Johnny: I haven't written as I've had an acute attack of kidney stones. Don't be alarmed. They haven't blocked my piss, but they're just painful as all Hell. I've been wrestling with something just like Jacob wrestled with the Angel of the Lord in the Bible. I know I have no right to ask, and you have a perfect right to tell me to piss up a rope, because it's your future. You see, I lied to you about the Van Gogh. The moment I saw it there on the wall of Dietrich's house I knew it wasn't a copy.*

*The frame was hand-carved wood and heavily gold leafed. The gilt bronze plaque at the bottom, everything about it screamed real. Just before I shipped back to the States, back then when you shipped out it was literally on a big boat, I had a buddy take a pretty good black and white photograph. I showed it to a German who was working at the Neue Pinakothek. He looked at me and said, "Where did you get this photograph?" I told him I found it in a file in the office of an SS general.*

*"I think I remember seeing the painting before the war, then again I could be mistaken. Why are you so interested?"*

*"No reason," I said. "I thought maybe it was in your museum."*

*"No," said the old man with a wistful expression on his face. "I wish it were."*

*"Do you think it's a copy?" I asked.*

*The man glared at me as if I'd said his mother was an ugly whore, and I had my answer. I told Emily it was a copy I'd bought on leave in Amsterdam, one of the few real lies I ever told her in forty years of marriage. I never showed it to your father, and there were years in which I never even looked at it once. I know it sounds bizarre, even insane, and when I think of living with it for all those years, I see my behavior as freakish and I can't explain it. I thought I'd show it to you, we'd sell it, and I'd give my share away. You'd be set for life, chase your dreams, found a law firm, buy a villa on the coast of Italy, see the world, your choice. The Internet made me decide to pursue a sale. After all, if anyone living on earth were missing a Van Gogh, it would have shown up somewhere on the Web. I've spent many days keying in Google searches, sent anonymous inquires to various museum curators, though, of course, never any photographs. I know nobody is looking for it. I also know that the end does not, and indeed cannot, be allowed to justify the means. I need to go public and reveal my shameful secret to the world. If my story disgraces me, I deserve it. I know you still have the painting, because you would have let me know if you sold it. I'm asking you to consign it to Park Avenue Galleries for a very public auction. Maybe Lucille could get some credit for convincing me to choose them over Christie's and Sotheby's.*

*I realize you might not believe a word I say after what I've told you, but I think you've met a perfectly wonderful girl, an authentic person with very little pretense about her. If you still want to go through with the sale, I understand. You gave your word to the man who bought Dietrich's pistol, and unlike mine, your word is still worth something. It's a hard thing after seeing yourself one way for eighty years, to find out you never really were that person after all. I'm not going to blame the devil or any outside influence in order to put distance between myself and my action as all too many people do. I can say categorically that Satan did not make me do it. Any evil that was present that day was inside me. I see that clearly. Neither do I blame the war or battle fatigue as we referred to it back then. Now the syndrome is referred to as post-traumatic stress disorder or PTSD. Oh, by the way, in the First World War they called it shellshock. I still don't really have a good explanation for why I did it. Maybe I was suffering from PTSD after all. No, it was an irresistible urge to own it, to take it home with me. Once I had it safely tucked away in my closet, it was like I had this amazing secret. One of the world's greatest art treasures was all mine. In a way, having it was like having Superman's cape. I might seem to the world like Hank Dryden, a mild-mannered reporter for the "Daily Planet" or vice president of the power company, but I had the most awesome, one piece art collection on earth. I alone knew that I was Superman.*

*I think I knew all along it was nothing more than an adolescent fantasy, kind of like fighting in the Battle of the Bulge at seventeen. I know this is probably the most pathetic letter you've ever received. You more than likely had me on a pedestal and now I'm lower than sperm whale shit on the bottom of the Marianas Trench, and that's kind of what I feel like right now. I really should just shoot myself and be done with it, however then you'd be the one to suffer, and I'd have taken the coward's way out of my richly deserved, public humiliation. Don't worry about me being suicidal. If kidney stones haven't made me do it, then being on Larry King won't either, although he'll have a field day interviewing such a disgrace to the untarnished image of the 'Greatest Generation.' You know every time I hear that jingoistic canting bullshit about how great my generation was, it makes me want to vomit my guts out. We were stupid and pig-ignorant, bombing Dresden, a 100% civilian target, nuking Hiroshima and Nagasaki, fighting the Japs over useless coral atolls in the Pacific, islands we could have just gone around leaving the remnants of the Jap army to eat lizards and fish until we took Japan.*

*Then Korea, which we created ourselves by permitting the Soviets to veto popular elections, elections we weren't so keen on either, the whole Cold War, McCarthy and his 'red scare,' all stupid, stupid, stupid. And through it all there was even stupider Henry Dryden with his ultimate war souvenir. I should have brought home a war bride instead. The problem was, I was already in love with your grandmother. Not that my being in love with her stopped me from enjoying the frauleins, a chapter of my life I only mentioned to her in passing, when it was more than just casual sex with one of them. That's just one more instance in which good old Henry is really nothing but a liar and a fraud. Well now you know your old Grandpa has feet of dogshit, not even clay. Rereading this email I see it as the effusion of a sick mind. If I were a religious fanatic, I'd see Luke's death as punishment for my sins, but I refuse to believe in that sort of God or that sort of karma. Your father was simply too good for this world like Vincent Van Gogh. Anyway, enough of this long rambling excuse for deceiving you, Johnny. I'm sorry, and that will either have to do or not do. Either way I will tell you, and I can only hope I have enough credibility left for you to believe me, when I say I love you with all my heart and nothing you can say or do will ever change that as long as I live. Hank.*

As a lawyer, John knew that most people, even those one thought were quite simple in both their lives and their personalities, were not like apples with one layer of skin, pulp, and a core with seeds. People were much more like onions, with layer upon layer, and one could go on peeling and rarely get to the inner core or truth.

Long before he received the email, when John was still in high school, he knew Hank wasn't a simple soul. John's mother always told him that despite his rather dull job, Hank was a very complex individual who thought about all sorts of metaphysical concepts, and that Luke used to say it was a pity that Hank never attended college, as he had a real inquiring mind and a high IQ. She told him stories of Hank marching in the vanguard of anti-war demonstrators wearing his sergeant's uniform. She considered Hank to be a hero at the time. Of course that was long before Edgar and the Republican fundraisers.

John couldn't help thinking Hank had played him for a fool and a patsy, though at the same time he realized it had been Hank's intention to make him a rich man. Not that the money effectively plastered the laceration of the betrayal, though to most people it would have been a soothing anodyne. John wasn't most people, then again as he'd told Lucille, the elements in the bodies of all humans had their origins in some distant star billions of years ago, even before the earth was formed, so the existence of the lowliest person on earth was an unimaginable miracle, greater than anything in the Bible, the Vedas, the Upanishads, or the teachings of Buddha. All things animate and inanimate were interconnected on a cosmic level and to think disparagingly of others using the term "most people" was dangerously inaccurate. A person could only distinguish himself by attitude, thought, and behavior.

Carol wasn't particularly shocked by the email. She believed there was always more to people than even their closest relations realized. She had been only slightly miffed at John for not letting her know about the Van Gogh from the beginning. She had no quarrel with Hank's position. In 1945, he was 17, fresh from months of trauma, and he didn't know any better. Officers and enlisted men were helping themselves to war souvenirs right out of homes and museums. Hank Dryden just happened upon the ultimate, the mother of all souvenirs.

She firmly believed that God not only marks the fall of small birds, but that He knows the outcome of a matter at its inception and scrutinizes and knows all human secrets. Hank was meant to take that painting and keep it safe all through the decades. Carol wasn't a Calvinist, thinking all human action was pre-destined and unalterable. There had to be an element of free will and choice, and it fell to John to exercise it. If John went through with the sale, the painting might remain secret for two more generations. "To her way of thinking, Hank had waited so long because in some fashion, as she understood it, the Van Gogh had become a part of him, of who he was, and how he saw himself. The painting wasn't evil like Wilde's Portrait of Dorian Grey. For Hank, the Van Gogh was more like any other talisman, a crucifix worn around the neck, or a lucky piece carried by a major league baseball player. Hank was nearly at the end of his life, the final scene in his own personal play, and he evidently thought it was time to let go of the Van Gogh. Carol smiled as she thought of it.

"Whatever are you smiling about?" John asked. "My grandfather, who is my father in fact, pretends he just happens to have this old painting in his closet, and it just might be a real Van Gogh. Sure it's a real long shot and he doesn't really know, but after all it should be checked out just in case. Anyway he tells his grandson, the public interest lawyer, the big sucker for any hard luck story, 'You take it with you and check it out, only be sure to be totally discreet and confidential because on the off chance it is genuine, I don't want to be pestered by the media. I'm too old for that circus. What did you say? They said it's a real Van Gogh?' I should have known something was rotten when he knew all about every Van Gogh ever sold at auction. He even told me he'd read about Jewish art collections being confiscated by the Nazi's and repatriated after the war. Wily old Henry Dryden, the only virgin in the whorehouse. With everything he told me, how could I have been so damn naive? I even told him that it seemed to me he knew far more about the legalities of stolen and confiscated art in wartime than I did. It wasn't exactly a popular subject at Loyola Law School. Whoever made the observation that what colors passion colors vision said a mouthful. Carol, you're looking at the biggest horse's ass in Los Angeles and that's saying quite a lot."

"Now, you're really exaggerating and in danger of indulging in self-pity, which is extremely unattractive in a man or a woman. You might feel like the biggest horse's ass, but that doesn't make you one. Like you said, feelings color perception. You love Hank, as well you should. He's your blood, and you're the son he loved so well and lost. Sure there's an age difference between you, though if you think of it, it's less than the one between you and any child you'll have if you had one right now."

John was still reeling from Hank's email when Carol's innocent comment about age differences stunned him. He'd always thought of Hank as so much older than he was. Carol wasn't quite correct. If he had a child in the next year, the age gap between his son or daughter and him would be exactly the same as between Hank and him. When the child was forty, John would be over eighty. Every year he waited would widen the gap. Thinking about it made him feel like he was suffocating, or about to have one of his panic attacks.

John sat silently as Carol said, "Well, I've had quite enough excitement for one day." As soon as the last word was spoken, she reconsidered, "On second thought, I'll wait to hear what you're going to do."

John had to prioritize quickly. He needed to reconcile what he needed to do with Lucille, Hank, and Angus. He was still hungry. The two tacos had only whetted his appetite. "First things first," he said as he reached for the handset. "I'm going to call Lucille."

"I like your priorities, John Dryden. Call her on her cell. I have the number if you need it."

"No, I've got it."

"Good. I'll be in my office."

## CHAPTER 24

# The Meeting

JOHN CALLED LUCILLE and told her that Hank had decided not to go through with the sale after all, and that he was in agreement with him, and that they were going to put it up at public auction.

"I hate to be the bearer of bad tidings," she said, "but I've seen it too many times. All sorts of people are going to claim ownership. There'll be lawsuits before the ink is dry on the consignment contract."

"I'm okay with that and so is Hank. He thought about it and now he wants all cards on the table, face up."

"As long as he's comfortable with his 15 minutes of fame, because the news media will have the proverbial field day with the story. It's a wonderful human interest tale."

"I figure I can shield him for quite a while. You know, a lawyer retained by a client who wishes to remain anonymous, that old bit. Either that or I could say my father bought it at a garage sale in Del Mar; no I'm just kidding. Seriously, if I consign it to Park Avenue will they defend my claim?"

"I know when Sotheby's and Christie's were in similar situations, attempting to auction major paintings with disputed titles, sometimes the sale was allowed to proceed and the litigation was over the monies generated, and other times the sale was stopped after the catalog was printed but before the actual sale. With a multimillion dollar commission from the buyer's premium alone, you can count on the auction house's law firm mounting a truly ferocious defense."

"That's exactly what I want, a ferocious defense by the very best litigators that I don't have to pay for."

"Defending the right to sell the property may or may not be part of the consignor's contract. Usually it reads, 'The seller warrants that he has title to the property,' or something like that."

"I can't guarantee anything other than that the property has been in the possession of the client for 60 years."

"You're the lawyer. I'm sure you can sit down with Christie's or Park Avenue's attorneys and work out something you both can live with."

"Is there any way you can take credit for my consigning the painting to Park Avenue?" This thought had never crossed Lucille's mind, though now that John mentioned it there was such a thing as an introductory commission, which was a gratuity paid to someone, often an estate attorney, for persuading someone to consign an important piece or collection to a particular auction gallery when the consignor wouldn't ordinarily have come to the gallery on his own. The introductory commission was normally set at a pre-agreed amount, based on either the reserve, the sale price, or a mutually agreed upon amount, but very rarely was it more than 3%. If the Drydens had clear title, and it was Lucille who introduced them and then induced them to consign the Van Gogh, the intro commission could easily have been 2% of one hundred million dollars. However with the potential cloud over the title, the auction house would be gambling whatever commission they paid out. Any reputable gallery would err on the side of caution under the circumstances. If there were to be any finder's fee, it would be contingent on the sale, and not paid immediately after the Drydens signed the contract as it usually was.

"I could ask for an introductory commission, however I work for the gallery, so it's an implied part of my job to attract property. Than again, I'm only a receptionist. Still, I did meet you through the gallery. There are all sorts of ethical considerations, not to mention Angus. I think in order to make it straight, I'd have to go with you to Sotheby's or Christie's, in which case if Park Avenue ever guessed it, I'd be fired and deserve to be. Of course even 1% would be more than I make as a receptionist in 35 years, not that I have any intention of working the desk for more than a year or two at the most."

"I haven't heard from Angus, although I do have an email I haven't opened."

"I can check your cell phone to see who called or you can call your voice mail."

"Why don't I call my voice mail, then I'll call you right back. What I'd like to do is leave here and come to Westwood. We need to go to your sushi place on Beverly Glen, that is if you're hungry and aren't tired of the place."

"No. To tell you the truth, I could eat there five times a week."

"Great. I'll call you right back."

"You better," she laughed. "I've been waiting all afternoon to hear from you."

"I fell asleep."

"I know, Carol told me."

"What else did she tell you?"

"Just girly stuff. Don't worry about it. Call me back. Bye."

John punched the numbers of his cell phone. Sure enough there were several calls from Angus, telling him to call him on his cell phone as soon as he could. John called Lucille and told her he was going to call Angus, then return Hank's email, after which he would make his way northwest through the traffic as best he could.

The office telephone rang as John hung up. Carol answered it, put Angus on hold, and told John over the intercom that Angus was on the line. John picked up the phone. "I've been calling you all day," said Angus somewhat annoyed.

"I'm sorry, I forgot my cell phone this morning."

"I've been calling your office, but it goes directly to voicemail until just now."

"The phone's been ringing off the hook with calls because of the suicide being on the news. My secretary did that so we could have some peace and quiet, and get some work done. I'm very sorry. I didn't mean to be incommunicado."

"Listen, I'm on the 105 East, passing the 110. I just picked Philippe up at LAX and if it's not too much of an imposition, we'd like to stop by and have a look at the Van Gogh before we head up to Beverly Hills."

John couldn't recall a time in his adult life when he'd been in a more awkward situation, except perhaps the time up in Napa with his inebriated fiancée. He'd had clients who were imprisoned and jailed after he defended them, which was awkward for him because he really cared deeply about his cases and understood that in most cases not involving violent crimes, incarceration was far more detrimental to society than it was beneficial. There were far too many instances of families forced to depend on a social safety net that was in tatters, and the burdens placed on suddenly single mothers were far more costly to society than any possible benefits. There were truly dangerous individuals who needed serious forced re-education and rehabilitation before being released back into society, though even they received little or none of the training they needed for successful re-entry. John had only defended three violent gang members, who in all probability would emerge from prison more hardened and more vicious than when they went in. Even in his dealings with these tattooed street toughs, John was inclined to see them as boys victimized by society rather than wild animals who needed to be locked up in cages for more years than they'd been alive.

"Angus," he said, and in the tone of that one word, Angus suddenly knew that something very bad had happened, like John's grandfather was in the hospital or worse. No one knew from one day to the next if he or she would live to greet the dawn, and since Henry Dryden was a WWII veteran, he had to be eighty plus, and an octogenarian could drop over at any time.

Angus was sick to his stomach, thinking, *I knew this was too good to be true*, and then, *Philippe's going to be very pissed off with me.*

"Angus, I just received an email from my grandfather. He's decided against a private sale."

"You've got to be kidding!"

"No, I'm afraid I'm not. I wish I were."

John knew Angus was beyond disappointment and there wasn't a thing he could do about it. Philippe was a very acute person and he could tell from Angus' tone and words that the deal was in mortal jeopardy. He had been involved in a sufficient number of transactions to have more than one deal that came unraveled at the penultimate stage. Still, calculating a risk-reward paradigm, he might lose two hundred thousand but balanced against the five million he would have made, it was nothing. Nevertheless, the money he spent would represent a significant loss and come from his own pocket.

"We'd still like to come to the office and see it."

"I'll wait for you," said John. Angus flipped his phone closed with his left hand.

"Shit," he said using the American pronunciation of the old Anglo Saxon expletive with a short vowel rather than the English long i.

"I take it there is a problem with the vendor," said Philippe rather mildly.

"Yes. His grandfather, the one who actually took the painting from Dietrich's home in May of 1945, has decided he wants it to be sold at public auction."

"He understands the sale and his ownership will more than likely be challenged in court, and he may easily lose the painting without any compensation, not to mention the attendant adverse publicity about his method of acquiring it?"

"I think they understand all that. I've explained all the possible permutations and scenarios of private and public sale. The grandson, whom you'll meet in a few minutes, is a lawyer. Not the high powered type, though he's sufficiently sharp to be aware of the perils involved in public auction."

"And the grandfather?"

"I've never even spoken with him, so I can't say much about him."

"You bought some things from him already?"

"A lovely Walther pistol, a presentation piece from Heinrich Himmler, and two of Dietrich's Knight's Cross documents in their presentation leather document cases." Angus said somewhat wistfully, "Unfortunately, not the Diamonds Document. There were only 27 of them awarded, you know."

"And they were happy with the prices you gave them?"

"They seemed to be. I paid them fairly close to retail. I just happened to have the ideal client."

"So you did well."

"Let's say I'll make a year's salary by the time everything's said and done."

"Good. So there's some rapport between you and the lawyer."

"I thought so until a few minutes ago."

"Cheer up," said Philippe. "It's far from hopeless. There's always hope until the contract's signed, and hope even after the ink's dry, though then it becomes far more difficult as you know. Backing out of a signed contract is an expensive and a messy proposition. Still, I've seen it happen."

"It's not something most clients are willing to undertake and that's a fact."

Angus drove up Long Beach Boulevard toward Tweedy, and as he did, Philippe was wondering how someone with a Van Gogh could work in such an obviously blighted neighborhood. There were terrible slums in Buenos Aires, however none of his clients lived or worked anywhere near their vicinity. When Angus pulled up to a meter on Tweedy and parked, Philippe was speechless.

"I never dreamt I'd see an unknown Van Gogh in a place remotely like this."

"I know exactly what you mean," said Angus. "When I came down here for the first time to buy the pistol, I was uncomfortable carrying the cash, I can tell you that. When I left the office, there were two Mexican thugs sitting on my bonnet."

Once all the pleasantries and introductions were completed, John brought out the Van Gogh. Philippe literally couldn't take his eyes off the painting. He was seated in John's swivel chair and the canvas was lying on the desktop still in the old cardboard folder. Philippe had slept quite well on the plane once it left Panama City, and although it was late, Buenos Aires time, like most Argentines, he was often up in the early morning hours dining in the Recoleta, and resting during the late afternoon. John and Angus were discussing the Knight's Cross documents, as John wanted to be sure Angus was satisfied, because Angus had been disagreeably surprised by the crease in the oak leaves award paper. Nothing was said by any of them about Hank's decision not to sell at the very last moment. Philippe had cautioned Angus not to say anything and to leave the attempt to resurrect the deal entirely up to him. Philippe was too experienced with the moods of the very rich; who would often change their minds about a purchase from one day to the next, to waste energy being be furious at Hank's change of heart. He had an impulse to tell Dryden that it was a copy Solomon Roth commissioned, that the original had been hand carried to Buenos Aires in 1939, and it was hanging in Esther Martinez, formerly Esther Roth's, dining room where he'd seen it two weeks ago. The urge was not easy to resist, because he could simply thank John and walk out, then in a month or two have Angus call him up and tell John the Roth granddaughter would like to purchase the copy for sentimental reasons since her grandfather had it painted by one of his artist friends who died at Majdanek in November 1943 after the rebellion at Sobibor. He hadn't spoken enough with Dryden to be sure if such a strategy would be successful.

Philippe wasn't dishonest. If he made the choice to execute his plan and John did sell it as a copy, Philippe would buy it, sell it for the fifty five million to Onishi, and pay John the fifty million telling him he'd made a mistake and Mrs. Martinez' painting was in fact the copy.

To categorize the painting as a masterpiece was an understatement. It was every bit as sublime as the best of Rembrandt's self-portraits, and that was the greatest praise Philippe could give to any self-portrait. In a way, as much as it was in his nature to prefer Rembrandt portraits for their painterly qualities, the abundantly rich colors the luxurious yet infinitely meticulous brushwork, the complete mastery of chiaroscuro, as well as the old master's penetrating profundity, this particular Van Gogh surpassed the 17th century titan. No artist could compete with Rembrandt's technical brilliance. It remains unsurpassed after nearly four centuries, and his series of self-portraits painted in the 1650's are universally regarded as the apex of achievement in the self-portrait genre of Western art. Rembrandt used multiple glazes of transparent color, and thick impasto, painstakingly applied to reproduce the most minute wrinkle and indentation in the flesh of the face, delineating more powerfully than any painter before or after him, the image of man tragically resigned to life's misfortunes, encompassing the intangibles of humility and love, and the sublime, philosophical acceptance of human frailty.

In this portrait, Philippe saw that Van Gogh, who had seen any number of Rembrandts during his years as a young art dealer in Holland and London, and mentioned them frequently in his letters to Theo, had realized a quality of emotion equally as deep and abiding as Rembrandt, and added a new dimension as well. There was a certain energy animating the sitter's face, hinting at exuberant joy amid all life's sorrows. This rendered the painting more of a positive statement than those of the Baroque master. Though Rembrandt achieved a great success in his late twenties, something that eluded Van Gogh all his life, Rembrandt also died in poverty and obscurity, all his children, and even his mistress, Hendrickje Stoffels, having pre-deceased him.

As these thoughts thronged through his mind, Philippe knew he couldn't in good conscience manipulate the situation in the way he probably should have. Five million dollars was a great deal of money. Philippe's gaze was riveted on the zinc white of Van Gogh's pupils, and he imagined himself in a darkened empty house; all alone in the bombed-out city of Munich. He would have unhesitatingly taken the painting with him. There were no witnesses and even if it were a crime, which was debatable given that the owner was an SS general, it was a victimless one. Then again, even Nazi's had children and so did Sepp Dietrich. He'd recently read a story in the *Wall Street Journal* about forty-year-old Katrin Himmler, the granddaughter of Ernst Himmler, Heinrich Himmler's brother. It turned out that Katrin's grandfather wasn't the apolitical man her grandmother told her about. Ernst was a member of the SS who joined in 1933, even before Heinrich carried out the assassination of Ernst Roehm, the chief of the SS and the SA, and Ernst Himmler had been a loyal member of the Nazi Party since 1931. Philippe appreciated the marvelous irony that Katrin Himmler was married to a Jew from Israel. Katrin's beloved grandmother, Paula, who vehemently denied any connection to her justly infamous brother-in-law actually made frequent telephone calls to the Reichsfuhrer SS in 1944 to have her family relocated out of harm's way as the Americans and British intensified their bombing of Berlin. Heinrich responded by hiding them safely in a Polish village. The fact that Esther Martinez and her brother, Chaim Roth, never made a claim for the Van Gogh with the Art Loss Register completely mystified Philippe.

*What did they have to lose?* he thought to himself. If they had reported it, he wouldn't be looking at it now, for he would have nothing whatsoever to do with a wanted work of art, except to assist the rightful owner in recovering it in any way he could, including reporting it to INTERPOL. How the Roths, given their degree of involvement in the art world, could possibly have allowed such a priceless gem to remain unknown and uncataloged since WWII. Truly the conumdrum presented by the painting's history and circumstances was fascinating. He'd deliberately not called on either of Roth's descendent prior to chartering the jet. Was it indeed the only painting left hanging in the Roth home in Munich, which was occupied by General Dietrich? Philippe wasn't clear on this part of the story because Angus, Hank, and John didn't know if it had been Roth's home before the war, although Hank thought it might have been. John told Philippe about all the ghostly images of the paintings that were on the walls from eye level to ceiling. Possibly the Van Gogh was left deliberately. Philippe understood why Goering wouldn't have taken it to Karinhalle. The Reichsmarshall would have found it profoundly disturbing. The image could be understood on many levels and one of them was as a mirror. Still, Goering and the other high Nazi officials were keenly aware of the value of important paintings that might not have suited their own aesthetics, and used to trade the unwanted and less salubrious but still valuable works of art for paintings and sculpture more amenable to their taste. They exchanged pieces with museums, governments, and with each other. Philippe was moved by the painting in such a way that he would have much preferred to commune with it alone, without Angus and Dryden in the room.

Philippe knew that Mr. Onishi would want the painting even if it were put up at public auction, however in that event the Japanese billionaire would bid on it himself, for he liked to think of himself as a wily and extremely clever bidder, which in fact he was not. Nothing Philippe had ever been able to say could ever convince him that allowing Philippe to bid for him would almost certainly save him one bid increment, and possibly two or even three, which at this level would save him millions. Onishi would not only take umbrage at anything more than the most polite and subtle suggestion that he permit Philippe to bid, he'd be mortally offended, the same way he would be if Philippe analyzed and criticized his play at the ten thousand dollar minimum baccarat table in Macao.

Few experiences in life were more exciting than bidding on an expensive lot at a live auction where split seconds equated to millions won or lost. Philippe had been on both sides of the auctioneer's podium for more than a dozen memorable contests, when two well-heeled bidders decided during the auction that they wanted the same painting, period. Egos and lust for possession made many an auction house's evening and sent the price of an otherwise good but not great work of art, to a world record for a particular artist. Not even the so-called world series of poker ever had the sort of stakes on the table that Park Avenue, Christie's, or Sotheby's offered when they put a high quality Matisse, Renoir, or Picasso up on the auction block. The winner's purse in any one of American horse racing's Triple Crown contests, the Belmont stakes, the Preakness, and the Kentucky Derby, was much less than each increment in a high stakes auction. At such an auction, ten seconds could see an increase of twenty million dollars. The auctioneers and the bidders would all be affected by the adrenalin rush such high stakes play engendered. Philippe thought the sensation equal to riding a horse in a major race, although the most the winner of an auction could expect in the form of a public demonstration by the crowd at a winning bid was a polite burst of applause from the people in the auction room.

Philippe would gladly forgo any commission and pay his own expenses to travel to New York, London, or Los Angeles just to bid for Mr. Onishi, to experience the sheer joy of matching wits and competing against other savvy agents as well as some of the wealthiest and powerful men and woman in the world, if and when the Van Gogh were sold. However, the notoriety that he would accrue from making the successful bid for what he was certain would be the new world record for any work of art, would add lustre to his business. The feeling of victory was sure to be close to the same sensation as kicking the winning goal in the final game of a World Cup match. He thought winning the bid on the Van Gogh would surpass the thrill of a gold medal at the Olympics, because there were dozens of Olympic events. There was only one world record painting and it was a mark that often stood for years.

Philippe bought expensive paintings and sculpture for his own account, however they were usually what the trade referred to as "sleepers." A sleeper was a work of art in an auction sale that for a variety of reasons and factors, such as condition, size, period, or sheer ignorance on the part of the auction gallery, dealers, collectors, and museums, somehow failed to attract bidders and sold either during or after the sale, if it was bought in, for a price that was thought to be in retrospect a bargain. Invariably the very same individuals and institutions who had ignored the piece prior to and during the sale were the first ones to write articles showering accolades upon it after some brave and perspicacious person followed his own knowledge and instincts, and bought the undervalued or unrecognized lot. Most any major sale had one or two paintings, sculpture, or drawings that sold for less, often substantially less than they should have. Even the cover lot of a sale could become a sleeper because it carried too high an initial reserve or estimate, which frightened off potential bidders.

Most galleries, Park Avenue, Sotheby's, Bonham's, and Christie's would extend fairly liberal credit terms to a dealer like Philippe, though once the account was unpaid after thirty days, interest was charged at two points over the bank rate, and seven or eight percent on a million dollars quickly eroded profits. There was any number of clients who refused to pay more than ten percent profit to a dealer who bought a lot at auction on general principle thinking they could have bought it themselves. Philippe's comment to them was always the same, "So why didn't you." Personally, he didn't care what anyone else paid for a given piece. What was important was how much the piece was worth to him. Hank had paid nothing for the Van Gogh and this meaningless to Philippe. He might dream of buying the Van Gogh for resale on his own account, but he had no illusions about his financial ability to actually do it. There were always the drug lords who offered to back him and he could fantasize about using 150 or 200 million of their money to buy the portrait at auction, though he would never act on his fancies. After the September 11 attacks, international scrutiny of large cash and third-party transactions made the major auction houses inquire into precisely where funds were coming from.

John was growing impatient. Chit chatting with Angus about Nazi documents was not what he wanted to be doing. Now that there wasn't going to be any sale of the Van Gogh, he wanted to be eating sushi and drinking a flask of good sake with Lucille, while he talked over the events of the day with the woman he loved. Much to his amazement he could honestly say to himself that he was in love with her after knowing her for two days. His mind cautioned him that he hadn't known her nearly long enough, that at his age such a precipitous plunge into the emotional depths was premature, not to mention potentially tragic. He believed in the old Chinese proverb that "He that goes up like a rocket shall fall back like a burned stick." John never considered himself to be one of those people ruled by his passions, at least not for the past five or six years. He did have a burning desire to see justice done in a world where there was precious little of it in a society preoccupied with legalistic constructs. Carol pointed out that he was looking for a mate who was more roommate, companion, and partner than an all-consuming love interest. This was the truth until he met Lucille. He was carrying on a conversation with Angus without thinking, because he was imagining on the taste of Lucille's mouth.

John approached Philippe and said in a firm tone, "Philippe, I apologize for bringing you here and wasting your time and money, but my grandfather is not the type of man I can pressure even if I wanted to, and as I feel I owe you the truth, I'm in agreement with his decision to sell it at public auction and let the chips fall where they may."

Philippe was about to tell Dryden the painting was a superb copy when at the very last second, much to his chagrin, he knew he couldn't do it. His choice not to had nothing to do with any ethical duty to Dryden, or to the old man who stole it to begin with, or to the memory and spirit of Vincent Van Gogh. He simply couldn't bring himself to say anything derogatory about the painting. Philippe liked money. There was no question about it. It was just that he loved works of art for more than their cash value at any given point in time, and it was this love that made him able to find the sleepers when others who were ruled by money couldn't see them.

"Mr. Dryden," Philippe began, "I won't insult your intelligence by saying that I'm not tremendously disappointed by this last-minute change of heart. I am. You have reneged on a gentleman's agreement with Angus here and I'm sure he's as stunned at this dramatic and sudden turn of events as I am. I won't bore you with details about the costs and inconvenience involved in flying from Buenos Aires to Los Angeles in a private jet. Nor will I tell you the sad story of how the money will come out of my pocket."

"So you weren't buying it for yourself?" said John.

"No, I was buying it for a client who already owns several Van Goghs and fell in love with yours."

"Perhaps something can be salvaged. Can't you and Angus work out an introductory commission for yourselves from Park Avenue or Sotheby's?"

"As Angus is employed by Park Avenue, he couldn't be directly involved. The real problem, to be quite frank, is the high degree of probability that any attempt at public sale will result in a flurry of lawsuits on the part of Roth heirs, Dietrich descendents, and God only knows who else. No one, and I speak for all the major galleries when I say this, is going to pay out a million dollars or more in introductory commissions as well as hundreds of thousands of dollars in legal fees to defend their right to sell the work in question."

"So you must think the painting is genuine."

Philippe smiled like the Cheshire cat in the Tenniel illustration of Alice in Wonderland. "Think it's an autograph work? My dear Mr. Dryden, I know it's genuine. I knew it from the moment I saw the pixels of the digital image assembling on my computer monitor. I'll tell you right now, driving here in the car I was so furious at having been brought up here under false pretenses and for nothing, that I was very tempted to tell you it was a copy, or rather a forgery commissioned by Solomon Roth so that his children could smuggle the original out of Germany, and that the original was hanging in the collection on one of the grandchildren in Argentina. I was planning to storm out of your office in disgust and have Angus approach you in a few weeks to see if you'd be interested in selling it as an excellent copy."

"So why didn't you? I don't know as if my grandfather would have sold it, but he might very well have."

"Aside from the fact that it would have been unethical, though you may believe me or not when I tell you, I would have paid you the fifty million later regardless, which would have rendered ethical considerations moot, the fact is that I simply find it impossible, given my abiding love for the art itself, to say that a work I know very well is authentic, is a fake. As absurd as it might sound to you, for me to do such a thing would be like murdering the painting or defacing it by slashing the canvas with a knife. The art business requires a modicum of chicanery from time to time, however without being pompous or accused of iconoclasm, I have lived my personal and professional life believing that deliberately telling a lie in order to better one's position in the world kills some part, however small, of the liar's soul. At my age, I have murdered quite enough of mine, and even five million dollars isn't enough money to make it worth killing any more of it."

"So what do you think of the painting?"

Philippe paused and gathered his thoughts. "It is, in my opinion, the finest of Van Gogh's self portraits, which makes it the finest painting of a single human being since Rembrandt. I'm not here to debate the merits of Van Gogh versus Rembrandt. It is truly a transcendently marvelous work, and when it finally sells at auction it will, and I say this with confidence, set a new world record. The only thing barring its path to stardom is the, shall we say, dubious way in which your grandfather acquired it. And of course how exactly did General Dietrich acquire it from Solomon Roth. I know that Roth bought it directly from Julien Tangy's daughter. No problem there. It's as good a title and provenance as a Van Gogh can have, except for the one oil painting Vincent sold while he was living."

"The one for 400 francs?" said John.

"I see someone's been doing his homework."

John nodded and then he looked at his watch. Philippe looked at Angus. "Shall we go to Beverly Hills? I don't know about you, Angus, but I'm hungry. You surely have a lovely restaurant in mind for this evening. Mr. Dryden, I thank you for allowing me to examine your magnificent Van Gogh. Naturally, I have very conflicted emotions. My client will be bitterly disappointed.. Let's hope he's not too miffed that he refuses to participate if and when it is sold publicly. One never knows how a billionaire will react to being thwarted."

"One never knows how anyone, rich or poor, will react to being thwarted. I will say that you have been more than gracious under the circumstances and you would have been perfectly justified in telling me to go to Hell. I'm happy you didn't and I would like you to act on my behalf in seeking the best possible terms for sale at Sotheby's, Park Avenue, Christie's, Bonham's, you know, which will give me the most favorable contract, and take whatever introductory commission you can work out. I think it's the very least I can do given the circumstances, and equally important, I know you will do what is best for the Van Gogh."

"I'd like some time to think about how this can be done, given that there's no real title other than sixty years of possession, which actually may not be as weak as it appears.

"Once again, please let me apologize for all your trouble."

"No, no, not at all," said Philippe pleasantly. "Perhaps there is a silver lining to this dark cloud after all."

"Here's my card," said John, handing Philippe one from the small upright silver holder on the left hand corner of his desk, another present from Carol. "You work it out with Angus and please let me know as soon as possible."

"Good night," said Philippe. "It was a pleasure meeting you."

"Angus," said John.

"I think you'd better walk us out just in case," said Angus. John locked the painting away in the blueprint cabinet and the three men walked out. When John got to Beverly Glen, Lucille was waiting for him outside the apartment building. He pulled into the driveway and she got in the Toyota.

"I haven't seen you all day. Aren't you going to kiss me?" she said in a playful tone. John placed his right hand behind her neck and gently pulled her towards him, and she flowed into his arms across the console. Her soft yielding mouth made him forget the tension of the hideous drive through rush hour Los Angeles traffic. His sexual thirst was in conflict with his hunger for food. Her tongue explored his gums for a few seconds and then she pulled away.

"I'm hungry," she said. "Another minute of kissing and I'd be so hot and bothered that we'd have to forget all about dinner, and I don't want to." John was having similar thoughts, even though he'd only eaten those two tacos.

He took the shift lever out of park into reverse and backed out into the northbound lane, then drove toward the dark, round mounds of the Santa Monica Mountains. On the way up Beverly Glen, John gave Lucille a detailed account of Hank's email, Carol's ethics lesson, and finally the meeting with Angus and Philippe. Lucille mostly listened, interjecting a comment or question here and there throughout the narrative; otherwise it would have been a monologue. In her heart she could have cared less about Dietrich or his son. She held to her position that the German people bore a collective responsibility for the Sho'ah, what non-Jews called the Holocaust. She categorically refused to do what all too many of what she thought of as apologists did, and see Hitler and Nazism as some unique phenomenon, totally out of context or character. The nation of Bach, Beethoven, Wagner, Heine, and Schiller was also the nation of Nietsche, Marx, Engels, Kierkegaard, Fichte, Hegel and others, philosophers, who with the exception of Marx, were no friends to European Jewry. Without the active cooperation of the German people there could have been no singling out of the Jews after 1933, first dispersing them and finally shipping them off like so many cattle to the death camps.

She expressed virtually no sympathy for Angus losing the multi-million dollar fee, or for Philippe having made the long costly journey in vain. They were both professionals and knew very well that not every deal works out as planned. To her, the most striking detail in the entire story was the attitude and behavior of her brand new boyfriend, John Dryden. In the past few hours he had quite literally lost millions of dollars, basically refused them, and throughout his recounting, he never once mentioned this even in passing. John had only to hand the cardboard folder with the painting, together with a signed bill of sale, with no guarantee of title or anything resembling such a warranty, and the money would have been wire-transferred to his bank. By mid-afternoon tomorrow at the very latest, John would be a comparatively wealthy man, and he didn't seem to care that he'd just turned down the opportunity. Lucille knew he loved Hank. She'd seen that for herself in Del Mar. Hank had made his feelings about the necessity of concealing his role in liberating the Van Gogh crystal clear, though he'd left the ultimate decision about the sale in John's hands, and if John had gone through with it and sold it to Philippe or Philippe's client, Hank would have accepted his share of the money and donated it as he'd planned to before his dramatic change of heart.

Lucille was by no means promiscuous. Neither was she a prude and in the last thirteen of her thirty years she'd known a fair number of lovers, several of whom she would just as soon forget, and two, whom she occasionally thought of with some regret for what might have been if things had worked out differently. Now John had miraculously entered her life like some deus ex machina out of a play by Sophocles. As he was speaking Lucille imagined herself in his place, calmly and deliberately turning down 25 million dollars, and though money was hardly one of the primary motivations in her life, if Hank were her grandfather, she didn't think she'd have resisted Philippe. There was so much good one could accomplish with all that money, from feeding the hungry, vaccinating children against malaria and encephalitis, to providing shelter for the homeless. The list was virtually limitless. She could buy a modest home and be the president of her own non-profit corporation. Even at 5%, the interest alone would exceed a million dollars a year without ever touching the principal.

"Any man," she began with a smile he couldn't see in the darkened car as it twisted through the canyon lit at long intervals by street lamps, and a pressure of her right hand on his right knew which he noticed, "who can be so blasé about turning down all that money must be either quite mad, ascetic, an unworldly dreamer, a special spiritual person or some combination of the four."

"I hardly think honoring my grandfather's wishes after all he's done for me and my mother back in the old days is any reason to congratulate me."

"I respectfully disagree. Your modesty is as becoming to you as your sweet defense of your grandfather. Remember, he was the one who demanded anonymity. Otherwise, you could have brought your old cardboard folder into Park Avenue and given Sondra and everyone else in the building the shock of their lives."

"Who is to say I can't still do that?"

"As much as I'd have loved to see the expression on her face when I called her to reception, I think it's wiser to allow Philippe to earn his introductory commission. If you go in and ask for a negative commission and no other charges, they'll give you this long speech about the buyer's premium having to be paid on all sales and how they were very sorry, but it simply wasn't done under any circumstances. With his connections they'll be forced to take him seriously and wouldn't dream of pulling a fast one."

"You mean to say that auction houses don't automatically give clients with Van Gogh's the best possible treatment?"

"Auction houses used to be family run businesses, but now they're run by accountants. Even Christie's, which is not a publicly held company but is owned by Francois Pinault, the French billionaire, still charges consignors' fees based on the total sales by the consignor in a given year. They charge for in-house digital photography, which costs them nothing. They charge for insurance, which costs nothing, and they'll conceal these charges in the contract. Philippe knows every trick in their playbook. He worked at Sotheby's for years. I've read about him in *Art and Auction*. He looks for sleepers at the Impressionist and Modern picture sales. Like nearly all really competent department heads eventually do, he went into private dealing."

"What's a negative commission?"

"A negative commission is where the auction house will give the consignor a portion of the buyer's premium. We talked about this yesterday, remember?"

Actually, John had forgotten. His head was a little foggy, though he was confident a few good pieces of sushi would quickly set it right. "I honestly don't recall, though I remember you saying you'd heard but didn't know if the auction houses gave the buyer a break on the ten percent premium."

"I thought we discussed negative commissions. Anyway, on a truly major piece the auction gallery can give the consignor a percentage of the buyer's premium as an incentive to choose to sell the item with them. A ten percent buyer's premium on a 100 million dollar painting leaves a lot of room for financial creativity." Lucille hesitated a moment then continued, "As much as I hate to say it, you and your grandfather might never see a penny of it for all your troubles."

"I've survived this long without being rich. Besides."

"Besides what?"

"I've gotten a year's income from selling Dietrich's pistol and documents in the past week, and I've met this special person, so I consider myself very fortunate, even blessed with or without the money for the Van Gogh."

In the past, Lucille suffered from a powerful tendency to over-romanticize the positive qualities of the men in her life, especially at the beginning of a relationship. As time passed she would initiate a testing process to determine if the man were emotionally, intellectually, and otherwise honest. The testing was like a woman in the produce section of a market tapping a melon with her finger to see if it were ripe but not rotten. Lucille was infinitely subtle in her probing and most of her lovers never knew she was testing them, or when they'd failed, which they almost always did to a greater or lesser degree.

Though it was far too early to begin the testing with John, the equanimity with which he'd accepted the loss of 25 million dollars was something that some women would view as apathy. However, that didn't apply in his case, because he was obviously completely engaged in living his life. To Lucille, his indifference to the mania for material gain was a very good sign. Materialism was something that had, in her opinion, replaced the need for and love of God in far too many people's lives. Americans took Jesus' admonition about not serving two masters, God and Mammon, seriously, resolving it by making the Divine indistinguishable from wealth. By serving God, they were guaranteed material wellbeing, and the greater the material reward the more assured one could be of God's favor. Television evangelists, books, DVD's, a multi-billion dollar industry was spawned and driven not by making people choose between God and money, but by conflating God and Mammon. Rather than making her cynical, Lucille thought the American obsession with multi-millionaire celebrities and celebrity multimillionaire was quite comical, but at the same time vile beyond belief. Only the other day she read about some sixty-year-old man, a billionaire in the roofing business, who died when he fell through his own roof, which was under construction. John had deliberately rejected the quintessential American dream of instant wealth, and she loved him for it.

As she listened to him saying how badly he felt about Angus losing out on his commission, she wondered why some bright girl hadn't taken him off the market and married him long ago. John was certainly handsome enough, though he was getting slightly long in the tooth. His fashion sense was nothing to write home about and he drove a decidedly middle-class car. His profession wasn't conducive to dating, though neither was it inimical to relationships either. Lucille really didn't know enough about lawyers, male or female, to judge. He worked out of his own office in Southgate so, assuming he didn't date his secretary, there was no opportunity for an office romance except with clients, which was unprofessional, so she really had answered her own question.

As far as the Sondra's of the world were concerned, he was a loser, possibly low-grade friendship material, but certainly not prime long-term relationship timber. John was a man who would place a premium on physical attractiveness, not that he would necessarily insist on the Barbie model, but an otherwise wonderful girl with a horseface wouldn't attract him as a potential mate, though he might surprise her. Beverly Glen was straightening out, and they were nearly to the exclusive strip mall and the restaurant.

"So, now that you've heard the whole sad story," said John as he turned left onto the street leading to the parking lot, "what do you think?" Lucille didn't answer immediately and John asked her, "Did I do the right thing, or am I strongly in the running for fool of the year honors?" The parking lot was quite full considering it was a weekday and nearly nine o'clock. They parked in the final row at the bottom of the sloping lot.

"You're taking a long time to answer my question."

"That's only because I'm trying to think of how to tell you how wonderful you are without giving you a swelled head. It's not that easy." In fact, John was having serious second thoughts about having turned Angus and Philippe down. This had nothing to do with the money. His regret was due to his having given Angus his word, what Philippe referred to as the word of a gentleman, and shaken hands on the deal. Not that a verbal agreement was enforceable in a court of law, although had Angus sued him and the matter gone before a judge or jury, John would have testified that he had indeed agreed to sell the painting and give Angus 5%. He was astonished that Philippe hadn't been more overtly abusive. Still, the comment about John's reneging on a gentlemen's agreement and by implication that John was not a man of his word stung more painfully than a wasp.

Lucille's praise him did little to soothe his wounded sense of honor. He didn't know whether he should share his second thoughts with her. His seller's remorse rested primarily on his having given Angus his word. This might come off seeming like arrogance and pride. The fact that it was the truth made it all the more prone to being misconstrued. It might appear to her that his word was more important to him than his grandfather. His word did mean more to him than the money, and not because keeping it was more valuable than the humanitarian uses the money could be put to. John would be the first to say his word was worthless in one sense. In another it was invaluable, as it allowed him to look in the mirror in the morning and evening and not be disgusted with the face that he saw staring back at him.

John set the parking brake and turned the ignition key, shutting off the engine and the lights. There was enough ambient light from the arc lamps on the perimeter of the parking lot to illuminate the interior of the Camry without the interior lamp. John looked over at Lucille, and the contrasting planes of light and shadow made her even more alluring to him than usual, dappled as if she were in a moonlit forest. She was thinking how strange life was that it was not just a Nazi's pistol, but an SS general's weapon that was the instrument that brought this honorable and decent man into her life. Surely life was infinitely more complicated than even the greatest minds ever conceived of, a wondrous tapestry woven instant by instant, present becoming past in a constant stream of the now. There would be time to talk of metaphysics at dinner between sushi and sake.

"Kiss me," she said.

## CHAPTER 25

# The Best of Times

IN THE WEEKS that followed, John was frequently put in mind of Charles Dickens's justly renowned opening sentence to his masterpiece, A Tale of Two Cities. They were for him as well, the best of times and the worst of times. The best was his relationship with Lucille. They had their disagreements. Lucille's antipathy towards Germans and Germany, which she voiced whenever the subject of the Van Gogh was broached, bothered John.

"How can you blame children and grandchildren, people you've never met, for what their parents or grandparents did? It's so Biblical. Like God visiting his wrath on the 4th generation in the Old Testament."

"First of all, there is no Old Testament. There is only one Testament and that is the Torah given to the Jews by Hashem. Why so-called Christians insist on calling the writings of men a testament of God, I'll never understand. Then again, I do. I have nothing against the rabbi Jesus. He was obviously a greatly beloved and learned scribe, a son of God as are we all. Without the marketing genius of another Jew, Saul of Damascus, Jesus and his teachings would have remained a minor sect of Judaism like the Essenes or the Qumran people who wrote the Dead Sea Scrolls. Saul and those who followed him collected popular features of the Jewish religion and the Roman religion, and adapted them. There are 613 commandments in the Torah. Too hard to remember and live up to, so reduce it to ten, easy to remember, and after all you've got ten fingers, so any illiterate can count to ten. Circumcision? No. Definitely not a good requirement for recruitment. Much too painful, especially for an adult. Circumcision would limit one's followers to Jews. No, throw that one out along with the 603 other commandments. Christians even borrow the days of the week from the Norse religion, the Eddas. Wednesday is Wotan's day. Thursday is Thor's day. Friday is Wotan's wife's Freya's day. Saturday is taken from the Roman religion, Saturn's day, Saturn being Zeus or Jupiter's father. Sunday, the day most Christians believe to be holy, though it isn't the day God rested on after creating the heavens and the earth, is obviously taken from the ancient Indo-Iranian god of light, whose cult is mentioned in the Indian Vedas from 1400 BCE where he is referred to as Mitra or Mithra. Mithra was worshipped from India to Britain and Germany. In 300 and 400AD, the Mithran religion, I refuse to call it a cult anymore than Judaism is a cult, was Christianity's chief competitor. The Christians took the day on which Mithra's birth was celebrated for more than a millennium, December 25th, and co-opted it for their god, Jesus. Then they placated the Romans by using the names of their gods, and their emperors who were worshipped as gods, for the months. June is for Juno, Jupiter's wife and queen of the gods. July is for Julius Caesar and August for Augustus, and of course March for Mars. The Christians took the Jewish Pesach or Passover and made it into Easter, the Shabbat wine and bread, and transformed them into the Eucharist."

John thought these spirited discussions were fascinating and though he didn't agree with Lucille's Germanophobia, he understood it. She was remarkably even-handed and didn't spare the Jews.

"Why America thinks it's necessary to support Israel is beyond me. Israel has the best-equipped military in the Middle East, and they have nuclear weapons. They can defend themselves against the Iranians or any other country in the region, except for Pakistan and Pakistan doesn't care about conquering Israel. America and Europe should forget all about the so-called Arab-Israeli conflict and stop meddling with their idiotic road maps. Like people are so stupid they believe in a road map to peace? Who thinks up this crap? Peace comes about when a military victory is followed by negotiations and trust, not artificially imposed frameworks. The Israelis won the victories, then they failed to win the trust of the defeated people and refused to negotiate in good faith. You can't assassinate religious leaders, bulldoze homes and olive groves, and then expect peace."

John listened, and as he did, he was reminded of Hank, who shared many of Lucille's positions regarding current events. Lucille brought the same fiery passion and intensity she had for the clash of ideas to her lovemaking. Initially John was slightly overwhelmed, and when he admitted the truth to himself, more than a little intimidated as well. After a few weeks of seeing her almost every night, he discovered a whole new language of sex that helped him to abandon his pre-existing notions from all his past relationships, and as he did so, his ardor began to keep pace with hers.

She took him with her once a week to a bath house in Koreatown on Olympic Boulevard east of Crenshaw, and introduced him to a wiry, middle-aged Korean man named Hee, who would proceed to adjust John's chi. After an hour of excruciating agony as Hee's steel fingers probed and pressured every nerve in his muscles and his organs, until he feared his stomach or bowels would rupture, he would dress, and within five minutes felt a surge of energy more powerful than any he had ever had from the most beneficial chiropractic adjustment.

"I've got to say," he told Lucille as they walked from the bathhouse to Soot Bul Jeep, one of the few Korean barbecue restaurants that used real charcoal and not bottled gas, "that your friend Hee hurts me to the point I just want to scream or punch him in the face, then when the pain stops, in a few minutes I feel like I'm twenty years old. No, I feel better than I did at twenty, and I'm ready to take on the world."

"That's the idea. You've certainly been quite the tiger in the bedroom and I like it."

"It's like I'm letting go of all my old inhibitions with you. My hang-ups are vanishing."

"And that's a good thing."

While his love for Lucille was blooming luxuriantly, certain other aspects of his life were becoming increasingly problematic. Incredible as it was, the Nahabedian's son and daughter filed a much-publicized, ten million dollar wrongful death action against him, alleging that John's behavior during the initial confrontation in the office had deranged their father, and that his Home Depot carpet had slipped on the linoleum floor causing Ahmed to lose his balance, fall, and shoot himself. The young Nahabedians also filed suit against Home Depot for not having a rubberized surface under the carpet, alleging that the 'rug was inherently unsafe'. However, the judge of the Los Angeles County Superior Court dismissed the complaint against Home Depot as frivolous. John appeared in court to have the action against him dismissed, but the judge ruled that because the complaint alleged John had punched Ahmed in the nose, the assault could have affected his judgment. After the preliminary hearing, John said to Carol, "Can you believe this shit?"

Carol said, "If a woman can collect a six-figure settlement from McDonalds for selling coffee that was too hot, when she spilled it on herself, a burglar can collect 400 thousand dollars from a New Jersey school board for 'negligently failing to have reinforcing wire in a skylight that he fell through' as he was attempting to burgle the school, and an armed robber collect damages from a homeowner who shoots him, need I go on?"

"No, I know the story all too well. In Europe, if you slip on a spilled liquid in a store, it's presumed to be your fault for not paying attention. If you fall through an open manhole, it's your fault. If your child drowns in the hotel swimming pool, it's your fault for not watching, not the hotel's fault for not having a lifeguard."

"Now you sound like a Republican congressman trying to reform the American theory of liability law where no one's responsible for any action or negligence as long as there's a deeper pocket somewhere."

"Well, you've got to admit, this suit is right up there with the most egregious abuses of the process. You were there. I didn't hit him once. He punched me in the nose and gave me a black eye!"

"And he wasn't waving a Glock at you and raving like a madman."

"Wait a minute, maybe we can countersue for him traumatizing you. Intentional infliction of emotional distress."

"Ahmed's dead. You can't sue a dead man."

"Death does dry up the liability stream. So now what do I do?"

"Well I'd say in your circumstances the old saying about the lawyer who handles his own case having a fool for a client applies. Your personal liability umbrella might cover this. Your malpractice policy won't, because Ahmed wasn't your client.

"I'll call Gloria Nunez. I'm sure she'll take the case. She owes me a favor. Also it's sufficiently high profile to appeal to her love of publicity, and who better to defend a old gringo like you than a young Hispanic female?"

"I still can't believe Judge Caperton didn't toss it."

"The Nahabedians are crafty; I'll give them that much. They were smart and hired a real old line, white bread, Los Angeles law firm. Then they lucked out and drew a real, old money, white bread judge."

"Well, you call Gloria. Maybe she can charm the old bastard into seeing reason and throwing this turkey out."

"More importantly, how's Hank?"

Carol saw John's eyes tear up. "He's better, that's what he told me when I called him this morning. I can tell this last attack really has him down. Even the latest news about the war doesn't seem to fire him up. No ranting and raving about how it's all a hoax to cover up the greatest theft in human history, over a trillion dollars and counting."

"I hope I'm not touching on a sore subject, but you don't think this has anything to do with the Van Gogh?"

To John's astonishment, Philippe and Park Avenue had protected Hank's identity quite successfully, and although the painting had made the expected headlines on CNN, Fox, BBC, MSNBC and Larry King, the chairman of Park Avenue stepped forward as the spokesman for the sale. Lord Lindsey, faultlessly urbane, looking more like the English Prime Minister than the head of an auction gallery, told viewers in his Cambridge accent that the painting had been privately held since the Second World War, and that the family had decided after much soul searching to share their masterpiece with the world, and that Park Avenue was honored to be chosen from among the great auction houses to offer it. He responded to sharp questions about reports that before the war the Van Gogh had belonged to Munich banker and collector, Solomon Roth, a victim of Nazi persecution, who perished at Auschwitz, by saying that the Roth family was well aware of the painting and referred all further questions about Solomon Roth to the Roth Foundation in Buenos Aires.

"Park Avenue Galleries, as well as our esteemed and distinguished competitors, Sotheby's, Christie's, and Bonham's are, shall I say, exquisitely sensitive to the whole issue of property that may have been taken illegally or under duress from victims of the Nazi terror. We funded and founded the Art Loss Register partly to ensure that art belonging to Germans and others prior to World War II can be tracked and returned to the rightful owners. We work closely with INTERPOL and other police agencies to ensure that the property offered for sale has good title. I might add that our respective firms have compiled a good record of just repatriation as the sale of property confiscated illegally by the Nazis from the Rothschild's at Christie's demonstrates. Several of the Rothschild pieces had been on display at the Kunsthistoriches Museum in Vienna prior to their return. We all, and I think I can speak for my competitors as well, make every legal and ethical effort to respect the rights of anyone with a legitimate claim to works of art. This Van Gogh self-portrait, which is without question, the single most important work of art to be offered for sale in the last half century, is no exception."

"No," said John. "I don't think the painting has anything to do with it. No one's even mentioned his name in connection with it."

"Are you sure? That e-mail was pretty intense. That was one hell of a secret to live with all of those years. I can't see how he did it. It was like having the Mona Lisa in your closet."

"You know, I'm not so sure Hank saw it that way. Even though that museum curator supposedly recognized the painting from the photograph, he might have just been trying to appear important.

"I honestly don't think he gave it all that much thought except in passing until a few weeks before he decided to show it to me and let me sell the pistol."

"It was obviously very much on his mind when he sent that e-mail. He had to realize he'd put you in a position where you were forced to choose between keeping your word and allowing him to expiate whatever burden of guilt he's been carrying around for the last 60 years. I don't think he thought of the trap you were in, though knowing both of you as I do, I will say I don't think he was doing you any great favor. Anyone but you, Don Quixote Dryden, would have told him it was too late, the money was paid and the deal was done and the GIVor whatever jet was in the air, headed south with the painting. Either Hank would get over it or he wouldn't, but regardless, he'd be 25 million dollars richer than he was when he got up that morning."

"What would you have done in my place?"

Carol looked at him with an unreadable expression on her face.

"I can honestly say I don't know the answer to that." They reached the parking lot off Hill Street near the courthouse where they parked early in the morning so they could eat breakfast before court.

"For someone who sounds so damn ambivalent, you sure made one hell of a convincing argument against my selling."

Carol's grin was more of a grimace. "It's easy to see and do what's right when it's someone else's money. I really don't know when push came to shove if I could have turned it down, but I knew that you could."

"Would you believe that I still have moments of regret?"

"Well, God be praised, you are human after all. What does Lucille say?"

"Actually I haven't talked to her all that much about my regrets. She's unhappy at the thought of any Dietrich relatives sharing in a windfall. It turns out the general had two sisters and two brothers, not to mention a son. Philippe has met with the Roth Foundation and their position still isn't completely clear. Evidently one of the Roths, either the grandson or the granddaughter, is dead set against sale, maintaining that Solomon would never have given up the painting except under duress. The other Roth is sure Grandpa gave it to Dietrich in exchange for visas and exit documents. I'm really out of the loop at this point, except for academic interest. I will say Philippe is keeping me posted, and having him represent us was one hundred percent the right move. He's earning whatever money he manages to get from Park Avenue."

John turned east on 1st Street to take the on-ramp to the 110 Harbor Freeway.

"One thing that bothers me about the whole thing is why the Roths or whoever they are by marriage never listed the painting with the Art Loss Register or any other organization. They're obviously connected to the art world at the highest level. Why sixty years of silence about a Van Gogh that must have been one of the prizes of Roth's collection?"

"I asked Philippe that same question in an email after he took the painting to Park Avenue in New York, and the story went public. He asked the lawyers and one of the great-granddaughters whom he knows personally, and they all gave him a resounding no comment."

"They can 'no comment' all they want. I still think there was something going on. So, do you think you'll ever see any money out of the sale?"

"I don't know, but I doubt it. Philippe says one of the major issues for the Roths is that Hank, of course they don't actually know his name, cut the canvas off the stretcher. To them, this is evidence of malicious intent. Philippe reminded the Roths of the restrictions on the size of items that GI's could bring back in duffel bags on a ship."

"So if Hank had taken it frame and all would they look at it as a proper 'liberation'?"

"Art thieves generally don't encumber themselves with frames. They cut the canvas, roll the paintings up, and flee, which is kind of what Hank did."

---

Hank Dryden left the hospital in Del Mar early in the morning after a heated disagreement with his physician, who was a lecturer on nephrology at the University of California San Diego Medical School. Dr. Watt warned him that though the latest chromotomography scans showed he'd passed the stone that hospitalized him by causing a blockage, there was a high probability of another, and it could result in another obstruction in the renal pelvis or the urethra, the tube that carries urine from the kidney to the bladder. The pain from renal colic, as Hank was only too well aware, was literally unendurable. Dr. Watt recommended surgery, as previous attempts to dissolve the stones weren't successful and ultrasound was never as effective as surgery in a case like his. Hank told Dr. Watt that he'd be damned, as he put it, "To allow myself to be filleted like a flounder at my age, for something that isn't imminently life threatening." The nephrologist told him that pain of such magnitude and intensity could have a decidedly negative impact on his central nervous system, and that a blockage might easily result in renal failure and irreversible damage to the kidney.

"That's why the Good Lord gave us two kidneys," said Hank. "In case one goes out. I'm tired of the stink of sickness in this place. It's making me lose interest in living at all. Do us both a favor and send me home."

"I'm strongly advising you to stay. I can schedule surgery for early tomorrow morning."

Hank snapped.

"I told you four times, I don't want surgery! I'm not scared of it! I just don't want it!"

"Henry, you're being stubborn."

"Fine, I'm a stubborn eighty-year-old man. So execute me. No surgery, and that's final!"

"Have you discussed this with your family?"

"No, and I'm not going to. Listen here, Dr. Watt. I know you're giving me what you know to be good advice, and I appreciate it. I'd like you to see it from my side. If I had this surgery, I'd be in here seven to ten days. If I stay here another two, I'll start thinking seriously about suicide. I'm an octogenarian. I fought in the Second World War. No surgery is going to make me young. I want to live whatever time I have left in my own home. Now would you please stop breaking my balls and let me go?"

"If you leave it will be against my explicit instructions. That will be in your file." Hank swung his legs over the edge of the hospital bed and sat up. He stood and untied the two thin strips of cloth that held his blue hospital gown, and calmly opened the white plastic-faced drawer of the dresser, removed his boxer shorts, and began dressing. There was an empty taxi at the hospital entrance and Hank took it home, and when the cab driver opened the door for him, Hank paid the man with a twenty-dollar bill, told him to "Keep the change." Hank was so happy he actually skipped up the driveway all the way to his front door much to the amusement of the taxi driver.

Hank walked into his bedroom, put on his New Balance walking shoes with the wide, white Velcro straps and walked right back out of the house to the beach. That morning the Pacific lived up to its name, with waves of slightly less than three feet breaking cleanly on the shore. It was only 7:35 a.m. on a weekday, so with the exception of a few female joggers who ran close to the Pacific Coast Highway, Hank had the strand nearest the water pretty much to himself, sharing it with a few industrious sandpipers and a small flock of sharp-beaked gulls. The salt air quickly washed away the cloying stink, which permeated the hospital an odor Hank thought was more noisome and noxious than raw sewage. Though the Del Mar Hospital was a clean, well-maintained modern facility, it still had the inevitable odor of the sickroom, even in the private and semi-private suites as they referred to them. It was the smell, as much as the hospital decor, hospital food, and hospital lighting that drove Hank out of the building against Dr. Watt's express orders.

He walked a mile to the south and was astonished at just how much a few days in bed had sapped his strength. He hadn't eaten the hospital food, which he thought was nauseating. The sight of the pasty mashed potatoes and iridescent gray meat smothered in some dark brown goop made him gag. On the Tuesday after he was admitted, John made a rare weekday appearance, bringing a rare roast beef sandwich from the Whole Foods Market as well as two pounds of organic cashews. Apart from the sandwich and the nuts, Hank hardly ate anything all week and even now he wasn't all that hungry.

The sea air and the two-mile ramble whetted his appetite. When he got home and looked in his refrigerator, he was nearly reduced to tears. John had stocked it with his favorite English Top Hat cheddar cheese, organic brown eggs, organic whole wheat bread, cranberry juice, and two six packs of Bohemia beer. Hank fixed a cheese sandwich on whole wheat toast, opened a bottle of beer, and silently thanked God he'd insisted on leaving the hospital. He called John on his cell phone to tell him he was home. John was a little incredulous, and was about to grill him to find out why the change of plans, when Hank had told him only the previous evening that Dr. Watt and he were considering surgery. Then John arrested his lawyer's impulse to cross-examine his grandfather. He remembered that Hank had lived for 80 years without his advice or assistance. If Hank were suffering from any significant impairment or diminution of his mental faculties, John would have called Dr. Watt and intervened, however Hank sounded very different than he had last night.

"You sound much better," said John.

"I started feeling better as soon as my feet touched the linoleum. Everything improved from the moment I walked out of the hospital. After a mile long walk on the beach I'm a whole new man. The cheddar and the beer helped, too. That was very thoughtful of you."

"Actually the groceries were more Lucille's idea. She never thought you'd stay for the surgery. I guess I knew you probably wouldn't either."

"Is that pretty girl pregnant yet?"

John was shocked. He often forgot that Hank could be amazingly frank concerning sexual matters, especially without his wife to act as a moderating influence and remind him of the social niceties and proprieties. John recovered his equanimity sufficiently to reply, "If she isn't, it's not for a lack of trying." Hank finished his beer. "I don't mean to make you uncomfortable. Let me put it like this. I'm kind of attached to seeing the Dryden line continue."

"Your sister had three children."

"Yes, she did. But they're not Drydens, they're Wilsons, and now the girls are whoever they married."

"We aren't even living together."

"That's not what I hear. Carol told me you're practically living in Lucille's apartment. You even went to the extent of moving your goldfish."

"All I have to say is Carol has a very big mouth."

"She didn't tell me anything Lucille didn't tell me weeks ago."

"I forgot that the three of you conspire behind my back."

"It's all for your own good. Since you're too damned altruistic to watch out for your own interests, we have to do it for you and in spite of you. Tell Lucille I'm sending something to her office. It should be there by 10:30 a.m. via Federal Express."

"Why don't you tell her yourself?"

"I figured you'd be seeing her this evening."

"All right, I'll tell her. I don't suppose you want to let me know what it is?"

"No, I want it to be a surprise."

"Have it your way. Do you want me to drive down tonight?"

"No, I really am feeling better. It's not like I would have checked myself out of the hospital if I were incapacitated. No matter what Dr. Watt says, I might be eccentric and old, but that doesn't mean I'm a fool."

"I never said you were and I don't know anybody who knows you thinks you are either except for Dr. Watt."

"No, you haven't, and I thank you for that. John, do you ever think we made the wrong decision by choosing a public sale?"

"No, I don't any more than twenty times a day. No seriously, it really wasn't up to me even though you left it in my hands."

"I know I did, and I want you to believe I feel nothing but regret for putting you in the position of having to break your word with Mr. Creswell. I know better than many men just how valuable a real man's word is to him. It must have hurt you and wounded you deeply in a part of your soul, and for that I'm very, very sorry. More than words can say, and I swear I never intended for it to happen that way."

"Grandpa, words are important to be sure, and I'm proud to say that my word is my bond, however you must know that I talked it over at length with my resident ethicist, Carol. Angus was well aware from our first meeting that the Van Gogh wasn't exactly your typical war trophy. Let me see," here John put his right thumb and index finger on the bridge of his nose to concentrate his thoughts. "As the language of the capture paper so eloquently phrases it, "I certify that I have personally examined the items of captured enemy equipment in the possession of Sergeant Henry Dryden and that the bearer is officially authorized by the Theater Commander, under the provisions of Section VI, EIR 155, WD 28 May 1945 to retain as his personal property the articled listed in Paragraph 2 below."

"You memorized all that?"

"It's legal stuff, so it's easy for me. My brain has special neural channels for any type of legal language, not that I'm able to remember the things I'd like to, such as poetry or French."

"You know, after I got the paper for the Walther and the books, I was tempted to type in 'one oil painting.' I saw other GI's shipping back used furniture, porcelain vases, music boxes and even a grand piano. That 'captured enemy equipment' label was applied to anything GI's wanted it to be."

"Well, if you'd had your captain add it to your capture paper, that would have given us a plausible legal argument, though I still think equipment would have to be rather broadly and liberally construed to extend to a painting."

"It's all water under the bridge at this point, besides..."

"Besides, what?"

"Frankly, I'm far more interested in a great-grandchild than I am in the Van Gogh."

John laughed rather loudly. "You'll need to talk to Lucille about that."

"I will when you come down on Saturday. You go for a walk on the beach and she and I will have a little chat."

"You're 100% sure you don't want me to come down tonight?"

"Yes I am. I'll be just fine now that I'm out of that hospital."

"All right, as long as you're sure."

"Trust me, John, I'm sure.

## CHAPTER 26

# The Rhinoceros Beetle

LUCILLE WAS AT her desk the next morning, when the Federal Express truck rolled up and double-parked in front of the gallery on Rodeo. Frank, the usual route driver, only parked in front when he had FedEx letters or boxes to deliver. Whenever he had large and heavy items such as property to be consigned, he parked in the alley behind the building. Frank was a pleasant Hispanic man in his late twenties, who used to flirt with Sondra and now he flirted with Lucille. The ex Beverly Hills detective opened the door for Frank, who came in with six letters and three FedEx boxes. Frank had a lovely smile and Lucille smiled back at him.

"How's my favorite receptionist on all Rodeo Drive?"

"I'm good, Frank. How's my favorite FedEx man?"

"What do you mean favorite? Are there other FedEx men?"

"No," she giggled. "There's only one."

"That's good," said Frank, who was punching numbers into his handheld computer and scanning the FedEx slips. "One of these boxes is for you."

"Me?" said Lucille, the astonishment plain in her tone and on her face. She'd only been working the desk for about two months, and she didn't have the slightest idea who would send a FedEx box to Park Avenue for her, unless it were John, and that made no sense. He'd sent bouquets of flowers to her work twice, which she thought was very sweet and romantic of him, but unnecessary. Frank finished logging the deliveries and handed Lucille her box. It was a large FedEx box and she looked at the FedEx carbon form inside the plastic pouch on the front of the cardboard to determine the sender.

"Who's Henry Dryden?" asked Frank. "Is he your boyfriend?"

Lucille smiled sweetly.

"No, as a matter of fact he's my boyfriend's grandfather."

"Do you know what it is?"

"I really don't have the vaguest idea."

"Then it's a surprise."

"That's an understatement."

Frank looked at his computer to check the time, because he didn't trust the elaborate antique clock on the wall. "I'd better run. I'm double-parked. See you tomorrow."

"See you, Frank. Have a good day and thanks for the package."

"It's always a pleasure."

Frank walked out and after he did, Lucille pulled the tab to open the box, and as usual the pull-tab tore along the perforation about half way, then broke off. The glue Federal Express uses to seal the flaps of their boxes is extremely powerful and tenacious. The cardboard will rip long before the adhesive gives way. Lucille tore furiously at the end of the box until at long last it opened, and then the telephone rang and she put the box down on the carpeted floor. The phone, which had been silent for nearly ten minutes, now rang without letup. There was an American Furniture and Decorations sale coming up in a few days, so consequently there were a number of telephone inquiries about various lots in the sale. The Internet was the favored means of communication between the under thirty demographic, and Park Avenue expert departments endorsed its use for condition reports, reserves, estimated sales prices, but a number of clients still wanted to hear the expert's voice on the telephone giving them the information they needed.

Finally there was a lull in the torrent of calls, and Lucille managed to extricate the contents, which were packed in small bubble wrap, taped rather solidly with fiberglass filament tape. People were passing by her desk and she was at pains to minimize the mess she was creating. She honestly couldn't imagine what Henry would be sending her, then she noticed a tiny white card envelope taped to the bubble that she'd overlooked, because it was so very diminutive, about a quarter the size of a postcard. The flap wasn't sealed, only tucked inside the envelope. Her name was written on the outside in rather neat block capitals. She opened the flap and there was a card inside. The card read, "You seemed to like the enclosed and I want you to have it. With my warmest regards, Henry Dryden." Lucille tried to remember the few times she'd been in Hank's home and what she'd admired, however her romance with John was very much of a whirlwind courtship and between all the chaos with the Van Gogh, Hank's hospitalization, the Nahabedian lawsuit, as well as the disruption of having John essentially move in with her, she couldn't recall exactly what it was that she liked that he would have sent her by Federal Express. Hank had used nearly as much filament tape as he had bubble wrap and without a box cutter or razor blade, removing the wrapping was impossible. It looked like a guarantee of broken fingernails, and Lucille's were already shorter than she liked them to be. There was a pair of scissors in the drawer of the Louis XVI bureau plat, though they were not good quality shears and tended to cut sideways on anything heavier than twenty-weight paper. The 3M filament tape was hard to cut under ideal circumstances with a good blade.

Lucille called Lewis in the shipping department to see if he could lend her one of his box cutters. Lewis, a serious, dignified, wise, and supremely kind 56-year-old black man was an expert at packing odd-sized fragile works of art so they would survive the roughest handling in shipping intact. He was only too happy to come out of the back with a box cutter. He took one look at Lucille's package and said, "Whoever packed that made darn sure it wasn't going to break in shipment. You had best let me unpack it."

"It's pretty well mummified, but I don't want to put you through any trouble."

"It's no trouble, no trouble at all. I'm happy to do it." He took the object and shook his head. "You're right. That's a lot of tape. Give me fifteen minutes." Lucille was actually relieved, then the phone began to ring again so she turned her attention to her work.

Lewis took Lucille's parcel back to the shipping room and began to slice through the tape, taking care not to cut through the bubble. He was as precise in the length, depth, and angle of his incisions as any surgeon. During his ten years with the gallery, he had never accidentally cut into any piece he unpacked and he fully intended to keep his record intact. He worked at a steel table topped with a 4x8 sheet of marine plywood that was covered with a thick gray wool carpet. Sondra walked in to measure a large, unframed, Ellsworth Kelly green acrylic on canvas that was being catalogued for a future auction featuring Contemporary Art.

"What are you doing?" she asked as she watched him making the final cuts in the filament tape Hank had wrapped so thoroughly around his gift to Lucille. Lewis had nothing against Sondra. She'd always been pleasant to him since the day she walked through the front door of the gallery. Some other receptionists who'd been the big boss' mistresses had been standoffish, even arrogant to him, however Sondra had always treated him with the same respect and unfailing courtesy she used with any department head. As a consequence, Lewis had no compunction about telling her what he was doing. He smiled as he put down the knife, which was no more than a hollow aluminum housing for a retractable single-edged razor blade, one he replaced frequently.

"It's something someone sent to Lucille." Lewis removed the bubble wrap and inside was more taped bubble wrap, only the inner wrap was taped with more care in a cross pattern rather than a series of haphazard bands. The object, whatever it was, seemed to be small, flat, and rectangular. Lewis took knife in hand once more and sliced precisely through all four bands of tape, and unwrapped the last of the bubble freeing the object inside. Sondra was watching intently as the semi-opaque plastic came off, and she couldn't believe what she was seeing. Lewis looked at it with curiosity. It was very small, perhaps three inches by five inches, in a thin, obviously ancient frame, under glass. Even with the frame it was only five by eight inches.

"Whoever wrapped it wasn't an artist with packing, but they sure made it so it wouldn't break in shipment." Lewis held it out at arm's length and contemplated the tiny image. Sondra had to exert an extraordinary degree of self-control to keep from snatching it from his powerful sinuous fingers. As soon as she thought a socially acceptable amount of time had passed, so she could speak without being thought as rude, she said politely, "May I see it?"

"Of course," said Lewis, handing her the tiny picture. The shipping room was well lit with fluorescent lamps overhead as well as a metal lamp with a 150-watt bulb clamped to one side of Lewis' work table. Sondra's heart was racing as she pulled the extendable metal lamp towards her so she could better see through the glass to the paper underneath. She found what she was looking for, the broad, distinctive chain and wire lines from the metal screen that was used to filter the rag fiber by hand, before Nicholas-Louis Robert invented the first machine for making paper in 1798. This piece of paper was plainly made of linen rags, a matted sheet on a wire screen from a water suspension, hence the chain and wire lines. Sondra turned it over and the brown paper glued to the back to prevent the entry of dust was ancient, very dry and brittle. There was a holographic inscription in black India ink, short, though written in a beautiful and elaborate script she thought was German. Sondra could make out the names Dietrich and Roth. There were three other words, which looked like 'Mit vielen dank,' something to do with thanks, not that it made any difference to her, because it was obviously far more recent than the image. In order to confirm what she believed the image might be, Sondra needed to remove the paper from the frame. Sondra had some formal training at the Art Institute of Chicago, still it was difficult to tell an etching, engraving, or a woodcut, from a drawing in silver point, pen, and bistre, heightened with white when the image was under a piece of old glass.

"Lewis, could you call Lucille and tell her to come back here?" The reception desk had to be manned during business hours. This was a firm, stated, gallery policy, one Sondra had temporarily forgotten in her excitement.

"No wait, I've got to call Erin first." Erin was a secretary in the Contemporary Art Department, so Lucille was surprised when she walked up and told her she would take the reception desk while Lucille met Sondra in the shipping room. Lucille handed over the headset and walked back to shipping, wondering what Sondra wanted. She didn't associate Sondra with Hank's mysterious gift, though as soon as she walked in Lucille recognized the wood frame Sondra was holding in her lovely, perfectly manicured hands. Lucille smiled. It was the old reproduction of Durer's print of the rhinoceros beetle. Sondra looked at Lucille.

"Do you have any idea what this is?" she asked almost feverishly.

"It's an old reproduction of a Durer print. I saw it in someone's home and admired it so he sent it here. Isn't that sweet?"

"I'm not so sure it's a copy."

"Oh, come on Sondra, that's ridiculous. Of course it is."

"It's got a presentation on the back."

Sondra handed it to Lucille, who turned it over and very nearly dropped it.

"Can you read it?" Sondra asked. "I got Dietrich and Roth, something about thanks."

Lucille's voice was weak, lacking its usual husky quality because her mouth was dry. "It says, 'To S. Dietrich with many thanks, S. Roth.'" Sondra looked at Lucille, whose face was pale rather than it's usual olive color.

"Are you feeling all right? Do you know who these people are?"

"I'm okay; I just can't believe it. This was given to an SS general by Solomon Roth."

Sondra immediately recognized the name. "You mean Solomon Roth as in the Roth Foundation. As in the Argentine Roths? Let's take it out of the frame and make sure I'm right."

"How can we do that without damaging the paper?"

"We'll cut around it. See where it's already out of the frame. Lewis, can you give me an X-Acto knife?"

"I'm not sure we should do this," said Lucille somewhat plaintively. "It was a gift from a very dear old gentleman."

Lewis handed Sondra a knurled handled, aluminum X-Acto knife. "Come on Lucille, you want to know as much as I do. Give me the print."

"I'm still not sure about cutting it open."

Sondra put out her right hand and took it from Lucille, who didn't hold onto it too hard, and allowed Sondra to take it, though she felt uneasy and ambivalent. Sondra sliced around the old fragile paper and handed it to Lucille. Underneath the paper, which had been glued to some very ancient pasteboard, was a piece of wafer thin, ancient, dark wood held into the frame by dark iron nails, though not very many of them, three on each side. "You would have had to take it out of the frame anyway. Look at all the foxing at the end of the left mandible and along the edges. Eventually the image would be damaged beyond repair. The glass is antique and doesn't reflect sunlight, and wood isn't a good backing as it absorbs moisture and leeches into the paper. Thank God they didn't mat it the last time it was framed or the nitric acid in the old paper could have caused even more problems. I know a really great paper conservator. She cleaned three Rembrandt drawings and a Goltzius etching and drypoint for the Getty last year. She'd probably pay you to work on a Durer."

Lucille knew that Sondra had her heart set on taking the paper out of the frame that instant. She also realized that there were dangers in leaving old paper under old glass without taking proper measures to conserve it, but somehow despite all Sondra's caveats, it had survived nearly 500 years, assuming Sondra was correct and it was an original.

"An original what?" thought Lucille, and suddenly she was nearly as anxious as Sondra.

"Go ahead, take it out," said Lucille.

"Lewis," said Sondra, "could you give me a small pair of pliers and a pair of wide tweezers?"

The pliers were a high grade, precision instrument from Sweden, and instead of tweezers, Lewis handed her a hemostat. Sondra carefully removed the first nail as though it were a splinter and held it up for Lucille to admire, as if she were some surgeon removing a foreign object from a human being.

"Look at that," she said with pride. "Square-cut, hand-forged, I'd say 18th century at the latest. Beautiful, just beautiful." Sondra dropped the tiny nail into Lucille's left palm then pulled out the remaining eleven nails one by one. She carefully lifted off the wood, and there was another piece of even darker and denser grained walnut underneath. Sondra turned the whole frame over and lifted up. The image was finally free of the frame, pressed down on Lewis' carpet by the glass which Sondra lifted off immediately.

"Lewis, do you have a magnifying glass?" Lewis gave her a good ten-power, large glass, with a carved ivory handle that had been given to him as a gift by the head of the decorative arts department.

Sondra bent her head down and scrutinized the diminutive piece of paper very carefully. Still conning the image, she said with a note of triumph in her tone, "Lucille, this is a drawing. It's not an etching, a woodcut, or a copper-plate engraving. See for yourself." Sondra handed the glass to her. She looked closely, straining to see where and if the textures overlapped and ink bled into the paper from a pen and not a plate, and having a very hard time. Try as she might, she didn't have Sondra's training and couldn't determine if it were a drawing, or an engraving heightened with pen and brush. Lucille handed the glass back to Sondra.

"I'm sorry, but I just don't have the expertise to see what you see. You're telling me this is an original drawing by Albrecht Durer?"

"I am indeed, and I want full credit for discovering it."

Lucille had no idea what Sondra was talking about as far as credit went.

"I'll be happy to tell anyone that you were the first to recognize it as a drawing and not a later engraving, if that's what you mean."

"You have to let me take it up to the Getty and show it to the curator for confirmation and get his blessing."

"Sondra, remember this was a gift from someone I hold in high esteem. I'm not sure I want to give it up right now. I just got it half an hour ago. Let me live with it for a few weeks and then maybe I can let you borrow it."

"I'm concerned," said Sondra, "With the condition of the paper, the staining and the foxing, it needs immediate conservation by a competent expert."

"Sondra, it's survived for 500 years. Surely it won't deteriorate in the next two weeks."

"See, Lucille. That's where you're wrong. It was basically sealed in the frame and now it's exposed to the elements including ozone. It's like a mummy in a tomb or the cave paintings at Lascaux. When the grotto was first discovered in September of 1940, the paintings were stunning. The colors, vibrant yellows, reds, browns, and blacks, were incredibly vivid, and they had been perfectly preserved for 18000 and maybe as many as 30,000 years. Within twenty years the colors lost their vividness and a green fungus grew over some of the paintings. They finally closed the grotto to the public in an effort to save them."

Lucille was horrified. She could almost see the colors on her drawing begin to fade before her eyes, and the stains and foxing grow in size and intensity. She looked at Sondra. "So knowing all this, why did you insist on taking it out of the frame?"

Sondra looked at Lucille as if she were an idiot. "Well, we had to know if it were a drawing or some reproduction."

"And you couldn't tell by looking through the glass?"

"Not with any high degree of certainty."

"Sondra, I want you to put it back in the frame as close to the way you found it as possible."

"That would be a mistake."

"It's my drawing and I want it put back the way it was."

"And I told you that a drawing like this needs to be professionally conserved."

Lucille was getting angry. She didn't care for the way Sondra was looking at her or the patronizing tone of voice she was using, as if Lucille were some fool with an undeserved treasure.

Lewis, who had been packing an unglazed T'ang dynasty, ceramic figure of an Earth spirit for shipment by Federal Express to a New York dealer in oriental art at the Manhattan Art and Antiques Center on Second Avenue, was listening as the conversation between Lucille and Sondra deteriorated. He had no intention of taking sides, as he liked both women, though he'd known Sondra for a longer time. If it came to blows, he would intervene as a neutral party. Lucille was obviously angry while Sondra was physically ill at the thought someone may have inadvertently sent Lucille a genuine Durer drawing as a present. The girl owed her a huge debt of gratitude for telling her it was an invaluable drawing worth seven figures and not a five hundred dollar $19^{th}$ century copy. The injustice of the situation and what she saw as Lucille's black ingratitude rankled her and she didn't really know how to effectively process her feelings.

"Do you have any idea how much this drawing is worth?"

"No, and it doesn't make any difference. It was a gift from a special person and to me, that's its true value. Now would you please do what I asked you to do?"

"No," said Sondra. "It's worth at least a million dollars. You think this belongs to you and that's the problem. Things like this belong to humanity and I'm not going to risk you damaging it. Lewis can give you two sheets of acid free paper, which will serve as a folder until you give it to a paper conservator who will clean and restore it, and use the old frame with conservation glass and a conservation backing. You have to let me take a picture of it, the frame, and the paper with the presentation and allow me write an article about my discovery for *Vanity Fair* or *Art and Auction*."

Lucille saw clearly enough through the prism of her anger to see that some or most of Sondra's catty attitude was due to disappointment that someone had unknowingly given her an extremely valuable work of art. This softened her fury, which had been on the verge of a violent eruption.

"You know, Sondra, maybe you're right. Take a picture and write your article, and if you think it needs to be put into a folder, please do it." Sondra, who had been so pissed off, she was ready to slap Lucille silly, took a deep breath and tried to relax. Lewis who had been on the brink of stepping in between the two girls, went back to concentrating on making certain the tall, projecting, ceramic flame above the Earth Spirit's head was cushioned in such a way that dropping the shipping box from waist level wouldn't snap it off. He knew what was needed, because he'd experimented with cheap reproductions of various porcelains, vases, bowls, figures, urns and the like to develop the most effective methods of cushioning odd-sized and shaped pieces, what he liked to call his "special needs" items. If the box or crate were thrown off the back of a loading dock or truck lift gate it might break regardless, however anything he packed would survive normal rough treatment undamaged.

After lunch, Lucille was at her desk when Sondra brought her the frame, the paper with Solomon Roth's presentation, and the folder she'd made up with the drawing inside. Sondra was smiling.

"I called the curator at the Getty and he said if you're ever interested in selling it, they would like to have a right of first refusal, assuming it passes their examination, which I guarantee you it will. I looked at the back and there's a tiny impressed mark, which shows that at one time it was in the Hapsburg Royal Collection. Sometime, I'd like to take you up to the Getty and let them look at it, that is if you don't mind."

"Sondra, I'd be happy to. It sounds like a great opportunity."

Sondra spoke with an uncharacteristic diffidence. "Whoever gave you this, there isn't any chance they have something else like it?"

Lucille thought to herself: *If you only knew the whole truth you'd probably have a cerebral hemorrhage. Turns out that the loser public interest lawyer wasn't such a loser after all, though you'll never know.*

"No," said Lucille sweetly. "The bug, as he called it, was the only thing he had."

"That's a shame," said Sondra.

"Yes," said Lucille. "It is, isn't it?"

THE END

CPSIA information can be obtained
at www.ICGtesting.com
Printed in the USA
BVOW09s1043040617
485997BV00001B/96/P

9 781608 448586